The sequel to *Th*

The Girl In A White Sari

Gigi Karagoz

Copyright © Gigi Karagoz 2021

The right of Gigi Karagoz to be identified as the author of this work has been asserted by her in accordance with the Copyright, Designs and Patents Act 1988.

All rights reserved. No part of this publication may be reproduced, transmitted, or stored in a retrieval system, in any form or by any means, without permission in writing from the publisher, nor be otherwise circulated in any form of binding or cover other than that in which it is published and without a similar condition being imposed on the subsequent purchaser.

The Girl in a White Sari is entirely a work of fiction. The author does not wish to cause offence, insult or to disparage any culture, religious beliefs or traditions of India and her people.

'You're the road of love, and at the end, my home.'

Rumi

Chapter One

London, September 2010

A SENSE OF knowing flooded through me. A momentary tug in my stomach made me catch my breath, and my heartbeat quickened just a little. I knew what it was, that flighty sound; an envelope floating down from the letterbox. A light, hopeful sound that belied the emotional weight of the contents and the changes they brought.

In the hallway, the sun streamed through the stained-glass panels in the front door, smearing the walls with red and turquoise light. Shooing a miaowing Billie out of the way, I picked up the cream envelope. Holding it to my nose, I breathed in, imagining there was some way to catch the scent of India, of the past. I carried the envelope to the kitchen and placed it on the table. Even though I'd already had the one strong coffee I allowed myself each day, I reached for my espresso pot. Another one wouldn't kill me, would it? The rich smell of Italian coffee swirled in the air, and leaning against the sink, I drank, not tasting anything.

Crossing the kitchen, I looked at my reflection in the glass door of eye-level oven. Tugging at the ends of my shoulder-length hair, I was glad the chestnut brown wasn't yet silvered. I pinched my jaw line and prodded my cheekbones.

'Not too bad, Mari. Not bad at all,' I said.

And how had the person who'd written my name on the envelope aged? My heart skittered, and twenty-three years' worth of regret was replaced by a gentler emotion. One that made me smile.

From the table, the envelope lured me. I picked it up, ran my thumb along the stripe of gold that decorated the edges. The postage stamp was obscured by the red lettering of the place and date stamp. Not that I could read the Hindi lettering, but it didn't matter, I knew which city it had been posted from.

Memories crashed in, taking me back to Shivpur, to the sound of gunfire bouncing off the rocks. Echoes of echoes, and sound upon sound that built up and up until my ears hummed with the vibrations. Then the sound changed, stuck on a slowly diminishing and quietening loop. I remembered the sharp metallic smell of blood that stung my nose and alerted my brain to the horror of what had happened.

Looking at the kitchen ceiling, I blinked rapidly, my fingers wiping the moisture from beneath my eyes. It had been such a long time ago, but I remembered every tiny detail and every emotion; disbelief, panic, horror. And relief that it wasn't me lying on the ground and bleeding into the sandstone dust, that it wasn't me taking my last breath.

Many things had changed since then. India's economy had strengthened, the beaches of Goa were now a package holiday destination, and travelling in India was mainstream, not the wild adventure it had been back in 1986. Calcutta was now Kolkata, Madras had changed to Chennai, and Bombay was Mumbai. But for me, it would always be Bombay.

With a deep breath, I slid my finger under the flap to open the envelope, and withdrew the red card printed with a gold, stylised line drawing of Ganesh, the elephant god, on the front.

My coffee grew cold, the wedding invitation still in my hand. Emotions swirled through me, pulling my thoughts all over the place, and my hand trembled. I read the card again. Names, date, venue; all there. Disappointment took centre stage; there was no note.

I hadn't had a letter from India for around ten, maybe eleven years. When the replies stopped coming, I stopped writing, choosing to believe the Buddhist theory that change is inevitable, and that nothing stays the same. Hadn't my life shown me that time and again? And yet, there was change again, in the form of a wedding invitation, and the promise behind it.

Opening my laptop, I checked BA and Air India's websites. Flight prices to Bombay weren't bad for November, and I scribbled down some details. Tapping my finger on the edge of the keyboard, I took a deep breath. I could just book it. I flexed my fingers, and typed in the date and destination, followed by my details. A heady excitement took over, but when the website asked me for my credit card details, I froze. This wasn't a decision I should make in a hurry; it involved Harry too.

An hour later, carrying a string bag full of groceries, and a carboard tray of take-away drinks, I closed Isabel's front door behind me. We'd been friends for years, despite my being ten years older than her, and she was like another sister to me. We had a copy of each other's front door key, for Billie feeding and plant-sitting duties when either of us went away. Or in that case, to bring in some shopping for her when she'd broken her leg.

'Where are you?' I called out, placing the bags on the kitchen worktop.

'Costa del Sofa,' Issy quipped. I followed her voice into the lounge, and handed her a coffee.

'Café Nero actually. There's a chocolate twist as well,' I said.

'You angel,' she said, taking her mid-morning breakfast from me. 'Thanks. Jon will be back later. He said he'd call me after the match finished, but you know what he's like. He'll get side-tracked talking cricket with someone, and forget to find out what shopping we need.'

'Isabel —'

'Although what they find to talk about is beyond me; it's so boring.'

'Issy, I've been invited to a wedding.' Perching on the armchair in the corner of the room, I sucked iced lemonade through a straw.

'When? Where? Whose?' Issy pulled the chocolate pastry out of the paper bag, and took a huge bite, bits of flaky pastry falling to her chest. 'So good.'

'November, India.'

Issy spluttered and coughed. 'No way. You're kidding?'

'Came this morning. I knew what it was before it hit the doormat. Of course, I want to go, but should I?'

'After all these years. Well, you usually have strong gut feelings, so what are they telling you?'

I rose from the chair, and stood in the weak autumn sunshine streaming through the window. Closing my eyes, I imagined the intense heat of the Indian sun, the monsoon rain, and the sounds of Bombay. And my heart remembered the idyllic weeks in Shivpur before the shooting.

'I almost booked the flight ticket this morning,' I said.

'Well, there you are,' Issy said. 'You just answered your own question.'

'But I'm not sure, which is why I want to talk to you about it.' I turned to face her.

'Honestly. Just go and have a holiday, and experience an Indian wedding. I would.'

'Isabel, come on, you know it's not as simple as that, not with the promise.' Sitting on the armchair, I crossed my legs, pulled at the seam of my jeans. 'I could be wrong, and that's all been forgotten. And if it has, I don't want to stir it all up again. But then, why would I get the invitation? Anyway, what'll I tell Harry?' I threw my arms wide, my bangles clattering.

'You can be honest with him, can't you?' Issy took another bite of her pastry.

'Can I?' My fingers trailed through my hair, twisting the

ends. 'We're on such an even keel right now. This will change everything.'

She tilted her head to one side, her direct gaze unsettlingly honest. 'Fair enough. Mari, if you don't want Harry to know the real reason you're going, you could tell him it's for work. That won't be so strange, will it? You work for a water charity; they must have projects in India.' She crumpled the pastry bag, licked the chocolate off her fingers. 'I feel like I'm talking you into this. But if it's Harry you're worrying about, I think he'll be fine. You underestimate how much he loves you, you know.'

'I hope you're right. Issy, an Indian wedding will be amazing. But…'

'Mari.' She shook her head, pulled a face. 'No *'buts.'* God, can you imagine your mother? She'll have a field day with this.'

'That has crossed my mind. It's mad; I haven't spoken to the old bat for over a decade, but nothing I do is ever right. Even after all this time, she's never forgiven me.'

'Is Harry still visiting her most weeks?' Issy said. I nodded. 'He's got to have a tough skin to do that.' She took the plastic lid off the take-away coffee cup, and sniffed it. 'Ah.'

'Harry says she's quite nice to him, which is staggering. Better late than never, I suppose. I'm glad she can see him for the darling he is.' I sat on the arm of the sofa, near Issy's feet. 'If I go to India and don't tell Harry, it'd be selfish. If I do tell him…that'd be selfish too. We never talk about any of that. And anyway, I mean, isn't it all too late? I should have…'

'You're overthinking it.' Issy sipped her coffee. 'Don't pre-empt how Harry may or may not react. This is your life. So, get your visa, get your ticket booked, and tell him you're off on your travels. See what happens over there, and deal with it then.'

'You are so bossy.' I wagged my finger at her, and leaned forward. 'Issy, what if…?' I bit my lip, raised my eyebrows.

'What if? You mean the promise? You already know the answer to that, or the invitation wouldn't have come, would it? So, the ball is in your court. I say, do something about it.'

The front door opened and heavy footsteps made their way down the hall.

'Hi Mari, see your Beetle's outside.' Jon popped his head round the door to the lounge. 'Let me dump my sports kit.'

Jon's Welsh accent was soothing, as was his bear-like presence. A moment later, he strode into the room and bent his six-foot frame to kiss his wife on the cheek. Issy reached up to him, brushed his untidy hair out of his eyes.

'Mari's off to India. For a wedding.' Issy grinned. 'But don't say anything to Harry. Let her tell him.'

'Isabel!' I threw my hands up in the air, glancing at the door, my ears straining. 'Jon, is Harry with you?'

'You're alright.' Jon said. 'He's on his phone outside.' I breathed out. 'Is this the wedding you've been waiting years to be invited to?' I nodded, and his eyes widened. 'Oh, the promise… well, it's about time.'

'Harry won't understand.' I shook my head. 'Not after all these years.'

'He'll handle it better than you think, Mari,' Jon said. 'He's a good man, is Harry.'

'Talking about me?' Harry strode into the room, all smiles, his black hair still wet from his post-cricket bath, or shower, or whatever they did in the changing rooms. 'Good or bad?'

Issy and I glanced at each other, and I shook my head in a tiny movement.

'I was just asking if you're staying for an Indian take-away tonight?' said Jon. 'Extra mango chutney, on me.'

Chapter Two

यात्रा

India, June 1986

MONSOON RAIN PUMMELLED at the roof, and thick, somnolent heat wrapped me, making me lazy, sticking me to the bed. I stretched my limbs, and turned onto my side. Daylight crept around the closed wooden shutters, and the heavy rain meant that it was probably afternoon. Reluctantly, I rose, stepped into my loose cotton *shalvar* trousers, and tied the cord low on my hips. Careful not to knock my nose stud, I pulled on my vest-top, easing it down over my sweat-sheened torso. My bangles tinkled, and I stopped, glancing over my shoulder.

On the bed, Arkanj turned over, throwing one arm above his head in an abandoned movement that stirred my belly with longing. It was tempting to wake him, slide myself over him again like I'd done every afternoon for the best part of a week. Instead, I lifted the creaking hasp, slid back the bolt and pushed open the double doors. I squinted in the light and stepped out onto the veranda, breathing in the smell of the rain. Turning to close the door behind me, I caught Arkanj's eye.

'Mari?' he said. 'Where are you going?'

'Bombay. I'm sure I told you,' I said, backing away. Cool raindrops dampened my hair and slithered down my bare arms. 'I need to go and pack my things.'

'You're leaving me, just like that?' Arkanj got off the bed, pulling the sheet with him, and reached out his hand. 'I thought we…' A smile played across his lips and he dropped the sheet to the floor. At five-foot-ten, he was exactly the same height as me, and I held his gaze, not wanting to look at what he was showing me. 'Come on, Mari. Stay.'

'It's been great, Ark.' I smiled, pulling my hair into a plait. There was no surge of emotion, no regret or connection, nothing. Ark's eyes hardened, and I shrugged, stepping further out into the rain. 'Sorry, I've got to go.'

Ark had been my lover for longer than any of the others. He was a medical student from Delhi, and a few years younger than me, and we'd had great fun together. But that was all it was. What was wrong with me? I craved love and intimacy but never managed to feel anything more than physical desire. During the eight weeks I'd been in Goa, it'd been the same, whoever's bed I'd woken up in. Trying to get Ryu out of my heart, and erase the awful memories of everything that happened in Japan wasn't easy. But the hedonistic beach life, the sex and the alcohol hadn't worked; it just left me hollow. Maybe I'd run out of emotion. Maybe that's what I deserved. Raising my arms, I leaned my head back, the rain washing my face.

Instead of heading back to my guesthouse, I walked along the empty beach. The sea thrashed wildly, the early monsoon wind whipping the waves into a frenzy of powerful foam. The water was calmer by the cluster of black rocks at the end of the bay, and leaving my clothes on the sand, I stepped into the sea. The waves tossed and turned me, crashing over me, while the undercurrents pulled at me like a needy lover.

The fourth time I went under, the pressure built in my chest, and I swallowed yet more water. Should I give in and let the sea take me? That way, I wouldn't need to think anymore, wouldn't need to hate myself anymore. I spread my arms wide, my head pounding. Just as I gave in, a huge wave pulled me up and threw me forwards, rolling me towards the beach. My heart hammered, and I crawled out of the sea. Seawater spewed out of my mouth, and I lay on the sand, looking up at the retreating clouds. Once my breathing steadied, and my chest stopped heaving, the tears came. Tracing my finger along the scar on the underside of my forearm, my insides twisted. My heart was still cloudy with Ryu, my conscience threaded with guilt over the two deaths I'd caused. And I liked it that way; it meant that I hadn't forgotten. The sea hadn't swallowed me, so it meant that I was destined to live with the pain and the layers of regret that had re-shaped me, and would no doubt re-shape me again.

On shaky legs, I struggled to pull my wet clothes onto my wet body, and then walked back to my guesthouse through trees and plants that glistened in the after-rain sun. Heat pulled the moisture out of the ground, making the air steamy, and I breathed in the damp, earthy smell. Within minutes, clouds rolled across the sky again, the thunder roared, and voluptuous raindrops pelted and poured.

At Bombay's Victoria Terminus, the crowds propelled me further inside the train station. At the dozen or so ticket windows, people pushed and shoved with no sense of personal space. I waited for ages at the wrong window, only to be told to go to another. With gritted teeth, I fought against the flow of people, and went to yet another window.

'Madam, you need to get a Tourist Quota ticket,' said the man behind the fourth window I tried. 'We have a system here. You can't just buy a ticket.'

'Can't just buy a ticket?' What kind of system was that? It wasn't the man's fault, so I forced a smile. 'Tourist quota. Okay. Where will I get that, please?' I said.

'Look.' He pointed upwards. 'Look for the sign. Tourist Quota.'

Crowds behind me surged wave-like, and I turned, pushed my way back through. I felt a hand on my breast and knocked it away, sure it was an accident. The wooden signs above the ticket windows were old, and painted with faded, tiny letters. I couldn't find one that said *'Tourist Quota.'*

Bewildered and frustrated, I left the ticket hall and sat on my bag, leaning against the cool marble wall near the station entrance. A surge of sadness engulfed me, and wrapping my arms around my knees, I leaned my head forward. The bus journey from Goa had taken more than twenty hours. Tiredness and frustration were never a good mix.

Moisture collected in my eyes, and I wiped it away to see a pair of turquoise-clad legs standing directly in front of me. I looked up. The rest of the body wore a knee-length tunic in the same colour. Late afternoon sunlight streamed through the entrance, bringing out the sheen and softness of the silk. If it hadn't been my favourite colour, I would never have noticed, never looked up.

'Miss, are you alright?' I looked up at a pair of dark eyes and a tentative smile on a bearded face. 'Are you in need of some assistance?' he said, his voice deep and resonant.

'I'm fine, thank you. I'm just frustrated that I can't get a ticket.' I smiled then, taking in his thick, almost curly hair that reached just below his collar bone. With no parting, it fell naturally, like a lion's mane.

'Where are you wanting to go? May I assist you and get you a ticket? I have some friends here.'

'Rajasthan. Somewhere in Rajasthan.'

'You could go to Udaipur. I have been there, so I can recommend that it's very lovely. The lake is relaxing, and it's a quiet town.' He moved his hands with every phrase, and I smiled. 'From there, I'm sure you may travel around Rajasthan and enjoy many wonderful things.'

'Udaipur?' I said.

He smiled, his teeth even and white between full lips, his eyes crinkling at the corners. He reminded me of a Moghul painting, with his big dark eyes and hooked nose. Striking; he was strikingly handsome. It was hard to put an age on him, but I guessed he was somewhere around thirty years old.

'All Rajasthan is full of palaces and peacocks.' He flicked his wrist. 'You will like it, I am sure. Udaipur is a good place to start.'

'Okay then, on your recommendation, I'll try and get a ticket to Udaipur.' I smiled up at him. 'Thank you.'

'Let me arrange it for you. If you like, you can give me the money. There will be just a small, small service charge, and I will come back, momentarily, with a ticket for you.' He squatted down beside me, his gaze intense. Waving his hand in a flamboyant, almost Italian gesture, he smiled. 'It's no trouble, really.'

Handing over the money, I watched him walk away and turn a corner. Maybe I had been scammed, but I'd only given him a few dollars' worth of rupees, so it wasn't the end of the world. Something told me that he'd come back, so I decided to wait a while. Worst case scenario, I could jump a taxi, find a guesthouse, and then a travel agent to help me get a train ticket. After fifteen minutes, my legs ached from sitting scrunched up, and I stood, just as his turquoise-self returned.

'Your train leaves at ten o'clock tonight. Second-class in the ladies-only compartment to Ahmedabad. Then change trains, and arrive in Udaipur tomorrow, middle of the day.' He handed me the ticket, and a few rupees, the turquoise silk of his sleeve shimmering. 'You gave me too much. I am Haresh. And your name, Miss?'

'Mari,' I said, glad I'd waited. 'Short for Marianna.'

He smiled again, and I felt something stir within me. He stood at least five inches taller than me, so he must have been six foot three or four. 'Thank you, Haresh.' Turquoise Haresh. I looked at the ticket, slightly disappointed. 'Tonight? I'd hoped to stay a few days and see the city.'

'That is entirely my mistake. I am sorry, I did not ask your preference. Now, you can go upstairs and avail yourself of the ladies' waiting room. I think you can freshen up for a few rupees, and they have luggage storage also.' He rubbed his jaw, looking at me. 'Then, if you allow, I will take you, and show you Bombay.'

'Thanks for the offer, but I'll stay here.' I glanced at him, suddenly shy.

'Oh, but Bombay is beautiful. Let me show you the beauty of Bombay. You surely cannot leave her without loving her.'

There was something likeable about him and his poetic way of talking. The train didn't leave until ten o'clock, and five hours was a long time to kill in a railway station, so why not? Haresh had probably made enough profit out of me not to have to hang around the station for the rest of the day, and judging by the silk clothing, he obviously did quite well as a ticket tout. It'd be interesting to know how much my ticket had actually cost, but I didn't ask. It was worth whatever extra I'd paid to actually get one.

Half an hour or so later, after I'd *'availed myself of the ladies' waiting room'* and changed into a pair of black shalwar and a short-sleeved top patterned with small grey elephants, I met Turquoise Haresh at the station's main entrance. He hailed an autorickshaw, and we climbed up into the vehicle that was similar to the three wheeled tuk-tuks I'd seen in Thailand. Haresh was too tall for the little autorickshaw, and had to lean forwards, legs wide, his forearms on his thighs. Turning to me, he smiled, and my insides flipped. He spoke to the driver, and we set off through the traffic.

The pavements were busy with people, the tarmac with vehicles, and cows roamed everywhere. Whole families clung on to motorbikes and scooters as they wove their way between trucks and buses. Horns beeped every millisecond, people shouted and laughed. The vibrancy and energy were tangible. I did a double-take when we passed an elephant painted with bright pink and blue flowers. The animal trundled along the road, ignoring the traffic that passed within inches of it. A group of women in jewel-coloured saris stopped a man pushing a handcart piled high with cauliflowers, and children played a game of tag so close to the traffic that I had to look away. The auto-driver turned a corner, and came to a stop behind a uniformed marching band, their drums and trumpets filling the air with a military beat. If this was everyday life, it was a shame to whizz past it all in an autorickshaw, I wanted to be part of it.

'Can we walk?' I said.

'Is it because you are worried about where I will take you in the auto, Mari? Please, I assure you that I have nothing untoward planned.' His frown eased when I shook my head.

'No, nothing like that,' I said. Haresh had a point; I was in a city I didn't know, with a good-looking man I didn't know, and he could be taking me anywhere. Glancing at him, I wasn't sure I'd mind where he took me. He smiled at me and I felt a flush of warmth. 'I just think it would be nice to walk. I'm really hungry too.'

Haresh paid for the auto, and we walked for a while, jostling with people as they bartered at hole-in-the-wall shops which sold everything from cooking pots to clothing. With his hand on the small of my back, he guided me through the crowds, bending his head towards me now and then to ask if I was okay. He took me down winding laneways of dilapidated, mildewed buildings, past ornate temples, and on into open spaces.

'There's a nice place to eat nearby. I know a short cut,' Haresh said. 'Please, follow.'

The deserted alley was long, narrow and bereft of sunlight. Ahead of me, Haresh's sandals slapped against the concrete as he walked, the sound echoing against the buildings that flanked each side of the alley. I slowed my pace. Fear flicked its tongue, and I held my breath. What was I thinking, following a man down a darkened alley? My heart pumped too fast, and my mouth was dry. The gap between Haresh and I widened as he continued down the alley, and I stopped walking. Glancing over my shoulder, I gauged the distance. Should I run back to the main road? Was he far enough away not to catch me?

A man walked towards us. Haresh looked over his shoulder at me, and nodded at the man. My hands curled into fists, and I took a few steps backwards. Blood rushed through my ears, and my breathing was rapid. There was nowhere to go, nowhere to run. I'd never get away from two of them. When the man went through a door just ahead of me, closing it behind him, I let out a long breath, bending forwards with my hands on my thighs.

'What is it?' Haresh said, walking back towards me. 'Is something wrong?'

'I don't…I need…' I rambled.

'We are almost there. Look.' Haresh pointed to the end of the alley, to where the sun shone, and people filled the street. 'Let's get you a cool drink.'

Fifty heavy paces later, we emerged from the alley into an open space. Tall trees cast dense shade on one side, and Haresh stood, watching me intently for a moment before buying some water from a doorway-sized shop.

'Thank you,' I said, taking the small plastic bottle from him. 'I just got too hot.' Blaming my almost-panic attack on the heat seemed like a reasonable excuse. The last thing I wanted was to offend Haresh, but more than that, I felt foolish.

Across the road, a young woman placed a single marigold on top of an open fronted box. Inside, a small statue with no features sat on top of a bright pink plinth. It was hard to make out what the statue was, but it was adorned with jasmine flowers, and sandalwood incense burned in front of it.

'Is it okay to take a photo? I said, digging for my Instamatic camera in the bottom of my cloth bag. 'I don't want to be disrespectful.'

'Yes, of course. Also, I can take one of you,' Haresh said. We crossed the road, and he reached for my camera. 'Shall I?'

'No, I don't like having my photo taken,' I said.

'But why? You are very…your green eyes. I am thinking that you are pretty, if you don't mind me saying.'

'I don't mind.' Smiling, I took a photo of the statue. 'Thank you.'

Haresh led me to a restaurant, pushed open the glass door, and gestured for me to go inside. The air-conditioning in the canteen-style eatery was wonderful after the humid heat of the streets.

Haresh ordered a *thali* for us both. Different foods in small bowls sat on one side of a round metal tray, a pile of rice on the other. My mouth watered at the delicious aromas, and I dug my spoon into the rice, then the vegetable curry. Haresh dolloped a spoonful of yellow dahl onto the edge of the rice and mixed it together on his tray with the fingers of his right hand. He transferred the food into his mouth easily, not dropping even one morsel into his neatly trimmed beard. I took the hint and tried to eat with my hand, but I struggled to tear off a piece of the warm flatbread, let alone get the rice and curry into my mouth. A flush of embarrassment crept up my neck when Haresh looked at my messy fingers and grinned.

'Are you feeding the elephants?' Haresh inclined his head, but didn't look directly at my chest where a glob of dahl had dropped. I laughed and dipped the end of a paper napkin into my water glass, dabbing at the mess.

When we'd finished eating, Haresh insisted on paying for our meal. He held the door of the restaurant open, and the humidity hit me like a wet blanket when I stepped onto the street. Dusk had fallen, and lights shone from every window. Neon signs in English and Hindi flickered into life, and the streetlights came on. We took a black and yellow taxi for a quick tour of impressive colonial buildings, lit up like monuments in the darkening evening.

In the suburb of Colaba, Haresh took me to a large Krishna Temple which was full of scrawny people who looked European or American, maybe Australian. The women wore drab coloured nylon saris, and the men were draped in orange robes, short pony-tails sticking out of their otherwise shaven heads. They sang something I couldn't understand, and it felt surreal and maybe a little false. Maybe they were opting out of real life, perhaps running away from something. But who was I to judge? That was exactly what I was doing; escaping reality, running away from my past, and all the trauma I'd lived through.

Passing the temple bookstand, I bought a thin book about the main Hindu gods and goddesses, hoping to learn a little about them.

'I was thinking of staying at an ashram,' I said. 'Or maybe volunteering somewhere. I need to create some good karma. But this place has put me off. It's more like a hippy commune.'

Haresh looked into my eyes, smiling as if he knew something about me that I didn't. 'There are many other ways to help your karma,' he said. 'Let's drink tea, *chai*, and I'll tell you.' He gestured to a chai stand on the other side of the road, and grabbed my hand. My stomach flipped at his touch, and we crossed the road, dodging traffic. 'Most towns have charitable organisations to help the poor,' he said. 'Also, you can find children's homes, or old peoples' shelters. But please, be careful of any widows' refuge. Not for your sake, but perhaps other Hindus won't be comfortable if you are associating with widows.'

'Oh?' I said. We sat on cracked plastic stools by the roadside, and Haresh spoke to the *chai-wallah*, the man who ran the tea stall. The chai-wallah's multi-coloured turban, and the pointy ends of his waxed moustache made him look like a panto villain, or a whacky magician. Traffic whizzed past, and the fumes caught in the back of my throat. I reached up to take my glass of chai from the chai-wallah, and sipped gratefully.

'There are some who consider widows to be very bad luck,' said Haresh. 'It's an old way of thinking; widows have no place in society after their husbands die. There cannot be a wife is there is no husband. And a bride goes to live with her husband's family when they marry, so she is reliant on them to look after her. It's not easy to understand, but ancient religious practices have become part of Indian culture. Not everyone today feels comfortable with this, but things are slow to change.'

'I read about *suttee*, where the widow threw herself onto her husband's funeral pyre.' I shuddered. 'Horrific.'

'Totally barbaric,' Haresh said. 'It was the Britishers who banned that, back in the eighteen-hundreds. But it's true that even nowadays, many widows still suffer. They are lucky if their husbands' families are keeping them, and taking care of them.' He drank his chai, holding the glass between thumb and forefinger. There was an elegance in his hands, something theatrical in their movement. 'But sometimes, they are not treated well. There are many stories of widows getting a thrashing, or being starved, or worse.' He looked at the ground, his brow creasing. 'In those cases, if the widow is not thrown out, she will mostly leave.'

'That sounds worse than bad luck,' I said. I wanted to say it sounded cruel, but travelling in a country didn't give me the right to judge its traditions. Imagining a heartbroken woman, mourning the death of her husband, and rejected by his family made me sad, even though I didn't fully understand. 'Their own children throw them out?'

Haresh shrugged, ran his hand through his hair, which fell back into place like something from a shampoo advert. 'It is like that. Sometimes it is to do with inheritance.' He tilted his head to one side, still frowning, looking at me intently. 'But mostly, it's because that is how it is. People don't think to question, they just stick to tradition. I am a little more open minded. I like to think I am not so traditional. My brother-in-law died, and it was my wish that my sister come and live with me. My wife, she was pregnant at that time, and was not in agreement.'

'I'm sorry.' I tried to keep my face neutral, not to show any shock or surprise. Families were tricky, I knew that. My mother threw me out when I was seventeen. Uncle Saturnino bought me a ticket to Sydney, gave me a couple of hundred pounds, and I hadn't been home since. Shaking the thought away, I sipped my chai, focusing on the sweetness infused with cardamom and ginger.

'My wife and I had many arguments about it,' said Haresh. 'She even threatened to go back to her family in Poona. I know that she was only using the superstition of bad luck as an excuse; for whatever reason, she didn't want my sister to be living with us.' He sucked air through his teeth. 'We were married only eleven months, and our first child was due at any moment. My sister stayed with her husband's parents and their other son for a while, but then I heard she ran away.'

'Do you know where she went?'

'I do not.' Haresh smiled, sadly. 'I looked for her for some time. I even went to Vrindavan.'

'What's that?'

'Vrindavan. It's a city just a few hours from Delhi. There are many widows' refuges there. Some charities are working to try and help them. It's a very holy city, with many, many temples,' he waved his hand in circles, 'and it attracts many, many widows. My sister wasn't there. There are widows' refuges across all of India. But I cannot search each and every one.'

'No. It sounds hard for her. And for you.'

'When our parents passed away, she was just eight years old, and I was thirteen. A few years later, I sent her to secondary school when we came to Bombay, and when it was time, I arranged a good marriage for her. It is a regretful thing that I did not help her when she needed me most.' He held the chai to his lips, sipping. Frowning, he looked at me. 'I am sorry, I should not be speaking of these things.'

'No, it's fine…it helps to talk. Especially to strangers. I do it a lot. I feel like they won't judge me, or think badly of me.'

'I think we are not strangers, actually.'

'And your child?' I said, the feeling coursing through me was more than a silent agreement. 'How old is it now?'

'My daughter, Tara, is three.' He smiled, straightened his shoulders and signalled for more chai.

'Tara…we have that name in English.'

'In Hindi, Tara means *'star'*.'

'I have a sister called Stella, and that means *'star'* too.'

We laughed. 'Tara is a little less than three,' Haresh said. 'My wife went home to her parents in Poona saying she could not manage the baby without her own mother. But really, it was because she was not happy here in Bombay.' Holding fresh chai in one hand, he flicked the other. 'We found that we did not like each other after the first days of marriage. So, you see? I could have helped my sister after all.'

Haresh looked wistful, and I felt sorry for him. What was the wife like? How could she be so cruel as to deprive him of his child? But then, look at my mother. By throwing me out, she'd deprived my father and my sisters of me. My heart ached at the thought of my twin sisters, Sofia and Stella. Haresh's story mirrored my own. We were both alone; I was estranged from my family, and so was he. He'd lost his sister, I'd lost mine. Perhaps he felt the same remorse and loneliness that I did. Maybe he lay awake at night wondering how his family were, and how he could heal the rift, just as I did.

'Don't give up,' I said. Something in my heart twitched, and I wanted to embrace him, tell him it would all be okay, even if it wouldn't be. 'Things will change. They always do.'

'Yes.' He slapped his thigh. 'And so, as we are trading secrets, tell me why is it that you are wanting to create some good karma. What did you do that was very wrong?' He laughed, his eyes playful.

'Two things. I have not spoken to my family for six years. My younger sister died in an accident, and my mother blames me. Then last year, my best friend, Kate, was killed while we were working in Japan. I...' Blinking away the tears, I placed the back of my fingers across my lips. 'Sorry.'

'No, I am the one who is sorry.' Haresh cleared his throat. 'You are suffering, and I was not intending to upset you further, Mari. You know, a person's time of birth, the events of their life, the time of death, everything is written. Everyone's story is written.' I looked away, watching a woman rub her child's face with the floaty end of her sari. 'We don't have to talk anymore, although if you want to, there is always time to listen.' Haresh briefly touched my arm. 'I'm sorry you have such a burden.'

'We both have sad stories, Haresh.' I smiled, standing up. 'Life, hey?' He stood, looking down at me. We stared at each other for a moment too long. 'Come on,' I said. 'Show me a little more of your beautiful Bombay.'

Just before ten, Haresh and I arrived back at the station, and joined the throngs of people waiting for trains. Rain pelted on the roofs that covered the platforms; we'd been lucky it'd stayed dry all afternoon. Standing under the light, I pulled my guidebook out of my bag, thumbing through it until I found Udaipur.

Haresh took the book from me and wrote his telephone number and address on the inside cover. 'When you come back to Bombay, come and find me,' he said, flashing a smile.

The train pulled in alongside the platform like a dragon, surrounded by smoke and puffs of steam. I followed Haresh until we found the ladies' carriage. I lifted my holdall, ready to board the train. Haresh leaned towards me, our eyes met and I held my breath.

'Thanks for everything today,' I said.

'It has been my pleasure. You know, I think it is written; our paths will cross again. You and I.' Haresh laughed. 'It's a shame that I cannot kiss you.'

'I wouldn't be offended,' I said, looking at his mouth.

'Ah, Mari. Affection in public is not permitted in India.' His smile floored me.

Something shifted in me, but I didn't answer, just looked at him. With his hand under my elbow, I stepped onto the train. Turquoise Haresh waved me off from the platform, a flash of peacock colour in the grey night.

Chapter Three
यात्रा

Shivpur 1986

MOVING THE FADED velvet armchair out of the way, I opened the window. The sound of children playing outside in the street drifted in with the breeze. It was still too hot, so I crossed to the alcove on the other side of my room. Gently pulling at a tassle on the end of the embroidered fabric that hung above the alcove, I crawled on the window-seat that was long enough to lie on, and as wide as a double bed. I opened one of four stained-glass windows, intending to open them all. In the narrow alley below, a woman in a white sari crouched on the ground, her head bobbed back and forth as the man she pleasured grunted. Closing the window quietly, I tried not to laugh.

I changed into a clean *kurta* tunic and shalwar, looped the *dupatta* scarf around my neck. Wiping the sweat from my lip, and hoping the lovers in the alley were finished, I opened all the windows, desperate for the breeze to cool the room.

Downstairs, I peered into Mr and Mrs Mehta's living room. She'd rented me her spare room, and insisted I think of her and her husband as family.

'Dolly Auntie? Can I pay for another week up front?' I said, still getting used to the reversed words.

'Another week?' said Dolly. She bustled out of her kitchen,

and into the hallway, wiping her floury hands on a cloth. 'I'm glad. Usually, if we have a guest, they only stay two or three nights. This will be your second week; are you not bored here in this small place.'

'Not at all.' I laughed. 'It's perfect for me after the month I spent in Rajasthan.' The slower pace of life in Shivpur was much needed after the bustle of the northern cities. 'I've been travelling since I left Japan at New Year, so that's what?' I counted on my fingers. 'Almost eight months. Even when I got to Goa in April, thinking I'd just relax on the same beach for weeks, I moved around. The longest I've spent anywhere was eight days in Jaisalmer. I'd like to stop for a while, just stay in one place for a few months.'

Dolly took the folded rupees, and tucked them into her *choli*, sari blouse. 'Good.' She smiled, her plump face creasing. 'You are welcome for as long as you want to stay. I'm making paratha, do you want some?'

'I'm off to Sharma's now. Maybe when I get back?'

'You are good to volunteer with the elderly. I'm not sure about these residential homes though. They are becoming very popular. Advertisements in the Times of India and all.' Dolly nodded. 'It just shows how our society is changing. Young people too busy working and what not to care for their elders.'

'The residents seem happy enough. There's a sense of community there. I like working in the kitchen with Kavita, although her food isn't as good as yours, Dolly Auntie.'

Dolly smiled, pulled her shoulders back. 'But the elderly are healthy?'

'Age related problems, I'm told. Not quite sure what that means, but they have helpers. Muddy said it's mostly forgetfulness; one lady made chai and left the gas on and the kitchen went on fire.'

'I have not seen Muddy for some time. Busy with his police work I expect.'

'I see Muddy everywhere,' I laughed. 'He's friends with the

manager, Kiran Lal, so he pops into Sharma's quite a bit. They were in the same school year together.'

The bus took me three kilometers through the boulder strewn landscape to Keshnagar, and I began the walk to Sharma's Residential Home for the Elderly. Fleetwood Mac's *'Don't Stop'* played on my Walkman, and I sang as I walked the narrow dirt strip that ran alongside the tarmac. Patches of shade from the palm trees that grew between the road and the fields stopped the intense sun from scorching me. My hair frizzed at the nape of my neck and temples, and sweat stuck my clothes to my skin. Dodging puddles left from the previous day's rain, I slipped in the drying mud that was still wet underneath a cracked surface, and regaining my balance, decided to take my chances with the traffic.

A minute later, Muddy pulled alongside me, cruising his Royal Enfield motorbike that purred like a panther.

'Wanna ride?' he said.

'Do you ever do any work, Muddy?' I said, taking my headphones off. 'You spend all your time riding around on your bike, or looking for me.'

'Police work is shift work, you know that.' He shifted forwards. 'I'm younger than you think I am, Mari. I want some fun while I'm still in my twenties. I'll be thirty all too soon. You should have some fun with me.'

All I could do was roll my eyes; I'd heard it all before.

Revving the bike, Muddy waited for me to climb on, and we roared off. Sitting side-saddle, with one hand resting on Muddy's shoulder, I tried to keep my balance. I wasn't confident enough to ride without holding on, but he ploughed through the traffic, and I watched his face in the wing mirror. Much easier to look at than the oncoming craziness of ox-drawn wagons, buses, autos, and people pushing overloaded handcarts.

Two women in white saris walked in single file along the tarmac, and Muddy gave them a wide berth. His hair moved in the wind, and he turned to say something that was snatched away before it reached my ears. Another group of women in white turned off the road, heading down a narrow track that led to a single-story building. Maybe it was a convent, and they were novice nuns, ready to give their lives to the devotion of Christ, or to tend the sick like Mother Theresa. There were plenty of Catholics in Goa, and I'd seen a church or two in Bombay.

A few minutes later, Muddy pulled up in front of a large two-storey building. A red and white painted sign said '*Sharma's Residential Home for the Elderly.*'

'Muddy,' I said, 'those ladies in white...I see them around the temple too. Are they missionaries? Nuns seem a bit out of place at a Hindu temple.'

'Nuns?' He laughed. 'No, they are widows. Hindu widows don't wear colour because they have given up all pleasures and vanities in life. It's called tonsure.' He glanced at me, a half-smile bringing his dimples to life. 'They live together in that house we passed. Some people believe they are cursed or unlucky.'

'Someone in Bombay told me that. It's sad; they lose their husbands and their families.'

'You see? Unlucky.'

I smiled, but I was thinking of Turquoise Haresh, and wondering what his lips would have felt like.

'Mari?' Muddy said.

'Sorry. So, what do the widows do at the temple?'

'They beg...they have to make a few rupees somehow, to buy food. Some will pray for you, or sing a devotional song. Sometimes the younger ones get paid... well, you know.'

I thought of the woman I'd seen in the alley. From being a wife, and possibly a mother, she'd been reduced to giving blow-jobs in back alleys just to survive. My stomach twisted with indignation that worldwide, women with no choices ended up selling their bodies. And that men were always there to buy them.

Muddy walked ahead of me along the narrow path and through the archway. Opening the wrought iron gate, he turned to me and smiled. Shoes off, we padded across the hall, the tiles cool under my feet.

Kiran greeted us at the entrance along with one of the residents, Leena, a small lady in a pale green sari. She carried a round brass tray in her delicate hands. The flame in the small dish of burning oil danced as she moved towards me. She reached up, and I ducked a little, so it was easier for her. Dabbing her middle finger into a dish of red powder, she dotted it between my eyebrows. Then Leena circled the tray clockwise, in front of me, three times.

'Good morning,' said Kiran. He ran his long, skinny fingers over his moustache. His short-sleeved shirt showed his thin arms which made me think of a daddy-long-legs. 'Everyone will be very happy you to see you again, Mari.'

'Thank you. What a lovely welcome,' I said. I'd only met Kiran once before, but he looked really familiar. Maybe I'd seen him on a bus or at the temple.

Kiran and Muddy chatted, and I followed Leena into the garden. The residents welcomed me with smiles and the interchangeable '*namaste*', or '*namaskar*'.

The residents sat on benches in the shade of leafy trees, and a few sat on swinging seats that reminded me of the Moghul paintings I'd seen in the palaces of Rajasthan. A group of women chatted around a wrought iron garden table, and two men played chess under a pink sun umbrella. On the veranda, a young man sat on a wooden sofa, reading a newspaper to the white haired-gentleman sitting next to him.

'Poor old chap,' said Leena. 'He's losing his sight. He likes the helper, Shreyas, to read to him every day.'

Leena took my arm, and we crossed the courtyard to the veranda.

'Please come and sit,' said Simran Chauhan, sitting a wicker chair on the veranda. Her blue chiffon sari rustled as she adjusted the fabric on her shoulder.

'Yes, join us,' said her companion, Vivika Singh, removing her reading glasses, and placing her book on the table in front of her.

'And you are how old?' asked Simran. Her smile wasn't genuine, and her sari rustled every time she moved.

'I'm almost twenty-four,' I said, pulling up another chair.

'Not married?' Gold bangles rattled down Simran's arms as she threw her hands up. 'At twenty-four?'

'Simran, let her be,' said Vivika. 'They do things differently, these modern girls.'

The morning passed quickly as we chatted about nothing important. Rekha, one of the helpers, brought us chai at eleven o'clock. After that, I helped Kavita in the kitchen by putting brinjal pickle into twenty-five small bowls; one for each resident. At one o'clock, Kavita and I dashed around, serving the residents their lunch of dahl, rice, and vegetable curry. Everyone ate in the fan-cooled dining room, away from the heat and the flies.

'Mari, come,' said Kavita, the cook. She stood at the door of her kitchen, her cotton sari dwarfing her tiny frame. 'You've been a great help to me again, dear. Thank you.'

'I enjoy it,' I said. 'I can stay and help wash the plates, if you like.' My mouth watered at the smell of the food, and I hoped Kavita would offer me some. She usually did, but I never liked to ask.

'No, no. I can manage. I'll ask one of the helpers.' Kavita looked at me sideways. 'We have to make do until someone else is hired. You won't be here forever. Young Shanti came every day to help me. But she stopped coming, and no one has seen her for more than one month.'

'Maybe she's unwell?' I said. The pile of plates I carried were heavy, and I placed them on the counter.

'Shanti's father came looking for her. He said her clothes were gone, and she'd run away.' Kavita twisted her hands together. 'Her friends and family don't know where she is. Or why she left.'

Cold ran through me, and my chest tightened. The agony of waiting and wondering when someone didn't come home wasn't something I'd wish on anyone. I took a deep breath, and pushed the memory to the back of my mind.

'It must be hard for her family,' I said. 'Did they tell the police?'

'There is only her father, and he is a poor man. He reported her missing, but she has not been found.' Kavita's eyes were moist. 'I feel sorry.' I put my hand or her arm. 'You're a nice girl Mari, and I'm glad you are here.' Kavita took a plate, and dolloped rice and vegetables on to it, before holding it out to me. 'Here, take this and sit with the residents.'

'Thanks. I'll enjoy this, it looks lovely.' I turned to leave.

'Mari, one thing,' Kavita said. 'I've been meaning to say. Be careful around Kiran.'

'What do you mean?' I said.

'He's a bad sort.' Kavita pulled a face, stepped closer to me. 'I think Kiran had something to do with Shanti going missing, and I've seen the way he looks at you. Now, go. Eat.'

Kavita went through the back door of the kitchen, and the rattle of metal pots echoed through the kitchen.

I stood at the dining room door, plate in hand. What did Kavita mean about Kiran? Had he upset the girl, Shanti? Maybe he'd given her a telling off. If her clothes were gone, maybe she'd just moved to another town to work.

Vivika, Simran, and Leena called to me from a table in the corner where they sat with their husbands. Not wanting to be rude, I joined them. They expertly ate with one hand, and I tried to copy them, gathering the rice and dahl with the tips of my fingers. My technique was improving, but I was still a messy eater. The ladies praised me, and their husbands talked amongst themselves about cricket and politics.

'I seem to have misplaced another gold bangle. I thought I had five, but now I have only four,' said Simran. 'And I'm sure I originally had six.'

'Oh, you've lost something again?' Leena said. 'You lost the book you were reading the other day. You leave things everywhere.'

'No, that was months ago,' said Vivika. 'Simran was worried

it might get wet during the first rain, remember?'

Simran's face creased. 'Yaar, old age is no fun.'

'Don't say anything,' said Leena. She leaned in close to me, spoke softly. 'But I think we need to keep an eye on Simran.'

'There's nothing wrong with my hearing,' said Simran. 'I'm fully…what's the word? Oh yes, compis methol.'

'Compos mentis.' Simran's husband corrected her without eye contact.

Vivika's husband smiled at me, a gold crown beside his incisor glinting in the light. 'You are a pretty one,' he said. 'Such fair skin. Like our daughter, she's very fair also.'

The bragging began then. The three women tried to outdo each other with tales of the good marriages they'd made for their sons. The conversation turned to the amount of wedding gold they'd given and received, and the clever grandsons they had; all of whom would make excellent doctors or lawyers or accountants once they finished their studies. Tall and handsome, they'd make good husbands too. Such good catches were sure to be popular with the match-makers. The granddaughters were all so fair-skinned and pretty, with sweet dispositions that would help secure good marriages, even in America. They could cook, sew, run a household, manage servants. It struck me that the British may have left India in the 1940s, but it seemed like they'd left some old-fashioned values behind. And I christened Vivika, Leena and Simaran, 'The Aunties.'

I visited Sharma's every other day, but each time it felt false, contrived. Helping Kavita was the only good I was doing. Drinking chai with wealthy women in silk saris didn't feel worthwhile at all. Maybe atoning wasn't supposed to make me feel good. One morning, I spent half an hour talking to Rahul and Sarita Sohal, who had just received a box of ripe mangoes from their son in Bangalore.

'Tell Kavita, the cook, to bring some plates so that we can all enjoy these mangoes,' said Sarita. Obviously, she'd had servants at home. 'These are the last of the season.'

Wandering through the dining room, I almost bumped into Kiran on his way out of the kitchen.

'You have arrived. Splendid,' he said. 'Excuse me, I must do some administration today. Excuse me.'

He rushed away, running his hand over his short hair. Where had I seen him before? It was at the edge of my mind, but I couldn't quite remember. Kavita stood at the preparation counter, her pink and purple sari dishevelled. She straightened the pleats of fabric on her shoulder, turning away from me.

'Morning, Kavita. Can I take some plates?' She didn't respond. 'Kavita?'

'Yes, yes, take what you want.' She still didn't turn, just waved her hand dismissively. She sniffed and wiped her eyes. 'Take them and go.'

Biting my lip, I stood for a moment, unsure what to do. Reaching up to the shelf, I lifted a small stack of stainless-steel plates. I stopped at the kitchen door and turned to see Kavita wipe her cheek with her *pallu*, the end of her sari. I carried the plates back to the Sohals, and needing knives, returned to the kitchen. Kavita was outside on the kitchen's terrace, crouched by the stand pipe, washing out a cooking pot.

'What happened? I saw Kiran leave. Did he upset you?' I said.

Kavita squinted at me, then raised her eyebrows. She focused on her pot, scrubbing at it again, even though it was clean. Turning on the tap, she caught water in her cupped hand and threw it over the tiled floor and walls. The drain gurgled thirstily.

'Kiran is very free with his hands, Mari. He thinks he has the right.' Kavita's voice was resigned, as if this was something she should just accept. 'Make sure you don't let him get too close to you.'

'You've tried to stop him?' I crouched beside her, handed her another pot from the pile.

'Many times. But, you know, this is a good job for me. My husband is the night guard here. He's here from eight in the evening until eight in the morning, just in case anything is needed. My children need food, clothes, school books.' Scrubbing harder at the pot, she sighed. 'Rent is high, also.'

'Doesn't mean Kiran can grope you,' I said.

'He is a fiend, and it's not like he's sex-starved.' She shook her head. 'His poor wife. I feel sorry for her. Everyone knows he visits brothels and pays for sex with the temple prostitutes.'

'Temple prostitutes?' I frowned.

'Sex and religion are closely linked, Mari. All part of life's renewal. Kiran even has sex with widows.'

Then it clicked. I remembered where I'd seen Kiran. He'd been with the woman in the white sari, in the alley behind my room. Running my hand over my forehead, I sighed.

'But widows are unlucky, so why would a man pay for sex with one?'

'Men need a lot of sex *nah*? Even a widow has something to interest a man.' She pointed between her legs. 'Men like to think they are so powerful. Sex and power; it's the same. Widow's bad luck doesn't touch them.'

'Kiran shouldn't be molesting you like this, Kavita,' I said.

'I know, but what to do? Also, he calls me a thief. I make a little extra food,' Kavita said, 'a simple dahl or some vegetables, and leave it for my best friend who lives in the widows' house. Otherwise, I don't know how she would survive. Kiran says I will lose my job, but he won't say anything if I'm nice to him. And if I lose my job, so will my husband.'

'What? Kiran can't blackmail you like that. Is your best friend the one he -?'

'No, not with Bhavna. She and I grew up all our lives together. Our mothers were also friends before we were born. My house is the small yellow one.' She pointed over her shoulder. 'Just behind here. Bhavna's family still live in the house across the field.'

'Life-long friends,' I said. That wasn't something I'd ever experienced. I'd lived in Australia, Spain and England before I was fifteen. 'And then?'

'Then Bhavna and her husband moved to Bangalore, and I didn't see her for ten years. Then I heard her husband died. Heart attack. Her mother-in-law threw her out, blaming Bhavna for her son's death.' My sharp intake of breath made Kavita glance at me. 'Quite normal.'

'Do you see her now?' I said.

'No, but I help by sending food. Mari, Kiran... he is not a good man. Some residents find their jewellery and money is missing. And he tells them they are imagining things, that they never had such jewellery or sums of money. And they doubt themselves, thinking he is right. They are forgetful and sometimes confused. But I know, I am sure, he is stealing.'

I told her what Simran had said about her gold bangles.

'You see, it happens from time to time. But that's not the worst thing. Shanti and Kiran were doing it, I am sure.'

Chattering and giggling heralded the caregivers' arrival at the kitchen door, ready for their chai-break. Manjula wore a green and orange sari, Rekha's was yellow and petrol blue, Puja's turquoise and magenta. They were a trio of birds of paradise.

'Doing it? You mean having sex?' I said.

'Yes. Okay, Mari. We'll talk again later, when we prepare lunch,' said Kavita.

Grabbing a couple of knives, I went back to the Sohals, seating myself next to Sarita. She glared at me, probably because I'd taken so long to come back with the knives. Once she had peeled and cut the mangoes, I handed out plates to the few residents who were in the courtyard.

'These are for you, dear,' said Sarita, handing me two mangoes. 'Take them back to your guesthouse, and enjoy them later.'

After lunch, I walked back to Keshnagar. The sky brooded, gathering heavy clouds, and I hoped I'd make it to the bus stop before it rained. A truck rumbled past, spewing up a cloud of dust as the wheels hit the narrow dirt path at the side of the road.

The helpers had been in and out of the kitchen all morning, so

Kavita hadn't had the chance to tell me about Kiran and Shanti. Perhaps he'd broken up with her, and she was heartbroken. A girl's virginity was highly prized in India; perhaps she'd been ashamed and couldn't face her family. That would be reason enough to run away.

And how dare Kiran molest Kavita? He was obviously a sexual predator. And what kind of man would steal from old people? My pace quickened, my thoughts tumbling. If I could get some proof that he was stealing, I could report him to the owners of Sharma's. And I had to find a way to make Kiran leave Kavita alone. But how? Maybe reporting him was the way for me to get some good karma. Two birds, one stone.

Leaving the mangoes Sarita had given me under the palm tree on the corner, I walked ahead, dodging a big brown cow as she headed for the undergrowth between the road and the fields beyond. Two women in white saris walked towards me. A man pushing a handcart as wide as a small car trundled behind them. Surely he couldn't see where he was going over the empty plastic containers piled onto his cart? He nearly knocked the women over, and they stood back as far as they could without stepping into the prickly undergrowth. I did the same when he passed me a moment later, and the women stayed still as I drew level with them.

'Hello, namaste,' I said.

The older lady didn't react, but the younger one smiled at me. At about five-foot-seven, she was taller than most Indian women I'd seen.

'Good afternoon, Miss,' the girl said, tucking a wayward strand of thick curly hair back into the bun it had escaped from.

The older lady said something in Hindi, and by the tone of her voice, she was telling the girl off.

'I left some mangoes under the tree,' I said. 'Please take them before that cow gets there.'

'Thank you,' the girl said.

The older woman reached the tree first, and retrieved the

mangoes. The girl waved at me, but her smile dropped when her companion slapped her arm.

Chapter Four
यात्रा

ON EITHER SIDE of the wide pathway that led to Shivpur's temple, women sat on groundsheets, the sequined edges of their brightly-coloured saris glittering in the morning sun. Others sat under makeshift tarpaulin shelters, and all of them sold something for the temple pilgrims; flower garlands, incense, tiny clay devotional lamps and the oil to burn in them. A woman in a yellow and gold sari called to me, holding up jasmine and marigold garlands. I stopped beside her, and handing over a few rupees, chose a short string of jasmine flowers. The flower seller stood behind me, and tucked the end of the string into my scrunchie so that the flowers covered my ponytail. Further towards the temple, I bought a glass of masala chai, and sat on a low stool, sharing the shade of the lady chai-wallah's red umbrella.

A tall girl smiled at me, and I smiled back. She took a step towards me, and I recognised her from the previous day, when I'd left the mangoes under the tree. She hesitated, and turned away. Perhaps she was shy, or worried that the older lady would tell her off again. It was a shame, I'd like to have talked to the girl. She looked about my age, and way too young to be a widow.

The air was hot and still, heavy with the rhythm of chanted prayers and the heady perfume of sandalwood. The temple bell rang out in a single clang that echoed against the boulders and rocks that surrounded it. Male pilgrims wearing only a white lungi around their lower halves, and three stripes of ash across their foreheads, walked solemnly through the temple entrance. Emotion surged through me, and the hairs on the back of my neck stood on end. I'd seen more than a few temples during the three months I'd been in India, but this one had a rawness, a simplicity about it that drew me back day after day.

Women in white saris moved amongst the crowd, speaking softly to one person, and then another, but nobody responded to them. The beggar man sat in his usual place by the temple entrance, his clothes worn and dirty. He scrabbled in the dust for the coins people dropped to the ground. I crouched beside him, and held out a few rupees. It was only then that I noticed the putrid stench coming from his bandaged foot.

To my shame, I dropped the coins on the ground, and backed away quickly. Maybe he needed antibiotics or some ointment. Or should I take him to a doctor? Why hadn't someone already done that for him? Smiling at me, the beggar picked up the coins, and I placed my hands in prayer position.

I followed the pilgrims though the entrance of the temple grounds, into an open courtyard. Groups of people gathered on the steps and flagstones, their quiet chatter drowned by chanted prayers. A child toddled, arms outstretched, trying to catch pigeons. Closed wooden doors flanked one side of the courtyard, their paint faded and peeling, and I perched on a doorstep drinking in the atmosphere. The serenity soothed me like a lover's caress, but the underlying vibrancy, the sense of life and all its joys was mesmerising.

Thick purple-black clouds rumbled overhead, bringing more monsoon rain. Langur monkeys ran along the flat roofs of the temple's outer buildings, swinging on the overhead electric cables, clambering up into the carved niches and crevices of the temple ready to take shelter.

Sitting there, I felt at peace for the first time in ages, and I thought back to when I was hiding in the mountains of Japan after Kate was killed, to when Asa told me that acceptance was the balm that heal all wounds. That kind lady popped into my head often; she'd done so much for me, even put herself at risk by taking me in. If Asa was right, and I managed to find acceptance, would I finally be able to let go of the past? Would my regret and remorse disappear, or just become something I could live with? I looked at my forearm, ran my finger along the still-vivid scar. What if the guilt continued to layer itself over everything until the colours changed and the light disappeared? What then?

Breathing in the smell of sandalwood incense, I wanted to sit at the temple forever, and it was only the fat, pelting rain, and the thought that Dolly Auntie would definitely have made something delicious, that sent me running through the streets back to the Mehtas'.

Early next morning, I waited for the bus to Keshnagar, specifically so that I could go to the pharmacy to buy something for the beggar. Two young men stood beside me at the bus stop, their arms around each other, staring at me. I turned away, and took my bottle of water out of my bag. Swigging a mouthful or two, I screwed the plastic lid back on the bottle, and opened my little book of Hindu gods. It was the third time I'd read it, and I was still unsure of who was who. It was complicated. There were so many gods and goddesses; Shiva and his wife Parvati, and their son the elephant-headed boy, Ganesh, then Krishna and Radha, Saraswathi, thousands more. All the deities were different incarnations of the same three gods; Brahma, Vishnu and Shiva, and each of those was an avatar of one supreme being. God.

Each deity had a specific divine quality, a specific manifestation of energy. The comparison wasn't direct, but they made me think of the Catholic saints my Spanish mother had taught me about. St Jude for lost causes, St Christopher for travel. Hindus had Kali to destroy what didn't work and rebuild it, Ganesh for good luck and overcoming problems. There were too many gods to remember, but Shiva and Parvati were my favourites because of their romance. I was a sucker for a romance. Parvati loved Shiva, but he wouldn't love her back. She waited years for him to fall in love with her, and finally they married. And it was believed that through their sexual union, life carried on, and the world kept turning. And whatever happened, whatever awful things I'd done, life did carry on.

In Keshnagar, the pharmacist was helpful, and I bought what he suggested, although we didn't know what the beggar's actual problem was. After a glass of chai at three different chai stands, I jumped the bus back to Shivpur. The journey was hot, dusty, and crowded. Three people were seated where two could fit, and sacks and bundles filled the aisle. I stood at the back, near the steps and the concertina doors of the rear exit. As the bus lurched, I altered my stance, trying to keep my balance. Someone's hand slid between my legs and squeezed.

'Get off me,' I yelled, turning to see who had done it. It could have been any one of the men who surrounded me, and I glared at them. 'Who just grabbed me?'

'What happened?' An older man in a checked shirt pushed through the crowd and stood beside me. 'Tell me, did someone bother you?'

'Someone just grabbed me between the legs.'

The man shouted something, and the bus came to a halt. The men at the back of the bus shouted and argued with each other, hands flying everywhere.

'Is this the culprit?' said the checked shirt man. 'He touched you?'

'I don't know.' I said. 'I didn't see who it was.'

There was more dialogue in heated tones, then the male passengers slapped and hit the person they blamed for groping me.

'He has admitted. We will put him down from the bus,' said the checked shirt man. 'This is not right that he has troubled you.'

The men bundled the culprit off the bus, slapping and kicking him until he fell to the ground. He shielded his head with his arms, but they kept kicking him.

'*Bas*, enough,' I yelled. 'Stop, please, that's enough.'

Nonchalantly, the men got back on the bus, and a seat was found for me. I accepted gratefully.

'You need to watch your behaviour,' said a woman across the aisle. 'If you stand with the men, what do you think will happen? They can't be expected to control themselves. Always stay with other ladies.' She tutted, and wagged her finger. 'What do you expect if you don't use your dupatta properly to cover yourself?'

She pulled at her own dupatta, and following her lead, I adjusted mine to drape over my chest. I didn't know the dupatta had a modesty purpose; I'd naively thought it was decorative, and had worn it like a scarf.

'Sorry,' I said.

Heat flooded my face. The excessive violence towards the culprit had upset me. Wasn't it a massive overreaction to beat and kick someone in the dirt like that? And yet I was being blamed for the fact he'd groped me. The need for gender segregation hadn't occurred to me for a short bus trip, and it should have. I'd used the Ladies' Retiring Room at the train station in Bombay, and Turquoise Haresh had booked me a berth in the ladies-only train compartment. Thinking of him brought a brief smile to my lips. I pulled my guidebook out of my bag and turned to the page where he'd written his name. Haresh Chandekar. Such a shame I hadn't spent longer in Bombay. But then, I'd probably never have come to Shivpur if I had. It wasn't mentioned in any of the guidebooks, and I was so glad I'd met the Aussie couple in Pushkar who'd told me about it.

Craning my neck out of the glassless window, I marvelled at the sandstone boulders piled up in mounds, or balanced on great slabs of rock. Rocks and boulders littered the landscape as far as I could see, and I imagined they had been scattered randomly, like marbles, by the hand of some giant, playful god.

Two ladies squeezed in next to me on the seat. The woman who had berated me a few minutes earlier said something to them in Hindi, and the lady beside me shot me a dirty look. Adjusting my position to give her some more room, I smiled. She scowled at me, so I looked out of the window again. I'd taken care to dress appropriately in the pilgrim town, keeping myself covered with long sleeved kurtas and trousers despite the heat. I'd left my strappy vest tops in Goa, knowing I needed to cover my shoulders away from the beaches. Evidently, I needed to be more vigilant, more understanding of the culture. The groping had angered me, but it had also made me aware of my vulnerability, and that was something I had thought I'd left behind in Japan.

Pushing the thought away, I was determined to be more careful, and I adjusted my dupatta again, making sure it draped modestly over my breasts. I tried to get my head round the fact that no public displays of affection were allowed, but men cuddled each other and walked hand in hand; sari-clad women covered their legs and shoulders, but exposed their torso, ribs to hips. And in a religious town, men received blow-jobs in back alleys. So many contradictions.

From Shivpur's bus stop, I walked through the village, past simple dwellings built of rough clay walls, or painted vicious salmon pink and lime green, like fake gems in costume jewellery. Children ran, dodging fresh cowpats that hadn't yet been collected to be dried and used instead of firewood.

When I reached the temple, I was relieved to see the beggar man was in his usual place. Rummaging in my big cloth bag, I found the bandages, gauze, antibiotic cream and tablets. I crouched opposite him, and placed each item on the ground between us.

'*Nain, nain*, no.' He waved his hand in front of his face.

Maybe he was embarrassed, or thought I'd ask him to pay for them. I smiled and tapped the packet of antibiotics. 'For your foot,' I said.

'Don't get too close.' I looked up at the man who had spoken. He moved his floppy fringe away from his eyes. 'You need to keep your distance.'

'Hi, Muddy.' How could he wear jeans in such fierce heat? 'Not on duty today?'

'Late shift for another two days. And the police station is as hot as hell during the day, so it's relief to be there in the evenings.'

'I got some things for this man. I think his foot must be badly infected.' I said. 'And his bandage is so dirty.'

'Mari, he has leprosy'

'Leprosy? I didn't think that still existed.' I stood and backed away from the beggar, tapping the dust from my lilac shalwar.

'It does,' he said. 'Sadly, those tablets won't help, but the bandages will be useful for him.'

'You know him?'

'He's been sitting in the same spot for as long as I can remember.' He smiled, his dimples adding to the charm. 'He manages. He has what he needs.'

Pulling my plaited hair forward over my shoulder, I smiled at the leper. 'Can I get him some food, or chai, or something?'

'Why not? So, when are you going to let me take you to see the sunset? I know a good spot. You keep finding excuses to refuse.' His tawny-gold eyes were unsettling, and I looked away.

'So, stop asking me, Muddy,' I said.

'Mari. Come on. Let me take you?'

'Alright. Maybe tomorrow,' I said, heading to the chai stand. 'I'll just get some chai and samosa for him,' I gestured to the beggar, 'then I'm meeting a friend.'

'Maybe tomorrow,' Muddy echoed. 'I'll find you.'

Looking over my shoulder, I smiled at Muddy. 'Why not?'

Chapter Five
यात्रा

LATER THAT WEEK, I got ready to meet Lucy. She and I had met at the temple a few days before. Naturally blonde, she stood out a mile, and we were drawn to each other's obvious foreignness in a village where there were few other tourists. She was staying in another house in the same street as the Mehtas'.

As it sometimes did, sadness nibbled at my core, and I blinked rapidly, keeping the tears away. There was no point in torturing myself, what was done, was done. I took the road out of the village, and climbed the hill, following the path that meandered through the boulders until I reached the viewpoint; a slanted slab of rock.

Lucy waved as I approached, her chubby arm wobbling slightly. We sat on the sun-warmed rock, looking down over the village. Dusk stole the edges of the day, and the sky turned from rose-gold to lilac. We sat quietly, listening to the sound of evening devotions at the temple waft up on the breeze. The sun slowly disappeared, taking the colour of the rocks with it. Everything turned to shadow-grey and silver, and the first stars pinpricked the darkening sky. In the village below, lights shone from windows and open doorways.

'What a place,' I said, letting out a deep breath. 'I'm so glad I came here. Although it took me three days from Jodpur via Bombay.' It had crossed my mind to go and find Turquoise Haresh in Bombay, but a storm had trapped me at the bus station, waiting for a bus which had been four hours late arriving, and six hours late departing.

'One day,' said Lucy, 'Shivpur will be in the Lonely Planet guidebook, and there'll be as many tourists as pilgrims visiting the temple.' She tucked her blonde hair behind her ears, and fiddled with her earring.

'It'll still be a wonderful place.' I sighed, drew my knees up to my chest.

'Are you okay? You look fed up,' she said.

'It's a long story.' I looked up at the final coral streaks of sunset and sighed. Chanted prayers echoed off the rocks, and the smell of cooking reminded me that I was hungry.

'I'm a good listener,' Lucy said, her voice soft. 'Comes with being a nurse. It helps to talk.'

'I know.' I glanced at her. She must have been a good nurse; she had that aura, that kind one. She reminded me of Mrs Jennings, my primary school nurse, who had a hug and a soothing word for every child with a scraped knee. 'It's hard, but I don't want sympathy or pity.' That would finish me off.

'Alright, whatever works for you.'

Taking a deep breath, I told Lucy how my already fractious relationship with my mother fell apart when she disowned me, blaming me for my sister's fatal accident. Then I told Lucy about Kate's murder, and what else had happened in Japan.

'My God,' said Lucy, her hand on my shoulder. 'I know you said no sympathy, but honestly, Mari. I wondered how you'd got that scar.'

'It still hurts sometimes.' I pulled the sleeve of my kurta down over my forearm. 'I could've prevented Kate's death. I mean, I knew it was going to happen but I did nothing to stop it. And Ryu.' I shrugged. 'He…I still can't believe…'

A shiver ran through me; someone was watching me. Turning my head, I looked around. Lucy and I were alone on the rock slab. But as I turned my head again, a man wearing a burnt orange turban, and swathed in red robes was standing on the pathway to the temple. He retreated, walking back between the rocks and boulders. Perhaps I imagined him.

'This is pretty heavy stuff,' said Lucy. 'I don't know how I'd cope dealing with that.' She stuck out her lower lip, then chewed on it.

'I'm fine most of the time, but now and again it washes over me, and I just feel so…sad.' I wiped my eyes with the end of my dupatta. 'And then there are the nightmares. They disturb me for days after.'

'Have you thought about some therapy?' Lucy said.

'You mean see a shrink? Maybe, when I get back to England. But I'd rather atone in my own way. That's why I volunteer. And I'll get some good karma. Anyway, enough. Come on, let's go and get something to eat. The smell of that food down there is just so good.' I was already running down the smooth rock towards the village, holding my dupatta aloft in one hand, letting it float on the breeze behind me.

After Lucy and I had eaten at the *dhaba*, a small eatery by the bus stop, we sauntered back towards the Mehtas'. Squinting in the glare of a motorbike's headlights, I smiled when it stopped beside us.

'Today is many days after tomorrow,' Muddy said, and I laughed. 'And that means you are late.' He dismounted his bike, heaved it to the side of the dusty road. 'Very late.'

Lucy looked at me, her eyebrows high, her eyes mischievous. I laughed again.

Solidly built, but not overweight, Muddy stood at around five-foot-eight; a couple of inches shorter than me. He swept his fringe out of his eyes and smiled.

'Hi, Muddy. This is my friend, Lucy.' I said.

'Shall we three drink chai?' Muddy said, smoothing his grey t-shirt that hung loosely over dark blue jeans. '*Chalo*, let's go. My older sister has a place close by. Let me invite you for chai.'

Muddy walked us back the way we had come, past houses with their doors and windows open. It was hard not to peek at the glimpses of local life seen through them. We reached a stone-brick house, and Muddy ushered us past a wrought iron gate, and through an ornate archway. Lucy and I followed him down a narrow hall, and out into an open-air courtyard. Looking up at shapely pillars that supported an upper-floor walkway, I nearly stepped into the fire pit in the middle of the stone-flagged floor.

'I thought you were taking us to a chai stall,' I said. Lights came on, illuminating the courtyard, and I ran my hand over the smooth carvings on one of the pillars. 'But this is your house?'

'Please, make yourselves comfortable.' He smiled, his eyes twinkling. 'I'll return in *ek* minute, one minute.' Shouting something in Hindi, he left.

A woman stuck her head out from behind a curtained doorway, her smile the same toothpaste-white as Muddy's. She exited the doorway backwards, sliding her feet into slippers that made no noise on the stone floor. She crossed the courtyard and disappeared into another doorway. A few bumps and bangs later, she emerged with a tray of chai and two bowls of something fried.

'That guy kept looking at you,' said Lucy. 'Those dimples. Who is he anyway?'

'Muddy. I met him about three weeks ago. We keep running into each other.' I shrugged, batting away a fluttering moth. 'He's always asking me to go and see the sunset with him.'

'Like a date?' said Lucy.

'I think so. But I need a break from men to be honest.' I sipped my chai and smiled at the woman who had made it for us.

'Please eat the pakoda, they are vegetables only. My name is Rhea, and this is my husband's family home.' She shot me look. 'And my brother's name is Rohan Mudgalkar. Police Sergeant Mudgalkar. Only his friends call him *Muddy*.'

I looked at Rhea, embarrassed that I'd spoken about her brother, and not even said *'hello'* to her.

'I'll remember that.' I said. 'Thank you, Rhea. The pakoda look delicious.'

'Are you from England?'

'Yes, but I live in Abu Dhabi,' said Lucy. 'I work in a private hospital.'

Lucy did most of the talking, and I skirted Rhea's questions about my family. When Muddy returned, Rhea made more chai, and we chatted for a while, mostly about where we'd been in India, and where we'd go next. Muddy kept looking at me and, trying not to smile, I avoided his gaze.

Later, Lucy and I walked slowly through the quiet streets. Lightening split the sky and thunder rolled in the distance. Our pace quickened, wanting to be home before the skies opened.

'He's nice, Mari, and he's definitely got the hots for you. It might do you good, take your mind off, you know...what you told me about.'

'I had plenty of taking my mind off things in Goa.'

Sleeping with someone did help. Even if that someone was just a body to cling to in the darkest part of the night. That was always the worst time for me - when the flashbacks crashed in and woke me. Panic, grief, or fear? I couldn't tell the difference, but it left me sweaty and shaky. Then I'd reach for the man beside me and the physical pleasure eased things for a while. But it couldn't erase the guilt, or remove Ryu from my mind or my heart.

'Slapper.' Lucy laughed.

'Hey!' I nudged her arm, laughing. 'I'll make up for my sins with all good karma I'm creating by volunteering, and helping lepers.'

Lucy needed to cash a travellers' cheque, so the next morning we took the bus to Keshnagar. We stood in the aisle at the front of the crowded bus with the other ladies, grateful for the glassless windows that allowed some movement of air.

The bus overtook trucks decorated with tinsel and plastic flowers. We skimmed past plodding bullock carts, their huge wooden wheels somnolently turning as the animals chewed cud. Skinny men on bicycles wobbled into oncoming traffic, and cars' horns beeped and honked. Lorries trumpeted, and I winced at the volume, amazed that my ears weren't bleeding. A red-turbaned man herded his goats along the side of the road, and passing vehicles threw up swathes of dust. I loved the heat, the chaos, the noise; they made my nerve endings sing with a thirst for life I hadn't thought I'd feel again.

We spilled off the bus at the bus station, and battled our way through the crowds. Lucy's face was flushed pink with the heat and after she'd got some cash, we sat on plastic stools at my favourite chai stand, where I loved the blend of spices they used. A samosa-wallah stopped beside us, transferring the large round tray of freshly fried pastries from his head to the ground.

'*Chaar,*' I said, holding up four fingers, then handing over the money. 'Nothing like them with chai. I've got a dilemma.'

'Tell me?' said Lucy. 'Is it Muddy?"

'No.' I tutted. 'In a nutshell; the guy who manages Sharma's is groping the cook, and saying he'll sack her if she complains. And a girl who used to work there has vanished. And the cook thinks he's involved. And then there's the missing jewellery.'

'No dilemma there, love,' said Lucy. 'Don't get involved. You've got enough to contend with.'

Of course, she was right. None of what was happening at Sharma's was anything to do with me. Except on a human level. And I wanted to help Kavita. I dipped the samosa into the mint and coriander chutney, and took a bite. The pastry was crisp, and the spiced vegetables inside deliciously warm.

Lucy laughed, and behind me, someone tugged at my pale pink dupatta, making the tiny bells sewn into the corners jingle. I glanced over my shoulder, my mouth full of samosa.

'Hi, Muddy,' said Lucy. 'You look nice in your uniform. Very nice.'

The dark sand colour of the police uniform didn't flatter Muddy's skin tone, but there was still something attractive about him. A pistol rested in the brown leather holster that hung off his belt, and three stars adorned his epaulets. With his fringe combed to one side, blending into the rest of his short hair, he looked completely different; tidy, official.

'You again,' I said, swallowing the last of my mouthful. 'Are you following me?' I tried not to laugh.

Muddy rested one hand on the table and looked down at me. 'Of course.' He placed his peak cap on his head.

'Why?'

'Why not?' His face was serious, but his eyes twinkled. 'Meet me tonight. Six o'clock, near the temple. Will you let me take you for a walk? We'll go to view the sunset.'

I shook my head and looked at Lucy. 'This again. I don't think so, Muddy,' I said.

'I'll see you at six.'

Muddy picked up a samosa, smiled, and walked away. Turning to watch him, noting his broad shoulders and solid legs, I laughed when he looked back at me.

'He's determined,' said Lucy, licking her fingers after finishing her samosas. 'And very sure of himself.'

'His honey-coloured eyes are, I grant you, very unusual. And that smile. He's attractive, but –'

Lucy grinned. 'Will you meet him later then?'

'Probably best if I don't.' I grinned back. And anyway, Muddy was friends with creepy Kiran, and that put me off him.

A large langur chattered its teeth on top of the chai stand's awning, and the chai-wallah hissed and waved his arms. I laughed as the monkey stared back, unfazed. Grabbing a broom, the chai-wallah poked the handle at the monkey, who ducked and screeched before loping off, trapezing itself along the electric cables.

Lucy and I left the chai stand, laughing, and walked through the bazaar, heading for the bus station. We dawdled, looking at the embroidered dupattas and costume jewellery, and I bought a dozen turquoise mirrored bangles. I'd have settled for two or three, but they came in packs of twelve; six for each wrist.

Sliding them over my hands, I held out my arms, and twisted my wrists, enjoying the tinkling sound they made and how they sparkled in the sunlight.

Children ran past, chasing each other, their laughter disappearing as fast as it had come. A group of teenaged schoolgirls, their long hair tied in looped plaits and fixed with red ribbons, walked behind us. Their voices were soft, and the rise and fall of their words sounded like singing.

'The small one is so sweet,' said one. 'Like a butterball.'

'And the tall one,' said another. 'Her hair...what colour is that?'

I smiled to myself, glad not to have to hide the features of my own physicality. Shoulders back and head up, I walked proudly. Gone were the days of skulking around, hiding my chestnut hair, hunched into an old green parka that had kept me hidden from the *yakuza*, the Japanese mafia.

Six o'clock came and went, and I lay reading a book on the window seat in my room, propped up with pillows from the bed. Black crows hopped on the tin roof across the alleyway, their claws tip-tapping like stiletto heels. There was a knock on my door. Lucy was early; we weren't going to eat dinner until later. Straightening my *lehenga*, I crossed the room, enjoying the way the heavy embroidery at the hem of the long skirt made it swish as I walked. I pulled back the squeaky bolt, opening the double doors inwards.

'Mari,' said Muddy. He leaned against the door frame, smiling so that his dimples showed. 'And where are you going dressed like that?'

Taking a step forward into the room, he stared at me, serious now. His stare was so intense, I dropped my gaze, took two steps backwards. He placed his hands on my bare waist, then ran them up my torso to where my choli finished under my bust.

'Muddy,' I said, my voice raspy.

'Yes?'

'Close the door,' I said. He grinned. 'On your way out.'

Chapter Six

London 2010

HARRY CAME CRASHING through the house, a whirlwind of energy and cricket whites. It was the same every Saturday from April to September. If he wasn't playing the sport, he watched it. Not that I minded, it gave me time to read or to catch up on some work. Sunday mornings though, were ours. Drinking coffee with the broadsheet papers strewn around us, we'd swap sections as we finished reading them, apart from the glossy magazines that always ended up by my feet, ready to flick through later.

'Did you win, darling?' I asked from the kitchen, pouring some stock over rice already in the saucepan.

Leaning against the doorway, Harry smiled. It still caught me off guard now and again how handsome he was. His chiselled features, his wide smile, his dark brown eyes. There was elegance in his stance which only got better as he got older. I should have been used to it, but sometimes I caught my breath, amazed that a man could be so beautiful.

'Rained off.' Harry shrugged. 'So, we all had a few pints. We'll still meet for practice, but that was the last match this season. That smells good. What are you making?'

'Something new. Uzbek style pilav. Got the idea for the spice mix from something I had over there.'

'So exotic. That's what I love about you,' he said, and I laughed. 'I smell lamb though, so what will you have?'

'Spiced lamb's roasting and the pilav is veggie. You know me, I won't go hungry. Wine or beer, Harry? Food'll be ready in about fifteen minutes.' I put the glass lid on the pan, and turned the flame low, watching the rice simmer.

Harry reached into the fridge, grabbed a bottle of Peroni. 'This for now.' He twisted off the top, and drank straight from the bottle, heading up the stairs. 'I'll be down in a bit.'

The words I wanted to say to him wouldn't come out of my mouth, so perhaps this wasn't the right time to discuss India. But it would have to be discussed, and soon.

Opening a bottle of red wine, I poured some into a glass, took it into the lounge. On the TV, some wannabe pop group sang on a talent show, and I let them distract me with their passable melody. The judges commented on their performance, one not too politely, and the audience hissed and booed. Vapid TV was exactly what I needed at that moment to distract me.

I placed my glass on the coffee table, the wine untouched. Sitting on the edge of the sofa, I twisted the ends of my hair, plaiting and unplaiting. The wedding invitation was hidden under a pile of post on top of the fridge, but it might as well have been in my hand. Maybe I was reading too much into it, and the wedding invitation was just that; a wedding invitation. But a promise had been made all those years ago, and the invitation was part of that. Then again, people broke promises all the time, didn't they?

Harry came thundering down the stairs. His height and build meant that he never moved quietly. He plonked himself beside me, slapping my thigh. 'What you watching, old girl? Not this rubbish again. Honestly, I can't believe you like this.' Grabbing the remote control, he flicked through the channels. 'I said I'd meet Jon at the Fair Oak later, just for an hour.'

'Right.' I said. I should tell him about India, but I wasn't ready. Mainly because I still hadn't made the decision to actually go.

'Call Isabel? You should both come along, have a catch-up. Do you good to have a few gins. It's got to be better than watching this crap.'

'Good idea.' Knowing Harry and Jon, they'd be engrossed in their cricket talk, so it'd be an ideal opportunity to talk to Issy.

After dinner, Harry and I walked fifteen minutes through the park, and met Jon and Issy outside the Fair Oak. It was still light, and evening was still and warm, so we sat at a wooden table in the beer garden. Harry went into the pub to buy our drinks. His generosity was one of the things I loved about him.

'Thank God the plaster cast's off. I'm starting physio next week,' said Issy, propping her crutches against the end of the table. 'I'm not up to a long walk yet, so Jon drove, which I thought was a good idea.'

'I have an even better idea,' said Jon. 'Don't fall off a ladder again. In fact, don't you be climbing up ladders. I've told you...'

'And I asked you three times to clean the gutters,' Issy snapped.

Harry brought the drinks over, and I moved to sit next to Issy, swapping places with Jon.

'I know you didn't tell Harry yet, but have you at least booked the flights?' said Issy. I shook my head. 'It's been two weeks. What's holding you back?'

'I know it was twenty-three years ago, but the promise still means something, to me anyway.' I sipped my gin, enjoying the fizz of the tonic in my mouth. 'I'm scared of the ramifications...' I tilted my head discreetly towards Harry.

'Make a decision; one way or the other.' Issy tutted, picking up her glass of red wine. 'Have you cleared it with work even?' I darted my eyes to the men, still engrossed in their own conversation, and shook my head. 'Check you can get the time off, and take it from there,' she said. 'No point in getting all worked up if you can't actually go.'

Working for a water charity gave me some degree of flexibility as it wasn't strictly a nine-five job when we had new projects starting. I'd accrued hours of unpaid overtime, which I could take back as time in lieu. Plus, I had some time booked off at the beginning of October, so I'd ask Alan, my boss, if I could just have a longer break.

'Yes, let's leave it to fate,' I said. 'If get the green light, I'll have no excuse, and I'll go. Just for the wedding. Forget the promise; I'm being ridiculous.'

'That's more like it,' said Issy, her hand on my arm.

'And one way or the other, I'll tell Harry.' I'd meant to keep my voice quiet.

'Yes please, I'll have another.'

I grinned at Issy and she rolled her eyes. At least Harry hadn't heard our actual conversation.

Chapter Seven
यात्रा

Shivpur, 1986

AT THE BUS station in Keshnagar, Lucy loaded her backpack into the luggage space at the back of the bus, shoving it in with sacks of rice and grain.

'Enjoy Rajasthan,' I said. 'You'll love it. Go to Jaisalmer; it's right at the end of the train line in the desert. And if you do, say '*hi*' to Shalu. He runs camel safaris out into the dunes. Spending the night under the stars, no light pollution, nothing, is just stunning. Anyway, Shalu 'll look after you.' I smiled at the memory. Probably best not to divulge just how he'd looked after me, but by the way Lucy was laughing, she must have worked it out. 'I mean finding you a room, Lucy. Just finding you a room, okay?'

'I will. Good luck with the good karma thing,' Lucy said. 'And go, on, get some Kama Sutra with this one.' She tilted her head, and I glanced over my shoulder. Muddy crossed the bus station, the orange stripe around his peaked cap bright in the intense sunlight.

'You are leaving?' said Muddy, looking from Lucy to me, and back again. 'Where are you going?'

'North. To the desert.' Lucy wiped her brow. 'Mari recommended a few places for me.'

'Mari, you are leaving also?' Muddy said. I shook my head,

and his face relaxed. 'That's good to hear. That's very good.'

Lucy and I laughed and hugged goodbye. She boarded the bus, and took her seat by the window. We waved as the bus groaned into life with a splutter of diesel, and drove away.

'Shall we have chai?' Muddy said. 'I thought you were leaving, it nearly broke my heart.'

'Okay, cheer me up. My only friend has just left,' I said.

At a chai stand near the bus station, Muddy and I sat opposite each other, glasses of chai in hand.

'How's the investigation going? The missing girl, Shanti,' I said. 'Kavita is a bit upset.'

'What did she tell you?' Muddy glared at me. 'There's nothing we can do. She ran away.'

'All Kavita said was that Shanti disappeared one day. Someone must know something,' I said. 'Did she have a boyfriend?' I didn't repeat what Kavita had told me.

'That's it,' said Muddy. 'The girl probably ran away with a lover. Leave it to the police, Mari. It's not your concern.'

It might not have been my concern, but knowing a girl was missing made me uneasy, and it was hard not to think of what happened to Kate.

After drinking chai with Muddy, I bought a kilo of rice, one of lentils, and another of chickpeas, and headed to Sharma's. My arms ached by the time I reached the tree on the corner where I'd left the mangoes. Placing the bags of food behind the tree so that it wasn't visible from the road, I stood at the top of the dirt path for a moment. In front of the widows' house, a woman pumped the handle of a well, then bent to lift the large container of water. Another woman joined her, and they laughed, carrying it towards the house. At least there was some laughter in the house of widows. How wrong I had been, thinking that they were nuns begging for donations, or there to convert Hindus to Catholicism. However harsh a nun's life was, the widows had it harsher. Bad luck had nothing to do with it; there was something tragic about casting a woman aside from society, death of a husband or not. Not being versed in Hindu scriptures, I didn't understand, but it was hard not be to judgemental. That was the danger of only knowing a small part of any story; a little knowledge is a dangerous thing.

Would it be better to take the food to them, or would I be breaking some taboo? I wasn't Hindu, so picking up the food again, I walked the hundred meters or so towards the house. When I reached the well at the front of the house, a flash of white caught my eye, and an elderly lady with white hair stood stock still in the doorway. Shouting something over her shoulder, she retreated back inside.

Voices echoed and saris rustled, then four or five women crowded into the doorway. The tall girl pushed through them, smiling broadly, and stepped towards me.

'Hello, I am Suhana,' she said, straightening her sari. 'Nice to meet you properly.'

'I brought these things for you and the other ladies.' I placed the two carrier bags on the ground. A young girl, who looked no more than fifteen picked them up, smiling at me. 'I hope I'm doing the right thing. Kavita at Sharma's –'

'Kavita? You know Kavita?' A smile broke across the face of another woman, her sari not so bright-white. 'She is my good friend. Tell me, how is she? And her husband?'

'She's fine, I haven't met her husband, but he's working at Sharma's too.'

'Thank you for the kind gift of food, but you should not be here,' said an elderly lady, the one who'd snapped at Suhana when I'd seen them on the road. 'This is no place for you.'

'Hiral Auntie,' said Suhana. 'Can't I speak with her? Just for a moment?'

With her grey hair scraped back into a bun, Hiral's face was elegant, her cheekbones high, and her eyes clear. She inclined her head, and Suhana smiled, stepping towards me. The other women followed Hiral inside the house.

'You'll be walking back to Keshnagar at about two o'clock?' Suhana said. I nodded. 'I have seen you, every few days, always at the same time. Wait for me, a little way down the road, so that Hiral Auntie doesn't see.'

'Yes. I'll wait for you.'

Suhana ran back into the house, and I turned, started walking back to the road.

'Wait, please.' Suhana called to me from the doorway. 'Pass a message to Kavita from her friend, Bhavna. She asks if she can have more of that brinjal bhaji.'

I opened the squeaky gate at Sharma's entrance, my teeth on edge at the sound, and found Kavita in the kitchen as usual. She was making chai. When she saw me, she smiled, and ushered me out into the pot washing courtyard.

'I'm sorry I said so many bad things about Kiran,' Kavita said. 'Please don't repeat anything, nah? If he hears, I will be fired.'

'Of course not, I won't say anything. But I've been wondering what I can do to help. There must be some way to stop him.'

'Don't cross him, Mari.' Kavita ran her hand across her mouth. 'He has some connection with unsavory people. And I am sure something happened to Shanti because of him.'

'Like what?' Frowning, I placed my hand on Kavita's arm.

'She was a pretty girl, clever too, but not educated. I don't know the whole story, but she was in love with a boy who broke her heart. Then a month or so later, Kiran asked to speak to her. She was gone for a long while, and I needed her in the kitchen, so I went to his office. The door wasn't closed and I could hear them both. They were doing it.'

Raising my finger to my lips, I peeked into the kitchen. One of the helpers was filling glasses with the chai Kavita had made minutes before. She and I waited for a moment, until the kitchen was empty again.

'And then? Did his wife find out or something?'

'Some months later, I overheard Kiran telling Shanti that

they'd go to Panjim to live. A week later, she was gone. But he is still here.'

'Maybe she's in Panjim, and he visits her there? But no, it's hours away.'

'Exactly, that can't be right.' Kavita said. She moved into the shade, pulling me with her. 'He lied to her, but where is she? At first, I thought maybe Shanti's father learned about her with these two men, and got angry. It would have ruined her chance for a good marriage. She was only seventeen.'

'You don't think her father killed her?' I twisted my hair, my stomach twisted itself. 'For family honour?'

'It's a possibility. But he is so distraught, and I hear that he sits at the police station every day, waiting for news, so I think not.'

'And the other man?' I said. 'The first boyfriend. Do you know who it was?'

'No one is sure who he is. There were some rumours. Maybe she is with him.' Kavita sighed. 'I hope she is with him. The police say they have no leads, nothing to investigate. People go missing all the time, they say. But it's like she didn't exist.'

'Did you tell the police about all this?' I asked, already knowing the answer. Kavita made a face. 'No. I get it. It's an awful story.' One that brought back memories of when Kate went missing. My heart stuttered, and I had to catch my breath. 'Let's hope Shanti's safe somewhere.'

Not knowing what else to say, I went to find Leena or one of the other residents. Instead, I was cornered by Kiran. He scratched his groin, and I averted my gaze.

'Mari, good morning. I wonder if you could come to the office?'

Kiran went ahead, and I followed him down the narrow corridor and into a small outer office. It was set out like an old-fashioned doctor's waiting room, with a large coffee table in the middle and half a dozen wooden chairs lining two walls. I stopped at the doorway to Kiran's office, and it wasn't until he moved behind his desk and motioned for me to sit in the chair opposite, that I realised I'd been primed to fight him off. My shoulders dropped, and I sat down, crossing my legs.

'Do you have any clerical experience at all?' Kiran's bulbous eyes made me uncomfortable, so I dropped my gaze. A sleek grey electric typewriter sat between us, flanked by reams of A4 and A5 paper.

'Not really, Kiran. I can't type either.'

'The twentieth century is coming to Sharma's. We are getting a first-class home computer next month, and I need to start sorting the residents' files. I have all their information, their next of kin details, that sort of thing, but I'm not very organised when it comes to keeping things tidy, in date order.'

'So, you want things put in date order, ready for the computer?'

'Yes. We have admission forms, receipts for medicines and provisions which all need to be put into date order. And the records of medical visits.' He rubbed his thumb along his moustache. 'They are mostly written in English, but you don't need to concern yourself with the content, just the date. Would you be able to do it?'

'I think so.'

'Good, good. It's very time-consuming, and I am busy with other things. But you have no previous accounting experience. Anyway, you don't need a degree in applied mathematics.' He chuckled, his hands resting on the desk.

'No, I'm not great with numbers really.' I lied. My first job had been at my Dad's restaurant when I was fifteen. For a couple of years, I'd prepared the bills on Fridays and Saturdays, and cashed-up at the end of the evening. 'But if it's just tidying the files and putting things into date order, I can do that, no worries.' If Kavita was right, and Kiran was stealing, it would be a good chance to find some proof. He might get the sack, which he deserved, and Kavita wouldn't have to endure his groping.

Kiran opened a drawer in his desk, handed me a small key. 'For the filing cabinet.' He pointed to the metal cabinet behind me. 'Perhaps you could start from the top and work down.' He pointed behind me. 'You can work through there on the coffee table. Just remember to replace the key when you leave.'

I stood and unlocked the cabinet, took an armful of manila files into the other room. Kiran left me to it, closing the outer office door behind him. The first thing I noticed was that the files weren't even in alphabetical order. Blowing out a breath, I wondered how someone could be so slap-dash. What did the man do all day? Apart from getting blow-jobs in back alleys.

The square air conditioning unit that was fixed into the window creaked and shuddered when I switched it on. The vents blew the air horizontally, so I moved them, directing the airflow upwards. The last thing I wanted was papers flying everywhere. In the first file that I opened, Ranjiv Sohal, and his wife Sarita's details had been typed onto separate admission forms. It was probably a bit nosey, but I read through their dates of birth, wedding date, next of kin details, and medications. Nothing riveting. There were receipts for doctor's visits, medications and shampoo, razor blades, and *sindoor*, the vermillion powder married women wore along the parting in their hair. Receipts from 1986 were mixed with ones as far back as 1982, and everything in between. Kiran was right; he was disorganised.

The receipts were spread out on the coffee table, and I popped into Kiran's office, looking for some paper clips. I rummaged through the top drawer of his desk, and grabbed a pad of sticky Post-its which might be useful. A few paper clips lurked in the drawer's corners, but I needed more. I opened the next drawer down, finding nothing but a jumble of typewriter ribbons and correction fluid. Scanning the room, I found a box of paperclips on the window sill, and took them back to my piles of receipts, and set to work.

It wasn't difficult; I organised the receipts into year, month and day, then separated each month's worth of receipts, and clipped them together in a little pile with a paper clip. I wrote the year and month on a Post-it, stuck it onto the first receipt. Once every month was done, I put them in order and placed them back in the file.

For the next hour or so, I worked through Leena and her husband's file, and then Vivika's. It was time-consuming and quite boring. Until I found a receipt signed by Vivika and Kiran. It stated that two pairs of gold earrings, three gemstone rings, and two gold necklaces had been deposited in the safe. I picked up Vivika's admission form in one hand, and the jewellery receipt in the other. At first glance, the signatures were the same, but looking more closely, the one on the jewellery receipt was more juddery, less smooth and flowing. If Kiran was stealing, maybe Vivika had deposited more jewellery. Had Kiran rewritten the receipt and forged the signature?

The office door opened, and I shuffled the paperwork back in order, closing the file, a too-bright smile pasted on my face.

'Lunch is almost ready, Mari,' said Kiran. He looked me up and down, pulling at his moustache. 'Please come. The residents are asking for you. And we have a new arrival, from Poona. He needs a little more help, so Shreyas will be staying close to him today.'

Kiran introduced me to Dinesh Desai, and left me to sit with him in the courtyard. I was glad; even if I hadn't known what Kiran was up to, he'd give me the creeps. The cicadas were noisy in the heat of the day, and the humidity was stifling.

'What a charming young woman you are, and so nice that you dress like Indian women,' said Dinesh. His white hair was brushed back and even from three feet away, I could smell the hair oil he used. He exuded wealth, not just because of the hefty gold bracelet around his wrist, and the chunky ruby ring he wore on his right hand.

'It's comfortable,' I said, wiping the sweat from my upper lip. 'And I'm staying in Shivpur, which is a holy place, so I like to be respectful.'

'I shall only be here temporarily,' said Dinesh. 'I live with my son, and he's gone to London for a three-month secondment. When he returns, I shall go home.'

'Shall we go through for lunch now?' I said.

I escorted Dinesh to a table in the dining room, and the Aunties and their husbands joined us. The Aunties cooed and clucked as they usually did, happy to welcome the dashing Dinesh. The Aunties stood around Dinesh, who sat like a maharajah in the middle of his female courtiers. The bright colours of their saris contrasted beautifully with Dinesh's white linen and hair.

'You all look lovely, let me take a photo,' I said. 'You look like film stars.'

I ran to the kitchen to grab my camera out of my bag. After I'd taken a couple of photos, that left only one on the reel of thirty-six shots. I must remember to get it developed at the camera shop near the bus station.

On my way back to Keshnagar after lunch, Suhana joined me on the road. We walked quickly for the first hundred meters or so, until we couldn't be seen from the widows' house.

'Would you like to go and have some ice cream?'

'Oh, no.' Suhana smiled sadly. 'In Hindi we say '*kulfi*.' I like it but I cannot. But thank you for asking. I think you don't understand how it is for widows.'

'I know a little, but obviously not enough. Sorry. I didn't think.'

'It's fine. Don't worry.' Suhana pulled my arm, bringing me away from the edge of the tarmack, and a huge truck that rumbled past. 'I am just happy to speak with someone my age.'

'Maybe you can teach me some Hindi? Is that what you speak?'

'I speak it. And Marathi.'

'How did you get here? I mean, why Keshnagar?' I wanted to know her story. She was too young to be a widow.

Suhana stopped walking, turned to face me, and her kind eyes looked sad. 'One day my husband was killed. A traffic accident. Two months later, I arrived here. My husband's parents were kind, but his brother was not. I missed my husband very much, even though we had been married only four months.'

I touched her arm in a gesture of comfort, but she moved an inch away from me, and my hand dropped. 'You poor thing.' I didn't know what else to say.

'Follow me.' She stepped through the undergrowth, pulling her sari close, and I did as she said. We walked across a field, towards a group of trees. 'Aarav was a kind man, he had a good job as an accountant for a large textile company in Bombay. His parents were good to me, and I was happy that my family had found me a good marriage. But Aarav left this world. So, I moved away.'

'That was it? You just left?'

'The day they told me he died, my life was over. They took me to our temple and shaved my head. Then my hair was sold to make money for the temple.' She flicked her wrist. 'I dressed in a white cotton sari, packed away all my bangles, my gold, even my sindoor. From that moment, I have lived a plain life.'

Suhana and I walked in silence until we reached the trees. My mind skittered back to almost a year before, when I'd cut fourteen inches off my long chestnut hair in an effort to disguise myself. My hair was my one vanity, my crowning glory, and it had broken my already shattered heart to cut it. I couldn't even imagine having to shave it off because my husband had died. But maybe that level of grief made vanity impossible.

'Did your in-laws ask you to leave, Suhana?' I said.

'No. But bother-in-law...' She shot a glance at me. 'He thought it...I...' Breathing out a long breath, she nodded. 'Yes, well, sex is a funny thing, isn't it?' Stunned into silence, I couldn't think of what to say. 'I did not encourage him in any way, really, I didn't.'

'And that's what made you leave.' I sniffed, suddenly tearful.

'My husband's parents did not believe that he forced me, and there was a big argument. Of course, they took their own son's side, and I couldn't endure it any longer. I had no choice. I left, sold my gold, and travelled here.'

'But couldn't you have started a new life somewhere else

with that money?'

'How? If I was a boy, yes. But no landlord would rent an apartment to a girl with no family. Not in any respectable area. A girl alone…no. Also, it's not possible to find work without someone to speak for you.'

'And your family? You couldn't go back to them?'

'No. That wasn't possible either. So, I live here now. And I am lucky to have a room to myself in the house. In some rooms there are two or three of us.'

We'd walked back the way we came, and reached the road, the heat of the afternoon pressing us into silence. Behind us, the roar of a motorbike and the sound of slowing wheels on gravel made me turn. Suhana was already walking back the way we had come, head down.

'Mari, I will drop you back to Shivpur,' said an unsmiling Muddy. 'Get on. Now.' He straightened his t-shirt and shifted forward on the bike.

'Hi, Muddy. I was wondering when I'd see you.'

'You've been thinking about me? Good. But Mari, don't get involved with widows, and especially not with that girl.'

'They bring bad luck?' I climbed on the bike, my arm sliding around his waist. 'Please take me for kulfi, I'm so hot.'

We ploughed along the road, and into Keshnagar. Muddy pulled up outside a small café with arched doorways that opened onto the street. I slid off the seat and stood on the pavement while he parked the bike.

'Mari.' Muddy looked from my face to my hair and back again. 'Let me be your friend.'

'You are, Muddy. I don't get on just anyone's bike you know.'

Inside the fan-cooled, wood-panelled café, rose and cardamom kulfi cooled me. The sweet flavours melded together so well, and the silky texture of the pale pink ice cream was divine. Muddy watched me, making me self-conscious. He smiled and looked away, then concentrated on his own kulfi. When he didn't watch me, I watched the sensuous way his lips pulled at the spoon full of kulfi, the way his tongue moved over it. As if he knew what I was thinking, he raised his eyebrows. I laughed, catching a drip of kulfi on my finger.

'What are you doing at work; anything interesting?' I asked, pushing my longing for sex out of my mind.

'We raided a gambling den close to Shivpur, shut it down. Makes a change from the usual domestic disputes over land or livestock there. Of course, Keshnagar has much more serious goings-on, like any city.'

'Serious goings-on?' I said. Keshnagar wasn't large enough to be called a city in my opinion; more like a large town. 'Really? Like what?'

'I can't say.' Muddy pointed at my empty plate. 'Another?' I nodded, and he signalled to the waiter. 'So, tell me. How is it at Sharma's?'

'I'm doing some simple administration for Kiran.' I smiled. 'They're getting a computer soon.'

'Administration?' Muddy frowned. 'Really?'

'Who owns Sharma's?' I said.

'Believe it or not, Mr Sharma.' Muddy smiled, his eyes mischievous. 'He was two years above me at school. He's done very well for himself, got another two premises. One in Panjim, one in Bangalore. Plans for one in Poona also. Keshnagar's elderly residents' home is his favourite because he's from here, still lives here in fact.'

White jacketed waiters served patrons who snapped their fingers for attention, waiting for sweet cakes, chai or iced-coffee while cigarette smoke swirled in the air. An elderly man brought my kulfi to the table, and I smiled my thanks.

'Mr Sharma's house is outside town,' said Muddy, 'behind high walls and a big iron gate. He even has guards outside.'

'Where do you live, Muddy?'

'Nowhere as grand. Until I marry, it's the police barracks. And that is a shame, as I can't have visitors.' He bit his bottom lip and narrowed his eyes.

I spluttered my kulfi, laughing. Grabbing a paper napkin, I wiped my lips. 'Honestly, you're relentless.'

'I have some leave next week,' said Muddy. 'Let's go to Malvan or Talashil. We can stay at a nice place near the sea and have a few days' holiday.'

'You and me?'

'Yes, it's not far. Just three or four hours. I'll hire a car and driver. We can be relaxed there. Not like here.' He sat back, one arm resting over the back of the chair. 'You know what I'm asking you, right? Shall we go?' He smiled that dimpled smile, and I was tempted to say '*yes*.'

'I don't think it's a good idea.'

'But I have such feelings for you, Mari. Let's be together.'

'Muddy...' I smiled, apologetically. 'No.'

'Tell me you are being coy, that you are just a shy girl. Can't you tell how much I like you? You must know, I want to be with you.'

'Look, we'll just stay friends, okay?' I stood up, ready to leave.

'I will make you change your mind. Come, let's go.' He paid at the cashier's desk. 'I'll drop you home.'

Chapter Eight
यात्रा

ON MY NEXT visit to Sharma's a few days later, I headed straight through the cool hallway towards the kitchen, hoping to find Kavita.

'Oh, there you are, dear.' Vivika approached, the silk of her sari rustling as she walked. 'Kiran has been keeping you away from us. We miss your company.'

'Me too,' I said. 'Shall we have chai?' I took her elbow, moving her away from the kitchen.

'Yes, come, we'll drink chai and chit chat.'

We joined Dinesh and a few of the other residents, and Rekha, one of the helpers, brought chai and lassi for us. I sipped my lassi, enjoying the sweet creamy taste, and listened as the women chatted in sing-song Hindi, peppered with English.

'Have you settled in, Dinesh?' I asked. He glanced at me, frowning.

'And you are?' he said, raising his finger. 'Have we met?'

'I met you a few days ago, when you first arrived. I'm Mari.'

'I won't be here long, you know. My son has been seconded to London for three months. On his return, I shall move back home.'

Leena patted the back of his right hand, and I glanced down. There was no ruby ring. No bracelet.

I excused myself, and stormed into Kiran's office. Taking some files from the cabinet, I stood for a moment, my mind whirring. I'd need more evidence that Kiran was stealing, and then I'd go to the police. Muddy and Kiran were friends, so I'd need to speak to another officer.

With the files spread out on the table in the outer office, I crouched down. Frowning with concentration, I took a close look at a few other files, comparing signatures. Those looked slightly wrong too. I checked dates, thinking that maybe the original signature had been made a long time before the later ones, and perhaps the residents' signatures were a little shakier recently. But the admission forms and the jewellery receipts had been signed on the same day.

Dinesh was the most recent arrival, so I took his file from the cabinet. There were only two pieces of paper in the file; his admission form that had been filled in on the day he arrived, and a receipt for his first month's payment, in advance. Where was the receipt for his ring and bracelet? My legs ached, so I knelt. Of course, it could be that Dinesh hadn't handed it in for safekeeping, and the jewellery was hidden away in a drawer in his room.

I left Kiran's office and went to find Kavita. She wasn't in the kitchen, but I followed the sound of running water that came from the rear courtyard.

'Morning,' I said, crouching beside her as she scrubbed the soil from potatoes and rinsed them under the tap. She threw each cleaned one into a metal pot. The noise was jarring. 'You okay?'

'I'm okay, thank you. Kiran just left. He makes me feel so dirty. He talks about wanting me to lick his thing. I won't do that.'

'Kavita, no.' I tutted. 'Does he...actually, you know?'

'No, no. He just talks about it, very crudely. Talk, talk, talk. Putting his hands everywhere under my clothes seems to be enough for him. And always here, in my kitchen. Dirty talk, here in my kitchen, where I make food for people.' She threw another potato into the pot. 'But sometimes I'm scared he won't keep control, and that he'll rape me.'

'We have to try and stop him, Kavita.' I took the knife

from the floor and slit open the top of a large paper sack, and rummaged inside. Handing two potatoes to her, I shifted my weight back on my heels. 'I could hang around, and maybe if he knows I've seen him, he might stop?'

She looked at me sideways. 'It will be my fault. He will say it is my fault for enticing him.'

'Can you tell him you'll speak to Mr Sharma? Or say you'll tell his wife.'

'Why don't you want to understand? I will be blamed, and then I'll have no chance of keeping this job. And neither will my husband. I have not mentioned all this to him.' She scrubbed the potato clean. 'I am so ashamed.' Sniffing, she wiped her hand under her nose. 'My husband would kill Kiran.'

'Kiran should be ashamed, not you. You haven't done anything wrong.'

'It is always the woman's fault. For inflaming the man. By a look, or a perfume, or the way she walks. Always the woman's fault.'

I'd been blamed when I'd been groped on the bus, and my stomach roiled. 'Then we need to tell the police Kiran is stealing.' Kavita's eyes widened when I told her about the signatures. 'When Dinesh arrived, he was wearing a really thick gold bracelet and a huge ruby ring.' I glanced over my shoulder, lowered my voice. 'He's not wearing them now, and there's no receipt in his file for them either. Do you think they're in his room? Could we ask Shreyas to check?'

'I'll ask Puja; she can look. She is my neighbours' daughter. I trust her.'

'Okay. I'll buy a calculator, and add up some of the receipts as well, because something isn't right there either.'

'Be careful, Mari.' Kavita turned off the tap, shook the water off her hands.

I smiled. 'I'm not afraid of Kiran.' Despite the scar on my arm, I'd stood up to the yakuza. 'He's small fry.'

On my next visit, I bought a notebook and a little calculator at the bazaar near the bus station. They were hidden in my cloth bag, along with a couple of biros.

The short walk to Sharma's that morning had exhausted me, and my legs were weak. Nausea swamped me, and my head swam. At the entrance, I leaned against the wall for a moment before I stepped out of my flip-flops. The smell of frying onions wafted from the kitchen, and made me feel worse. Holding my breath, I headed towards the kitchen.

'Morning, Kavita,' I said.

She winked at me, a beckoned me to the courtyard outside the kitchen. Following her out there, I glanced over my shoulder to make sure no one else was around.

'Puja checked Dinesh's room.' Kavita smiled. 'Like we thought, no jewellery. Not anywhere. She looked in every place while Shreyas was bathing Dinesh. Nothing there.'

'Okay, that's good.' I tutted. 'Well, not good; poor Dinesh. I'll get the film in my camera developed. Those photos I took of Dinesh and the Aunties will show he had the jewellery when he arrived. It gives us real evidence. So, let me get to the office and see what else I can find.'

'Yes. Good idea. You are a good girl, Mari.' Kavita patted my arm.

'Kavita?' Kiran called from the kitchen. 'Where are you?'

'Yes?' she said, and raised her eyebrows.

Should I stay in case he groped her? I hesitated until Kavita shooed me out of the gate at the end of the rear courtyard. Running barefoot down the side of the building, I slowed down, nausea threatening. It must have been the lassi I had at the bus station. Perhaps the yogurt had been a bit off. Reaching the front entrance, I casually walked down the hall and back into the kitchen as though I'd only just arrived.

'Morning,' I said, glaring at Kiran. 'I'll carry on with the files in your office, Kiran, and then I'll come and sit with the residents.'

'Yes,' he said, and moved away from Kavita. It took all my

self-control not to rip his head off. 'I'll be going to temple now.'

In his office, I set to work. I made a note of everything I thought was dodgy so that later when I went to the police with it, they'd know what to look for. Most of the residents' files were now all in date order and collated, so I had time to trawl through and collect more information. The more evidence I had, the better.

In Leena's file, I found a doctor's receipt for a visit. It had the doctor's address stamped on it and the date, name, and apartment number written in blue biro. The amount was written in black as if it had been filled out by someone else. Had Kiran paid the doctor one amount and then charged Leena more? There were numerous receipts for medicines, some of them duplicated within a few days of each other. I was no doctor, but I knew that a seven-day course of Amoxycillin was usual, so why were there two receipts for the same drug, for the same person three days apart? The more I looked into the receipts in the other files too, the more suspicious receipts I found. One other thing struck me; the receipts were mostly the same type; like they'd been peeled off the same receipt pad. Then I checked the numbers on the top right-hand corner of each one. 000106 for the first antibiotic and 000107 for the next. Surely every pharmacy, doctor, food shop, laundry, and so on would have their own receipt pads? If Kiran had his own receipt pad, I needed to find it.

Looking down the corridor, I made sure Kiran wasn't coming back in case he hadn't left for temple yet. I ran back to his office and scanned the shelves behind his desk, moving the clock, and the photos of him and his bird-like wife out of the way to see if it was hidden anywhere. Standing on tiptoe I reached up and patted my hand along the top of the bookshelf in case it was up there. My head spun, and sweat streamed down my back. I thought I was going to pass out. Footsteps echoed from the corridor and I turned, my heart in my mouth. Kiran was already in the outer room. Taking deep breaths, I tried to stay calm and non-plussed.

'Looking for something, Mari?' said Kiran. His eyes narrowed as he looked at me standing in the doorway to his office.

'Oh, Kiran. Hi. That's nice. Is it new?' I nodded at the blue and white striped shirt he wore. 'Just needed the hole punch.' I raised my hand to show him what I'd grabbed off his desk in a panic, seconds before he'd seen me.

Suhana found me sitting under the palm tree on the corner of the lane to the widow's house. The humid heat was unbearable, and I needed the shade after just a five-minute walk from Sharma's.

'Are you fine, Mari?' she said, her face creased with concern. 'You don't look good.'

'I'm just overheated,' I said. I stood, and leaned against the tree. 'Just feel a bit woozy.'

'Come. Come.' She took my hand, and we walked slowly down the lane. I leaned into her a little, just to steady myself. 'I will give you *nimbu pani*. Sweet and salty lemon water will make you better.'

'But that lady, Hirmal? She won't be happy if I come in.'

'Let me check, but I'm sure no one is home from temple yet.'

Suhana left me at the entrance for a moment and went into the widows' house. She came out smiling, ushered me into a small room near the entrance. It was simple; just a narrow bed, and a low wooden shelf unit. Folded white saris filled the top shelf, and choli hung on wire hangers from the curtainless rail above the small window. On the middle shelf, a box of something, a bottle of shampoo, and a pink bar of Lux soap.

I sat on the bed, and Suhana lifted my legs onto it, then left the room. I lay down, glad of the lesser heat inside the small shady room. Suhana came back, wrapped wet cloths around my ankles, and fanned the air near my head with a rattan heart shaped-fan. My eyes were heavy, I couldn't keep them open.

Later I woke, my heart racing from the nightmare I'd just had. The smell of blood was real, the sound of it dripping on the mat, the weight of my attacker kneeling on my chest as the knife cut through my flesh; all so real. Sitting upright, I dislodged the cloths on my forehead and feet, my breath steadying. It took me a moment to realise where I was. Dusky light filled the room, and a mosquito buzzed near my ear. Swatting it away, I took one deep breath after another, calming my heart. Even though I knew it was a dream, I checked the underside of my forearm, running my thumb over the healed scar that still pricked and dragged.

'Suhana?' I stood, feeling better, and took a tentative step towards the doorway. 'Suhana?' The dizziness has subsided, but my legs were still jelly-like.

Suhana came into the room carrying a pink plastic jug filled with liquid, and I sat on the bed again.

'Good, you are rested. Here, please drink this. *Nimbu pani*. Lemon juice, water, salt, and sugar. While you slept, I went to buy the lemons, and a little salt and sugar. We don't usually have them. You will soon feel fine.' She poured the drink into a small glass. 'Slowly drink, not fastly.' While I sipped the cool drink, she closed the door. 'My friends are all back from the temple now. They don't know you are here. Stay quiet, okay? Better that Himal Auntie doesn't see you.'

'Thank you. I didn't mean to sleep. I'll drink this and go.'

'No, no, no.' She flicked her wrist in that gesture I saw so often, her palm upwards, facing me. 'Wait, and drink a little more. I don't want to hear that you were found in a bad way on the roadside.'

'Suhana, where are your family, your parents?' I asked her. Whatever their traditions, how could they not take her back?

She lifted the glass bowl from a paraffin lamp and lit the wick. When she replaced the glass, the warm glow was brighter than I'd thought it would be. 'No parents, but my brother is in Bombay. I miss him. And my school.'

'You were a teacher?'

'Yes, for first year pupils. The little ones were so much fun, so naughty. But I am in a different phase of my life now.'

There was no bitterness in her voice, no sense of the injustice her husband's death had caused her. I wanted to believe what Asa had told me, that acceptance was the balm that heals all wounds.

To me, that made sense, but looking at Suhana, it seemed that her acceptance went deeper. It was a natural reaction to an expected situation. No questions, no self-pity, just total acceptance. It must be liberating to have that embedded in your psyche, but that didn't alter the fact that what happened to her, and the other widows, made me uncomfortable. Religion and culture aside, as a human being, I couldn't help feeling it wasn't right. I stretched my arms, glanced at my watch.

'It's nearly nine o'clock. Have I missed the last bus to Shivpur? I guess I can get an auto.'

'No, Mari. You must stay here. You won't find autos outside Keshnagar now. It's too dark outside, you can't walk there. Wait, I'll bring food.'

A few minutes late she came back carrying a tin thali tray. The watery yellow dahl looked unappetising, so did the small potato still in its wrinkled skin. I didn't want to be ungrateful, but I couldn't face food.

'I'm sorry, but I'm not hungry. You have it, Suhana.'

'I have eaten. This is for you. Please.'

'*Dhanyavad,* thank you.' It dawned on me that maybe this was part of her own meal, so I broke the potato apart, and dipped it into the dahl. It was hard not to show my surprise when it got to my mouth. 'No spice? No garlic?'

'Not permitted. Everything must be plain. We can't have spice in case it makes our blood hot, you understand? Widows cannot have any pleasure. We live in tonsure.'

When I finished the meal, Suhana took away the tray. 'I'll sleep with Bhavna. But be careful when you leave that no one sees you, *theek hai*? Okay?'

'Thank you Suhana, goodnight.'

'Finish the nimbu pani in the jug.' She pointed to her shelves and closed the door behind her. 'Close the lamp when you are ready.'

It was only then that I noticed the large box of condoms next to her shampoo on the shelf, and I was really confused.

Chapter Nine
यात्रा

I TAPPED ON the Mehtas' sitting room doorframe. Mr Mehta grunted in greeting from the sofa opposite the door. All I could see were his legs, wrapped in a checked lungi, his hands on either side of the newspaper he was reading, and the top of his white-haired head.

'Ah, you got the *bhindi* for me.' Dolly popped her head around the kitchen door, wiping her hands on a tea cloth. 'Such a good girl. Thank you.' Her round face creased as she smiled.

'It was so busy in Keshnagar, and so humid,' I said. 'The sky's black over there. I just got to the bus before it rained.'

'Good. That means it won't rain here today.'

'Why not?' I handed her the bag of bhindi, okra, and followed her into the kitchen, placing a wad of rupees next to the electric spice grinder on the counter. 'Here; room money for the next two weeks.'

'Thank you, dear.' Dolly put the money in a plastic jar and placed it on the shelf next to tubs of lentils and chickpeas. 'When it rains in Keshnagar, it doesn't rain in Shivpur. And the other way around. No one knows why. Was the bus crowded?' She frowned. 'No one troubled you, I hope.'

'No, I stay at the front with the women now.' After all, I wouldn't want to be blamed for a man's lustful grope. It still rankled that women were at fault when men couldn't control themselves. 'I'm getting used to being stared at too.'

Dolly took a large plastic bowl from under the counter, placed it on the floor, and tipped the dark green vegetables into it. Crouching next to it, she picked out the leaves and twigs.

'I'll see you when dinner is ready, *theek hai*?'

'I can stay and help make the food with you?' Dolly shook her head. 'Okay, I'll go and see the holy man, Babba-ji.'

'Be careful in the rocks, *beti*, sometimes the monkeys that reside there are a little threatening.'

I liked how she called me *beti*, which meant *child*. 'How far up is the cave he lives in?' I said.

'Go behind the temple and you'll find it. There's a natural path, so just keep going up between the rocks. At the top, you'll find two boulders leaning together. Babba-ji's cave is through there. Take water with you, and be back before it becomes dark.'

Climbing higher through the rocks and boulders, I passed small shrines, sometimes no more than a mound of big stones and a blob of tinfoil adorning the rocks. There were more elaborate shrines; a trident held up by a pile of rocks, or red and yellow stripes painted onto a flat stone and propped up against a pile of pebbles. Hindus chose their personal favourite manifestations of God to worship, and here in Shivpur, they chose Shiva.

Noises came from close by, and I stopped, not sure if I should go any further. Perhaps it was the monkeys. I walked slowly, eyes darting, ready to run from marauding primates. Weaving my way through the rocks, I stopped dead. A man was shagging a woman from behind, her red and pink sari hoisted out of the way as she bent over a boulder. I backed away slowly so that they wouldn't know they'd been seen. Out of the corner of my eye, a man in a blue and white striped shirt caught my attention. Stifling a gasp, I clasped my hand over my mouth. Kiran stood at a distance, pretending not to watch them. I ducked behind a large rock, peeking out a minute or so later when the noises stopped. The woman straightened her sari. Kiran counted the money the man handed him, gave some to her, and pocketed the rest. All three walked in my direction, and I crouched down, holding my breath. Their footsteps scuffled past me, and they made their way down the path. I sat back against the rock, twisting the ends of my hair. When I thought it was okay to move without being seen, I came out from my hiding place. The three of them had separated and were heading towards the temple via different paths.

Kiran. My stomach roiled thinking of Kavita and the residents of Sharma's. Disgusting man. My dislike of him ran through me like hot lava. I couldn't let him get away with what he was doing. I knew that Kiran and Muddy were old school friends, but I'd tell him what Kiran was doing. Friendship couldn't take precedence over something so vile. Hopefully Muddy would speak to Mr Sharma and get Kiran fired. It was the least I could do for Kavita. I stepped over rocks and took the sandy path between the boulders, heading up the hill to find Babba-ji.

On the days that I didn't go to Sharma's, I found things to occupy myself. I drank chai with Dolly, sitting on her kitchen floor while she sat on the opposite side of a basket of lentils or vegetables that needed preparing for our meals. She taught a little about Indian cookery, and I helped her as much as she'd allow. Paying her a few rupees on top of the room rent meant that she fed me, and her food was amazingly good.

'How long have you and Raju Uncle been married?' I asked.

'More than twenty-five years. My husband was station master at Keshnagar for thirty years.' Dolly smiled, her shoulders back. 'Good government job, and he retired this year on a pension.'

'And now he watches the news and listens to the cricket.' I podded peas, letting them rain into the bowl between my knees, and dropping the pods onto the floor beside me.

'Tisk. Let him. My daughter, Anjali, is only a little younger than you. She married less than three years ago. Her husband is so nice, he is Bangalore assistant sub-station manager.' There was pride, and sadness in her voice. 'My grandson is almost two now.'

'It's nice that you have a grandchild.' She must miss her only daughter, but I wondered why she and Raju Uncle were never in the same room. 'Do you see much of the boy?'

'So far away, not easy to go and come regularly.' Dolly sighed. 'Mari, when my grandson marries, I will invite you to his wedding. And you will wear a sari, not shalwar. Always you wear shalwar kameez, but a sari is so elegant, and you are tall, so it will look good on you.'

'Saris are lovely, but I'd probably trip over all that fabric. Shalwar are easier for me. But maybe one day I'll try and wear a sari.'

'At my grandson's wedding, okay?'

'Okay.' I laughed.

Days passed so easily, and a sort of routine emerged without me planning it. I hung out by the ghats at the river in the mornings, watching women wash their saris, and the temple elephant have her bath. Later, I retreated to my room to sleep or read, or I'd just sit on the window seat and listen to Duran Duran or Fleetwood Mac on my Walkman.

With both windows open, the breeze cooled the room. I always flopped on the bed, ignoring the squeaks and creaks it made whenever I moved, and dozed through the stifling hot afternoons. I listened to the lullaby of the rain and waited for it to stop. Once it was cooler, I walked to the temple and sat on the stone steps in the outer courtyard. It soothed me to sit there quietly in the dusk, listening to the prayers being chanted, and the clanging of the temple bell. Most days, if it wasn't raining, I'd get on the back of Muddy's bike, and he'd take me for lunch, or chai or kulfi. And on the days that I went to Sharma's, I always met Suhana on my way back to bus station. We'd find a tree to sit under and we'd talk about life, and love, and sometimes she taught me some Hindi. She'd smile when I made mistakes, and patiently explain it all to me again. It was such a shame that she couldn't continue teaching children, just because her husband died. I loved India, but she was flawed. Majestic, romantic, but flawed.

One morning, I changed my routine a little. After breakfast of paratha and chai, I stayed in my room, listening to music. '*Songbird*' made me cry. Would I ever feel love like that? Had I actually loved Ryu, or simply woven the emotion out of loneliness and lust? Whatever I'd felt for him, it had become twisted by Kate's death. Needing to erase my self-induced sadness, I changed the tape for Duran Duran's album, '*Rio*'. I stepped across the room, moving my feet to the upbeat rhythm, I sang along to '*Hold back the Rain*' and broke in to a full-on dance. The irony of the title wasn't lost on me when the heavens opened, and I replayed the song again.

When the rain stopped, I ventured outside, and bought a garland of marigold flowers from a young boy near the temple. They were for Dolly, who hung a fresh garland of them across the top of her front door every morning, and threw the old ones out onto the street for passing cows to eat. I stopped at the chai stand near the temple. A woman stared hard at me, rushing over to me as I crouched on a tiny plastic stool under the red umbrella.

'Hello. How are you? Remember me? Muddy's sister. I wanted to see you. I left a message for you at your guesthouse.'

'Rhea, was it? Nice to see you again.' I stood, offered to buy her chai. 'Sorry, I didn't get any message.'

We sat together, sipping tea in silence. Cows wandered past, slowing chewing their cud, meandering with all the time in the world. They stopped on the corner, and a mother cow licked her tiny calf, her tongue almost as big as its head.

'I don't want to offend you, but I must speak up. People are telling me, they see you and Muddy together. All the time. You and him,' Rhea said. 'Really, when he told me, I –'

'What did he tell you?' I pushed my mirrored bangles up and down my forearm, the tinkling sound calming me.

'He's talking about feelings. Feelings. I ask you!'

'We're just friends, Rhea. We enjoy each other's company.'

She flicked her wrist, turning her palm outwards at shoulder height. 'Shivpur is a religious town, and you need to have some respect for our culture. Everyone knows what you Western girls get up to in Goa.' Her voice got louder. 'This is not Goa. Those types of things don't happen here.'

'What?' I said. 'There's nothing like that going on. I know he likes me, but honestly, we really are just friends.'

'Then leave him alone. Do you know the trouble you are causing? Everyone is gossiping. He is a police officer; he needs to be careful of his reputation. He needs a good Indian wife. Not a Goa tourist.'

'Fine.' Leaving my chai unfinished, I stood, my head held high. I straightened my silver kurta, swathed my embroidered dupatta across my chest and stepped away.

'My parents have already fixed his marriage,' Rhea said. 'We'll speak to the pandit, bring the date forward.'

My pace increased, and indignation curled my hands into fists. Good thing I hadn't got involved with Muddy, but I liked him enough to be annoyed. More annoying was the fact that I'd left the marigold garland on the ground by the chai stand, and there was no way I was going back to get it.

Later in Keshnagar, the Hindi and English sign pointed me to the old café that Muddy had taken me to, and my newly acquired favourite, rose and cardamom kulfi was served by a gentle old man in a white jacket. The combination of flavours was exquisite, and somehow very Indian. I stayed for a while, reading a chapter or two of a paperback; something by Jackie Collins that Lucy had left me. Kulfi finished, I picked up the bill, drank the water that had been placed on my table. Standing at the wooden cashier's desk near the door, waiting to pay, noise from outside caught my attention.

I craned my head around the arched doorway, and stepped out onto the pavement. Three or four policemen crowded around someone on the ground, beating him with their batons. People ran from all sides, yelling and shouting, kicking at the man on the ground. With my hands over my mouth, I stood transfixed, horrified. Wasn't it illegal for the police to do something like that?

'What happened? What did he do?' I asked my waiter who'd joined me on the street.

'The crowd is saying he stole something from a shop down there. Come back inside, Miss. Come.'

'Why are they beating him?' My stomach roiled at the violence. 'They could just arrest him.'

'A beating is better than a night in the cells. He'll remember it longer.'

Just as I turned to go inside, the policemen moved away. Two were laughing. One of them was Muddy.

Chapter Ten
यात्रा

DOLLY CALLED TO me as I shuffled my feet out of my new toe loop sandals, and left them by the front door. Peering around the doorway into her kitchen, I smiled at her as I knocked a string of dried chilies with my head.

'Afternoon, Dolly Auntie,' I said, untangling myself from them.

'Here. Pakoda. Potato and onion. I made them freshly.' Dolly handed me a metal plate, and I sat on the tiled floor to eat them, as I'd done many times before. Her kindness and generosity had increased over the six weeks or so I'd been living in her house. 'Your police-wallah came looking for you again, beti.'

'He's not my police-wallah, Dolly Auntie. He's just...' I was going to say he was a friend. But I wasn't even sure about that. I bit into the crispy pakoda as Dolly plonked a metal cup of chai on the floor next to me. 'Anyway, I don't have time to see him now. I'm at Sharma's most days. I have a lot to do there.'

'You are a good girl, Mari. It's nice, you want to help others. But all that walking, no wonder you are so skinny. Take more pakoda. I'll go and come, I must give some to Raju Uncle.'

The sound of the radio was loud from their sitting room. 'Cricket again,' I said. 'Why don't you sit in there with him?'

'If I speak, he says I am disturbing him, or that he can't hear the commentary, or he can't concentrate on what he is reading. No matter, I like my kitchen. I have much to do in here.' Her smile was resigned. 'Eat up, dear. Please. You need some fat on your bones, like me.' She pinched the roll of flesh exposed by her sari at her waist, giggled, and took the pakoda to her husband. She was back in a flash. 'More chai. You don't drink enough either.'

I'd always been a good weight, but I wasn't skinny. Delhi belly had struck more than once, and I guessed it was the tap water I drank at Sharma's. I knew it came from a storage tank at the back of the building. My weight was maintained by the amount of fried food I was eating. Pakoda, samosa, fried bindhi, jalebi; I enjoyed them all. And then there was the almost daily kulfi.

'I think I sweat out everything I consume,' I said. 'It's just so hot.'

'Not long now. Another two weeks only,' said Dolly. 'It will be cooler, and the rain will stop, and then I can dry this year's chilies on the roof.'

'Hang on. What's the date now?'

'August twenty.'

'I'll need to get my visa sorted, it runs out at the beginning of October.' I shook my head. 'I can't believe I've been in India for over four months.'

'Ask your police-wallah about your visa, Mari.' Dolly smiled and raised her eyebrows. 'He will definitely oblige you.'

Annoyingly, she was right. My avoidance tactics had worked for a few weeks since I'd seen him beating that poor man on the street, and I didn't relish the thought of seeing Muddy again, but I didn't know who else to ask.

A little later I sat on the armchair in my room, with my arms leaning on the window frame. Where I should go next? I needed to make a plan. Out of nowhere, the thunder rolled and the lightning flashed in a sky that had been clear just ten minutes before. Monsoon rain bounced off every surface, and water gushed from the roofs and into the gutters. Two little boys played with paper boats, floating them in the deluge that suddenly flooded the streets, laughing as their boats raced along.

Stretching my arms out of the window, I enjoyed the coolness of the rain, turning my hands skywards to catch it.

Changing into the green silk kurta I used as a nightshirt, I lay on the window seat. The pitter-patter of the rain on the corrugated tin roof on the opposite side of the alley was strangely soporific. Suhana had taught me the Hindi word for the sound; *rhimjhim*.

Was it time for me to move on to Nepal, or perhaps Burma? Turning onto my back, I looked up at the tassels of the wall hanging above the alcove moving in the breeze. Perhaps I could head to Dharamshala next, enjoy the cool air and the high altitude of the low Himalaya before the snows of winter closed the roads. And if the Dalai Lama was in residence in McLeod Ganj, I'd go and listen to his teachings, even if they were in Tibetan. Just to be in his presence would be a wonderful thing. A year earlier, when Kate and I had planned travelling across Asia together, Dharamshala had been top of my list for places to go once we reached India. How had I got so side-tracked?

I dug my travellers' cheques out of my bag and counted them. There was still over two thousand dollars' worth. I'd hardly spent any money while I'd been in India. Everything cost so little anyway, even travel and guesthouses. At that rate, I reckoned that I could probably stay another year.

India was a big country, and I'd seen so little of it in the four and a half months I'd been there. I'd wasted so much time in Goa, but then I'd needed the escapism, needed time to heal. Imagine how much more of India I could see in another year. So, I needed to figure out how could I arrange a new visa.

I pulled my holdall out from under the bed, unzipped it, and unwrapped the guidebook from my faded Levi's jacket. Just the sight of the jacket brought back memories of Japan. I ran my hands over the denim, fiddling with the flat metal buttons. Perhaps I should throw it away, but I'd probably need it when I headed north. Crawling onto the creaking bed, I flicked through the guidebook, and smiled when I saw where Turquoise

Haresh had written his name. Haresh Chandekar. *Chand* was the Hindi word for the moon; *chandini* meant moonlight. What did Chandekar mean?

Turning the pages, I found the information I was looking for. It was possible to apply for a new six-month Indian visa in Kathmandu. There was a bus I could take from Delhi, that travelled up through the foothills of the Himalayas, and into Nepal. That'd be hairy, to say the least, and I imagined twisty-bendy narrow roads and full sick bags. But the guidebook gave me the address of the visa office, and that was all I needed right then. It seemed a faff to leave a country to come back into it; maybe there was another way, but nothing was mentioned in the guidebook.

My fingers traced the scrawled comments and asterisks Kate had written through the guidebook. Would she have liked India? Thinking of her reminded me of who I was, and everything that had happened. I ran my thumb along my scar that had faded from angry red to dark pink. It might not be as vivid as it had been, but my nightmares still were. Add the guilt I felt completed the trifecta of things I'd probably carry to my grave. The guilt was the hardest thing to deal with.

Turning onto my side, I faced the open window. The fan above me, and the wind from the storm cooled me as I lay there. Above the alcove, the wall hanging flapped with every gust of air, its tiny sewn on mirrors catching the light. My tears dried as I cried them and eventually, I slept.

I woke at dusk, when the storm had blown herself out, leaving the air fresher, and my mind clearer. In the morning, I'd go to Keshnagar, ask for Muddy at the police station, and see what he could do about extending my visa. If there was a chance that I could get it sorted locally, great. If not I'd head to Dharamshala, then onto Nepal. Either way, I'd leave in a week or ten days, and that would be enough time to give Muddy the evidence I was collecting against Kiran.

On the corner of the road to the temple, a huge black and cream cow chewed at a pile of wilting marigolds, and I dodged her on my way to the bus stop. I heard the familiar deep roar of a Royal Enfield motorbike and turned to face it. Muddy must have been off duty again; he wore navy chinos and a light blue polo shirt.

'Where are you these days, Mari?' His dimples showed themselves through the stubble on his cheeks. 'I miss you.'

'You need a shave,' I said.

'I know. I've been working on a murder case for three days straight, so have not left the station. I'll go to the barber later. I came to ask if I can take you for kulfi.'

'A murder?' My solar plexus twitched. 'Is it the missing girl, Shanti? What happened?'

'You are so worried about someone you don't even know.' Muddy frowned. 'It's nothing to do with her, but you know I can't discuss details. Things happen in Keshnagar, just like in any other Indian city.'

'Fair enough. Okay, it's too early for kulfi. But I wanted to talk to you anyway.' I climbed on behind him, using his shoulder to lever myself up. 'Chalo.'

Instead of leaning into his body as I usually would, I kept an inch or so away from him, contact minimal, just my hand on his shoulder. Impossible as it was to chat on a motorbike anyway, the silence was heavy. When he skirted a man herding some scrawny goats along the roadside, I had to hold on, and my arm circled Muddy's waist. My mind flittered from one thing to another, not sure what to tell him about Kiran, about what Rhea had said, or even that I'd seen him beating that man. By the time we reached the café, I decided to just ask him about my visa.

Muddy and I drank strong, milky coffee. He watched me, and I avoided his gaze. He sat back in his chair, head to one side.

'You hate me now?' Muddy said. 'Did someone say something to you?'

'You know Rhea did. Look, that doesn't matter. I need to

ask you something.'

His shoulders tensed, and he leaned one elbow on the table, his honey-coloured gaze direct. 'You can ask me anything, Mari. My friend is out of town, and I have the key to his apartment. We can be alone. Shall we go there today? We can talk privately.'

'We can talk here, Muddy.'

'But I want to…you know, be with you. Alone.' He smiled that dimpled smile of his.

'No.' Strangely, I was tempted. But how could I be attracted to him after what I'd seen him do? 'No. But I wonder if you can help me? I need to extend my visa.'

'If that means you will stay longer, I'll find a way. Come, chalo. Let's go to the apartment. And after,' he grinned, 'we can talk more. And then, I will call someone. He will tell me how to get your visa extended, okay?' He stared at me, and I stared back.

'Just find out and let me know,' I said. 'Leave a message with Dolly Auntie.'

'I don't want to do that. Come with me.' Muddy sucked air in through his teeth, closing his eyes for a moment. 'Oh, Mari. I have waited so long for you. Come on, let's be together.' Leaning towards me, he lowered his voice. 'I want to be naked and sweaty with you.'

He smiled then, ran his finger along my arm, and I was so tempted, I could feel my own heat building at the thought of it.

'I'll get the bus back to Shivpur.' I stood to leave, and Muddy dropped his head, groaning.

Chapter Eleven
यात्रा

THE PRE-DAWN SOUNDS of brooms being swept through houses and onto the street woke me as usual, but instead of turning over and going back to sleep, energy coursed through me, and I felt invigorated. Washing and dressing, I made my way out of the house, and walked towards the temple. The pathway behind it wasn't steep at first, but the higher I climbed into the boulders, the narrower it became, and the more often I had to use my hands to clamber over the rocks.

The sun was still behind the mountain, and the light was ethereal, greying everything out in silver-blue. Small birds chirped, and I jumped back as a lizard scuttled across my path. I stopped for a moment and looked back the way I'd come. Below me, the village bustled with people; kids waiting on the corner to be picked up by the Keshnagar school bus, women setting up their stalls under rolled back tarpaulins, others cleaning their front steps with water, and men heading to temple in their white dhoti for morning prayers.

As the sun peeked over the boulders, like the diamond ring of an eclipse, everything came alive. The tarpaulins turned red, green, yellow; saris showed their pinks and oranges, their mustards and blues. Greenery amongst the stones looked brighter, the dust washed away by the night's rain.

Turning back, I looked up, wondering how much further I needed to go, and I kept on climbing. At the top of the path, two huge boulders leaned against each other, and I knew by the smell of sandalwood incense that I was close. Twice before I'd tried to find the cave but never had. Taking the narrow path to the right of the two boulders, I covered my head with my dupatta, out of respect.

Babba-ji sat crossed-legged, wrapped in a dark red shawl. His turban was burnt orange, and his forehead was covered in three white stripes of ash on either side of a red vertical line.

'Namaste, Babba-ji,' I said, my hands in prayer position. He smiled, gathering his dreadlocks, and moving them over his shoulder.

'Namaste, welcome. Although nothing here. Just me.' He laughed, his teeth yellow and uncared for. 'I see you every day, at the temple.'

'I've seen you too, and I wanted to meet you.'

I placed the packet of incense and the vegetable paratha wrapped in foil that Dolly had made, as well as a small bag of raw peanuts on the coir mat that Babba-ji was sitting on.

'Have you come to ask the meaning of what I am doing?' Babba-ji chuckled. 'Why I choose to live this way? I am very interesting to you?'

'I don't want to be nosy, but yes, you are very interesting.' I smiled and he gestured to the ground. I sat opposite him. 'All I know is that you are a Babba-ji, a saddhu, and that you are very respected and revered by everyone in the village.'

'So, you come with some good knowledge already.' He uncrossed his legs, shook them out. His feet were crusted with hard skin from what I assumed was years of walking barefoot.

'India makes me feel reflective, although I'm not a really a religious person –'

'But you believe in something. I feel that from you.' He tilted his head, looked at me through narrowed eyes. 'Don't deny who you are. Allow yourself to connect with the divine within. And when you see things, don't be afraid.'

'How did you know?' I said. Babba-ji smiled. 'Anyway, I don't '*see*'; I just know. But that hasn't happened since...' I wanted to tell him that I hadn't had any kind of premonition since before Kate died, that I hadn't replaced my lost Tarot cards, that my knowings hardly happened anymore, but my throat was tight, and the words wouldn't come.

'What do you need to let go of, so that you can embrace this life? To earn *moksha?*'

'I don't know what that is, sorry.' I took a lighter out of my bag, lit a stick of incense, and stuck it between two small stones. The smoke danced and drifted in the air.

'Moksha is freedom. Release from the cycle of death and rebirth. It's what all Hindus want; for this life to be the last.'

My heart twitched. Moksha was Samsara, the Buddhist concept of liberation through enlightenment. I'd learned about it from a monk in Bangkok. He'd explained that we suffer because we form attachments, and that because nothing is permanent and things must change, then suffering is inevitable.

'And you live without possessions –'

'Because greed, desire, and material things hold you back from moksha.'

'Buddhism has the same –'

'Similar, not the same.' Babba-ji laughed. 'Subtle differences, but we are all looking for nirvana, nah? We are all tired of day to day living, the expected painful death, the same struggles in the next life. I talked with an American once.' He nodded, moving his dreadlocks again. 'That man referred to moksha as... now what was it?' He scratched his chin under his long grey beard. 'Ah, I remember. Getting off the hamster wheel.'

I smiled. 'Good analogy.'

Babba-ji laughed, slapping his thighs. 'I don't know what is a hamster. He explained to me but in my mind's eye, I see a rat in a cage, running around on a wheel.' He circled his hand in the air. 'Round and around, round and around.'

Above us, myna birds flew, cawing, and we both looked up. The sky lost its milkiness as the sun rose higher, searing its heat through the wispy grey clouds.

'I don't know how to get off the wheel. And maybe I'm not ready, I have to fix things in this life first.'

'That's the point. Fix. Fix. Do what you can. But if not resolved, you'll try again in your next lifetime. But be careful not to create more things you need to fix.' He rotated his hand in the air. 'The wheel, see? What is it you want for your life, girl?'

'Love. Happiness. Peace. Simple things.' I adjusted my legs, patting the dust from my shalwar.

'Young people! Always it's romance they worry about. Yet life is longer than any romance, nah?'

I laughed. He was probably right. 'So, tell me, where did you learn your English?'

'At school in Mysore. My family was quite well to do. But I changed my perception of life after my mother died. I decided to live a simple life of devotion, instead of making rich people richer.'

The temple bell rang, and chanted prayers drifted on the breeze.

'I should go.' I knelt and placed a few folded rupees on his mat.

'Come again. Take God's blessing with you.' Babba-ji touched my forehead, and I wiped tears from my eyes.

Late in the afternoon that day, after kulfi at the café, Muddy took me to the viewpoint to watch the sunset. The rocks changed from ochre to pink as the light played over them. A troupe of langurs ran amok across the temple pillars and buildings in the village, their tails erect like dodgem car poles. We sat on a sun-warm rock, Muddy's hand resting discreetly in the small of my back.

'Don't leave,' Muddy said. 'You can stay longer.'

'There are other parts of India I want to see.'

'And if I ask you to stay?' He touched my face, and I shifted away. 'For me, Mari.'

'But you have a marriage arranged. You're not thinking straight, Muddy.'

'What is there to think? I know what I feel, what I want. I told you, how I feel about you. I have made up my mind.'

Streaks of lilac and coral, grey and indigo streaked the sky, and the first stars appeared. I stood, made my back to the pathway; there was no reason to stay now the sun had gone. Muddy followed me, our footsteps on the pebbly path the only sound. My silence should have been enough, and I hoped it made him understand that I didn't feel the same as he did.

We walked back to the Mehtas' and stood outside. Muddy looked at me, a tentative smile creasing his eyes. 'No? You don't love me?'

'I really like you, as a friend. But that's all. Love?' I looked away. 'I can't believe…look, if I've given you the wrong signals, I'm sorry, but I don't feel like that for you.'

Dolly bustled out of the door, thrusting her feet into slip-on sandals.

'Hello, Dolly Auntie,' I said, glad of the distraction. When Muddy left without saying anything, I felt bad. I hadn't meant to hurt him, just hadn't taken him seriously. It hadn't happened to me before; I was usually the one in love, the one that got hurt. It had been the same with Ryu, and that was still fresh enough to tear at my heart.

'No bloody water again,' Dolly said. 'Let's go to where the men are meeting. We can listen to their plan for the village.'

Water had been sporadic in the village for the last week or so. Something about pipes bursting somewhere. The river water wasn't safe for drinking, so the *Panchayat* called a meeting. The elected group of village leaders sat on a raised dais that had been set up between the temple and the river. Bright lights hung from cables threaded through the trees, shining on the Panchayat. With their Nehru caps and long white kurtas over pristine dhoti, they looked so different from the other men. It was also their air of importance that set them apart.

'We will collect water from various wells, and clear streams in our district,' said the *Sarpanch* through a booming microphone. The Sarpanch owned the barbershop and had been elected as head of the Panchayat.

The crowd murmured in agreement, sitting on plastic chairs, drinking chai that was provided for everyone. Dolly and I stood at the back, half-hidden by a tree. She translated everything for me, patting my hand as she spoke quietly.

'I can offer my bullock cart,' said an elderly man in the middle of the crowd, raising his hand.

Everyone clapped and clapped again when another three carts were offered.

'We'll set out at six o'clock in the morning,' said the Sarpanch, 'Every two days, until this water crisis is over. Starting tomorrow. Whatever we collect will be divided between every household. Per capita.' He flicked his wrist. 'Don't think that what you collect is for yourself only. We will give the same amount of water to each person, regardless of age. One baby will get the same measure as a working man. Per capita. But every household must send at least one person to help collect the water.'

The discussion turned to what the water could be carried in, and it was heart-warming to see everyone contribute ideas. The sense of community was humbling. But the absence of women at the meeting was galling.

Dolly and I left the men to work out the details, and went to check on an elderly couple who lived in a thatched shack on the edge of the village. They were alone and frail, so we took their water butt, carrying it between us, back to the village, ready for the morning.

'Dolly,' I said. 'I'll be leaving within the next week, as soon as I book a bus ticket to Bombay. I can't rely on Muddy to help with the visa.'

'Oh. Of course, of course. You must go, I understand.'

The way she said it made me think she didn't want me to go.

The following morning, in the dawn light, Dolly and I helped with the loading of earthenware jugs and plastic containers of all sizes next to plastic demijohns and water butts on the bullock carts. The farmers had decorated their bullocks' horns with ribbons, and strings of marigolds hung round the animals' broad necks, as well as along the edges of the carts. I walked with Dolly and the other villagers, alongside the carts as they headed out of the village and into the rocky countryside, towards wells in fields, and streams that fed the river. Kids sat between the demijohns, and someone banged a drum, started to sing a warbling song. Everyone joined in. I had no idea what they were singing about, but I clapped along. Eventually, the carts broke file, heading out in four different directions.

When our cart reached a well, Dolly and I joined the others, and gathered containers, planning to fill the largest ones first. The women tied rope or thick string around the necks of earthenware vessels, and through the handles of plastic buckets. The larger containers were placed around the well, ready to be filled. A dozen or so women, plus Dolly and I leaned over the waist height mud-brick wall of the well. There was a skill to twisting the rope so that the bucket dunked into the water and filled up, but mine kept floating on the surface. I struggled for ages, trying to dip the bucket in the water, and when I managed to fill it and haul it up, the other women cheered. We filled the larger containers, bucketful by bucketful, trying not to waste a drop. When they were full, the men carried them away, hefting them onto the cart. It was a slow process, and one that could be speeded up if the men helped us women at the well.

My shoulders ached, and I ran my forearm across my face, the sleeve of my kurta wet and cool against my skin. Looking up at the sky, I grimaced against the brightness, wishing I had sunglasses, and hoping it would rain. Dipping my cupped hand into my bucket, I drank handful after handful of water.

From the other side of the well, Rhea watched me, the disdain on her face making me blush. I focused on dipping my empty bucket back into the water.

'Why are you here?' Rhea said, pushing through the other women to stand beside me, her hands on her hips. 'Why are you? This is not your place.'

'I just wanted to help,' I said, my hands wide in supplication. 'And there's an old couple, neither of them could manage this, so I'm here instead of them.'

'Interfering Britisher.' Rhea tutted.

'I'm leaving in a few days. You don't need to worry, Rhea.'

'Bas, bas,' said Dolly. 'Enough. Leave her, Rhea, she means well. Come, Mari, let's sit in the shade. We can rest for a while.' Rhea said something in Hindi, and Dolly made a sound with her teeth.

'What did she say?' I asked. Dolly and I sat on the ground, and I shuffled my bottom back against the wheel of the cart, leaned against it in a small patch of shade. One of the bullocks snorted, thrashing his head before he settled again.

'Not to be repeated, dear.' Dolly smiled. 'Your police-wallah, though, he thinks differently about you than she does.'

'We are just friends, so what's her bloody problem?'

'He thinks differently about that. You should go home, get married; you are a good age for marriage.' Dolly smiled. 'And so pretty. Any man would be happy to have you, I think.'

'I'm unlucky in love, Dolly Auntie. Maybe my karma means I won't ever find true love with the right man at the right time.'

'Did you love someone? At home?'

'In Japan. But it wasn't possible. It turned out he wasn't the person I thought he was.'

'Heartbroken?' Dolly shook her head. 'It happens. You'll find someone else. I am sure. Shall I take you to the astrologer? We'll go together, and see what he says.' Her bangles rattled as she moved her hands. 'Really, we should go. Find out what is written for you.'

'I don't want to know. What if he predicts a future I don't want? I'd rather wait for the surprise.'

'You can't avoid your fate. What's written, is written. Poor Muddy. Better he marries a local girl, hai na?'

'That would please Rhea. I hope he's happy. But I only ever liked him as a friend. I didn't encourage him, really, I didn't.'

'But you did, beti. By spending so much time with him, driving all around on his motorbike, coffee and kulfi in Keshnagar.' Dolly looked at me. 'All of that is encouragement. Did you do it with him?'

'Dolly! No.' I spluttered. 'No.' I glanced at her. 'He did ask me, many times. I have to admit I did think about it.'

Dolly threw her head back and laughed.

'No one would blame you. Dreamy. It's the dimples.' She tweaked her own cheeks. 'Adorable. Love will find you, Mari. I believe that. And so should you.'

'I'm going back to help. Let someone else take a rest,' I said.

When all the containers were filled, and the carts loaded, we walked the three or four kilometres back to Shivpur. There was no singing on the way back, and the early afternoon heat made me more tired than I actually was. By time I got back to my room, I was shaking and sweating and puking.

Chapter Twelve

London 2010

My office desk was tidy, just a photo of me and Harry on his last birthday, a turquoise coffee mug, and the usual computer hardware.

Alan, my boss, was in his glass-walled office, shouting down the phone. He raised his hand when he saw me walk past, and rolled his eyes. His tie was askew, his shirt only half-tucked into his corduroy trousers. It might not be the right time to broach the subject of me taking extended leave. Our project in Senegal was almost wrapped up, and the new one in Ethiopia was underway, so I knew it would be fine for me to be out of the office for three or four weeks.

'Mari, coffee?' said Julie, popping her head into my office. Her pink tie-dye clothes and wild hair reminded me of myself in my twenties when I'd been travelling all over Asia. 'Jam doughnuts too. Alan brought them in at lunchtime.'

'Do you have to ask?' I smiled, and Julie laughed.

I was busy that afternoon, making phone calls and sending out requests for meetings. Scheduling a presentation at Marlborough College was a highlight of my day. We'd get some good funding from them, I was sure. As one of the most prestigious private schools in the UK, they were known for their philanthropy to the large Non-Governmental Organisations. We were a small charity, and worked with the big players who came to us for our expertise in getting clean, running water to the places that needed it most.

'Alan?' I caught his eye as he passed my desk, a coffee mug in his hand. 'Can I have a word?'

'Follow me into my office then, and bring your hidden stash of ginger biscuits.'

Grabbing the biscuits from my desk draw, I asked Julie to answer my phone if it rang, and headed into Alan's office.

'Put your boss hat on please,' I said and closed the door. Sitting opposite him, I rolled the unopened packet of biscuits across his desk. 'I got Marlborough for the school loos project.'

'Well done, you. Marvellous.' He opened the biscuits, held the packet out to me, but I shook my head. 'And Comic Relief?'

'Not yet, but I'm hopeful. Of course, they love that it's for kids. The fact that it's five boys' loos and five girls' loos seemed to tick their equality boxes too. Okay.' I took a deep breath. 'Friend hat on now, please.'

'As long as you don't ask me for a raise.' Crumbs dropped from his mouth, and he brushed them away. He frowned. 'What's wrong? Harry?'

'In a way. I mean, it does concern him. I need you to give me extra leave. I'll be happy to take it unpaid, although I reckon I'm owed at least two weeks in lieu. Anyway, I basically need three, maybe four weeks off in November.'

'I thought you were going travelling around Crete in October. Has something changed? Wait.' He tapped at his keyboard, peered at the screen. 'Maggie's away in Chad; she's got to oversee the office set up and then hand over to the man on the ground over there.'

'She's back on November third. If I cancel October's leave, I can go when she gets back.' Pushing my hair behind my ears, I leaned forwards. 'It's important, Alan. You know I wouldn't ask if it wasn't.'

The phone on his desk rang, and he picked up the receiver. Looking at me apologetically, he spoke into the mouthpiece. I pointed to myself and then to the door, but he shook his head.

He'd probably agree to let me have more time off; he was more like a friend than a boss after all the years we'd worked together. But then again, work was work.

I'd met Alan and his then-wife, Angie, eighteen years ago. They had started the charity, *Water Well Together*, known as *WWT*, a few years before that. Desperate for a job, I'd blagged an interview, and was over the moon when they agreed to hire me as a receptionist. I did the photocopying, made the tea, dealt with the post; all the usual tasks. But it meant I learned the ropes of working for a charity, and a few years later I was promoted to an administration role, and then to assistant campaign manager. With my travel experience, Angie asked me to go to Nepal with her so that I could gain the first-hand experience of running a project. Harry hadn't wanted me to go, and I wasn't too keen either. The memories I had of Nepal weren't the greatest, but it was for work, and I didn't have a choice. And now, fifteen years later, Harry was used to my work-related travels, and I had become a senior project manager.

Alan ended his call, slurped his coffee. 'Sorry about that.'

'It's fine, Alan.'

'Go on then, tell me, what's this all about, Mari.' Biting into a biscuit, Alan rolled his eyes. 'My waistline won't thank you later.'

'I've been invited to a wedding in India. I need to go to India. And I want to take Harry with me.'

'Bloody hell.'

Chapter Thirteen
यात्रा

Shivpur, 1986

THE BATHROOM BECAME my place of residence. I couldn't leave it for more than a few minutes. Laying on my bed, as the fan dried the moisture that covered my body, I felt another spasm low in my gut that told me my digestive system still had more to get rid of. The bathroom bucket of water was empty; I was embarrassed by the stench and the fact I had nothing to swill the squat loo with. Leaning against the wall, I turned the tap, hoping for the gurgle and splutter and eventual gush of water. Nothing came.

On the second day that I was ill, Dolly called the doctor in from Keshnagar. She opened my door, came into my room, the doctor followed behind with his black Gladstone bag.

The doctor sat on the edge of the bed, and the springs squeaked in protest. I sat up, but dizziness assaulted me, and I lay back. When he raised my green silk kurta, to examine my stomach, Dolly Auntie looked away.

'Doctor?' Dolly came to the other side of the bed and took hold of my hand. 'What is it?'

'Most probably a parasitical infection,' he said. 'A few people are sick from the well water. Did she drink any without boiling it first?' Dolly nodded. He scribbled on a prescription pad and ripped it off. 'Doxycycline for ten days. Lots of nimbu pani.

Paracetamol for any fever. She'll be fine.'

'I'm going to Bombay tomorrow,' I said.

'I disagree,' said the doctor. 'Better to stay here. Rest and recovery. Maybe one week later you can go, okay?'

The antibiotics took three days to kick in, and gradually I felt better. Dolly cooked me *khichdi,* lentil and rice porridge, and checked on me throughout the day. Muddy brought two fresh coconuts from Keshnagar every afternoon. They helped with rehydration; I drank one in the afternoon, and the other the next morning. He brought me a tatty old paperback he'd found somewhere, as well as sachets of rehydration salts, sweets, and salted cashews. Patiently, he waited downstairs with the Mehtas. I was well enough to see him, but I couldn't face him, knowing I'd hurt him. But he was a glutton for punishment, and every afternoon for a week, he visited.

A day or so later, I woke in the morning craving chai and samosas, and I knew I was better. While in the bathroom, I checked if there was water. Laughing as the clean, cold liquid poured over me, I showered, knowing I would never take running water for granted again. When I was dressed, I made my way downstairs to the kitchen.

'I need fresh air,' I said. 'I'll walk a little.'

'Good that you are up,' said Dolly. 'Don't go too far. Maybe I should come also?'

'I feel okay, Dolly Auntie, honestly. I'll just go to the temple, sit on the steps while it's still cool.' Draping my dupatta across my shoulders, and pulling it down over my chest, I smiled at her. 'I'm hoping to see my friend, Suhana.'

'Bring her for chai, beti. Any friend of yours is welcome. Who is this girl?'

'She's the same age as me, and her husband died after they'd only been married for four months.'

'Oh no, poor thing. So, she's a widow?' Dolly's smile faded. 'Please don't tell me about the bad luck. She's such an intelligent girl, but she's got no chance of any kind of life.' I leaned against the door frame. 'I don't want to be disrespectful to Indian culture, but it stinks.'

'I also don't believe in this tonsure, it's outdated and quite brutal.' She tutted. 'Not every family is the same in their observance of these old traditions, you know. Poor girl, and so young. Beti, I can't have her for chai – the neighbours…'

'I don't think she'd come anyway.' I moved away from the door. 'See you in a bit.'

'Okay. Ten minutes only, or I will come and take you back here.'

'Yes, Dolly Auntie.'

'Your police-wallah will be here at four o'clock, like every day. And the water is back. Look.' She turned the tap on and off, on and off, laughing as the water splashed. 'Such a good thing.'

On my way to the temple, I almost collided with a cow. It eyed me, tossing its horns, so I turned a different corner.

After masala chai and an oh-so-tasty samosa, I bought another two of the hot pastries, and the seller wrapped them in newspaper for me. I headed to the temple entrance, and gave the samosas to the leper. He put his hands in prayer position and smiled. I found a quiet spot in the shade, and sat on a rock behind the flower sellers, watching as life bustled around the entrance. Scanning the crowds, I looked for Suhana.

Monkeys swung themselves on long arms across the buildings, and I waited for the temple elephant to appear. Every morning, pilgrims gave money for her blessing; for a few rupees, she'd place her trunk on their head as a sign of good luck. I held my camera ready; I wanted to finish the roll of film. Babba-ji stood by the rocks, and he raised his hand when he saw me, closed his eyes, and said something. Hopefully, he was saying a prayer for me. If I'd had the energy, I would have gone and spoken to him.

Kiran emerged from the temple; it was duplicitous for him to be a religious man. Perhaps Hindus prayed to atone, and for forgiveness the way Catholics did. If that was the case, Kiran had a lot of praying to do. He bought a short string of jasmine, and stood in the shade, chatting to another man who joined him there. Kiran pocketed something the man gave him. A girl in a white sari approached me, and with the low sun shining in my eyes, it took me a moment to realise it was Suhana.

'Mari, I am so happy to see you.' Her smile was wide, her eyes bright. 'I hear you have been ill,' she said. 'You are fine now?'

'I came here hoping I'd find you. I'm better, thank you.' I moved the fabric of my lehenga out of the way, the sequins woven into the embroidery catching the light. I patted the step beside me, expecting her to sit. But she shook her head, glancing over her shoulder.

'Your clothes are very fine; are you going to a wedding?'

'No.' I laughed. 'I just like it. But is it too much, you know, as a foreigner?'

'No, you look very nice.'

'And you, have you sung any prayers yet this morning?'

'Not yet. But I will if someone wants to pay me. I have missed our walks and chats.'

Suhana touched a little pouch that hung on a string around her waist and hid it under the folds of her sari. She smiled, and I snapped her photo. I'd get the roll of film developed; the photos I took of Dinesh and the Aunties would show his jewellery, and I had to finish what I'd started.

'Me too.' I pulled a few rupees out of my bag, placed them beside me. 'If you'd like some chai, Suhana? Or a samosa?'

'Thank you, no. I will see you near Sharma's? Will you go again soon?'

Before I could reply, an elderly man approached her, spoke a few words. Suhana went towards the temple with him, smiling back at me over her shoulder. At least she'd have a few rupees today. Literally singing for her supper. I sat a while longer until tiredness engulfed me, and I rose, ready to walk the few streets back home. Kiran's companion walked into the rocks, probably on his way home after praying. Looking around for a moment,

Kiran raised his hand slightly.

'Leela,' he said.

Immediately, a woman wearing a red and pink sari passed him and followed the other man into the rocks. I knew what that was about; it was the same woman as last time, the one I'd seen the first time I looked for Babba-ji. Kiran pimping Leela; that was something else the police should be dealing with.

I stood, ready to head back, but my legs needed a little more rest, so I sat again. That's when Kiran saw me. He walked towards me, his skinny legs clad in tight jeans. He was all smiles. My insides turned cold. Did he know that I knew he was a pimp? I decided to play it cool, act normally.

'Oh, I see you are better. That's very good news indeed.' Kiran scratched his nose. 'The residents are concerned, and asking about you daily.'

Peering up at him, I shaded my eyes from the sun. 'I hope to come tomorrow. I think I'll take an auto rather than wait for the bus and then walk.'

'Yes, yes, take an auto. I can arrange payment for that, a sundry expense. The residents will be so happy to see you again. They like you immensely.'

'I enjoy their company. How is Kavita?' I twisted my hair around my finger.

'She keeps to her kitchen; I don't know what she does in there all day. But her food is good enough.'

His dismissive tone was galling, especially knowing what he did to Kavita, but then again, I shouldn't be surprised.

'I'll come tomorrow then, and finish organising those files for you,' I said. 'There's not much more to do.'

'Okay, I must go now. See you. Bye.' He smiled, walked away, and stopped to speak to Suhana as she exited the temple. She inclined her head, and her smile was warm.

A flicker of something ran through me, but I didn't give it much headroom. I was too busy thinking about reporting Kiran. One more trawl through the files, and I'd have enough proof of what he was doing. The bigger picture was between him and his conscience, but he had to leave Kavita alone, stop molesting her, and stop stealing from the residents. If I could make that happen, I'd leave Shivpur happy, knowing I'd done something good.

When I got back to the Mehtas', Muddy's bike was parked outside. Kicking off my flip-flops, I stepped into the hallway, peered round the sitting-room door.

'Here she is, here she is,' said Dolly. 'I was just going to send Muddy to fetch you.'

Muddy looked at me, his smile as charming as the first time I'd seen it. 'Hi. Thanks for coming every day,' I said. 'Dolly Auntie has taken really good care of me. I'm so grateful.'

'Tisk,' said Dolly, and shuffled out of the room.

'I'm so happy you are well again.' Muddy stood, walked towards me. 'Come, let me take you for chai.'

'I'm a little tired, Muddy.'

'You just need to sit on the bike, Mari, I'll be the one driving.'

Before I knew it, Muddy ushered me outside, and I didn't resist. I climbed on his bike, and we roared out of the village, towards Keshnagar. We pulled up at a roadside chai stand, and sat at a rickety table while the chai-wallah made masala chai.

'I hear some bad news,' said Muddy. 'Dolly said you are leaving soon, when you are properly recovered.'

I smiled, tapped my finger on the table. 'I have exactly a month and two days left on my visa. I'm going to Bombay the day after tomorrow. My plan is to head north east, go to Dharamshala then onto McLeod Ganj, and cross the border into Nepal before the visa expires. Then I'll get another one.'

'Sorry I could not help you with that. Will you come back here?' Muddy sipped his chai, his eyes burning into mine.

'You can help me with something else.' My hand reached across the table, touched his fingers lightly. 'As a policeman.'

He nodded periodically as I told him that Kiran was stealing, about the missing jewellery, the falsified receipts and the sexual harassment of Kavita.

'This is not good. But it's very commonplace here. Petty theft. And your friend, Kavita's situation is also very commonplace. She will be blamed. She is the worker, and he is the boss. Do you see?'

'Are you saying that because Kiran is your friend?' I leaned forward, looked directly into his eyes.

'I know him very well, and I can't imagine he is a thief. But no one can know someone inside out. Kavita is a handsome woman, maybe she has teased him a little?'

'What? No. I've seen her crying because she's so ashamed of what he's done to her. She told me she's scared he will actually rape her, Muddy. You have to stop him.'

'Okay, I can speak to him about that, stop anything happening again. Tell me about the stealing.'

'The receipts aren't for much, twenty rupees here, fifty rupees there. But the jewellery is valuable. Especially Dinesh's. And anyway, being commonplace doesn't make it right,' I leaned forwards. 'And Kavita's a wife and mother; she shouldn't be molested by Kiran.'

'You are one hundred percent sure? About the jewellery theft? That's weightier.'

'Yes. And once I get the photos developed, I'll have actual proof. I've written down everything that doesn't add up in a notebook, receipt numbers, amounts, dates, where I think he's forged signatures. It's easy for the police to find everything; I've pinned them all together in each file. I'm going to Sharma's tomorrow, and I'll take a look at his sundry expenses. But what I really need to do, is check the jewellery safe, check what's in it against the receipts, but I expect it's already been sold. But Dinesh's might be in there. The ring was huge, and the bracelet was an inch thick. Must be worth a fortune.'

'Leave the safe to the police,' said Muddy. 'That's not for you to get involved in. Bring your notebook and all the evidence you have to the station tomorrow. I'll take it from there.'

Muddy paid the chai-wallah, and we walked to the bike. I stood in front of it while he climbed on, and put the key in the ignition.

'What?' he said.

'Do you think I'll need to stay a day or so longer, if the police needed to question me at all, or sign statements?'

'No. I'll take care of everything. You are a good girl, Mari.' He ran his fingers up my forearm. 'Let's go somewhere we can be alone.'

Laughing, I moved my arm away. I felt a tug, a longing. It had been months since I'd been with anyone, and I looked at him for a long time. Would it be such a terrible thing to sleep with him?

'No, Muddy.' I bit my lip. 'But maybe this will do...' I leaned over and kissed his lips briefly. Moving away, I climbed onto the bike behind him. 'Happy now?'

'No.' He laughed

Chapter Fourteen
यात्रा

THE NEXT DAY, I hid the notebook in my cloth bag, and closed the door to Kiran's office on my way out. The information I needed was all in there; each resident's name headed a page, followed by a list of receipt numbers, the amounts, what they were for, and a brief description of what was wrong. The main evidence was the lack of a receipt for Dinesh's jewellery. Kiran couldn't deny Dinesh had that ring when he arrived, even if the poor man wouldn't remember. I prayed that one of the photos I'd taken of Dinesh and the Aunties showed the ring and bracelet clearly. I'd let the police have the negatives too, in case they needed copies.

Lunch took forever, and the goodbyes longer. I felt sad, knowing that I wouldn't be seeing Kavita and the residents again.

'We are all so disappointed that you are leaving us,' said Leena, 'but we've so enjoyed your company.'

'We have, we have,' said Vivika. 'Send us a postcard from Dharamshala. And if you meet the Dalai Lama, ask him to bless us all, here at Sharma's.'

'I will.' I said. 'Take care, all of you. I promise I'll send you cards.'

Taking my empty plates and bowls into the kitchen, I placed them on the counter. 'Kavita, can I speak to you?'

Straightening her pallu, she jerked her head towards the rear courtyard, and I followed her.

'I'm meeting Muddy at two-thirty tomorrow afternoon,' I said.

'I'll give him my notebook, and the photos of Dinesh. Muddy said he'll open an investigation, and then, maybe Kiran will get into the trouble he deserves.'

'I hope so. But Mr Sharma will probably use his influence; Kiran is his brother-in-law after all. But if he sends Kiran to work somewhere else, that will be enough for me. I can't stand his hands on me anymore. I held a knife yesterday, and he did not come near me.' I hugged her. 'Okay, okay,' she pulled away, brushing her fingers under her eyes. 'I will miss you.'

Turning, I walked out of the back entrance. I stopped for a moment, and looked over my shoulder. Knowing I'd done all I could wasn't good enough; I needed to know the outcome. Then I thought of Asa, and knew that acceptance was the only thing I could take away. Acceptance that I had at least tried to help. That had to be enough.

I met Suhana by the big palm tree. She was quiet, not her usual self. She dragged her feet along the road, twisting the end of her white pallu.

'Are you going to tell me what's wrong?' I said.

'I am sad because you are leaving. And also, there is something. But I don't want to tell you in case you think I am a bad person,' she said. 'I have a problem, and I don't know what to do.'

'How could you be a bad person?' I almost laughed, but I could see her face was dark, troubled. 'Tell me, maybe I can help?'

'There's a man. He says he can give me a better life, but I'm not sure.'

'He wants to marry you, Suhana?' I smiled, thrilled that this lovely girl would be able to shed her widow's white sari and enter the world of the living again.

'No, not marry. Just look after me.'

Trucks and buses passed us, spewing plumes of diesel and dust. We both turned our heads away from the traffic.

'Let's go and sit under the trees, it's too noisy here,' I said.

I followed Suhana through a gap in some scrubby bushes,

and we walked across an empty field to a cluster of thin trees. Their shade was welcome as usual. Suhana gathered a handful of twigs, used them as a makeshift broom to sweep away the goat droppings that littered the ground. Sitting together under the tree, there was just the noise of cicadas and the distant traffic.

'So, he doesn't want to marry you?' I said.

'He promises to look after me.' Suhana was coy, avoiding my gaze.

A cold sensation ran through me. 'Look after you how?'

'That's what I don't want to tell you...but please understand, Mari. I have to make money somehow. Or I can't eat. I do it sometimes,' she glanced at me from under lowered lashes, 'if I don't get money at the temple.'

'Suhana...' I reached for her hand, but she moved it away.

'He says I can make more money, much more, if I go to this other place. And he will look after me there. Find me nice men only. Rich ones. He promised.'

'There must be another way.'

'What other way? I know of none. I let him do it to me. I don't mind. He is kind and he always uses condoms.' Suhana shook her head, her eyes wide. 'He says he loves me and doesn't want me to do it with the other men here because he knows them.'

My fingers pressed into my lips. It wasn't my place to judge, and I had no solution to offer. I took a deep breath. 'Are there many other men?'

'There was one other before, for a long time. I loved him, and he was very tender with me. He promised to take me to another town, where he could introduce me as his wife, and we'd start a new life. But something changed his mind, I don't know what.'

'You loved him? Oh, I am sorry, Suhana. It's awful to have your heartbroken. I know.'

'After that, I thought it doesn't matter anymore, so when my new friend asked me, I did it with him too.'

'So, your new friend doesn't want you to...be with other men here, because he knows them. But he's okay for you to be with men he doesn't know? Suhana, where is this place he wants to take you?'

'Panjim. Goa. There are casinos, plenty of rich men. If I go there, I can wear colour again, eat tasty food. I can live in a house with other girls, not old widow women. And I can make good money.'

'Is he going with you to Panjim?' I asked, fiddling with the tiny pebbles I found under my fingers. Something nagged at me; the story sounded familiar as it hovered at the edge of my mind, but I focused on Suhana. 'How will he look after you there, if you're living with other girls?'

'He will take me there, introduce me to the owner. He says I need him to recommend me, or I can't go there. Then he will leave. He will visit when he can. I know he loves me. He is sweet and kind, and will not abandon me.'

'Suhana,' I grabbed her hand. 'It's a brothel. He's sending you to a brothel. Oh, my God. No.'

'You make it sound bad. But this is a natural part of life, Mari. And I have few options. I can beg or I can give pleasure to men.'

Again, her acceptance humbled me. My stomach turned over, thinking of this girl working in a brothel. What kind of life was that? How long would she last? What would happen when her looks faded?

'You said you have a brother in Bombay?' I said. 'Can't you try and speak to him, maybe he can help you?'

'I have not spoken to my brother since my husband died. It's been more than three years. And my friend says there will only be one, or maybe two men each day. I don't mind. The money will be good.'

Brothels kept their whores busier than one or two clients a day, I was sure of that, but maybe it was a genuine arrangement. What was I thinking? This man was probably going to sell Suhana to the brothel and she'd never see him again. And she'd end up with some horrible disease, possibly AIDS, after servicing hundreds of men every week. Trying to stay calm, I batted away a persistent fly.

'Were you close to your brother?' I asked.

'Oh yes, he is kind and nice. Very smart, also. And so handsome. That's why we moved to Bombay from Poona. He was acting in films.'

'Can you contact him?'

'If he is living still in the same chawl, maybe.'

'Living where?' I frowned.

'Oh, a chawl is special to Bombay, not anywhere else in India. It's an apartment building. You enter the chawl from the street, straight into the open courtyard in the middle.' She drew an oblong with her hands. 'Three floors, maybe four. There's a walkway that runs around each floor on the courtyard side so people can reach their apartments. Two or three rooms. Usually, the apartment has a balcony on the other side, overlooking the street outside. Chawl.'

I tried to picture what she was describing, but it sounded like a prison block, apart from the open courtyard and the balconies. 'So, do you remember the address of this chowl? Maybe you can go back there.'

'Chawl. Haresh wanted me to live with him after Aarav died, but his wife didn't want me. She was pregnant, so she would not allow a widow in her home. I think they argued a lot, and she threatened to go back to Poona.'

My sharp intake of breath made Suhana look at me. I scooched across the ground, pebbles and dust flying, to kneel opposite her. My mouth hung open, and I knew my eyes were wide.

'What's your brother's name?' I said, clasping her hands, my heart beating fast. 'You said Haresh? Is he Haresh...' My mind raced, trying to remember his last name. Something to do with the moon. Chand; that was it. 'Haresh Chandekar? He works at Victoria Terminus?'

'Yes, Haresh Chandekar. But he works close by the station, not in it. How can you know this?'

'He's really tall; maybe six foot-three.' I raised my hand a few inches above my head.

'Five. His hair is not so curly as mine, and he doesn't shave. You know my brother?' Her face creased, and she moved her hand across her eyes.

'Haresh Chandekar. Oh, my God.' I slapped my forehead. 'I call him Turquoise Haresh. I met him in Bombay, spent half a day with him. He got me a train ticket to Udaipur.'

'Wait. How do know my brother?' Her voice was hushed. Tears wet her face, and she brushed them away. 'This is so wonderful. How is his business? Is he well? And his child? Was it born well? Boy? Girl? Sorry, sorry, I have so much to ask. And why turquoise?'

'It's okay. I don't know how much I can tell you, but he was wearing turquoise silk, so I think his business is doing well. He must get tickets for a lot of people like me.' I smiled, but Suhana frowned. 'He said his daughter is two…no, three. His wife took her back to Poona, and he doesn't see much of her.'

'Oh. That is not good. That woman wasn't a good match for him; he made the mistake to marry someone he didn't love. She had such a sour character.'

'He spoke about you, you know. He told me how bad he felt that he couldn't find you when you left your husband's parents. He even went to Vrin…some holy town where lots of widows live.'

'Vrindavan. I didn't go there. I heard bad things about the squalor. So, I came here. He was looking for me?' Suhana put her hand on her heart.

'Yes. Suhana, maybe you can go home. To Bombay, to your brother, Haresh.'

'But he didn't take me to live with him before, so why would he accept me now. Especially if he learns what I have become, and what I do with that man for money.'

'You said it was Haresh's wife who didn't agree; that's what he told me as well. And his wife is in Poona. I'll bring his address and phone number to you, it's written in my guidebook.' I held her hands, leaning forwards. 'Call him, ask him if you can home.'

'Do you think so?' She looked at me, her brow creased, her eyes heavy. I nodded, smiling. 'Yes. I think I can go home. But, can you call my brother, please? The telephone office won't let me in.'

'Of course, and as soon as I speak to him, I'll come back here and find you, okay? But I need to go back to Shivpur; my guidebook's in my room.'

Later, every time I called Haresh from the Mehtas' phone in the sitting room, the line either didn't connect, or it rang out, unanswered. I booked multiple calls through the operator every hour until way past midnight, and the next day until lunchtime, when I needed to go to Keshnagar to pick up my photos and take them to Muddy. I'd try again from the phone office or the tobacco shop in town, and if I still couldn't get through, I decided I would go to the chawl in Bombay as soon as I arrived there. Poor Suhana, she must have been going loopy waiting for me for me to bring her news.

Ripping open the packet of developed photos, I smiled at the one I'd taken of Suhana at the temple, and breathed out when I saw the ones of Dinesh and the Aunties. Thank God, both had come out well. I held them in my hands, victorious. There he was, Dinesh, resplendent in white linen, surrounded by the glamorous Aunties, his right wrist sporting a thick bracelet and his finger, a ruby ring fit for a maharaja.

I walked the five blocks to the police station. Muddy met me at the entrance; he must have been waiting for me. Glancing at my watch, I saw that I was bang on time. Without a word, he led me down a corridor full of people, and showed me into the office he shared with another officer.

There was so much noise, so much commotion in the corridor, that I was glad to take a seat at Muddy's big wooden desk in the slightly quieter office. One side of the desk was piled high with manila folders; the other was taken up with a typewriter and a telephone. The tri-colour flag of India adorned the wall behind the desk, and beside it was a map of the area, pinned by the corners, the edges moving slightly in the breeze of the ceiling fan.

Muddy moved behind the desk, sat down, and clicked his fingers at me. 'Show me.' I handed over my notebook and the photos. His demeanour was so different in uniform; professional, I supposed. With his floppy fringe slicked back, his face looked older. 'Is this all?'

'Yes, but it's detailed. Like I told you, everything you need is in there. It –'

'This is a very harsh allegation. Can you be one hundred percent sure?' He still hadn't looked at me. 'Did you witness anything first hand?'

Shuffling noises came from behind me, and I glanced over my shoulder to see the other officer put on his peaked cap and leave.

'I need to be professional,' Muddy said. 'I don't want them to give the investigation to someone else.'

'My bus leaves tonight at six,' I said. 'Can you take this investigation forwards without me?'

'Shall I use my police power to make you stay, Mari?'

'We've talked about this, Muddy.' I looked at the ceiling.

'Okay, go. But I will remember you, and your sweet kiss always.' He cleared his throat. 'Yes, I will make the necessary investigations.' He stood. 'Thank you for bringing this to me. I will take it from here.'

He ushered me out of the office, and through the crowded corridor to the entrance where two police officers stood. They glanced at us, and Muddy turned, walked back down the corridor. I hadn't expected a grand goodbye, but I couldn't believe he didn't say anything at all. Chewing my lip, I left the police station. Perhaps I really had hurt him, but it was more likely to do with pride. And the fact that his colleagues were watching.

An idea popped into my head, and I crossed the road to a

clothing shop, and half an hour later emerged with a carrier bag. Jumping an auto, I asked the driver to drop me just before Sharma's, and then I walked back to the palm tree on the corner of the lane to the widows' house. Bhavna, Kavita's friend, saw me and waved. A few minutes later, Suhana joined me on the corner.

We walked quickly to the group of trees we usually sat under. As she cleared the ground again, she glanced at the large carrier bag in my hand. I gave it to her, smiling.

'For when you go to Bombay. It's my favourite colour, and I thought it would look nice on you.' We sat opposite each other. 'The choli is my size, so it should fit you. There's a pink and yellow shalwar kameez as well. I didn't know what you'd prefer. Please don't be offended, but I put some money in there too, just for the bus ticket, and whatever food you need on the journey.'

'Mari, that's such wonderful news.' Suhana pulled the sari out of the bag, held it against her. The lime green paisley pattern on the turquoise background looked gorgeous in the sunlight. 'Will I go with you tonight? Will my brother meet us at the bus station, or -?'

'Oh, God, no. I'm so sorry.' My stomach sank. 'I haven't spoken to him. He either doesn't answer, or the line doesn't connect.'

Suhana dropped to the ground beside me, hung her head, pretending to examine the sari which lay bunched in her lap. 'I thought…'

'I'm sorry. I didn't think.' Looking at the cloudless sky, I felt awful that I'd misled her. 'But yes, come with me, and we'll go to the chowl.'

'Chawl.'

'Yes, chawl. I'll take you to your brother, okay?' I tried to meet her gaze, but she avoided mine. 'Suhana?'

'I cannot go without assurance. He may refuse to meet me, and then how will I survive in Bombay? If I leave here, I won't be able to return. Another widow will take my place. And that man, my friend, will not give me a second chance. If I don't agree to go to Panjim next week, he says he can't help me. He is pressing me.'

'Then just stay here.' I snapped a small twig in my fingers, tapped the ground with the end of it. 'What if...I go and find your brother when I get to Bombay? I'll speak to him, then you can go there.'

'You are so foolish. Kind, but foolish. Mari, what if he learns what I have done with men.'

'We won't tell him, and how else would he find out? Two days. Give me two days. I'm going tonight, then one day to find Haresh and one day for him to get here. If he's not here by Friday...or maybe I can get a message to you. My friend's a police –'

'Sergeant? Yes, everyone knows about you and Muddy. His sister is very against you. I heard her calling you a *'British slut'* the other day.'

'She can fuck off.' Suhana looked startled. 'Sorry, and anyway, there's nothing between him and me. We're really just friends.'

'But he's so charming, so nice. You don't like him?' She twisted the end of her sari. 'Really?'

'Look, enough about Muddy.' I drew my knees up, leaned back against the tree. 'I get it, you don't want to risk leaving Keshnagar. So, I'll go to Bombay and find Haresh, okay? If he's happy for you to go home, I'll get a message to you in a few days. Give me time to find him. Then you can go there.'

'But if he doesn't?'

'Please, just stay here. You manage don't you?' I frowned. 'It could be a lot worse in Panjim.'

'I don't want to make my friend angry. Maybe he'll stop helping me here. Once a week, I get a good amount of rupee from him. More than I can make in two or three days at the temple.' She turned her head away. 'He is my good friend, also.'

'Do you like him, Suhana? Is that it?'

'I did not like it the first time.'

'But I mean *him*. Do you like the man?'

'A little, because he is kind. He isn't handsome like the man

I loved before, but he is nice to me. I don't mind what we do, sometimes I enjoy it. Except when someone is watching.'

My hand flew towards my mouth, but I dropped it halfway. 'Someone watches? Who watches you?'

'Not every time. But when he wants someone to watch us, he pays Leela. He likes it if she touches and licks him first before he puts his thing in me, and then she must say…how manly he is, how big his thing is, how hard he is doing it to me, all good things about Kiran until it's over.'

'Kiran?' I held my breath. 'From Sharma's?' Suhana smiled and nodded. 'The man who pays you for sex is Kiran Lal?'

Chapter Fifteen
यात्रा

As soon as the bus got me into Bombay, I headed for the train station, Victoria Terminus. If I was lucky, Turquoise Haresh would be there, touting tickets for tourists. Of course, there was no sign of the man I'd come to find. Maybe he was showing some other people around Bombay. I waited around the ticket hall and the entrance for nearly two hours that morning, but Haresh didn't show up, so there was no choice but to go to his chawl.

Tired and grubby, I needed a quick shower and a change of clothes after my long bus ride from Keshnagar via Bangalore. The woman in charge of the ladies' waiting room at the station didn't want to let me in without a train ticket, but I offered her some rupees, and I was granted access. Unzipping my holdall, I pulled out the first thing I found; my aqua lehenga. By the time I was ready, I was starving. That could wait; I needed to find Suhana's brother.

When the taxi driver pulled up outside the address that I'd given him, a small group of children of around ten or twelve years old gathered around the vehicle. Inadvertently, I'd interrupted some game they were playing on the dusty waste ground outside the chawl. I opened the car door, and the kids moved back, allowing me to walk towards the chawl itself. Hefting my holdall from one hand to the other, I walked towards the building. It was three storeys high, with some balconies enclosed by metal grilles, and others hung with washing. I presumed each balcony belonged to a separate apartment, so there must have been four per floor. The kids followed behind with whispers and giggles from the girls, and silence from the boys. Hoping it was pure curiosity and not malice that made them follow me, I looked for an entrance to the building. It was a good thing that Suhana had described the layout of a chawl, otherwise I wouldn't have known to go under the archway and into the inner courtyard so that I could find Haresh's apartment.

'Namaste. You are lost, I think,' said a lady in a pink and grey sari, her loose black hair reaching her waist. Leaning out of an open doorway just inside the entrance, she smiled. 'Can I help?'

'Namaste,' I said, putting down my holdall. 'I'm looking for Haresh Chandekar.'

'Top floor. Number thirty-two. Take that staircase over there.' She pointed diagonally across the paved courtyard.

I glanced up at the open walkways on all four sides of the building. Washing hung everywhere, and bikes leaned against the railings, their handles poking through like snipers' gun barrels. The chawl had looked smaller from the outside, but there were more than thirty apartments. Voices echoed around the courtyard as women chatted on the upper floors, and Hindi music played somewhere. People peered over the walkways, talking, laughing. Kids ran across the courtyard, dodging two scooters parked to one side, and a mother washed her toddler at a stand pipe in the corner.

'Thank you,' I said and took a few steps into the sunlight. A little black and ginger cat rubbed herself against my legs, before laying down in a patch of shade under a wooden bench.

'Oh, sorry,' the woman said. 'I'm not thinking. Haresh won't be there now. He's out.' Turning to ask her if she knew when he'd be back, I smiled. It seemed like all the residents of the chawl were standing with her, staring at me. 'Why do you want him?'

'Just visiting,' I said. 'Just visiting.'

'Come back after dark. He'll be home then,' said the woman,

braiding her hair into a thick plait.

'Leyra, no.' An elderly man in a white dhoti and cotton vest said. 'Haresh is at the shop today. Tell her where it is. She can go there now. Maybe her visit is urgent.'

'Thank you. May I have the shop's address?' I asked. Leyra ducked into an open doorway, and I stood, waiting. She came back and thrust a piece of paper with something scrawled on it at me. Her glass bangles jangled as much as mine as I took it from her. 'Where is this?'

'Near Victoria Terminus,' she said, smiling. 'Let us find you an auto.'

My entourage escorted me back outside, and one of the boys ran off. Three minutes later he was back, an auto pootling slowly behind him. I waved as I left, nervous that I would soon see Turquoise Haresh, and be able to tell him I'd found his sister. One thing I wouldn't be telling him, was what she did with Kiran. Was I doing the right thing, trying to reunite Haresh and Suhana? What if he didn't want to see her?

The auto dropped me outside an electronics shop. Maybe Haresh worked here part-time or was helping out. Desktop computer terminals with integral keyboards filled the double-fronted shop window. Then I spotted a sign in Hindi or Marathi, I wasn't sure, that was mounted across the top of the doorway next to one in English that said '*Electric Chandekar*'. Maybe it was a family business, and he just touted train tickets for extra income. Pushing open the door, I stepped into a fan-cooled shop. He stood at the back, six foot five of sage-green kurta and trousers, moving boxes from one side of the room to the other. When he turned, my belly jolted; I'd forgotten how good-looking he was, and the effect he had on me. Strangely, I was disappointed he wasn't wearing the colour I'd named him after.

'Haresh?' I said.

He smiled, and put down the box he was carrying.

'How was Udaipur?' His voice was deeper than I remembered. 'I hope it delighted you?' Taking my hand, he smiled down at me.

'Perfect recommendation, thank you.' Haresh nodded. 'I went to your chawl, and the people there gave me this address.' I moved my hand out of his, dropping my gaze. 'I hope it's okay.'

'Well, I did say you should come and find me. And so, here you are. Lovely that you are surprising me like this,' He shook his hair back. His smile was warm and his eyes creased at the corners. 'Looking like a maharani.' The way he looked at me made me feel like one. 'I don't think you are here to purchase a home computer, so shall we have chai?'

'Can I buy you lunch? I'm hungry.' Haresh laughed. 'I travelled from Keshnagar last night, arrived here a few hours ago.'

'Keshnagar…is it far?' I nodded. 'We can go now and eat. I'll close the shop.' He grabbed a set of keys from behind the cashier's desk. 'Come.'

'Won't your boss mind?' I asked.

'This is my shop, Mari; I can close if I choose.' Outside, he locked the door, and pulled down the metal shutter, securing it at the bottom with a padlock. 'Shall we walk?' He took my holdall from me. 'I'll carry this for you.'

'I thought you were a ticket tout at the station,' I said.

He threw his head back and laughed, his hair blue-black in the sunlight. Ryu popped into my head, but I dismissed the thought before it fully formed.

'Ticket tout. That's so sweet,' said Haresh. 'I have this shop, a workshop for repairs, and a small electronics factory. The shop's manager has a family thing, so I came here this morning.'

'Why did you get me a train ticket that day?' I looked up at him, at the face that should have been enough to get him into Hollywood.

'First, I saw a girl crying. How can I not help? And then I saw how beautiful you are, with your green eyes.' His eyes moved over my face, and I felt the heat of a blush. 'I felt…How can I not help? My friend is the assistant manager of the ticket office, so I had gone there to drink chai with him. I saw you, I asked him to help, and your service charge went to the clerk who issued your ticket.'

'And I'm so glad that you did help. Thank you.'

'And that day, we became friends.' Haresh smiled. 'I remember.'

We walked along busy streets, chatting about Rajasthan, and I only had good things to say. In the back of my mind, I was going over how much I should tell Haresh about Suhana, and I didn't want to blurt it out, wanted to wait until the right moment. Like the first time I'd met him, he guided me with his hand, kept checking I was alright. Maybe it was his height, or his looks, or his hair, but I felt I was walking with a god and, when he smiled at me, I felt like his goddess.

'Where are we going?' I asked, letting him lead the way. The sequins and silver embroidery on my lehenga sparkled in the sunlight, and I felt magical.

'First, to where my scooter is parked, and then I'll take you to a small dhaba that I know.' He looked back at me, smiling 'The food is very tasty there. All veg. No non-veg. I'm sure you will enjoy it.'

That might be a better place to tell him, instead of on a busy street. I bit my lip. What if he didn't care that I'd found Suhana? There was a chance he'd tell me to mind my own business. But then I'd seen the sadness in his eyes when he'd told me about her.

When we reached his red Vespa scooter, he pulled it off its stand and started the engine. He sat forward on the double seat, and I climbed on, side-saddle, behind him. We drove through the traffic, and I closed my eyes as other vehicles came within millimetres of us. My body tensed as Haresh swerved around a hand cart piled high with hessian sacks. Whatever they were filled with must have been heavy; it took two men to push the cart.

At the dhaba, Haresh was greeted with smiles and namastes. Sitting on the opposite side of the table, I kept glancing at him. Having something so monumental to tell him caused the butterflies in my stomach. There wasn't a menu; the waiter just wrote down whatever it was that Haresh said.

'Do you drink beer, Haresh?' I said. 'I've been in a pilgrimage town for almost two months. I could murder a beer.'

'I will join you.' Haresh said, and spoke to the waiter who brought over a small bottle of Kingfisher and two glasses.

When the food arrived, it smelled so good that I couldn't wait to tuck in. I took the lid off the round plastic box, took out a warm roti, and spooned some dry-fried okra onto my metal plate. Haresh spooned some yellow dahl onto my plate, and then some paneer and peas that came in a fragrant gravy.

The food was amazing, not just because I was ravenous. There was something in the way every dish used different spices, and each one complimented the others. We chatted about Haresh's business, Rajasthan, and the water shortage in Shivpur. Was it time to tell him? Something stopped me; I couldn't do it. I didn't know where to start.

Dragging the last piece of my roti across the plate, I mopped up the last of the paneer. Haresh watched me and smiled.

'What?' I said, darting my eyes from side to side.

'You have mastered eating with your hand.' He gestured to my fingers. 'Look, no mess this time.'

'God, you remember that?' I flushed at the memory of being embarrassed. Maybe it was the glass of beer I'd just finished or the way he looked at me, but my face was hot.

'How could I forget? I have wondered often when I would see you again. You and I...' Haresh said. 'I knew it, the first time I saw you. And, now here you are, with me.'

I nodded, heat flushing through me.

The dhaba was full over the lunchtime period, people came and went, most of them stopping to say a few words to Haresh. He and I sat there for ages, talking and drinking chai. His laugh came easily, and I liked his flamboyant hand gestures. And I liked how he made me feel.

'Everyone knows you,' I said.

'I eat here regularly. I live two streets away. Will you stay long in Bombay?' He looked at me, and I couldn't look away.

'No,' I said. 'Actually, I was going to ask you to help me get a ticket to Delhi for tomorrow, but now I know that's not your real job.'

Haresh laughed. 'Ticket tout. So funny. You are very sweet. I can speak to my manager friend, find a nice ticket to Delhi for you.'

'Thank you.' I took a deep breath, leaning forwards. 'There's something I need to tell you.'

'I'll just pay, and then we can go to the station, get your ticket.'

Butterflies skittered across my stomach as I waited for Haresh to pay the bill, trying not to stare at his strong hooked nose, and his full lips. His eyes were gentle and honest, but what if he decided not to take Suhana in? Maybe too much time had passed. Too much pain and regret might cloud his decision.

'Ready?' Haresh gestured to the door, but I stood facing him. 'What was it that you are wanting to tell me?'

'Haresh, it's about your sister, Suhana.'

'My sister?' He frowned, and when I nodded, his eyes widened. Looking around him, he rubbed his hand over his face. 'Come, we need to speak privately.'

Outside the restaurant, Haresh walked quickly to his Vespa, and put my holdall between his feet on the footboard. I climbed up, and sat side-saddle, half-smiling when he reached behind him and grabbed my hand. Pulling my arm around his waist, he placed my hand on his stomach, and held it there for a while, waiting for a gap in the traffic so he could pull out onto the road.

The kids at the chawl were playing cricket, the ball flaying up dust as it hit the ground. They gathered around us as Haresh parked his Vespa. Thunder rolled in the distance, and the sky darkened. Haresh and I walked through the archway, and crossed the courtyard. I followed him up three steep flights of wooden stairs to the third floor.

Plastic chairs, kids' toys, and cooking pots flanked the already narrow walkways. Every window had metal bars across it, and every door was open, some with floor-length curtains drawn across them. People came and went, and the chawl bustled with life.

Leaving our shoes outside, I followed Haresh through double doors painted rose-pink, and straight into the living room of his apartment. The ceilings were high, and fans at either end whirred to life as Haresh flicked switches by the front door.

Haresh placed my holdall in the small kitchen, and stood there with his back to me for a moment. My fingers twirled a strand of my hair. Spider plants lined the kitchen window sill which was flanked by thin cotton curtains. Reaching into my bag, I pulled out the photo I'd taken of Suhana at the temple.

'Tell me,' Haresh said, walking into the living room. He sat on the hard backed sofa, and the expression in his eyes wasn't a joyful one.

'Haresh,' I sat beside him, placed my hand on his arm, my bangles tinkling, and showed him the photo.

'My God. It really is Suhana.' He took the photo, stared at it, then looked at me. 'My sister. Where? Where is she?'

'In a widows' house just outside Keshnagar. Sometimes, she sings at the temple in Shivpur. She's my friend, Haresh.'

'Your friend?' He stared at me, his chin trembling. 'Where is that place?'

'Southern Maharashtra, inland, near the Goan border.'

'She's...' His face was wet, but he smiled. He placed the photo on the low table in front of the sofa. 'Mari. When? When was this?'

'I took the photo three days ago, and last saw her yesterday. I kept calling the phone number you wrote in my guidebook, but there was never an answer, so I came here to find you.'

'Phone has not been working for, I don't know, some weeks now.' He held my hands. 'But why is it that have you come here, and not Suhana? Ah, she thinks my wife –'

'No, she knows that your wife is in Poona. I wanted to bring Suhana with me, and even bought her a sari so she could travel on the bus.'

'How far away is this place?'

'The bus from Keshnagar to Bangalore is about three hours, and then thirteen hours from Bangalore to here.'

'Suhana didn't come?' He wiped his nose on the back of his hand. 'Why?' His shoulders shook, but he cried quietly.

'She wasn't sure…she didn't think you'd…' In the kitchen, I took two glasses from a metal shelf. Holding one under the spout of the demijohn of filtered water, I pressed the pump, and the water gurgled out. Two women stood outside the window, and they giggled when I smiled. Drinking quickly, I filled the other glass and took it with me. Smoothing down my hair, I took off my dupatta, draping it over the wooden arm of the sofa. I placed the glass in Haresh's hand, and he gulped the water down. 'She was scared to leave Keshnagar. If she came here and…couldn't see you, it would've been hard for her to go back. She said she'd lose her place in the widows' house.' I picked my bag up off the floor, rummaged for a packet of tissues, and handed them to Haresh.

'You found my sister. I thought the worst had happened. But she's well.' Haresh wiped his eyes, and I sat beside him. 'Will she come now?'

I nodded. 'I'll call a friend there, get him to take her a message.'
'Thank you.'

Haresh put his arms around me, and I sank into his embrace. I just held him, stroking his hair. When his breathing steadied, and his shoulders stopped shaking, he let go of me and looked into my eyes.

'Where's the nearest working phone?' I cleared my throat. 'I'll call my friend.'

'I will go to Keshnagar, and bring my sister back. Thank you, but I don't want to be relying on someone else to take a message. It's better if I go myself.'

I looked at my watch. 'It's three o'clock. Will there be a bus?'

'This is India. There will always be a bus.' Haresh went to the door, opened it, and shouted something. A voice answered from down in the courtyard, and Haresh went out onto the walkway. The discussion continued for a minute or so, including the word

'*Bangalore*' more than once. I couldn't take my eyes off him. The way his hair moved, the way he stood, then clutched the railing as he leaned over it, still shouting to someone below. He turned and smiled. 'Maharani, I'll go and come.'

Peeking out of the doorway, I caught the eye of an elderly lady sitting on a plastic stool outside her front door. She raised a hand and smiled. Across the other side of the chawl, on the walkway, a group of ladies chatted. One gave another a plate of something, covered with a cloth. They glanced at me, and carried on talking. TVs and radios blasted their noise from different apartments.

Back in the apartment, I stepped through one of the doors off the living room. Trailing my fingers across the top of a dust-free chest of drawers, I walked past two single beds, and out onto the balcony. A piece of floral fabric hung from the roof, the ends tied to the balcony railings, giving some shade, or perhaps privacy. A rolled up, thin mattress leaned against the wall. Maybe Haresh liked to sleep on it when the nights were too hot to be indoors. Laughter floated up from the waste ground below, and I stood for a moment watching the children chasing each other, before I came back through the doors into the living room.

Heavy textbooks with Hindi titles were piled on each other on the open shelves of a TV cabinet. Pulling a thin red photo album off a shelf, I flicked open a page, but before I had a chance to look at the pictures, Haresh's face appeared at the kitchen window. I bit my lip, flushed warm with nosy-parker guilt, and slid the album back.

'How come everyone leaves all the doors and windows open?' I said, turning to pick up one of many small trophies that graced the cabinet. A cricket bat leaned against one side of it. No surprise there; no self-respecting Indian wouldn't play cricket.

'For the breeze. It's too hot otherwise.' Haresh came into the apartment. 'It's quite safe. We all watch out for each other here in the chawl. Mari, eight o'clock tonight.' Haresh closed the doors, pulled the curtains across the kitchen window and rushed to me, spun me around, his hands on my bare waist. 'The first available bus to Bangalore will be leaving then.'

'That's great. There's a bus every hour during the day to Keshnagar from there. So, this time tomorrow, you could already be on your way back here with Suhana.' I smiled, letting go of his arms.

'You have done a wonderful thing, Mari.'

'I just wanted to help.'

Haresh took a step closer to me, planting a kiss on my forehead, holding me to him for a moment. He leaned back, and looked down at me. My heart thumped, and my eyes dropped his gaze, staring at his mouth.

'So,' he walked away from me, held out his hand. 'Come, I think we both need to rest.' I took his hand and followed him into the bedroom I hadn't been in. 'This is my room. Please, you can rest here, and I will use the other room.'

That wasn't what I'd expected, but even so, I smiled at him. 'Okay.'

Tapping his hand on the door, he stopped on his way out of the room, turned to me. 'You are so lovely. Sleep a little, Maharani.'

When he'd gone, I undressed and crawled onto the double bed in my underwear. I starfished the bed, legs and arms stretched out, and let the ceiling fan cool my skin. Perhaps it was a good thing that he'd gone to the other room, but I wished he hadn't. Maybe he was being respectful, especially as there wasn't much privacy in the chawl. Everyone's doors and windows were permanently open, how did they manage it? Turning onto my side, I stared at the bedroom door. Maybe lovers waited for the cover of darkness before they crept into each other's beds.

Somewhere in the chawl, a child squealed, and the engine of a scooter pootled to life. Women chatted and the kids on the waste ground shouted and laughed. Was Haresh already asleep in the other room? With all the noise, I doubted it. Perhaps he lay awake, wondering if I was too? I closed my eyes, wanting to sleep, but I could sense him there, on the other side of the living room. My skin prickled with electricity, and my stomach tightened. It was tempting to be brazen, and just go to him, but something held me back. I'd been brazen enough in Goa. At first I'd tried to copy Kate's carefree attitude to sexual partners. It wasn't really my style, but after the first few one-night stands, I actually enjoyed the anonymity of casual sex. When I first met Ark, I'd taken his hand, and told him, quite graphically, what I wanted him to do to me. And we'd had a great five or six days together. But I couldn't be so forward with Haresh, and I didn't know why. Maybe it was because sex with the guys in Goa had just been the kind of sex that scratched the proverbial itch. But Haresh didn't make me want to have sex for the sake of it; he made me want to have sex with him. It was more than desire, more than lust, but I couldn't put a word to the energy that pulled me to him.

The afternoon heat built, and the activity in the chawl lessened. As it quietened, my heavy eyes closed, and I drifted into an almost-sleep. After a while, I turned onto my back and stretched my arms above my head. Sleep didn't want to join me, and Haresh didn't want to join me either. Thirsty, I rose and dressed, and headed to the kitchen.

'Is everything okay?' Haresh said from the other bedroom.

I stood still, didn't dare look into the room he spoke from. 'Yes, I'm just getting some water. Do you want some?'

'Please.' Haresh came to the bedroom door wearing a white lungi slung around his hips. Leaning against the frame, he smiled. My face flushed, and I averted my eyes from his bare chest, but not before I'd seen the dark hair that covered it and ran down below his belly button. 'Let me, I am also thirsty,' he said.

Following Haresh into the kitchen, I stood against the kitchen counter and took the glass of water from his hand.

'I have been thinking. Instead of Delhi, why don't you come with me to Keshnagar?' he said, standing close. My heart beat fast, and I looked up at his dark eyes.

'I'm heading north, to McLeod Ganj, then Nepal. I need to

be out of the country in a month.'

'Then there is an abundance of time.' He took my hand, drawing me to him. 'Take me to the place where Suhana is living. Help me bring her home to Bombay.'

'I suppose I could...but I don't see why you need my help.' He put his hands on my shoulders, and kissed my lips, the smell of sandalwood rising from his hair. My insides flipped, and my heartbeat quickened. 'I mean,' I said, 'I can explain exactly where the house is.' I moved my hand across his chest, wanting my lips to follow.

'And if my sister is not there, how will I find her?' Haresh's lips teased mine. 'I don't know the town, or the area.' He ran his hands down my back, his mouth on my neck. My heartbeat fluttered, and my eyes closed. 'How can I go there alone? Please, will you help me?'

'Find Sergeant Mudgalkar, he'll help you.' Haresh's fingers moved over my breasts. 'He...'

Haresh kissed me, his mouth gentle, his tongue insistant. He took me out of my clothes, pressed me against the wall with his body. 'Come with me to Keshnagar. For some reason, I need you with me, Mari.' He untied his lungi, and half-carried me to the sofa. 'Bedroom is too far,' he said.

Haresh got up and padded across to the bathroom. The water ran, and he sang along to the loud Hindi music coming from somewhere close by, making me smile. Filling a glass from the demijohn, I stood in the kitchen, drinking thirstily. My body still trembled, sex-drunk from the things he'd done to me on the sofa.

'I am needing to eat.' Haresh came out of the bathroom, rubbing a small towel over his arms. He stood behind me, nuzzling my neck, his arms wrapped around me. I placed my glass on the counter, enjoying his damp skin that was cool against mine, which still burned. My stomach clenched when his fingers moved over it, and I parted my legs. 'Would you like something? I'll go and fetch paratha or samosa, and then make some chai for us, okay?' He slid hid hand between my thighs, and I gasped, letting my head fall back against his chest. 'Mari. I want you again, but we don't have much time.'

'It doesn't have to take long,' I said, turning to face him.

'That is a very good point,' he said, lifting me onto the counter, and wrapping my legs around him.

After another shower, Haresh dressed, and I grabbed a kurta and shalwar from my bag, and headed to the bathroom. Haresh stood watching me, smiling and running his hand through his quickly drying hair, the curl-waves already forming. It was only then I noticed the layers cut into it. He bit his lip, and looked at the ceiling, his fist gently pounding his heart as he moved his body in time to the music. He danced, hands gesturing and shoulders shaking.

I stood at the bathroom door, laughing.

'My poor heart. I am lost already.' His eyes skimmed over my body, and he smiled. 'Wash and dress. Don't be naked when I come with the food, or you will be impossible to resist.' He put his hands on my waist and kissed my lips. 'And, Mari. Thank you for finding Suhana. I can't thank you enough.'

'I think you just did.' I laughed.

'I will thank you again, and then again. Lock the door behind me, okay?'

A moment after I finished sluicing myself with buckets of tepid water, the phone rang. Turning the tap off, I stood listening. Should I answer it? Wrapped in a towel that barely covered me, I moved towards the sound. My feet slid on the tiled floor, and I grabbed the doorframe of the spare room. By the time I reached the phone, it stopped ringing. I turned to leave, and it rang again. The cream Bakelite receiver was heavy in my hand. 'Hello?' I said. 'Hello, this is Haresh Chandekar's house.' Static crackled on the line, and I couldn't hear anything else. Then the phone went dead.

Chapter Sixteen
यात्रा

HARESH AND I sat on the floor, either side of the low table, drinking chai and eating freshly cooked vegetable samosa. The combination was one of my favourites, and I was famished. Between bites, I told Haresh how Dolly Auntie looked after me after we'd brought water to the village, and that I felt sorry that she and her husband never seemed to communicate. When I told him how Suhana had cared for me when I'd been suffering from heatstroke, his eyes misted.

'My sister is a very kind person.' Haresh smiled. 'I'm glad she has you for a friend.'

'Suhana and I met and talked every few days, whenever I went to Sharma's,' I said. 'She was always so cheerful, so accepting of how her life was.'

'Sometimes we have to accept things as they are, even if we don't like them.' He raised his glass to his lips, sipped his chai.

Looking at Haresh, my heart skipped a beat. When he smiled at me, I was flooded with warmth, and convinced myself that it was because I'd done something good; connecting the dots to help reunite him with his sister. Even though I tried thinking that Haresh and I were nothing more than a lovely, very sexy afternoon, I knew I was lying to myself.

'I have to telephone my factory and ask my chief manager, Bhupinder, to watch everything for a few days. Then, I'll go to Keshnagar.' Haresh stood, adjusted his lungi, and went to fill the water glasses. 'The bus is leaving in less than two hours. Bus station is quite far, I must be leaving soon. Will you also come?'

'I can't.' My eyes fixed on his. My mouth said one thing, my whole body another.

'I was considering to travel by train, but it takes longer, and so many changes. Bus is the best way. You know, I bought two tickets.' His dark eyes looked at me, and he sighed. 'If you won't come, I hope you will stay here until I return with my sister. Leyra downstairs will help you if you are needing something. Right, I should pack.'

I followed him into his bedroom, and he pulled a small suitcase that looked like something from the 1960s out from under his bed. He packed a clean lungi and a couple of kurta suits.

'You wore that the first time I met you,' I said, gesturing to the turquoise silk clothing. 'It's my favourite colour.'

'Ah, so that's why you looked at me? For the colour only.' He grabbed me, pulled me to him. 'You see? *Naseep*. Fate. Come to Keshnagar. We'll bring my sister home together.'

'Turquoise Haresh.' I said. 'That's how I think of you.'

He laughed, moved my hair away from my face. Longing flooded me, Haresh stared at me, and I couldn't look away. His mouth was demanding, and I didn't resist. He pulled away, and turned back to his suitcase.

'I'll come with you,' I said. Something compelled me to go with him, there wasn't a choice.

Smiling, he took a comb off a shelf, as well as a can of deodorant, and put them into the elasticated side pocket of the suitcase. From under his mattress, he pulled a thick wad of rupees, tucked it into his trouser pocket under the knee-length burgundy kurta.

'Righty ho. I'll get my toothbrush, and then we need to go, or we'll be getting late. Are you ready?'

Picking up my dupatta, I draped it across my chest, letting the ends flow down my back. Haresh picked up our bags, and we headed down the stairs, passing his neighbours who all smiled at me. He spoke to them, laughing and smiling, and they called to him from all over the chawl. The place buzzed with life. Most of the doors and windows were still wide open, and people gathered outside each other's homes, chatting and drinking chai. I couldn't imagine living with such a lack of privacy, but then I also envied their ease with each other, their sense of community. I'd lived in isolation for so long. But the chawl felt like a real neighbourhood, and that meant people might know each other's business, but they would have each other's backs.

In the taxi, Haresh held my hand. 'They were very excited when I told them that you are my sister's friend and that we are going to get her. I hope you don't mind.'

'Why would I mind?' I slid myself closer to him as the taxi's wheels spun dust into the air like candyfloss.

'Because you are more than just my sister's friend. It is written that we were to meet. Do you think so, Mari?'

My life used to revolve around a belief in the power of the universe, fate, and destiny. I'd given up reading Tarot cards, given up tuning in to my innermost knowings when Kate died. But sitting in the taxi with Haresh Chandekar, with my soul soothed and my heart unclouded, I began to believe in it all again.

'To help bring Suhana home? Yes,' I said.

'I meant you and I.' Haresh's hand tightened over mine.

In a thunderstorm, Haresh and I boarded the eight o'clock evening express bus that would get us to Bangalore at nine the next morning. From there, we'd catch another bus for the last three hours of the journey to Keshnagar. I didn't relish the thought of another long bus journey, but with Haresh by my side, it didn't seem so bad. He needed to sit in the middle of the long seat across the back of the bus, so he could stretch his long legs into the aisle. That meant I got stuck between him and an old man who hogged the window seat. Thank God for the rest stops every few hours, where we could use the loo, buy some water, chai, and either samosa or pakoda.

Haresh and I talked into the early hours. At one point, I dozed with my head against his arm, lulled by the sound of tires on wet tarmac, and dreaming in fits and starts of Suhana, Kate, and my sisters.

We reached Bangalore after thirteen long, bumpy, uncomfortable hours. Hungry, we sat in the bus station cafeteria eating paneer cutlet and rice for breakfast. The chai was too milky and too sweet, but Haresh drank mine as well as his own.

'What about your neighbours?' I asked, spearing a piece of breaded paneer onto my plastic fork. 'Do they know Suhana is a widow?'

He frowned. 'I will just introduce Suhana as my younger sister. If she wants, I'll find her another husband, or maybe she can be a teacher again. My chawl, it's a good community, but it's better no one is knowing the truth. I don't want my sister to face any prejudice.'

'How long have you lived there?'

'I moved there after my wife and daughter left. My neighbours don't know about that. I must sound very dishonest.' Haresh pulled a face. 'I assure you, it wasn't a malicious thing, not to tell them, but I was very upset and I didn't want anyone to pity me.'

'And are you still upset after three years?' I couldn't look at him. 'Has it got easier for you?'

'Time is important for these things. Yes, it's easier, and no, it's not. For wife, I don't care, but my daughter…'

'I'm surprised your wife's parents took her back,' I said. Traditionally, a woman's role was that of a dutiful daughter, then an obedient wife to her husband in her in-laws' home. It rankled that a woman couldn't be a person in her own right, that she had to have a defined role subservient to a man. Then again, maybe it wasn't so alien; pre-1960s Britain had been similar; the man was the wage earner, and the woman stayed at home to cook, clean, and raise the children.

'Wife's family love her too much,' Haresh said. 'She is a little spoiled.'

'But she won't let you see Tara?'

'I visited many times. Poor Tara, she is so small.' Haresh shrugged. 'She isn't remembering who I am, and gets a little teary. Of course, wife gets angry, saying I am distressing the child. Tara is better with her mother for now. She has her grandparents there, her aunts and cousins also. I am alone in Bombay, working every day, so it wouldn't be right to keep her with me.'

A cold feeling ran through me, and I concentrated on my food. How could I have ignored the fact he was married and had a child? Even if his wife wasn't around, it didn't mean he was free. What was I thinking? I shouldn't have slept with him. The paneer tasted of cardboard, and I swallowed quickly. Simple justification would be the heat of the moment, his joy at knowing his sister was safe was a strong aphrodisiac, one I didn't even try to resist. But it went deeper than that; there was such energy between Haresh and me that it was almost tangible. And now we were travelling across India together.

'I'm sorry, Haresh.' I touched his arm across the table. 'It's not easy.'

'Tara is so small, so young.' Haresh said. 'Maybe, it can be different when she's older.'

'Suhana told me you went to Bombay because you wanted to get into films.' I changed the subject. Looking at his body, his hair, that mouth, heat flushed through me. 'I think you'd look great on-screen.'

'I have been in lots of films. I've been on location many times for films they were shooting in Rajasthan. Because I am tall like a Rajput, although I am a proud Maharashtrian. Small parts only.' He smiled at me, his chocolate candy eyes warm. 'I have played a maharaja, and wore a splendid turban, with a peacock feather.' He made a flamboyant gesture, above his head. 'I have played various doctors in hospitals, a body on the roadside, a waiter, and also the heroine's brother, neighbours, the hero's friend, a child's uncle.' He flicked his wrist. 'A basketball player, a villain many times, it goes on. But I never played the leading role, the hero.'

'Is that why you stopped?' I sucked Limca through a paper straw. 'Because you wanted to be the hero?'

'No.' He leaned forward at an angle, one elbow on the table.

'Don't move,' I said. I scrabbled in my bag for my camera and raised it ready to take a photo. 'Might be better if you smile.' He laughed, and I took the picture.

'Anyway, leading ladies are small, petite. Probably their height is being about five foot two, or three. I am six foot five. They come only to here.' He placed the edge of his hand at heart height. 'Not good for the camera angle, and too difficult for the close-ups. And the dance sequences look ridiculous with me being so much taller than everyone else. If the ladies were tall like you, there would be no problem.'

'That's such a shame. So, can't you carry on taking small roles?'

'I left it.' Shrugging his shoulders, Haresh finished his chai. 'To marry. The money I had saved from my films and my inheritance bought my factory. We build small computer parts for an American company called Apple. Wife wanted a steady income, and it was going well before she left. Then after two years, I started the workshop for businesses who need their computers fixing, and last year I opened my shop, *'Electric Chandekar.'*

'Don't you miss acting though? I'd love to see your films. Must be fun to be an actor.'

'Yes I miss it, but it was my choice to change career. Some things cannot be. And some things can.' He ran his fingers across the back of my hand and grinned. 'Where will we stay in Keshnagar? I think we should stay one night, to rest before we bring Suhana back to Bombay.'

'There are a few hotels, but I stayed in Shivpur, so I don't know what they're like.'

The tannoy announced the bus was ready for its passengers, and we left the cafeteria. After stowing the luggage, we climbed aboard and found our seats at the back.

'We'll take two rooms. Officially one for Suhana and you, and one for me.' His fingers brushed the hair away from my face. 'I can't wait to see my sister again. We will have a good dinner somewhere.' He smiled. His mouth was so close to mine, I could hardly breathe. 'You can sneak into my room.'

'Sneak? Do you think Suhana will disapprove?' I said.

'No, it's just that an unmarried couple cannot be alone in a hotel room together. It is morally unacceptable.'

'Morally unacceptable.' I laughed. 'It's illegal?'

'No, but the police are often involved. The man will face a fine, and the woman, she will be shamed. We'll be careful. Wait until Suhana is sleeping, no one will know. I'll be with you tonight, and every night until you leave India. I will get your train ticket to Delhi, or maybe a plane ticket from Bombay to Kathmandu. That way, you can leave the day before your visa ends. You can stay with me and Suhana until then.'

'Yes,' I said, looking into his eyes. It felt right. And McLeod Ganj and the Dalai Lama would still be there when I came back to India from Nepal. Another month wouldn't make a difference; there'd still be time before the snows came.

The Krisha Hotel in Keshnagar gave us two rooms on the same floor. We took our luggage upstairs, but didn't unpack it. The double bed was rock hard as I sat, jarring my already stiff hips. Two overnight bus journeys in three days were enough for anyone. I stood again, turned on the air conditioning unit, holding my hands in front of the cool air. Bending, I closed my eyes and let the air blow onto my face.

Haresh put his arms around me, and I turned. 'Thank you, Mari. You have saved not only my sister but also me.'

'Haresh.' I sank into his embrace, my heart expanding.

'When Suhana vanished, I was feeling very guilty. I am a good man, I know, but I was wrong at that time. If my wife had not been about to birth our child and so against a widow in the house, I would have brought Suhana to live with us. But I was thinking only of my child.'

'Which was right.' I moved away from him, stood by the window, and looked out onto the street below. The kulfi café was at the far end of the street, and I suddenly craved cardamom and rose sweetness.

'Six months after my daughter was born, I was still trying to find Suhana, and that's when I travelled to Vrindavan, the city of widows, to find her.' He stood beside me and took my hand, kissed the back of my fingers. 'And when I returned to home, wife was gone. My daughter was gone.' I put my arms around him, felt his heart thumping. 'I lost everything. Because brother-in-law died, I too lost everything.'

'I don't know what to say.' My eyes met his.

'When I met you, you told me you were wanting to do something to help people. I knew then that you were a different kind of person, with a good heart. And I am right. Look what you have done for Suhana, and for me.'

He kissed my neck and I sighed, letting my head fall back. Moving my dupatta out of the way, his lips followed the scooped neckline of my kurta, his fingers trailing over my breasts.

'There isn't time,' I said.

'No, I wasn't thinking to be doing that now. I just needed to kiss my Maharani a little.' He grinned. 'Chalo. Where will she be now?'

'She usually met me at around two in the afternoon near the house, when I left Sharma's.' I looked at my watch. 'It's just one o'clock now. She might still be at the temple.'

'Then we shall start there.'

The auto took us straight to the temple entrance. Pilgrims were few in the fierce heat of midday. The leper was asleep in his usual spot, but there was no sign of any of the widows, let alone Suhana. We skirted the temple grounds a few times, looking amongst the pillars and outer shrines. Haresh suggested we split up, so he went one way and I went the other. Backtracking, I headed out of the temple. The hair on the back of my neck stood on end, and I felt someone watching me. I looked up at the boulders. Babba-ji stood there and inclined his head when I raised my hand in greeting. I walked towards the chai stand and the little stalls selling flowers and incense. The chai lady sat under her red umbrella as usual, and handed me a clay cup without me asking. I squatted down, sharing her shade, my eyes on the temple, waiting for Haresh.

What was keeping him? I wandered over to the samosa-wallah, and bought four. The leper was still asleep, so I left them on the ground beside him. I paced for a while, then went back for another glass of chai. When Haresh finally appeared, my heart flipped. His hair moved as he walked, and his stride was determined. He saw me and smiled.

The chai lady nudged me, looked at me questioningly.

'*Mere dost,*' I said. *My friend.* She laughed, made a high-pitched noise, and patted my arm. So, it wasn't just me then. 'Do you want chai, Haresh?'

'I made a *puja*, said some prayers,' he said.

'I can see that,' I looked at the vertical red mark between his eyebrows.

He took the chai from the lady, squatted beside me. Holding the clay pot between forefinger and thumb, he sipped the chai, and I thought back to the first time I'd met him, when we'd drunk chai together. His fingers fascinated me then, and did so even more now that I knew how they felt on my skin.

'Suhana is not here,' he said. 'We'll go to the house, and wait there for her. Come, let's go.' He stood and took some rupees out of his pocket, gave them to the chai lady with a smile.

We headed towards the corner to find an auto. 'It's too early,' I said. 'She won't be there.' Why did I feel so nervous? The sensation that something bad was going to happen almost floored me. Terror made my legs shake, and I stopped walking. With my hands on my thighs, I leaned forwards, my breath caught. 'Haresh.'

'What is it, darling? Are you unwell? Come.'

With one hand under my elbow, he walked close to me until we reached the corner, where a few autos waited. I waited for my breath to steady, and for my heart to stop palpitating. Haresh spoke to the auto driver and I turned to see Babba-ji standing a few meters away, resplendent in orange and red.

'Babba-ji,' I said. 'What is this?'

'You cannot change what is written. Fate,' he answered, and walked away.

Haresh and I climbed into the auto. He had to bend almost double to fit. I told him to tell the driver to take us to Sharma's. My body and my mind felt separated, I couldn't shake the panic. The auto raced up the hill towards Keshnagar. Haresh leaned forwards, his forearms on his thighs, looking out of the open side of the auto.

'What kind of landscape is this?' Haresh turned to me, took my hand. 'It's beautiful. I didn't notice on the way here, but it's truly very spectacular.'

I could only nod. My mind still racing, trying to work out why the abject fear I felt wouldn't go away. If it was some sort of premonition, I didn't want it. They were a thing of my past that I didn't want back again. It wasn't like they were ever specific enough to allow me to stop something happening. Was that what Babba-ji meant?

We hopped out of the auto just before Sharma's and walked back the way we'd come. The auto driver looked at us as if we were nuts when he turned the vehicle and drove back down the road. We dodged cow pats and trucks as we walked along the road, and when we reached the palm tree on the corner, I stopped.

'This is it, Haresh.' I stood in front of him, my hands on his arms. 'Down there.' He looked down the track to the single-storey building. 'What do you want to do?'

'I was praying in the temple, thanking God for you, and for my sister. Thanking him for taking away my guilt, and allowing me to be feeling happy for the first time in three years. But I am a little nervous.'

I reached up and touched his face. He put his hand over mine, turned his face, pressing his lips to my palm. 'Shall I go and get her?' I said. He nodded. 'Haresh?'

'Yes, darling?' His eyes darted everywhere, looking behind me at the house.

'Don't you want to go? Would it be better if family take her from there?'

'You are family, Mari. Go, please. I don't want to wait more.'

I ran down the lane. 'Suhana? Suhana?' Going into the building, I called again for her. As I reached her room, Bhavna met me at the door.

'Hello, how are you? I heard you went to Bombay, but you are again here.'

I touched her arm. 'Yes, where's Suhana?' I pushed open the door, stepped into Suhana's room. I looked at where she kept her saris, folded so neatly. And the shelf where she kept her toiletries. They were all empty. 'Bhavna, where are her things?'

'She gave all to me before she left.'

'Do you know where she went?' I left the room, heading to the entrance. 'When did she leave?' I said over my shoulder.

'Maybe last night, or this morning. I don't know.'

Rushing out of the building, my feet picked up speed. I called to Haresh, and he ran towards me, meeting me halfway to the house.

'We're too late,' I covered my mouth with the back of my hand, failing to stop my sobs. 'She's gone.'

Haresh put his arm around my shoulders, hugged me to him, but I stepped away, conscious of watching eyes.

'Do they know where?' he asked me, his hands on my arms, bending his knees to look directly into my eyes. 'Where could she go alone?'

'Kiran will know.' I walked so fast that I was almost running, my bag bouncing against my thigh. 'I'll fucking kill the bastard.'

'Who is Kiran? Mari. Stop for ek minute, okay?' Grabbing me from behind, he whirled me to face him. 'Tell me.'

Chapter Seventeen
यात्रा

REACHING THE ENTRANCE to Sharma's, I stopped. Haresh looked at me, his eyes worried. My guts twisted, thinking that what I was about to tell him could change everything.

'This is where I came to help with the residents. Well, not help. I just had tea with them. Kiran Lal runs the place.' I pushed my hair back from my face. 'He asked me to do some administration for him, and I found out that he is a thief, and he molests my friend, Kavita, the cook. He also pimps at least one girl, maybe more, I don't know. The day before I came to Bombay, I reported him to the police, gave them evidence that he's stealing the residents' money, and their expensive jewellery.'

'But what does Suhana have to do with this place?' Haresh frowned.

'It's not the place, Haresh.' I touched his arm, and took a deep breath. 'God, I don't know how to tell you this...Kiran said he would look after her. I mean...'

'Don't tell me that.' Haresh took a step back from me. His hands together in prayer position, he raised them to cover his mouth. 'Did he make her –'

'Suhana told me the day before I left that he found a place in Panjim where she could live and work. I tried to convince her to come with me instead.'

He shook his head. 'And she's not at the house...so you think he already has taken her there? To that place?'

'Let's go and ask him.' It was only when I turned to walk up the path that I realised that the wrought iron gate was locked. 'What?' I shook the padlock, hoping it would come open.

'Everywhere is closed up,' said Haresh, coming from the side of the building. 'All windows, closed.' His mouth was pressed into a hard line and he flicked his hands up. 'Another entrance at the back, also closed.'

'This is really weird, Haresh. I was here four days ago.' I looked up at him. 'What can have happened in four days?'

He looked up to the sky, his hands on his hips. 'Where can I find this Kiran?'

'That's just it. I don't know.' I shrugged my shoulders. 'Wait. Kavita lives in a yellow house somewhere behind here. She'll know what happened. Come on.'

We ran around the side of the building, I scanned the fields behind and pointed to the small yellow house. Haresh strode ahead of me, and we made our way down narrow dirt paths between the fields. Crows cawed in the trees, their witchy cackles ominous under the grey sky. Scrubby bushes dragged at our clothes as we rushed towards Kavita's house, and my dupatta caught on a twig. I ripped it off, tearing a hole in the fabric.

'Haresh, wait.' I stood in front of him outside Kavita's house. A few chickens clucked, pecking at the dirt behind a scrawny tree. 'Kavita is my friend, so let me speak to her first.' He nodded, stood slightly behind me. Looking up at the flat roof, where washing flapped on a line, I hoped she was home.

Kavita peeked out from behind a curtain that covered the doorway.

'Mari?' Kavita said, and eyed Haresh, looking from him to me and back again. 'You didn't go to Bombay?'

'I did, but I came back. Kavita, this is Haresh Chandekar. He's my friend.'

'Namaste, Kavita-didi,' Haresh placed his hands together in greeting, and she did the same. 'We need to find Kiran Lal. Mari thinks he has done something with my sister.'

'Bloody Kiran!' Kavita almost spat the words. 'Wait, sit. I will make chai and I will tell you all.' Haresh and I looked at each other. 'Go. Sit. Sit.' She waved towards a *charpoi* bed, along the side of the house. 'Husband is sleeping inside. I will bring chai. Are you hungry? I have some bhaji.'

'Kavita, I don't think there is time for chai,' I said, standing my ground.

'Mari, let her make some chai for us. We have time to sit, and there is always time to listen.' Haresh touched my arm, his voice soft.

If he could stay calm, maybe I should try to do the same. Suhana was his sister after all, not mine. But where was she? I felt tears welling. I sniffed, straightened my shoulders, and sat next to Haresh on the charpoi. If we had caught an earlier bus, if I'd told Haresh as soon as I found him, maybe we would have got to Keshnagar before Suhana left.

Kavita returned with chai, and we took the glasses off the melamine tray she offered. She dragged a plastic chair across the ground and sat opposite us. We sipped the chai, sweet and strong, heady with the flavour of cardamom. I waited for Kavita to start talking, to tell us where Kiran was. Haresh took a bite of potato bhaji, but I couldn't face food.

'The day after you left for Bombay,' Kavita said, 'Mr Sharma came. He and Kiran were arguing in the office. My neighbours' daughter, Puja, listened at the door.' She giggled. 'The men spoke something about money and the jewellery. Muddy also came, and there was a loud discussion. Your name was mentioned more than once, Mari.' She sipped her tea, tapped the side of her chair. 'Then, after some hours, all three men were gone. And one by one, the residents' families came, took them away. Some were even sent by taxi to Sharma's in Panjim, some went back to their own homes. By yesterday, the whole place is empty.' She flicked out her hands. 'Everyone is gone. And this morning, Sharma's men locked the doors. Sharma's is now closed down for renovation.'

'But why? I don't understand.'

'You told Muddy everything that was going on,' Kavita said. 'He told Sharma.'

'Muddy wouldn't...he was involved somehow?' I said. 'There can't have been that much money skimmed off, could there? And why not just sack Kiran? It seems excessive to close the place completely.' I rubbed my forehead.

'Easier,' said Kavita. 'Sharma didn't want a scandal caused by his brother-in-law. It would have been very damaging for all his businesses, and his political ambitions. Better to find an excuse to close the place. Even temporarily.'

Haresh leaned forward, elbows on his knees. 'Please, who are Muddy and Sharma?'

'Police Sergeant Mudgalkar, and Mr Sharma is a very rich, powerful, and political man,' said Kavita. 'He has some goon connections.'

'And this Kiran? Where is he?'

'At his home. Are you the son of one of our residents?'

'I am not. I am looking for my sister.'

'Kavita,' I said, 'Haresh's sister, Suhana, is one of Bhavna's friends. In the widow's house. Kiran has been...' I glanced at Haresh.

'Aiii, that man.' Kavita whacked the arm of her chair. 'He never stops.' She narrowed her eyes at me. 'I told you to stay away from those women.'

'Kavita,' Haresh said. 'Mari has helped me locate my sister. I looked for her for more than one year. Now I have come here to take her back to Bombay, but we fear Kiran has sent her to a brothel.' He shook his hair back, sat straight. 'I want to speak with him urgently.'

Kavita nodded. 'Is it the one in Panjim?'

'Yes, how did you know?' I said.

'Shanti has come home,' Kavita looked at the ground. 'She told her father everything that happened. Muddy had also been playing around with her. He promised her everything and broke her heart. Then Kiran involved himself with her like I told you. Promised her a new life with him in Panjim and sold her to the brothel. She got out of there, and came home. Poor girl; she is ruined now.'

'What?' My mouth open, I stared at Kavita. Was Muddy the one Suhana said she was with before Kiran? I felt sick. 'We've got to get to Suhana back.'

'I must be finding Kiran,' said Haresh. 'Learn exactly where he has taken her.' His face was calm, but his shoulders were tensed, his fingers curled into his palms. 'Do you know where we can find him?'

Kavita went inside the house, came back with an address written on a piece of bright pink paper. Haresh thanked her, took my hand, and we walked towards the path.

'Wait.' I turned. 'What will you do now, Kavita. You and your husband have lost your jobs.' My insides twisted with guilt.

'Tisk, no problem.' She smiled. 'We work now for Sharma. I will go early morning to their big house, make breakfast, help the little ones get ready for school, and then do some cleaning. Husband is a driver now.'

'That's good news. I'm glad.'

It went some way to salve my conscience, but I didn't ask about the helpers. What would they do now Sharma's was closed? All I'd wanted was to stop Kiran. People had lost their jobs, and those poor elderly people had been moved around like luggage because I had taken the moral high ground over a pervy, petty thief. But no, he was more than that; selling girls to a brothel made him an evil bastard.

The rain started before we reached Kiran's house, a modest two-storey add-on to another building. The front protruded out onto the street a little further than the one it was attached to. Haresh and I stood, drenched in the rain. Not sure whether or not I should leave things to him or try and help, I stayed still when he approached the front door.

'Yes, stay here, darling.' Haresh turned back to me, and moved a strand of wet hair away from my face. 'I will ask politely, and I hope Kiran gives me an answer.'

Haresh pounded on the door, and a thin woman in a salmon pink kurta with coral shalwar opened it, pulling her dupatta over her head.

'Yes?' she said, looking at me, and then speaking to Haresh in Hindi. She called over her shoulder, and Kiran appeared at the door.

'Kiran?' Haresh drew himself up to his full height, dwarfing Kiran. 'Where is my sister? Which filthy whorehouse did you take her to?'

'You!' Kiran pointed at me, came towards me, his hand raised. 'What have you done? Who are you to interfere?'

Haresh's arm flew out, blocking Kiran's path. 'Don't be thinking to even touch her.' Kiran dodged him, making a beeline for me, the rain plastering his hair to his head. Haresh stepped in front of him, his body taught. 'Leave her, Kiran. I asked you... where did you take my sister? Where is my sister?'

'Whoring probably.' He spat on the ground, then jerked his head towards me. 'Like she did with Muddy.'

One punch and Kiran groaned, blood running over this moustache, and the punch second had him staggering, water splashing as he fell backwards onto the rain-soaked ground. Haresh knelt, pounding Kiran's face again and again. His wife screamed, and neighbours came running. A few men tried to drag Haresh away, but he shook them off.

Haresh sat on Kiran's chest, one hand around his scrawny neck. 'Where did you take Suhana.' Haresh's kurta was stuck to his back with the rain, and water dripped from the ends of his long hair.

'Nowhere. Nowhere.' Kiran's spidery hands scrabbled at Haresh's, trying to free himself.

'I will ask you again. Where is my sister?' Kiran coughed, Haresh loosened his grip.

'I don't know, yaar, I didn't see her for…for some days.'

Letting go of Kiran, Haresh stood, dragged the man to his feet. Kiran cowered, his arms above his head, ready to stave off more blows. But Haresh stood back. Kiran's wife was crying, and she grabbed his shirt. She thumped his back, yelling at him, raindrops darkening her clothing. Poor woman, perhaps she hadn't known what Kiran was doing. The neighbours stood crowded to one side of Kiran's house, and I glanced at their faces. Something in their expressions told me they were enjoying the drama.

'Was Kiran inappropriate with you, Miss?' said a young man, his moustache wispy, like a teenager's. He held a black umbrella over my head. 'We all know he is very free with the ladies. I am sorry for you. Good that your husband has given him a thrashing.'

All I could do was smile, but it didn't reach my eyes. Part of me was shocked at the brutality, part of me thoroughly condoned it; I even understood the neighbours' enjoyment. Haresh shook his wrist, and splayed his fingers, rubbing the blood from his knuckles.

'And the last time you saw her?' Haresh stood close to Kiran, his gaze bearing down on him.

'Three days ago, she was begging at the temple. God promise.' With fingers and thumb pressed together, he touched his throat. 'I didn't take her anywhere.'

'Then where is she?' I said, stepping forwards.

'You should have kept your mouth shut.' Kiran took a step towards me. 'What gives you the right…' Haresh moved his hand a few inches, raised his eyebrows, and Kiran backed away. 'Bloody Britisher bitch.'

Haresh landed another punch, and blood flew from Kiran's mouth and nose. 'That's for Shanti.'

The crowd parted to let me and Haresh through, some of the men patted him on the back and spoke to him in Marathi. He didn't answer, his jaw and shoulders still tight. I walked behind him until we were back on the main road. He stopped and turned to me, his eyes dark and his lips pressed together.

'I must apologise,' Haresh said and I took his hand to examine his bruised knuckles, the rain washing the blood away as fast as it appeared. 'That's not something you should be seeing. I am so angry with that man, for what he has done. He won't even be punished if he has connections. What kind of person sells lonely girls to a brothel…'

'Do you think he's lying about Suhana?' I said, twisting my wet hair into a plait. 'Where is she?' I shivered, my rain-soaked clothes cold on my body.

'He said "*God promise*", so perhaps he is not lying.'

'What does that mean?'

'It's something like..' Haresh looked at the sky. 'Maybe, "*I promise in God's name*", or "*I swear to God.*" We take that expression very seriously.'

'So, where the hell is Suhana?' I said, my teeth starting to chatter.

'I still have family, cousins, uncles and aunties in Poona. If Suhana thinks I don't want her…but, she didn't go there when my wife…' Haresh walked ahead, and I ran to catch up with him.

'So call them, see if she's there.' We stepped around a giant puddle. The rain stopped, and the sky was already clearing.

'Mari, I don't know their telephone numbers.' Haresh's voice was harsh. 'Sorry. Sorry. I am not sure they even live in the same places now. It's more than three years since I contacted them after my brother-in-law died.'

'Kiran's a scumbag. Why would he sell girls to a brothel when he's related to the richest man in town?' I was chilled to the bone, and rubbed my arms.

'Come, you need to change your clothing. Greed can drive a man. You know, what he has done is illegal. Probably we can't help any other girl still in Panjim, but he's pimping Leela, and Shanti perhaps will tell the police. I think that if I report these things to the police, they will have to arrest him. His goon contacts may not be able to help on that front.'

'Goon?' I said.

'Gangster.'

'What? Like mafia?' I was stunned when Haresh nodded. 'Even in a town like Keshnagar?' That explained what Muddy had told me months ago about shady dealings.

'Everywhere, darling. Come, you are shivering. Let's go back. I need to report Suhana as a missing person.'

'Okay, then. Let's go to the police.'

Chapter Eighteen
यात्रा

London, 2010

My twin sisters and their husbands were coming for Sunday morning coffee. We all lived in West London, so it wasn't difficult to see each other regularly anyway, but the whole family getting together was a monthly ritual. I pushed back the bi-fold doors that separated my lounge-diner from the kitchen, creating one large room, and checked my watch.

They weren't due for another half hour, so I rummaged in the understairs cupboard while Harry was upstairs in the shower. Shooing Billie away, I pulled the photo album out of a box. Flicking through the pages, I found what I was looking for.

The photo had migrated from a frame on my bedside cabinet, to the bottom of a drawer, and finally into the album. Its journey had taken around seven years after I'd come back to England. Each time I'd moved the photo, the habit of hope had broken a little bit more, until it only existed as a memory.

Unpeeling the film that held the photo in place, I lifted it from the page. The face that looked back at me, was still young, still in its prime. The way his hair fell to his collar bone, the angle he was sitting at, the even, white teeth, all of him was etched in my mind anyway. Especially his eyes. I didn't need a photo to remind me, but every now and again, I looked at the only one I had of him. If I closed my eyes, I heard his voice, so deep and warm, and the soft way he spoke to me. The ends of my fingers tingled, and I remembered the feel of his skin, and his thick, almost curly hair. My heart expanded, nothing had changed. I'd honour my promise; but would he? Was he even asking me?

Sighing, I placed the photo back in the album, and turned the page, looking for Suhana's photo. How was she now? I wished I knew. With the album back in its box, I picked Billie up, and went through to the lounge. I sat for a minute, stroking her long ginger and white fur, and she purred like a little motorbike when I scratched behind her black ears. Eventually, she hopped off my lap. I picked up my electric blue iPod, and scrolled down until I found what I wanted. Popping the iPod on its dock on the mantlepiece, I pressed *shuffle*.

The albums *'Rio'* and *'Rumours'* had been the soundtrack to my eight months in India. Every track brought a different memory of a specific time when I'd listened to it. The imagery that the memories brought were film-like, dream-like. And even that morning, in West London, *'Songbird'* took my breath away, and the sadness I'd felt twenty-three years before hit me like a truck. My eyes were moist, and my heart hurt. It might not be the best idea to lose myself in nostalgia, but it might help me justify my decision. I wandered through to the kitchen, wiped my eyes, and blew my nose.

The doorbell rang.

'It's on the latch,' I called, opening the fridge. I unwrapped some extra mature cheddar, and cut a small chunk off. I chopped the corner off that, dropping it to the floor for Billie who snaffled it up.

'Morning, Mari,' said Will. I waved my hand, my mouth full of cheese.

'Cheese, at this time of the morning?' Sofia kissed my cheek. 'Are we late, or early?' Will raised an eyebrow at me, and I raised one back. 'Or bang on time, like I told Will we would be?' She slammed a box on the kitchen table. 'Pastries. The ones you like from Waitrose.'

I could hear Harry and Will talking, and glanced past the dining table, and into the lounge. Knowing them, it would be computers or sport.

'What's with you?' I said. 'Don't spat at Will all day today, I don't think I can stand it.'

'He's just…'

'He's just a lovely man, who adores you, Sofia.' I placed mugs on a tray, poured water from the kettle into a large cafetiere. 'And spatting at him won't help.'

'Like you're a marriage expert,' she huffed, bending to stoke Billie who rubbed herself against Sofia's leg.

'If you're going to be a bitch all day, you can leave now. I'm not in the mood for it, Sof.'

'Sorry.' She shrugged. 'I think it's the fertility hormones that make me cranky. If this round doesn't work, we'll have to give up. It's so expensive.'

'Stella and I told you we can re-mortgage this house; it's a third yours anyway.'

'I know, thank you, but Will and I decided that this is the third and final round. And we can adopt. Plenty of kids need a family. I'm thirty-seven, for God's sake. If we leave it much longer, don't want to be mistaken for my child's grannie at the school gate.'

'You wouldn't mind, not really. Not if that child, adopted or not, was yours.' I took milk from the fridge. 'Plenty of women are having kids later in life, Sof.'

'I'm already later in life.' We both laughed.

'You make me feel ancient. I'm ten years older than you.' Sofia rolled her eyes. 'When will you know if it's worked this time?' I said, unwrapping the sticky pastries.

'End of next week, something like that. And *you* are so amazing, and glamorous and together, that it doesn't matter how old you are.'

If only she knew. Smiling at her, I placed one pastry on the plate, then another. A fluttery feeling ran across my body, and I knew instinctively that she was pregnant. It wasn't for me to tell her; it'd be nicer if she found out in private when she was with Will and the pee-on-a-stick pregnancy test.

Placing the tray of mugs on the dining table, I stepped into the lounge and bent to collect the Sunday papers off the living room floor. I glared at Harry. He grimaced, and picked up the rest, piling them to one side of the wood burner.

'Coffee and pastries on the dining table,' said Sofia. 'Hurry up, before Mari eats them all.'

'Mari,' Stella's voice cut through the chatter. 'Best you move anything breakable. The boys are a nightmare today.'

Sticking my head into the hall, I smiled at Ali and Mehmet, five and seven years old, and so cute, I'd forgive them anything. I crouched down in the lounge doorway and they ran to hug me. 'Gremlins, goblins, or good boys today?'

'Good boys, good boys,' they said in unison. Running into the lounge, they pounced on Will and Harry. Billie shot up the stairs, seeking a quiet sanctuary in one of the bedrooms.

Stella and Sofia stood chatting, their dark brown heads together, their arms around each other's waists. It made me think of when they were small, when they were never more than a foot away from each other, talking in their own identical twin language.

'We need to leave at about three,' said Stella. 'Kenan's flight gets in around the same time, so we should be there when he clears customs.' Sitting in the armchair, she had one son on her lap, the other squeezed in next to her.

'One of the benefits of living close to Heathrow,' Harry said.

'How's his family in Izmir?' Will asked. 'You should have gone, Stel. Your in-laws adore you.'

'It's the gremlins.' Stella ruffled Mehmet's hair. 'Four hours on a plane? Nope. Not until they behave like people.'

'We are people, *Ane*.' Ali looked up at her, using the Turkish word for mother. She hugged him to her and laughed. Sofia looked away, and I felt her sadness, her longing for a child. 'People. People.' The boys chanted. 'Can we go in the garden,

Auntie Mari?'

'Yes, go. Please go.' I said, and we all laughed. The boys followed me into the kitchen, hopping around me as I unlocked the door that led to the garden.

Filling the kettle again, in case anyone wanted more coffee, I watched the boys race around the garden, burning off their excessive energy. Smiling, I remembered the kids playing cricket in Bombay, even in the rain, their enthusiasm never waning despite the deluge and the mud. They'd be grown up now, probably married with children of their own.

I pulled the wedding invitation out from under a pile of post on top of the fridge. The return address was different, so the bride-to-be's parents must have moved house. Shame there wasn't a phone number, but then, I'd never be brave enough to make the call. There was an email address though. I could write an email; that would be easier. But what would I say?

'Are you making more coffee?' Sofia came into the kitchen. 'You okay? You seem distracted.'

Quickly replacing the invitation, I leaned back against the fridge. 'I'm fine. Just watching the boys. Did you go to see Mum this morning? How is she?'

'No change.' Sofia shrugged. 'She's asleep most of the time.'

'That's palliative care for you.'

'You should make your peace with her before she...before it's too late. You'll regret it if you don't.'

'What does it matter after such a long time?' I threw out my hands, my thin gold bangles tinkling. 'I have no relationship with her. I accepted that ages ago, and made my peace with it.'

Stella stood in the doorway, empty cafetiere in hand. 'Not this again, Sofia,' she said. 'You mean well, we all know that, but you know what Mum's like. You can't blame Mari for not wanting to see go and see her.'

Rinsing the cafetiere, I made more coffee, took it into the lounge. I perched on the arm of the sofa, next to Harry. He raised his eyebrows at me, and I shook my head. Stella and Sofia were still talking in the kitchen, and I tried hard not to listen. We'd had this conversation more than once over the last three or four months, and I didn't want it again.

I remembered the first time I'd taken Harry to meet the family, and everyone instantly loved him. Except for Mum. She refused to interact, or say anything nice, just looked at him like he was dirt on the bottom of her shoe. That was the final straw for me; that's what finally broke my already cracked heart. And for the last twenty-two years, I had not set foot inside her house, nor her in mine. I'd seen her at my sisters' weddings and Dad's funeral, but we'd stayed on opposite sides of the venues.

'I know I keep saying you should see Mum, Mari,' said Sofia coming through from the kitchen. She sat in the chair by the window, leaning back against the cushions. 'But, it's different this time.'

'When I was there last week, they said it wouldn't be long,' said Stella. 'I need to take the boys in again, so they can say goodbye.'

'Are you sure you want to do that? I mean, they're very young.' Will looked horrified. 'It might scar them for life.' He placed his coffee mug down on the side table. 'Just my opinion.'

'Valid one,' said Sofia. 'They're too young, Stel.' From the garden, shouts and laughter wafted through the house. 'Listen to them; the innocence of youth.'

'You sound like a bitter old lady,' said Harry, and we all laughed.

'Marianna.' Sofia said, and we all turned to look at her. 'It's different this time because…Mum's actually asking for you.'

I looked around the room, at the stunned faces. 'Why? I have nothing to say to her, and there's nothing that she can say that I could possibly want to hear,' I said, twisting my hair around my fingers. 'Factor in her resentment towards me for the last thirty years since Elena died, and all the things she's said and done, and there's no point in carrying on this conversation,' I said.

'Think about it.' Harry looked at me, his brown eyes concerned. 'There's this phrase you use…that there's always time to listen. And you know, it's never too late to build a bridge.'

'Well said, Harry. I'm glad Mum's mellowed towards you,' said Sofia. 'And it's wonderful how kind you've been to her since she's had cancer. She didn't deserve it after the way she treated you for all those years.'

'No, she didn't,' said Stella, refilling the coffee mugs. 'She not an easy person, even when she's on your side. God, I had some battles with her over marrying Kenan, I mean, he's not even a practising Muslim. Now it's all about how badly we bring up the boys.'

'When did you last speak to her? It's got to be ten years?' said Harry, looking at me. 'Or more. I can't remember.'

'It was when Mari was maid of honour at my wedding,' said Stella. 'So, it's eleven years. What happened then? She said something awful to you…'

'She just dripped her usual anti-Mari poison,' I said.

'She didn't like what you were wearing,' Sofia said. 'She said ethnic clothing looked cheap, especially on an aging woman. But that was nothing less than she'd expected from you or something like that.'

'I think the word whore was used,' said Will. Sofia leaned into him smiling. 'I took her aside and asked her to play nicely.'

'It's too late,' I said. My chest tightened, and my palms were moist. 'It doesn't matter anymore. Honestly, I'm fine not seeing her. I don't need to make any grand gesture and say goodbye.'

'Maybe she does, though,' said Harry.

'And she's still our Mum, whatever she's done.' Sofia looked at me. 'You should go, Mari.' She nodded. 'Do you want me to come with you?'

'We three could go together,' said Stella.

I looked from one to the other. 'I love you guys, but I can't. I just can't.'

Chapter Nineteen
यात्रा

Shivpur, 1986

After a hot shower and a change of clothes, I waited in the old café for Haresh. Sipping chai, I warmed my still cold hands on the cup. All I'd wanted was to help Suhana reunite with her brother; just as in my heart of hearts, I wanted to reunite with my twin sisters, Sofia and Stella. How had it all gone wrong?

Would it be overdramatic to say that Suhana was missing? My heart contracted, and my breath caught in my throat. I remembered those first few days when Kate didn't come home. Emotions crashed in, leaving me breathless and panicky. What the hell? There I was, eleven months later, in another country, and another girl was missing. I should've insisted that Suhana come with me to Bombay, I shouldn't have left her.

Nausea swamped me, sweat trickling down my back. Just reaching the bathroom in time, I threw up. Tears wet my face, and I held my hair back when I retched again. If I hadn't left my sister alone, she probably wouldn't have drowned. And I'd left Kate alone on our way back from Ryu's the night she went missing, and look what happened to her. I shouldn't have left her alone either. Guilt had eaten me alive since then, and whichever way I looked at it, Kate died because of me. If Suhana…if something bad happened to Suhana… please, God, don't let the same thing happen again. What if Suhana was lying in a ditch somewhere, slowly dying? What if history was repeating itself? Was this what Babba-ji meant when he said I couldn't change fate? I threw up again.

The washbasin was tiny, and I bent to rinse my mouth, spilling water down the front of my kurta. I couldn't look at my reflection in the plastic-framed mirror that hung above it. Kiran was no yakuza boss, and perhaps Suhana had left of her own free will. It was feasible; she knew Kiran wanted to send her to the brothel. Maybe she'd decided not to go, and maybe not trusting me to find her brother, decided she'd leave of her own accord. She could have gone to another temple town in another state, rather than be forced to go to that brothel with Kiran. Yes. That had to be it. I straightened my kurta, and tidied my hair, my hands still shaking. My legs trembled as I walked back to the table, and my vision was slightly blurred.

It was over an hour before Haresh strode through the arched doorway. My memories had done their work, and I was trying to keep it together, trying not to hyperventilate and cry.

'Done,' he said. 'Are you alright, Maharani?' Haresh pulled out a chair and sat beside me at the table, his hand on my back. 'You look not well.'

'Just worried. What did they say?' I forced a smile, glad he was with me.

'I spoke with a Sub-Inspector Mahesh. I have reported Suhana as missing. He will get the police in Panjim to check the brothels for her and any other girl from Keshnagar. I paid a lot of *baksheesh,* bribe money, to make him do it. If there are any other girls there, the police will get them out. He suggested that perhaps Suhana has gone to another widow's place, perhaps after a disagreement with the others here, or that she left because she didn't want to go to Panjim.' He ran his hand through his hair, smiled sadly. 'Hopefully, that is what had happened. Also, he will escalate my complaint about Kiran and see to it. He said Kiran is known to them, and that they are trying to clamp down on prostitution near the temple. They will question him regarding it all.'

'Good.' I said, scanning his face. 'You look less stressed.'

'I've done what I can.' Haresh grimaced and shook his wrist, flexing his fingers. 'You know, I can't remember the last time I hit someone. Maybe ten years ago, when I was nineteen. I hit a cricket umpire when he falsely called me out.' He looked around. 'Nice place.'

'Try the kulfi. Rose and cardamom; it's my favourite.' I smiled. 'I wanted to bring Suhana here, just to give her something nice, but she refused.'

'Plain life, no pleasure.' Haresh turned and spoke to the white-jacketed waiter and a few minutes later two pale pink kulfi arrived. 'I must call Bhupinder. Just to make sure everything is okay with my business. Then I think we should book our bus tickets, and return tomorrow to Bombay. There's nothing else to do.'

I pulled my chair closer to his, needing to feel his warmth, and leaned my elbow on the table. My spoon still in hand, the kulfi melted slowly. 'Let me go back to the widow's house.' I said. 'I'll talk to all of them, especially Hirmal Auntie. I only saw Bhavna earlier.' I couldn't just leave it. I'd dragged Haresh all the way from Bombay for nothing, given him false hope, and I felt like shit. 'Maybe someone knows something.' Kulfi dripped down my hand, he caught it and licked it off his finger, his eyes locked with mine.

'Mari? Beti?' I turned to the voice. 'Oh, my dear girl, *kya hua*? What happened?' said Dolly. 'You didn't go to Bombay?'

'Dolly Auntie, I did, but I came back for a few days, I'm helping - '

'Haresh Chandekar,' he said, standing, palms pressed together. 'Namaste. I am Mari's friend. We've come to find my sister.'

'She is lost? How can I help?' Dolly adjusted the pallu of her blue sari, glancing up at Haresh, then at me.

'It's complicated,' I said.

'Then you will need all the help you can get. May I sit? Then you can tell me, and I and Raju Uncle will help, okay?'

'My sister is a widow, you may not wish to help.' Haresh smiled, sitting again. 'But please, we'd be delighted for you to join us. Mari has told me how kind you have been with her.'

'It's nothing. She's easy to be kind to, nah?' Dolly smiled at me, raised her eyebrows. 'We miss her, now her room is empty.'

'No new guest?' I said.

'No. So, tell me, is this the girl you told me about, Mari? Your young friend who was married for just four months?' Her gaze was intent, her hand on my arm. I nodded. She sucked air through her teeth. 'Yaar, a human is a human, a girl is a girl.'

We told her the story; well, I did most of the talking, and Haresh sipped the chai he'd ordered for us. Dolly nodded, made tutting sounds.

'The temple prostitutes come and go. We all know they are there, and we all ignore it. I don't know this Kiran, but he sounds like a bad sort. That poor girl he sold, did her family not look for her? And those poor elders, but really, they have families to take care of them. The children should do their best by their parents now.' She placed her glass of chai on the table. 'And good that Suhana got away before Kiran could carry out his plan. I am sure she will be somewhere safe by now. Have you searched everywhere close by?'

'Yes, Auntie,' said Haresh. 'We have done everything we could. When Mari found me in Bombay, my heart was full knowing my sister was found. But hope has become fragile now.'

'I just wanted to help, but I made everything worse.' I sniffed, blinking quickly. 'Look at the devastation I've caused. I'm so sorry.'

'No, no, don't say that. I didn't mean to sound…it's not your fault.' Haresh's voice and his eyes were soft. Under the table, he took my hand. People had told me *'it's not your fault'* so many times; when my sister died, when Kate died. And Haresh was telling me the same thing while Suhana was missing. 'Auntie,' he said, 'please tell her.'

'He is correct, beti. You tried to be helpful to many people. And you have saved the old from this Kiran. And the cook. And you spoke with your friend, and it seems that she chose not to follow Kiran to that place. She will be better for it. You see, everything you have done is good.'

'Yes,' I said. Haresh still held my hand under the table, and I smiled at him. 'I'm sorry to bring you all this way for nothing.'

'For nothing?' Haresh looked at me. 'This has not been nothing.' My heart boomed, and I wanted to sink into his arms, never let go.

'You two, so sweet.' Dolly giggled, looking away. 'I should be going. Raju Uncle will be worried if I'm getting late. What will you do now?'

'We have rooms here, at the Krishna Hotel. I was thinking to return to Bombay tonight, but that means Mari will have made the journey three times in three days. Too much I think, so we'll go tomorrow instead. Excuse me for ek minute, I want to call my business. I saw a phone across the road. I'll go and come.'

He stood, and Dolly gasped as he walked away. 'So dishy.' She turned to me. 'Mari, remember I told you love would find you? The way he looks at you. Goodness gracious, it's exactly the way my husband looked at me when we first met. I still remember. Twenty-five years on.'

'I've only known Haresh three days, Dolly Auntie, but...' I shrugged, palms upwards.

'Three minutes can be enough time to know, nah? Will you stay with him in Bombay? If he marries you, come here and visit us again.' She undid the clasp of her shiny handbag that looked like something the Queen of England would carry, and scrabbled inside. She pulled out a pen and wrote on a paper napkin. 'Our telephone number. Let me know what happens, beti.'

We stood, and I hugged her. 'Goodbye, again. It was so lovely to see you.' I tucked the napkin into my cloth bag.

'He's coming back. My God, beti, look at him. If I was younger...okay, I have to go.' She and Haresh exchanged a few words at the doorway, and both came rushing back to me. Dolly's arms flapped like a bird, her handbag just missing a chai drinker's head.

Haresh put his hands on the table. 'She's in Bombay, Mari. Suhana is safely in Bombay.'

'This is great news,' Dolly said. 'You see, all is well. Now you two can relax. I'm very happy for you. Okay, bye. Bye.'

Neither Haresh or I replied. We finished our tea, grinning at each other with relief. He stood, and I grabbed my bag, followed him out of the café. Ten meters down the road, we stopped when the waiter called after us.

'Could you kindly settle the bill, sir?' the waiter said. 'I think you have forgotten.'

'Of course, I am so sorry. So sorry.' Haresh glanced at the handwritten bill, took some rupees from his pocket. The waiter took them, looked up at Haresh. 'No need for change. Please, for the inconvenience.'

The waiter smiled and returned to the café, and we walked on towards the Krishna Hotel.

'So, did you speak to her? Is she at your apartment?'

'I didn't speak to Suhana,' Haresh said, 'but she arrived yesterday afternoon at my factory, asking for me. Bhupinder didn't know I even had a sister, so he shooed her away, thinking she was a scammer or some kind of beggar.'

Traffic horns honked, and people pushed past us on the busy street. I stopped by a shop doorway, just to get some space so that I could focus on what he was telling me.

'And now?' I said, holding the sleeve of his kurta, my eyes drawn by the undone buttons at the neck which revealed six inches or so of his chest. 'Where is she now?'

'She spoke at length with Bhupinder, about my wife and Tara, my film work, things only someone close to me could know. Even which school and university I went to. So, he took her to my chawl.' He moved a strand of my hair away from my face, stood close.

'So, they know she's a widow?' I imagined her being turned away from the chawl, left to roam the streets of Bombay, alone and scared. We'd never have a chance of finding her.

'No. She's clever.' He laughed, tapped the side of his temple. 'Suhana told them that she's my sister, originally from Poona, and that she has left her abusive husband in Bangalore. And Mari, Bhupinder said she was wearing a beautiful turquoise and green sari.'

'The one I gave her.' My fingers brushed tears from under my eyes. The whole day had been so fraught, so exhausting, I couldn't hold them back. Relief washed over me, sweet and heady.

'The one you gave her, Mari. You see? What a great thing you have done. Without that, she would not be able to travel.'

'She's waiting for you there, in Bombay, when we came to find her here.' Laughing, I threw up my hands. 'It's *pagal*. Crazy.'

'Look.' I turned to see what he referred to; the window of a jewellery shop. 'I will buy you something to celebrate. What would you like, my darling?'

'How about…that anklet?' I pointed to a thin silver chain, tiny bells hanging off the length of it. 'I want to jingle when I walk.'

'Okay, Maharani, come. You should try it on.'

Buying a little silver anklet took time. Haresh wanted me to try on lots, and walk the length of the shop, so he could hear the sound they made. His choice was more elaborate than I'd have liked; a thin chain with loops of bells hanging off it. But all the anklets were so pretty, and I liked every one, so was happy for him to choose one for me. He fastened it around my ankle, his touch sending shivers through me. Then we settled in for the bartering, the chai drinking, and the banter.

'I've bought another, for Suhana.' Haresh looked at me. 'My house will be noisy.' My heart flipped, and then my stomach growled. He laughed, and paid the shop owner, and put a little velvet bag into his trouser pocket. 'Hungry again? Me too, let's eat.'

Back at the Krishna Hotel, I emerged from the bathroom wearing only the anklet and my knee-length green silk kurta. Already showered, Haresh was on the bed, wearing a lungi, and sitting propped up with the pillows behind his back.

'You are very tired, I think?' he said.

I shook my head, crawling onto the bed. He kissed my forehead, moved my hair back from my face. I knelt beside him, my fingers tracing the hair on his chest, my tongue running down his stomach to his belly button. Moving his lungi aside, I looked up at him, and his breathing changed. He stroked my hair, sighing. After a while, he moved away, got up and dragged me to the edge of the bed. Kneeling on the floor between my feet, he pushed my knees further apart, his eyes intense. He lowered his head to kiss my thighs.

'Lie back, darling,' he said.

Pleasure built as I lost myself to his mouth and his fingers, and I clawed at the sheet. He moved his hands underneath my hips, and my back arched; I knew it wouldn't be long. Maybe he sensed that, because he stopped what he was doing, and stood up, leaving me gasping. Our eyes didn't leave each other's. He lifted the water glass from the bedside cabinet and held it out for me. Shaking my head, my heart beat like crazy. Slowly, he put the glass back, still holding my gaze. He lay down, so I crawled up beside him, and he took me in his arms.

'Haresh?' I whispered. I waited for something more to happen, but nothing did, and I thought he'd fallen asleep. He must have been so tired after the journey from Bombay, the anticipation, followed by disappointment, the anger, the fighting. I snuggled in, needing sleep myself, happy just being in his arms. Then, in one movement, Haresh pulled me under him. I held his hair back from his face and he kissed me, his fingers trailing down my body, touching the sweet place that sent electricity through my whole being. He took me to the edge and back more than once until it was almost torture. When he finally eased himself into me, it was like nothing I'd ever known. He took control of every position and movement, leaving me shaking and almost sobbing. When he came, his release seemed as intense for him as mine had been for me.

I woke, with his arms around me, and the sheet twisted between our feet. Haresh's breathing was deep and rhythmic, his sleep peaceful. I ran my hand over his chest, feeling his heartbeat. He stirred, and pulled me closer. His skin smelled of sandalwood, and I closed my eyes again, smiling.

'Mari, stop, you are dreaming.' Haresh's deep voice edged into my conscience and I woke, shaking all over. 'Okay, darling, you are okay. I am here.'

It took me a moment to realise where I was, that I was safe, and that the nightmare was over. I switched the bedside lamp on, my hand still trembling. My breathing was rapid, and Haresh hugged me to him for a moment, stroking my hair. He held me at arms-length, looking into my eyes.

'I'm okay,' I said. 'Just a dream. Just a dream.'

'You are sure?'

'It happens a lot, sorry.' I examined my scar; I always did after a nightmare. Just to make sure the cuts were healed.

From the minibar on the other side of the room, he took a small bottle of water. Handing it to me, he sat on the edge of the bed, watching me drink. I nodded, sipping the water.

'What happened?' he said, one arm around my shoulders. He ran his fingers over my scar. 'How did this happen to you?'

'I'll tell you. Later.' I leaned forwards and kissed him, and his reaction was instant. Climbing onto his lap, I guided him into me, the silk of my kurta whispering against my skin as he pushed it up over my hips.

With an almighty crash, the door of the room flew open, the main light went on, and I looked over my shoulder to see three police officers in the doorway.

'Perfect,' said one, in a voice I recognised.

'Beautiful, what a picture,' said another.

Chapter Twenty
यात्रा

HARESH MOVED QUICKLY, lifting me off him, and grabbing the sheet to cover himself. Adjusting my kurta, I stood, my eyes adjusting to the harsh light, mortified at the leering expressions on the police officers' faces.

'Get up, you dog,' Muddy said. 'And you, filthy whore, cover yourself.'

'What the hell?' I said. 'Get out.'

'Mari, take your clothing to the bathroom and dress,' said Haresh. 'What is going on, officer? You can't barge in here like this.'

'We are arresting you, Haresh Chandekar, for the assault and battery of Kiran Lal. Also, for trying to evade payment at a café.' Muddy smirked. 'And, happily, I am arresting you both for immoral and lewd behaviour in a hotel room. You are not married, and this,' he gestured to the bed, 'is not allowed.'

Haresh held out his hands palms up. 'Officer, take me, I knew the risk, but please leave the girl out of it. Mari, go and dress.'

When I came out of the bathroom, Haresh was dressed, handcuffs around his wrists. I glared at Muddy, who ignored me. One of the other officers pulled my hands in front of me, clicking he handcuffs closed around one wrist, then the other. Opening my mouth to speak, I closed it; I had no voice. We were led from the room, down the stairs at the end of the corridor, and out of the hotel. Haresh spoke non-stop, in Hindi, and then Marathi.

Glancing over his shoulder at me, he said. 'I'm sorry, Mari. He won't listen –'

'Shut up.' Muddy thwacked Haresh's arm with his baton. Haresh cringed, tried to dodge another blow.

We were ushered roughly through onlookers towards two white police jeeps. It amazed me how quickly a crowd could form.

'Mari...' Haresh looked at me.

I didn't get the chance to respond. Muddy and his fellow officers bundled Haresh into the back of one jeep, and me into the other.

At the back of the station, they rushed Haresh ahead of me, took him into a room at the end of the corridor. The officers pushed me into another room, two doors up, nearer the entrance. The door clanged shut, and I was alone.

Apart from a concrete bench built into the wall, and a metal bucket in the corner, the room was empty. A line of breeze blocks separated the wall from the ceiling on all four sides. A real prison cell; my God, I was in handcuffs in a prison cell. For what? I sat, stood, paced for what seemed ages, but when I looked at my watch, it had only been ten minutes. Haresh had broken the law by punching Kiran, and I knew nothing of the Indian judicial system, had no idea of what could happen to him. And the immoral behaviour charge?

Shudders ran through me. Three men had seen me half-naked, having sex. I covered my face with my hands. Why did it have to be Muddy? There must have been other officers on duty? I sat, stood, and paced again.

Somewhere in the building, I could hear shouting, and then scuffles, thwacks. I moved from one side of the room to the other, trying to work out which breezeblock the sound was coming from. Sickening noises of something hard hitting flesh filtered through the wall, and I realised they were coming from the end of the corridor.

'Haresh! Haresh!' I shouted. 'Don't fight back.' I stood on the concrete bench, shouted through the breezeblock. 'Don't fight back.'

'Mari. Stay quiet,' Muddy yelled, and I heard nothing more than the blows and the grunts and the cries.

'Muddy, stop. Don't hit him.' I slapped my hands against the wall, the handcuffs digging into my wrists. 'Please stop hitting him.' Sobbing, I sank down, sitting cross-legged on the bench. 'Please, Muddy, stop. Stop.'

Everything went quiet. I stood on the bench again, listening through the breezeblock to faint moans.

'Haresh. Haresh. Can you hear me?' I waited for an answer. 'Haresh?'

The door of my cell opened, and I jumped down. Muddy strode in, tapping his baton against his thigh. A younger officer stood behind him, trying not to smirk.

'Can you take these cuffs off? They hurt,' I said. Muddy shook his head. 'You shitty bastard,' I said. 'How could you –'

Muddy's slap came out of nowhere, and I gasped. 'Warning.' He raised his forefinger. 'Do not insult a police officer. What do you think you were doing? Who is that man to you?' He spoke to the other officer, who moved towards the door.

'No, please don't leave,' I said, but the officer closed the door behind him. I sighed, sat on the bench, and leaned my head back against the wall, my face still stinging.

'You left here three days ago, and come back with him, and stay together in a hotel? I waited two months for you. Whore.'

I raised my cuffed hands in front of my face. Muddy grabbed them, pulled me to stand in front of him. His thumb rubbed hard along my lower lip, and he pinched my nipple, twisting it.

'Get off me.' I pushed him away, moved to the other side of the cell. 'You said you have feelings for me, so please, stop all this.'

'Feelings?' Muddy looked at me, his eyes narrow. 'Every man says that to try and get inside a woman. I should fuck you right there.' He jerked his head towards the bench, and his fringe flopped forwards. 'Even after you had that Bombay bastard inside you. It looked good, too.' He moved towards me, his eyes hard.

'I like your white arse. You know, it's not technically illegal, but we can still fine you for being together in a hotel room.'

'So fine us, let us go,' I wiped the moisture from my eyes, my ear ringing from his slap. He grabbed my hair, pulling my head one way and then the other. I cried out, tears streaming. 'Muddy, stop. Please.'

'Us? Us?' He laughed. 'You, yes, maybe in the morning. But your lover, well, I can fine him, or send him to prison. I am still deciding. His offense is a serious one. Kiran Lal has raised a complaint against Chandekar. Slander and assault.'

'Go and find Leela. Kavita. Shanti. They'll tell you about your friend Kiran.'

'You are so naïve, Mari. You think I don't know Leela? And her friends; Laxmi, Padma. I don't remember all their names.' He grabbed my breast, and squeezed hard, his fingers digging in. 'They look after the police officers occasionally. We go to the bar they work from, get rid of the other patrons. Then we buy the whores booze, and they dance, strip for us, put on a nice girl on girl show.' He pulled a condom out of his pocket, and my heart froze. 'The drunker they get, the more fun it is. We take in a big box of these, and we all have a good time. I like Padma best.' He thrust his pelvis forwards and backwards. 'From behind. And your Bombay bastard's bitch sister? She loved it, begged for more. Really nice too, especially for free. Stupid girl actually believed I was going to build a new life with her. As if I'd marry a whoring widow. When I got bored with her, I passed her on to Kiran.'

'You did the same with Shanti. You disgust me.'

'What Kiran did has nothing to do with me. Come on, let's get your clothes off.'

Muddy grabbed my wrists, pulled me towards him, trying to kiss me. The cuffs dug in, pain shooting up my forearms, and I twisted myself away from him, trying to dodge his mouth. 'Muddy, stop, get off me.'

'Come on, you did it for him.' He pulled at the hem of my kurta, trying to lift it. 'Why can't you do it for me? Huh?'

'Stop, please. Don't. No.'

One of Muddy's hands snaked under my kurta, moving up my ribcage, the other held me to him. He pressed himself against me, and I could feel his erection. His thumb rubbed over my nipple. Oh, God. I pushed at his shoulders, but I couldn't get him off me. My breath was jagged, and my vision cloudy.

'Stop, Muddy. No. get off me.'

I spat in his face. He wiped it away, laughing. When he pushed me back against the wall, I kicked at him, hit his shoulder, but the cuffs made made my attempt feeble.

'And tonight? I see you with someone else. What a nice, juicy show that was.' He thrust his hand between my legs. 'You make me crazy with jealousy. I'm going to really enjoy fucking you.'

'Get off me,' I yelled. 'Help me, someone. Please.' Using his body weight to pin me to the wall, he untied the drawstring of my shalwar, put his hand inside. 'No. No.' I sobbed. His fingers dug into my thighs, and I kept them clamped shut and pounded on his back, pulled at his hair.

'Let me see if you are still wet for that Bombay bastard.' He tried to force my feet apart, kissing my neck. 'I can smell you, I want to feel…' The door opened, and Muddy moved away from me, pushing his fringe back. I grabbed my shalwar to stop them from falling down. Crying, I moved to the bench before my legs gave way.

'Sergeant Mudgalkar, I think that's enough, sir.' The young officer unlocked the cuffs, removing them gently. Berry-coloured bruises circled my wrists like painful bangles. He handed me a plastic cup of tepid water, looking intently into my eyes. 'She might tell the newspapers. After all, she's a Britisher.'

'Thank you,' I said and glugged the water down in two mouthfuls. 'He's right, Muddy. If you touch me again, or Haresh, I will tell everyone. The papers, the TV reporters, the British Embassy. Everyone.'

'Cool off in here,' Muddy said. 'You were hysterical, and I had to slap you to bring you to your senses. I'll let the kicks and scratches go. You were not yourself. And you let me touch you, you liked it. Because as everyone knows, we are old friends, aren't we?'

When he left, I breathed out. Thank God the officer had intervened. How far would Muddy have gone? Surely... no, he was just trying, and succeeding, to intimidate me. Shaking, I sat, gently moving my swollen wrists. I stood on the bench again, calling to Haresh through the breezeblocks, but there was no answer. I screamed then, kicking at the door. Rage engulfed me, and I slapped my hands on the door, time and again, yelling for them to let me out. Kicking and shouting brought no one, did no good, and exhausted, I slid to the floor, burying my face in my hands. Crawling to the bench, I lay on my side, and closed my eyes, trying to stop the shaking.

Hours later, the young officer brought me a thali tray of watery food and a cup of chai. 'Here, you must be hungry.' He placed it beside me on the bench.

'Dhanyevad. Haresh?'

'The doctor is attending him now,' he said. 'He'll survive. Bruising, cuts, nothing more. Are you also in need of medical attention?' He looked at my bruised wrists.

'No, I'm fine. Thank you for opening the door when you did earlier.'

'Sergeant Mudgalkar is not happy.' The officer looked over his shoulder, lowered his voice. 'He suffered some humiliation in front of all of us when we found you...' Shrugging, he smiled. 'We liked to tease Sergeant when he was taking you everywhere on his motorbike. We even placed bets, and he lost significant money when you didn't let him... sorry.'

'But to arrest us...' I shook my head. 'For something that isn't even illegal?'

'Well, it's morally not acceptable. We came to the hotel looking for Chandekar for the assault charge. To find you together, well... Sergeant says it is a bonus. Look, is there perhaps someone I can call for you? If they pay the fines, we will have to let you go.'

'In my bag at the hotel, there's a napkin with my Auntie's phone number on it. Dolly and Raju Mehta. They live in Shivpur. They might help us.'

'All your belongings are being brought here this morning. Also, Mr Chandekar's.' The officer walked towards the door. 'Leave it with me, I will make the call for you.'

The door closed, and I paced the cell. Haresh needed a doctor? Sobs wracked me as I crouched over the bucket, peeing. I sat down on the hard bench and pushed the food away. The chai wasn't very hot, so I drank it in a few gulps. Immediately, I brought it back up, spewing the liquid into the metal bucket.

'Maharani? Mari?' Haresh called to me. 'I can hear you are unwell, please call for them. Get a doctor.'

Standing close to the breezeblock, I placed my hand on the wall for support. 'I'm fine. You? Are you hurt badly? Haresh…' I placed my hand over my mouth.

'Don't cry, darling. It will all be fine. Kuch nai hoga. Nothing will happen. They will let us go, soon. Rest now, okay?'

Chapter Twenty-One
यात्रा

THE ELECTRIC LIGHT reflected off Raju Uncle's glasses, and Dolly Auntie straightened her pallu. They talked quietly to each other. The clock in the entrance of the police station struck two, and I tried to walk straight.

'Beti!' Dolly touched my cheek gently, and I winced. 'Sergeant Mudgalkar is not such a good man. I am so sorry for you all. Come, we have your things in a taxi, come to our home and recover there. We will take care of you.'

'The hotels won't accept you,' Raju Uncle said, pushing his glasses up his nose. 'And you are in no fit state to be travelling anywhere. You are welcome with us, please. Come.' It was the first time he had ever spoken to me, and the moisture in my eyes spilled over.

'I need to wait for Haresh, I can't leave him.' I sniffed, wiping my nose on my dupatta, and looked at my feet. 'They've kept us here for fifteen hours. Thank you, but I'll stay here until they release him.'

'He is already at our home, Mari dear. I came to collect him more than three hours ago.' Raju patted my arm. 'Come, child, come.'

I remembered Asa, saying those exact three words to me. '*Come, child, come.*' She had taken me into her home in the mountains. Her kindness had given me the strength to recover from Kates's death, and my attack. I also found the will to live.

Although Asa tried to teach me about acceptance, it was always something just out of my grasp.

My tears didn't stop until we reached Shivpur, sitting in the back of the taxi with Dolly. The tears were born of horror and relief. And also of gratitude. How much kindness I'd already had from this couple, and now they had taken Haresh and me in. Like Asa had taken me in. And my tears echoed all the tears I'd cried in Japan.

'How bad is he?' I asked, wiping my face.

'His eyebrow needed three stitches, and there's some bruising on his body. Also, his feet where they struck him with wet bamboo,' said Dolly, patting my hand. 'Nothing broken.'

'Wet bamboo? I said. 'His feet?'

'Wet bamboo hurts like hell. And the soles of the feet are a very tender part of the body,' Raju said, turning to speak to me from the front seat. 'Nothing that won't heal in a few days, so don't worry. He is exhausted, as you must be. We will care for him, with good simple food, some medicines, and he can take plenty of rest. And for you too, some rest is a good idea, I think.'

'I've put turmeric paste all over the bruises,' Dolly said. 'It will help with the swelling.'

'Also, I got our family doctor to check him over, the same one who came to see you,' Raju said. 'I think the police doctor might not be vigilant to spot something. I was worried about a concussion, but the doctor says there is none.'

I closed my eyes, fighting nausea, as the tears and the shaking started again.

We arrived back at the Mehtas' house, and Raju carried my bag up the stairs.

'Is Haresh in my old room?' I said.

'Go up and see him,' said Dolly, 'But, beti, you'll need to be sleeping down here, okay? I'll make a bed for you tonight on the sofa, nah?'

'Of course. Thank you. I'll sleep on the floor if I need to.'

'Leave your bag upstairs. It will be easier, not so much space in the sitting room. And later, I'll put turmeric on your wrists. They look bad.'

Upstairs, I peered through the open door. Haresh stirred, looked across at me, his dark eyes pain-filled. Stepping close to the bed, I stood, not knowing what to say. Raju smiled and patted my arm as he left the room.

'You're here.' Haresh took my hand. 'I was listening for your anklet. Are you alright?' Gasping, he tried to sit up but didn't get very far. 'I've been waiting for you, worrying that he would not let you go.' His eyes searched my face, and he looked at my hands, grimacing when he frowned. 'Your wrists…'

Perching on the edge of the bed, I leaned forward to kiss Haresh's lips, and my hand shook as I stroked back his long, thick hair. The bruises on his face were vivid red and purple-blue, and under his chest hair, more bruises swelled. I bit my lip, my chin trembling. Thick red welts patterned his upper arms, and three black stitches ran along the edge of his left eyebrow. Everything was smeared with earthy ochre turmeric paste.

'I am so sorry.' I fought back tears. 'I could hear him beating you. I think he did this because of me.'

'He told me that you and he…were lovers for two months? Mari, tell me it's not true.'

'He's lying. God promise.' I smiled. 'He tried for two months, ask Dolly Aunty. But we were only ever friends. I wasn't interested in him in that way. I…he said he had feelings, but I didn't.'

'I am thinking that Mudgalkar is in Sharma's pocket,' said Haresh, 'to protect Kiran.'

'They all went to school together,' I said. 'And although Muddy says he wasn't involved with the brothel…he knew about what Kiran was doing.'

'I beat Kiran, so my arrest is justified. But the beating… Mudgalkar is jealous of you and I.' He sighed, lifted my hand to his lips. 'Honestly, I'd do the same. I want to kill him now for touching you.' His face creased, his chin trembling.

'Don't,' I said, touching his face as gently as I could.

'I could hear everything. I thought he would… You were shouting, crying, asking him to stop. But he would not.' I took Haresh's hand. His eyes were full, tears brimming over. 'It was hell. I could do nothing. He had me tied to a chair with a gag in my mouth. And I could hear you screaming.' His breath juddered. 'My poor love. How bad…did he…?'

'He didn't get the chance to do anything.' I shook my head.

'He told me that he and Suhana… did you know? But not for money. He said she loved him.'

'She did love him. But he broke her heart.'

He breathed out, closed his eyes. 'Bastard. I should not have been in the hotel room with you. Forgive me.'

Moving closer, I tried to hold him, but he tensed at my touch. So, we sat, just holding hands, the pain in my wrists ignored.

'There's nothing to forgive, Haresh. What about the assault charge on Kiran? How come they let you go?'

'Hefty fine. I need to pay within one week. Bhupinder will handle it from Bombay. Oh, God. Darling, can you pass me the water?' Haresh sniffed. 'I waited for you to come back, but now I need to take some tablets for the pain. The doctor said they will make me sedated.' I held the glass while he drank the water, and swallowed the tablet. 'Lay down with me, I need you beside me while I sleep.'

'I can't. Dolly says I've got to sleep downstairs. On the sofa.' Haresh smiled. 'Sleep, okay? I'll bring food up to you later.' I kissed his forehead, avoiding the stitches, and let myself out of the room, not wanting to leave his side.

For the next three days, Haresh was in considerable pain. He couldn't get out of bed or walk without sweating and groaning. It broke my heart to see him suffer because of what Muddy had done. Twice a day, with gentle sweeps of a wet cloth, I washed his body clean and reapplied the fresh earth-smelling turmeric paste Dolly prepared. It helped my bruised wrists as well.

Haresh asked Raju to call Bhupinder in Bombay, explaining

that we'd been delayed, but not why. Raju just said that Haresh was unwell and wasn't able to travel for a few more days. Haresh would call himself in a few days. He'd need to arrange the money to pay the fine.

On the fourth day, just before breakfast, I helped Haresh into the bathroom. Wearing a lungi around his lower half, he sat on a low stool in the bathroom while I washed his hair and his upper body with buckets of water I filled from the tap. The sandalwood scented shampoo was rich and luxurious, and I moved my fingers into his hair, gently stroking it back from his face, massaging his scalp. My own clothes were soaked, and leaving him to finish washing, I nipped back into the room to change. When he came out of the bathroom, I helped him dress in a comfortable lunghi and a loose cotton shirt.

I wanted to go to Keshnagar to get strong pain killers and anti-inflammatory tablets, as well as antiseptic cream from the pharmacy. The turmeric paste was doing its job, but I figured traditional medicine alongside it couldn't do any harm.

'Do you want to go downstairs, Haresh? You could sit with Raju,' I said, combing his hair while he sat in the armchair by the window. My fingers followed the comb, and he leaned his head back, his eyes closed.

'Yes, I would like to do that. He seems a very good man, and I must at least offer some thanks for what he's done to help us.' I moved around the chair to stand in front of him, bent to kiss his lips. 'Mari, send someone else to the pharmacy. I don't want Muddy to see you. You shouldn't go alone.' Haresh looked at me. 'I'm in…'

'I'll ask Dolly to come with me. Treat her to some kulfi. I'm craving that rose and cardamom flavour.'

Downstairs, the door of the sitting room was open as usual, and Haresh knocked on the doorframe. The Mehtas were sitting side by side on the sofa, holding hands and laughing softly.

'Come in, we are just looking at our photo album. Remembering when we were young and in head-over-heels in love,' said Dolly.

Haresh cleared his throat. 'I'm not wanting to disturb, Raju Uncle. Sir, I just…'

'Sit, boy. We can listen to the radio. Cricket match,' Raju said, and Dolly rolled her eyes. I laughed.

'Of course. I play for a local team in Bombay.' Haresh slowly lowered himself into the armchair. 'First batsman.'

Leaving the men to their talk of cricket, Dolly and I took ourselves off to Keshnagar.

On the sixth day after our release from prison, Haresh and I walked to the ghats by the river in the early morning sunshine. He leaned on me, and I was glad his bruises had changed to yellow-green. The stitches were looking less angry too. His feet still hurt, and I cursed Muddy time and again for what he'd done.

Most of each day was spent in what had become Haresh's room. We sat opposite each other on the window seat, legs crossed, and we talked all day. Dolly regularly brought us nimbu pani, or chai, or something tasty to eat.

If the Mehtas knew I had been sleeping on the creaky bed with Haresh in the afternoon, they didn't say a word. Haresh and I didn't even think of doing anything to disrespect their home. We hadn't even kissed properly, let alone anything else. But as his bruises healed, and his mobility increased, he'd take me in his arms, and we'd lie there and listen to the rhimjhim. I'd fall asleep happy and content; just being with him was enough.

We made sure we were sitting on the window seat by five every afternoon. That was when Raju Uncle tapped on the door and brought in his transistor radio. He'd gather his lungi under him, and sit on the window seat with Haresh, while I was banished to the armchair. We listened to All India Radio and the BBC World Service news bulletins. We heard how Reagan and Gorbachev had met at the Reykjavik Summit in Iceland. I smiled, remembering my stance on global disarmament, how I'd even had a bag with the CND logo embroidered on it. The rest of the world seemed so far away, and things like nuclear weapons irrelevant in Shivpur.

A news bulletin announced that the Dalai Lama had just returned from a ten-day visit to the USSR. I really wanted to see His Holiness in McLeod Ganj, but thinking of travelling away from Haresh was too surreal a concept. But I couldn't stay in Shivpur forever.

In the evenings we joined the Mehtas for a meal in the kitchen, and I'd help Dolly clean up and prepare chai while Raju and Haresh disappeared into the sitting room to read the newspaper, *The Times of India*.

Haresh's recovery took eight days, and he was brighter in himself as well as walking without too much discomfort by then. That morning, I sat between his legs, leaning back against him on the window seat. He ran his fingers through the ends of my hair, which made me sleepy, and I just breathed in the warmth of him, absorbing him into my every cell. We listened to Duran Duran's album *Rio* on my Walkman, Haresh holding the earphones in position so that we could both hear the music. '*Your Own Way*' reminded me that I was running out of time, and needed to leave India in just over two weeks.

'I need to get to Delhi soon,' I said. 'And then McLeod Ganj.'

'Not before I take you to the Taj Mahal.' Haresh shifted slightly, and I turned my head to look at him. 'The most romantic place, built for love.'

'Have you been there?' If I stretched up a few inches, I could kiss his mouth. He knew what I was thinking, and bent his head, kissing my lips.

'No, but my parents got engaged there. Such a nice story they told me and my sister. Both families gathered outside the monument, and there was music and flowers. Mum was acting shy, which is expected, but Dad couldn't wait. He just grabbed her hand and told everyone he had found his love.'

'Wasn't the marriage arranged?'

'Of course, but they fell in love anyway.' His arms tightened around me. 'Some things are written. Like you and I. Darling, I think they would have liked you.'

'What happened to them, Haresh?'

'My parents were university lecturers, in Poona,' he said. 'They were killed outright in a traffic accident with a truck. They were going to a conference for some charitable works they were doing for street kids.'

'You were thirteen. And Suhana was eight.'

'You remember?' He kissed the side of my face, lacing his fingers with mine. 'And we went to live with my father's brother and his family. I think it was hard for them to have us there; they had four kids of their own. To give their time, I mean; my father left enough money. But they were kind and sent us to good schools, so we had the best education.'

My hand stroked his shins where the fabric of his lungi fell open, the hair silky smooth under my fingers. 'So, when did you go to Bombay?'

'At aged eighteen. Suhana came with me and finished her education there. By then, I was already making some films in between finishing my electronics engineering degree. And you know the rest.' He took my hand, traced his fingers over mine. 'And now, your turn.'

'Not much to tell. Spanish mother, English father. I'm the oldest of four girls; there's one set of twins who are almost fourteen now. My other sister, Elena...she died when she was fifteen. I was two years older.'

'What happened?'

'She fell in the shower, knocked herself out, and drowned in three inches of water.'

'No. So sad to die young. He shifted his position behind me, and I leaned forwards, taking my weight off him. 'I am sorry for your family.'

'Thing is, Mum blamed me.' I turned so that I was sitting, feet on the floor. 'Elena and I were alone in the house; I was downstairs the whole time. Elena had been driving me mad all morning, and I'd ignored her when she called me. We were best friends, but we squabbled a lot too.' I shrugged. 'I ignored her, not realising she actually needed me. And she died.'

'How could you know?' Haresh put his arm around my shoulders and moved to sit beside me. 'Accidents are accidents.' He turned his head to look at me, and I smiled at him. He touched my face, and my eyes closed for a moment.

'My mother said I wasn't her daughter and made me leave the house. And that's why I've not seen my family for almost six years.'

'Are you okay with that?' Haresh trailed his fingers up and down my arm.

'I am now. One day, I will go back to England, and by then maybe we can reconcile. Who knows?'

Haresh reached under my hair, stroking the back of my neck. His mouth was so close to mine, and our eyes locked. I could feel the heat growing in my blood, pulsing through me, and I reached up to kiss him. His mouth was gentle, his tongue slow, and we pulled away from each other when Dolly opened the door.

'What is going on here? I see you are all recovered now,' Dolly said sternly. 'Seems you are fine, nah?'

Haresh stood and straightened his kurta. 'Sorry, Auntie.'

Then Dolly smiled, raising her eyebrows. 'I have to go out for five minutes,' she said. 'Then, you come downstairs. I will be out for five minutes only, okay?' She left, closing the door quietly, and her footsteps pattered down the stairs. 'Five minutes.'

We stood waiting for the front door to close, and Haresh undid my choli, and I dropped it on the window seat. His mouth was soft on my skin, his tongue hot on my nipples. Fumbling with my lehenga, he cursed. I stopped his hand and shaking my head, pulled the fabric up, gathering it at my waist before I sat on the window seat. He sat beside me, kissing me, touching me, until I gasped. Gently pushing me down, he untied his lungi, and slid himself into me. He pushed my legs back, moving slowly.

'Mari? Haresh? I'm back. Are you coming down?' Dolly Auntie called from the bottom of the stairs.

'Ek minute, Auntie,' I called back. 'Haresh,' I whispered. He stared into my eyes, and then his mouth was on mine, his kisses deep. We stopped, breathing hard.

'I don't want to…finish. It feels too good.' He kissed my throat. 'Mari, I…'

Wanting more of his mouth, I kissed him. We moved together, sweat sliding over us. The pleasure was intense, rolling me towards the edge, and I clung to him as he took me over it.

'Shhh, Mari.' Haresh laughed and a minute later, it was my turn to tell him to be quiet.

Giggling, we took it in turns to quickly wash in the bathroom. When we were dressed, we both went downstairs.

'Chai is almost ready, go sit. Raju Uncle will be back shortly,' Dolly said from the kitchen.

'Thank you, as always,' said Haresh. 'May I use your phone, please. I need to call Bombay. I'll give you…' He fumbled in his pocket for some rupees.

'Use it, use it, no problem.'

In the kitchen, I plated up some snacks, and Dolly poured the chai through a strainer. She kept giggling.

'What?' I said, smiling. Hoping she wouldn't say she'd heard us.

'I said five minutes. It was twelve.' She nudged me, and I nearly dropped the snacks. 'You lucky girl. Take the pleasure while you can. After children, it stops a little. Your priority will change.'

'I'm sorry.' I placed my hands on my flushed cheeks. 'I know you didn't want us to sleep together in your house.'

'Sleep? What sleep?' She pointed upwards. 'Room is above. I had to go and wait in the sitting room after I called you to come down.' She laughed, her hands on her ample hips.

'Don't, you're making me blush,' I said, laughing. My hands hid my face.

'You were already blushing when you came down. Love blush. He had better be marrying you.' She wiped her face, laughing again, and holding her sides.

'Stop, Dolly Auntie, please.'

'Oh, beti.' Adjusting her sari, she looked at me, suddenly serious. 'You two love each other, I think.'

'He hasn't said.' I shrugged.

'He doesn't need to say it. Can't you see in it his eyes? The way he speaks to you.' She took hold of my hands. 'When Uncle Raju collected him from the police station that morning, Haresh refused to leave. The man could not stand up even, and he did not want to leave you. If that's not love, what is?'

'Oh, God.' My heart swelled, full to bursting. With my hand over my mouth, I blinked the tears back.

'Marry him. Make children. Live a happy life. You love him?' I nodded. 'Good. Otherwise, no twelve minutes, nah?' Our laughter filled the kitchen.

'All is well.' Haresh came to the doorway, leaning against it, blocking the light. 'Suhana is staying with my neighbours, Manu and his wife.' He glanced at me, smiling. 'Leyra. You met her, Mari. No one has a spare key to my apartment, you see. They are all waiting for me to go back now. And my business also needs my attention. Bhupinder is raising the cash for the fine.'

'Are you ready for the journey?' said Dolly. 'You can stay longer if you need to.' She flapped her hand at him, and he moved aside. She took the chai and snacks into the sitting room, just as Raju arrived, and we followed her into the sitting room.

'Sir, I think we will be taking the bus to Bangalore this evening,' Haresh said and sat on the sofa. 'Thank you for all you have done for us. Please, let me cover any expenses you have incurred.'

'Mari's fine was substantial,' said Raju. 'I'll be happy if you can settle that amount.' He fumbled in his pocket, and handed Haresh a receipt.

'I don't have that much with me, but if I could use your phone again, I'll ask Bhupinder to make a transfer to your bank account.' Raju nodded. 'And for the room, the food, doctors fee, taxi money?'

'I won't hear of it.' Raju raised one hand, adjusted his lungi with the other. 'No need. Good to see you recovered. The pain is less?'

'Much less. Not much at all.' Haresh looked at me and smiled. My blush deepened, and I smiled, looking away. 'I need to return home now. My sister is waiting.'

Late in the afternoon, we were packed and ready to go. I hugged Dolly and shook hands with Raju. They walked us to the corner of the temple street where the autos waited.

'You were wearing this kurta when I first met you,' I said, running my hand along the turquoise silk on Haresh's arm.

'You like it?' Haresh said. I nodded. 'And you were wearing black trousers and a shirt with hungry elephants on it.' We laughed. 'But I like you better in colour. Like when you found me in Mumbai. I turned around, and there you were, looking so…' he bent to my ear, 'delectable.'

Haresh spoke to the auto driver, and I was sure I heard Dolly say something to Raju about twelve minutes. They giggled, and she held onto her husband's arm. Haresh placed our bags in the auto, and I placed one foot in the back of the vehicle, ready to climb in. A car drew up on the other side of the road, a little way in front of the auto. Kiran got out, leaving the door open. A white police jeep pulled up behind his car, the spinning orange light on the roof flashing. A moment later, Muddy and five other officers spilled out on the street. Now what? I moved next to Haresh, looking up at him, but he didn't meet my gaze.

'How dare you besmirch my reputation?' Kiran said, his face twisted with hatred. He staggered slightly as he stood there, and leaned back against the car. He walked a few unsteady steps towards us, speaking Hindi. 'I have lost everything because of you.'

The police walkie-talkie trilled, and I looked at Muddy, but he stared at Kiran.

'Mari, go back to Raju Uncle's,' Haresh said, his shoulders tensed. He took my arm, and steered me towards the Mehtas, raised his eyebrows at Raju. 'Take the women away.'

'No, Haresh, don't hit him again,' I said, pulling away. 'Please, let's just get in the auto. We can just go.'

'Do as I say, Maharani.' Haresh walked three paces away from me, towards Kiran. 'Please, darling,' he said and shot me a look. 'Please.'

The auto driver roared away, the wheels spraying up small stones and dust, and in my peripheral vision, people ran in all directions. Muddy and his officers moved closer.

'You British bitch. You have ruined everything for me.' Kiran's words were slurred, and he waved his right arm around, his fist clenched. Haresh stepped slowly toward him. 'My wife has gone to live at her sister's. I have no job. My brother-in-law also has cut ties with me. Even Leela has someone else to help arrange her clients. Do you know what you have done?'

'Chandekar,' said Muddy. 'What do you think are you doing?'

'Muddy? What's going on?' I shouted. 'We paid the fines; just let us leave.' He ignored me, focusing on Kiran and Haresh.

'Raju Uncle, get the women away,' Haresh said over his shoulder, and then put his arms out, raised his hands at chest height. 'Come on, Kiran *bhaya*, brother, you don't really want to be doing this.'

'I heard that English bitch gives a man a good, good time.' Kiran laughed, high pitched, and not natural. 'Lovely arse too, I believe. But you should stay away from her, or she'll ruin your life. As unlucky as the stupid widow girl she took away from me. I need more whiskey.'

A silent crowd gathered on the other side of the car; the men's faces expectant as they waited silently for something to happen. The police officers' feet scuffled on the stony ground as they moved in a line, closer to Haresh and Kiran. Time slowed, became as heavy as the clouds that gathered overhead. I looked from one police officer to another, trying to understand what was happening.

'Raju Uncle. Now,' Haresh shouted, his deep voice booming. He took another step towards Kiran.

Raju ushered Dolly away, but I stayed put, frowning as the police took position around Kiran and Haresh.

'What money I could have made from her,' Kiran slurred, waving his hand. 'Such a pretty young thing. Many would have paid good money for her. Like the kitchen assistant. Always good money for the pretty ones.'

Haresh's fists clenched, and I prayed he wouldn't hit Kiran. Muddy spoke to his officers, and they circled Haresh and Kiran. One by one they drew their pistols from the holsters on their belts. My heart beat so fast, and I ran my hands down my thighs, leaning them on my knees while I caught my breath. What was going on?

I remembered the sensation I'd had standing in the very same spot a week ago when fear and dread had almost taken my legs from under me. Was this it? Looking up at the boulders, I saw a flash of red-orange against the sandstone. Babba-ji moved forwards, and although he was far away, I could feel he was looking straight at me.

The police moved in closer, and Kiran pointed at me. Everyone stopped moving, except Haresh, who took a tiny step towards Kiran. Muddy spoke again to his officers, who raised their weapons. Kiran waved his arm, and sunlight reflected off something in his hand as he pointed at me. I clamped my hands to my mouth, stifling a scream. My whole body shook and my mouth went dry.

'Nobody move,' Muddy shouted. 'Kiran, put down the gun.'

'Not until I kill her, damn Britisher. I have no life, thanks to her interfering.' He pointed the gun at me again, his legs unsteady.

'Mari, back away. Slowly,' Muddy said over his shoulder as he moved backwards towards me, his gun trained on Kiran. 'I've got you covered.'

My legs wouldn't work. I stood rooted to the spot, while in what seemed like slow motion, Haresh lunged for Kiran's gun, and a shot rang out. Within the same second, another shot, and I ducked down, crouching on the ground with my hands over my ears. Deafening echoes of echoes, sound upon sound, bounced off the boulders. Noise built up and up until my ears hummed with the vibration. Then, the sound changed and seemed stuck on a slowly diminishing and quietening loop. And the smell; the sharp metallic smell of blood that stung my nose, and alerted my brain to the horror of what had happened. Haresh lay slumped over Kiran, blood spilling onto the ground and staining the turquoise silk of his kurta.

Chapter Twenty-Two
यात्रा

THE BALLPOINT PEN ran out mid-signature, and the police officer handed me another one, tutting. Scrawling my name across the bottom of the page, I hoped this was the last document I needed to sign, but of course, it was all in triplicate, and I had to sign the other two copies as well. Perhaps I was still in shock, but it was all like a surreal dream. I looked at the ceiling, blinking back tears. Sniffing, I looked down at my hands, at the smears of dried blood that made my stomach lurch.

Dolly and Raju sat at another desk in the Keshnagar police station, no doubt going through the same process as I was, signing witness statement after witness statement. It was endless; the questioning, the remarks, the judgement in the eyes of the police officers. My last dealings with the police has been in Japan, and they had been far from sympathetic in the beginning. But when they realised that I was innocent, that I hadn't killed Kate, their attitude had changed. At every stage, the interviews had been carried out with nothing but honorific based politeness. Here, the police were argumentative, bordering on aggressive. Perhaps it was because one of their own had been shot. Muddy had been taken to the hospital and the bullet was being removed from his shoulder.

My ears still buzzed from the shots that were fired, from the echoes that bounced around for what seemed like hours. The glare from the overhead strip light burned into my brain, and I needed to lay down.

'You're free to go, Miss.' The officer stood, gathered his papers, and signalled to a constable. 'Go on, go home. We are done. So many other witness statements to take. I'll be here all bloody night.'

My legs shook as I stood, and turning, I almost lost my balance. Haresh's hand caught my elbow, and he steadied me. I gazed at him, shook my head.

'I know,' he said. 'Let's go. I need to change my clothes. This blood is making me feel not good.'

'We missed the bus,' I said. 'There's another at two am. Let's get that one. I want to leave here as soon as possible.'

'I agree, totally.' Haresh looked down at me, moved my hair back off my shoulders. 'But maybe we should rest tonight. It has been an ordeal, and I for one, am exhausted.'

'Yes, come. Your room is your room tonight,' said Dolly. 'And you need to shower, get the blood off you.'

'We've caused you so much trouble, I can't thank you enough.' I smiled at her, and then my legs gave way, and Haresh helped me to a chair.

'Take a deep breath, Mari. You are okay, I am here with you.' Haresh crouched down, looking into my eyes. 'It's over now.'

I closed my eyes, and leaned my forehead against his shoulder, waiting for Raju to bring the taxi and take us home.

It wasn't until later, when I was in the bathroom upstairs at the Mehtas', that the tears came. I sat on the low stool, my head in my hands, reliving the last few moments of Kiran's life.

When I saw Haresh slumped over Kiran, when I saw the blood, I thought Haresh was dead. Muddy was also on the ground, blood seeping into his uniform. A police officer ran to the jeep, spoke on the two-way radio. He came back, pressed a wad of something onto Muddy's shoulder to stem the bleeding. Raju stood beside Dolly, his hand on her shoulder while she knelt in the dirt, holding Muddy's hand. And I couldn't move;

I saw everything like I was watching a film, and I stayed rooted to the spot.

The other officers stood over Haresh and Kiran, and one of them pushed Kiran's gun away with the end of his baton. The other one crouched down and said something. Haresh moved, and the officers helped him up. He turned to me, his kurta covered in blood, and I ran to him, sobbing.

'It's not my blood, Mari. It's not mine,' Haresh said. I ran my hands over him, looking for a bullet hole in his clothes. 'It's not mine.'

Kiran's frog eyes stared unseeing at the sky, the blood still seeping from his chest. One of the officers placed the gun into an evidence bag and covered Kiran's face with a piece of cloth.

'The bullet missed you? How did it miss you? Muddy aimed straight at Kiran, and then you moved in front of him.' My blood-stained hands patted Haresh's arms, his chest. 'I don't understand.'

'I felt it. Look.' His fingers opened a rip in the upper sleeve of his kurta, revealing a thick welt of burned red skin. 'When I tried to grab Kiran's gun, I felt it.' We looked at each other, eyes wide, and I put my hand over my mouth.

A police van drew up, followed by two ambulances. We were ushered into the van, along with a dozen others from the crowd, and taken to the police station in Keshnagar.

In the bathroom, with the cool water washing over me, I realised what Babba-ji had meant; that I'd couldn't stop what was written, couldn't stop fate. But what good was knowing that? There wasn't any way I could have stopped anything from happening anyway. Muddy was in the hospital, Kiran was dead. I cried, trying not to make a sound, scrubbing my nails with a little brush to get the blood out from under them. Drying myself with a towel, I wrapped it around me and went into our room.

'I thought Kiran would kill you, I really thought he would,' Haresh said. He was sitting in the armchair, looking out of the window. In profile, the lamplight made him look serious, and as I walked towards him, I saw the wetness in his eyes. 'I thank God, he did not.'

I stood behind Haresh, finger-combing his hair, and bent to kiss the top of his head. 'It was awful. When I saw you laying on top of Kiran, and all that blood. I thought I'd lost you.' I sniffed, and he looked around at me.

'That will never happen, Maharani.'

Haresh stood, took the towel off my body, letting it drop to the floor. Taking my hand, he led me to the window seat and lay me down, his mouth on mine. He was strong, demanding, and in control, but it didn't feel like love. It was over quickly, and when we started again a short while later, it was the same. Only that time, we both cried afterwards.

Sleep was impossible, even though I was exhausted. My mind went over and over everything, again and again. I couldn't figure out who's gun had fired first; Muddy's or Kiran's. Did it even matter? Why was I fixated on that tiny detail? Haresh stirred, turned over onto his side. I was glad he could sleep, and glad that Raju had let me stay in the same room. But wait, if Haresh hadn't moved Kiran's gun, Muddy wouldn't have got shot. Was I standing to the right or left of Muddy? Would the bullet have hit me anyway? Circles, I was going round in circles. Whichever way I looked at it, whether Haresh had moved Kiran's gun or not, Muddy was standing in front of me, protecting me. Muddy had saved my life. The gratitude I felt was overwhelming, especially in juxtaposition to what I knew about him, let alone what he'd done to Haresh in the police cell, and to me. My fingers constantly wiped my eyes, and I needed to blow my nose.

I sat up, moving slowly so that the bed didn't creak, and careful not to disturb Haresh, I went to the bathroom. Looking in the mirror, I remembered how my mother had said I was cursed. It felt like she was right. What was wrong with me that such awful things happened wherever I went? Maybe I could blame death for following me, or maybe I had to take responsibility for the dramas that played out around me.

Haresh slept until mid-morning, and I lay beside him, drifting in and out of awareness.

'Are you decent?' Dolly tapped on the door. 'Can I come in? I have chai and pakoda for you.'

'We shall come down in a moment, Auntie,' said Haresh, and we scrabbled for clothes.

'Theek hai, come when you are ready. Raju Uncle booked your bus tickets for this afternoon. And he called your Bhupinder to explain you have been delayed again. I threw away your clothes, Haresh. The blood did not come out.'

'Thank you. Please, do not worry.' Haresh stood, the sheet wrapped around his lower half, his hair all over the place. 'The clothes do not matter.'

'Come down, breakfast is here for you.' Her footsteps on the stairs were soft.

Shaking my head, I left the bed and lay back on the window seat, my arms reaching for Haresh. He smiled and dropped the sheet. Breakfast could wait.

As much as I wanted to leave Shivpur, I also wanted to stay. For the last week, bit by bit, kiss by kiss, I'd built myself a world, a dream existence where there was just Haresh and me. But the real world beckoned, and time was marching on. In two weeks, I'd need to leave, and cross the border into Nepal. But how, when there was a bond between Haresh and me that was different to anything else I'd experienced with a man. It was more than special. I'd felt it in Bombay, but laying in his arms that morning, it was deeper, and stronger after everything that had happened to us.

Goodbyes were never easy, and as much as the Mehtas had been kind and been so helpful, I wondered if they were glad to see us go.

'Write to me from Bombay,' said Dolly. 'I want to know how

things turn out for you.' She nudged her husband's arm. 'Big love story, nah?'

'I will,' I laughed. 'And don't forget to write back.'

The Mehtas waved us off, and the bus pulled away. I braced myself for the long journey back to Bombay. This was the last time Haresh and I would be together; I knew that. Once we got to Bombay, he'd reunite with his sister, and it would be better to leave them in private for that. I planned to find a guesthouse, hopefully not too far away, and maybe I'd visit them in the chawl for chai, or meet them at a dhaba somewhere for lunch. My throat was tight, and I fought back tears.

Haresh called Bhupinder from Bangalore to let him know he'd be back the next morning. When we arrived at the chawl after taking an auto from the bus station, we were greeted at the entrance by Manu and his wife, Leyra, the neighbours who had taken Suhana in for the last ten days. A small crowd of other neighbours formed at the entrance, behind Suhana, who stood there in her turquoise and lime green sari. She wore glass bangles and had a green bindi between her brows. I looked from her to Haresh and back again. Neither of them moved, they just stood looking at each other.

'Ek minute,' I said to the auto driver, and I placed Haresh's suitcase on the ground behind him. I needed to say goodbye, but I didn't want to intrude, so I waited by the auto, for the right moment.

Haresh took a few steps towards Suhana, and scooped her into his arms, twirling her around and around. They both laughed, and the neighbours cheered and clapped. He turned to me, his smile wide and joyful, and my heart skipped.

'Come, meet my sister, Suhana.' He extended his arm towards me. 'Suhana, meet Mari.'

'I know her. She is my very best friend,' said Suhana. She smiled and hugged me. 'Thank you, from my heart, thank you.'

'I'm glad I could help,' I said and looked at Haresh.

He handed some money to the auto driver, who left my holdall next to Haresh's suitcase. 'Come, let's go home.' The neighbours went inside, chatting and laughing.

'I'll leave you to it,' I said. 'I'll call in a few days, and maybe we can meet –'

Haresh stood in front of me, but I couldn't look at him. My heart raced, and I didn't want the emotions to surface, to spill over. Every part of me wanted to stay with him, was compelled to stay with him, but I knew I should go.

'Why would you say such a thing?' Haresh's voice was quiet. 'I told you; you will stay with me.' When he touched my hand, I looked up at him. There were no words to describe the look in his eyes. 'Don't go.'

Suhana and I followed Haresh into the chawl. We kept looking at each other and grinning. She looked so different without her white sari. Haresh carried our bags up the three flights of stairs, and we almost ran into the back of him when he stopped dead. The walkway was decked out with garlands of marigolds. They hung around the rose-pink doors of Haresh's apartment, the kitchen window, and more of the gold-coloured flowers were draped around the railings.

'To welcome you home after your journey, and for your good health.' Suhana touched Haresh's arm. 'I was worried when I heard you were unwell. You have some stitches.' She frowned. 'Accident of some kind?'

'I will tell you when we are inside. Come.' Haresh put the key in the padlock and turned it. Removing it from the hasp, he placed it on the window sill. Leaving our shoes by the door, Suhana and I stepped inside. 'First, I will fetch your things from downstairs, sister. Then we will talk and drink chai.'

Suhana walked around the apartment, looking in the bedrooms and the bathroom, opening the cupboard in the kitchen, running her hands along the shelves on the wall.

'It's big for a chawl apartment, and he has made a nice home,' she said. 'I like the pale blue colour on the walls.'

'I can't believe you are here, Suhana,' I said. 'I'm so happy to see you in Bombay.'

'I too. I cannot believe it. But what happened there to delay you? Something serious? I can tell by your face.'

'Let Haresh tell you everything, okay. You should hear it from him. I'll drink chai, and then I'll go.'

'Go? Again?' Haresh said. He stood in the doorway, frowning. He brought a small vinyl shopping bag into the apartment. 'Sister, I will buy you many saris, okay. Every colour you like, and everything else you need. I can't believe this is all you are owning.'

'Everything I have is from Mari. Shall I make chai?' Suhana said, and she grinned when Haresh nodded.

'Mari, I told you.' He spoke softly while Suhana clattered about in the kitchen. 'Stay with me.'

'But...' I pointed towards the kitchen. He shook his head, gestured to himself and then me, and pointed to his room. 'No. I...' He held his hand out to me, so I followed him into his room.

'You keep speaking about leaving. Why? I don't understand.' Haresh placed his hands on my waist, looked down at me.

'You just found your sister after three years, Haresh. There must be so much you need to talk about. She's been through a lot, she needs all your attention now.'

'There's plenty of time to talk. But you are needing to rest. I think what happened in Shivpur has disturbed you greatly. You hardly spoke on the journey here, you would not eat.' Holding me, he stroked my hair. 'I know you...if you don't eat, you are not yourself. The shock will pass, darling. Stay here, rest. And then we'll see.'

I nodded, followed him back into the other room just as Suhana brought three glasses of chai on a small tray.

'I tried hard to remember how much masala and sugar to put in. It's been a long time since I made proper chai.'

Haresh and Suhana talked in Hindi, and I went out onto the walkway. Down in the courtyard, a group of elderly men played cards on a folding table, and a woman washed clothes at the standpipe. People came and went, and the chawl buzzed with noise. A teenaged girl dragged her cycle up three flights of stairs and leaned it against the railings of the walkway. She grinned at me, and I smiled back.

I turned and looked through the kitchen window. Suhana's hands covered her face, and her shoulders shook. Haresh sat next to her, his head bent, hands between his knees. Biting my lip, I blinked back tears, my heart aching for both of them.

In the kitchen, I filled two glasses with water, and placed them on the table in front of the sofa. Neither Suhana or Haresh looked up, so I left them talking, and went to the balcony. I unfolded the mattress and lay down. The call to prayer, the *ezan* sang out from the *masjid*, the mosque at the end of the street, and I drifted close to sleep for a while. My mind was too busy, frantically flitting from one thought to another. Focusing on the cool breeze didn't distract me. If Haresh hadn't grabbed Kiran's gun; if Muddy hadn't been standing exactly where he was…I stared up at the underside of the roof. Sleep wouldn't come. The kids played cricket on the patch of ground outside, and I turned on my side to watch them. When the sky tipped itself down on them, they carried on playing. I smiled; kids in Europe would be running for cover, but not here. Rain splashed on me, and I retreated inside the apartment, pulling the mattress with me. Haresh moved to make room for me on the sofa, and I sat beside him.

'I'll make more chai,' Suhana said. 'You've been sleeping, it will refresh you.'

'She's been telling me about the widows' house, and how she has been managing to live for three years.'

Haresh looked at me. He clenched his jaw, and I reached to touch him, but withdrew my hand, glancing at Suhana, who had her back to us in the kitchen.

'It can't have been easy for her,' I said.

'I can't believe she had to…thank God you found her, Mari. Thank God I found you. And I'm glad for what happened in Shivpur.'

With a tray of fresh chai in her hands, Suhana looked from one of us to the other and back. 'And now you can tell me; what exactly did happen in Shivpur?'

By the time Haresh finished telling the story of what happened to Kiran, Suhana's untouched chai was cold, a scummy film forming on the top.

'Muddy shot Kiran because he was going to shoot Mari. Oh, my goodness. Kiran is dead?' Suhana shook her head. 'All this happened because you found out what he was doing at Sharma's, and because you stopped me going to the…to Panjim? But I don't understand, something is missing from your story.'

'What do you mean?' I said.

'How is it that my brother's face is bruised and he has stitches? If you thrashed Kiran, brother, I can't believe he did that to you.'

'There is something else we need to tell you,' said Haresh, taking my hand. 'I love this woman. And I think you love me too?' His eyes burned into mine. I nodded. He smiled, ran his hand through his hair. 'I was afraid you would say that you did not. Mudgalkar found us in a hotel room together. He added that to the charges when he arrested me for beating Kiran.' He gestured to his face. 'And he beat me for being with Mari because he wanted her.'

'What? You two love each other?' Suhana said, her frown deep.

Silence filled the room, and I didn't dare look at either one of them. Haresh sat quietly, his hand covering mine. Suhana didn't say a word, but I could feel her looking at me.

'Yes, I love him,' I said.

'Muddy caught you together?' Suhana said. 'In a hotel room. You mean…?'

I blushed, and Haresh cleared his throat. Suhana laughed, throwing her head back, and stamping her feet on the floor.

'So, you are in love? I am so happy. This is a good day. I will make a puja, to thank Shiva for everything.'

'Mari, put your things in Suhana's room,' Haresh said. 'I have to go and talk to Mr Bhose, explain that you will be staying here for some time.' He touched my face and walked out of the door. He turned, and with one hand on each side of the door frame, leaned into the apartment, his smile wide. 'I cannot believe how my life has changed in just ten days.' And he was gone.

'Who is Mr Bhose?' I asked Suhana.

'He owns the chawl. Haresh will be paying rent to him. I met him at Manu and Leyra's when he came to meet me. He has some political aspirations, very pro-Maharashtra. He has found me a job in a school also. It's two bus journeys away, but it's a good chance for me. I start on Monday. I will be a teacher again.'

'Oh, my God, that's fantastic.' I looked at her. The kohl around her eyes made them look brighter. 'Your life has also changed in ten days. And mine, Suhana.'

'You love Haresh, really?'

'I know. I'm surprised too, but yes.'

'And Muddy found you together. Actually…?' I nodded, my eyes closed. 'Oh, my goodness, he will have been very angry. He is very possessive of women.' Suhana flicked a glance at me. 'He and I…at one time, I had some feelings for him. He's the one I told you about, the one before Kiran. But don't tell Haresh, please.'

'Suhana, Muddy told us. There's nothing your brother doesn't know.' I took her hands. 'But that's the past, and you don't have to do that anymore. Does Mr Bhose, the landlord, have to agree to me staying here?'

'One; you are a foreigner, and two; Haresh is a single man as far as they know. Three; you can be arrested, but you already know that.' She laughed, grinning from ear to ear. 'For propriety's sake, do as Haresh says, and leave your things in my room. People come in and out of each other's apartment. Chawl life is like that; there's not much privacy. You are my friend, so all will be well. I spoke about you anyway, said you had helped me find my brother. If anyone asks you, we met in Bangalore, not Keshnagar, okay?'

I nodded, looking at the girl whose life had transformed in just a few days, by a chance meeting on a roadside with me. How quickly things could change. I remembered that nothing was permanent, and that things could change again, at any time. There were only two weeks until I needed to leave; two weeks here in the chawl, and I was determined to enjoy every single second.

Chapter Twenty-Three
यात्रा

HINDI FILM MUSIC played on a new radio-cassette player Haresh had bought for Suhana. She showed me again how to move my hands, and place my feet just so. The hip movements were easier to do once I worked out that I needed to shift my weight onto the alternate foot.

'See, now stamp your foot a little, the anklet will jingle. Yes, now push out the other hip...yes.' I followed her instructions. 'Now, turn. And back.'

I lost my balance, and we both laughed. 'It's getting too hot now,' I said. 'Let's stop. Haresh will be home soon.'

Looking at my watch, I was glad it was almost midday, and that Haresh would be back in an hour or so. I hated not being with him, but he'd been away from his business for almost two weeks, and of course, there were things he needed to see to. Plus, he was having his stitches out.

'Do you want to learn how to make yellow dahl and beetroot sabzi?' Suhana said from the kitchen. 'I think today I will be lazy, and buy the roti. It's Saturday after all.'

Haresh and I had only got back from Shivpur the day before, and I was glad Suhana had already settled in, as if she'd always lived there. She'd woken us earlier that morning, tapping on the door to tell us that chai and potato paratha was waiting for us.

'Tell me what to do and I'll do it all,' I said. 'You already cooked breakfast.'

'You want to impress him, nah?' Suhana grinned. 'I'm so happy about you and my brother. It's like a fairy tale. Right. So. First, grate the ginger and then the garlic, then mash them to a paste. Then crush the spices on the board with the pestle.'

'I know. It is a fairy tale.' Warmth spread through me just thinking about Haresh, and I followed Suhana's instructions, releasing subtle fragrances into the kitchen.

'Will you stay long? Yes, now rinse the lentils, and add the ghee to the pan.' Suhana turned the lever on the Calor gas canister and lit the burner with a match. 'Now the spices.'

The freshly crushed cardamom and coriander seeds gave off a smell as fragrant as any perfume. Whole mustard seeds spat when I tossed them into the ghee. Suhana opened the lid of a tin box, revealing a patchwork of colour in square compartments, all housing ground spices. Yellow turmeric, red chili powder, donkey brown masala. She spooned in a little of each, adding chopped onion and green chilies into the pot.

'Two weeks.' I turned on the tap, stuck the tray of lentils under the gentle flow, swooshing them with my hand, and draining off the water now and again, the way Dolly had shown me.

'Only two weeks? And then? Stir the spices, you don't want to burn them. Now, a spoonful of water, just for tempering.'

'I don't know.' Sadness pinched at the edges of my happiness, but I wouldn't let it invade. 'I don't know.'

Within thirty minutes I had created two delicious dishes under Suhana's guidance. She nipped out to get some roti from the man on the corner of the road outside the chawl.

In the bathroom, I combed my hair, ready to plait it, and a watery feeling washed over me. My stomach flittered and I felt otherworldly as if I was about to faint. My hands on the basin steadied me, and I looked in the mirror, noting the freckles on my nose, the tiny gold nose stud, and the olive-green colour of my eyes. It had been a long while since I'd looked into a mirror and liked what I saw.

'Darling? Mari?' Haresh's deep voice brought a smile to my

lips, and I closed the bathroom door behind me, stepping into the kitchen.

'Hi.' I went into his arms, and he kissed me, his mouth warm and slow. His hands ran down my back, and he grabbed my bum.

'I missed you. Can't wait for afternoon sleep time.' Haresh laughed as I batted his arm. 'I need to go back to the office for some hours later on. But I'll be free all day tomorrow.'

I ran my finger gently across the scar above his eyebrow. 'Did it hurt when they took them out?'

'No,' Haresh kissed me again.

Suhana cleared her throat, and we jumped apart. 'You need to be careful. The neighbours might see.' She placed the hot roti on the worktop, unwrapped them from the newspaper. 'Can we go to Chowpatti tomorrow? I want to see the sea.'

'Anything you want, sister. Here.' Haresh lifted a large package from beside the door, hefted it onto the sofa. I sat next to it, happy to see Suhana's wide smile. 'I bought six saris for you. And three shalwar kameez. All dupattas and choli, underskirts, everything is there. Three pairs of *chapal*, sandals also.'

Suhana beamed at him, sat on the floor, and ripped open the brown paper parcel. 'Oh, thank you, brother.' Colour spilled everywhere; red and pink, green and yellow, navy and mustard, floral patterns, and subtle prints. Some were embellished with embroidery, others were plain cotton. 'I love them all.'

Covering her face with her hands, her shoulders shook. Haresh crouched beside her, his hand on her arm.

'What is it?' He glanced at me, throwing out a hand in a questioning gesture. I shook my head, shrugging. 'Sister?'

'I can't believe it's over... all that time, I was so lonely. Bhavna and the other widows were the same. Mostly, we tried to take care of each other, but there were arguments and some jealousy. Like when Muddy bought me a new white sari.'

Haresh stood and paced the room, his hands on his hips. 'Don't talk about that time.' Suhana and I looked at him, startled by his harsh tone. 'Sorry. Please forget all that has happened.

Just focus on this new life you are starting, here in Bombay. It's better, theek hai.'

Suhana wiped her eyes with her pallu. 'Yes, look, not even one white sari here. And the sari you gave me, Mari, will be my favourite for a long time. The day I left Keshnagar, wearing this,' she pointed to herself, 'I felt like a different girl. A free girl.'

Haresh smiled at me and picked up another package from beside the door. 'And this one is for you.' He handed it to me. 'I want to see you in a sari, Maharani.'

Opening the package, I gasped. I stood, draping the length of sea-green fabric over my arm, the silk cool against my skin. The edges had a thick border of heavy, beaded embroidery in pale gold and silver, with a darker teal running through it. The pallu was a work of art; eighteen inches of elaborate paisley design. It weighed a ton, and I knew it was expensive.

'No, Haresh.' I spoke quietly. 'Give this to Suhana. I'll take a cotton one.' I looked at her, surrounded by fabric, busy matching shalwar to dupattas. 'It's too much.'

'It's special, Benares silk.' He moved a strand of my hair behind my ear. 'Nothing else could do for you.'

'It's stunning, but let Suhana have it.'

'Mari, I can't take that one,' said Suhana, her eyes moist. 'It's a wedding sari.'

Sunday afternoon at Chowpatty Beach was a carnival of noise and humanity. What seemed like thousands of people crowded along Marine Drive and the beach itself. They stood in groups, chatting and laughing, or sat together on the sand. At the water's edge, children chased waves, their screams and yells lost against the backdrop of music and chatter.

Suhana and I walked either side of Haresh along the seafront in the cool of the cloudy, late afternoon. The sky was grey, although the rain held off, and the horizon blurred into the sea.

Cars honked, vying for parking spaces, and throngs of people milled in every direction, talking and laughing. A group of teenaged boys followed us, each one saying '*hello*' over and over again, until Haresh said something to them, and they sauntered off in another direction.

Chowpatty was made up of pockets of industry everywhere you looked; boys collected parking money from drivers wanting to park opposite the sea; at the traffic lights, men selling small bottles of water walked between the cars; makeshift stalls sold small plastic toys; and a boy collected money from onlookers as a tiny girl walked a tightrope. Food stalls lined the side of the road, and others were being set up on the beach itself. The smell of fried spicy food invaded every breath.

'Hungry?' Haresh asked, his hand under my elbow.

'Always,' I replied, and Suhana nodded.

'I can't believe I am here, at Chowpatty, with my brother and my didi,' Suhana darted in front of Haresh and held onto my arm.

Suhana called me '*didi*', which meant *elder sister*.

'And tomorrow you start work,' Haresh said, smiling. 'The past is a long time ago.'

'Thank God,' I said, my stomach lurching at the thought of it. I pushed my hair back, my hand shaking. Would I ever stop having such physical reactions to horrible memories?

'Did you try *vada pav*?' he said. 'Shall we?' He gestured to a shack across the road, and we crossed easily when the cars stopped at the red traffic light.

The roadside stall was busy. To the side, two men sat on low stools flattening balls of spiced mashed potato, dipping them in batter, and deep-frying them. Over a second cauldron, a man dripped a handful of liquid batter which formed short wormlike shapes as it hit the hot oil. At the counter, another two men served customers. One of them slit open a soft bap bun and sloshed on green chutney and some finely sliced red onion. He handed it to the other man who put a mashed potato fritter into the bun, slathered it with red chutney, and piled on a handful of crispy batter strips.

'Extra chili for me,' Suhana said.

Watching her tuck into the vada pav was joyful. After three

years of plain food, everything must have been an explosion of taste for her. She closed her eyes, and the expression on her face made me smile, and I nudged Haresh.

'Sister, shall I get you one more?' She nodded, her mouth still full. 'And you, my darling?'

'No. I'm fine.' I watched a little girl of no more than four or five dodge between the unmoving cars at the traffic lights. Holding up a handful of jasmine garlands, she went from driver's side to passenger's, trying to sell them. 'Haresh, I'm going to buy those...that child needs to get off the road.'

Haresh put his hand on my arm. 'Don't. The money won't stay with her. She'll be part of a gang of street beggars, and somewhere, someone is sending the children out to get what they can.'

'But she's...' I wanted to say "*a baby, not much older than your daughter,*" but I stopped myself. My eyes filled, and I blinked back the tears.

'Whoever is running the gang makes the money. It's hard to understand, I know. Let's buy her a vada pav instead.'

Haresh bought another two, and I took one to the little girl. She looked up at me, huge eyes in a dirty face. She placed her jasmine garlands on the pavement, and crouched down beside them, devouring the vada pav. Everything in me wanted to pick her up and take her home. I looked over my shoulder at Haresh. By the expression on his face, I knew he was thinking the same as I was, and about his daughter, Tara.

Once Suhana had finished eating, we carried our shoes and walked onto the beach itself. I folded my arms, feeling the refreshing breeze off the Arabian Sea, and the cool sand under my feet. The strange watery sensation I'd had the day before washed over me again, making me feel dreamlike. I was breathless for a minute or so.

'Maybe we'll see the sunset,' Suhana said. 'Mari-didi?' She turned, looking back up the beach at me.

'What is it, darling? Why are you not coming?' Haresh frowned, walking back towards me.

'Just admiring the view,' I lied, not realising that I had stopped walking. Haresh had said the shock of Kiran's shooting would wear off, and he was right, but it was taking its time.

Haresh stood close, and we walked to the edge of the sea, just as the clouds parted and the orange sun shone through. Crowds of people paddled in the sea, although no one swam. Kids squealed and ran into the water until it reached their knees, and then ran out again. The waves lapped gently, and the seagulls whirled overhead, crying mournfully. Suhana lifted the hem of her peach-coloured sari and ran along the sand, her long plait bouncing between her shoulders.

'Shall we?' Haresh said. We walked along the water's edge, the cold water lapping over my toes. I stopped for a moment to roll up the legs of my shalwar. 'I am thinking.' Haresh stopped and turned to face me. 'You can go to Nepal, get your new visa, and then come back. Here. To me.'

'For six months?' I said, stepping close to him. 'With you?'

'You love me, don't you?' He took my hand, kissed my fingers quickly, before I snatched my hand away, looking around us. I nodded. I reached up to touch his cheek just where his beard finished. 'So, give me your answer. Will you stay?'

Looking at him then, I knew we were bonded by something unseen, something unknown.

'I want to, but then what happens in another six months, when my visa runs out again?' A wave of cool water hit my shins, and another my knees.

'Let's not worry about that now. I am making some plans.' Smiling, he nudged me with his arm. 'But first, go to Nepal, and then come home to me. Yes?'

'Yes,' I said. 'I'll come back to you.'

Lifting me, he swung me around, and I squealed, scared that he'd drop me into the cold seawater, or that a policeman would appear and arrest us. Haresh laughed and put me down on the sand. Suhana ran towards us and flopped next to me, breathless

'Such good air here, isn't it? I love this place,' she said.

With Haresh on one side of me, discreetly holding my hand, and Suhana's arm linked through mine on the other, we sat watching the sun descend behind the built-up skyline of Bombay at the end of the bay. My heart was so full, I could have cried. It had been such a long time since I'd felt truly loved and wanted, and as if I had family.

Suhana was up the next morning at dawn, sweeping a broom through the apartment, and rattling around in the kitchen. It was her first day in her new job, and I guessed she was excited. I hadn't slept well, and I padded, yawning into the kitchen in my green kurta, my anklet tinkling as I walked. The air smelt of sandalwood, and three incense sticks still burned in front of a little statue of Shiva on a small shelf by the door.

'No need for to you get up, Mari-didi. Please, I'm sorry to have disturbed you. I've made paratha, and there are peas and mushroom for your lunch.' She clipped the handle of her three-tiered *tiffin* lunch box closed. 'I'll take mine to school with me. And here, pakoda for breakfast.'

'You don't have to do all this. I can cook the few dishes Dolly Auntie taught me. And those I learned from you.'

'I am enjoying cooking tasty food, it's not hard work. Anyway, pakoda are from outside.' She smiled, putting her tiffin into a thermal carrier.

'Are you excited?' I asked, pouring chai into a glass. The liquid was hot and sweet, and I loved the cardamom she'd laced it with. 'Or a bit nervous?'

'Both. I know I am lucky. When I think of my life before…I am scared somehow it will follow me here.' She bit her lip.

'No one will ever know.' I lowered my voice, not wanting Haresh to hear. 'Kiran, Muddy, none of it matters now. This is the first day of the rest of your life. You are free, Suhana.'

Haresh stuck his dishevelled head round the bedroom door. 'Ek minute, let me dress.'

Suhana caught my eye. I looked away, blushing.

'So, good luck today. I hope you love them all as much as they will love you,' Haresh said, pulling his kurta down over his lungi, and running his fingers through his hair. 'I'm proud of you, sister.'

'What will you do today?' she said, looking from me to him and back again. We both smiled. 'Oh, forget I asked. Okay, see you later.'

Haresh stood at the front door, and once Suhana had gone, he bolted it shut.

'I want today to be just you and I, darling. Like at Dolly Auntie's.' I stood in the doorway to his room, and he took a bedsheet from the cupboard and both pillows from the bed. 'Come.'

'Don't you need to go to work?' I stood, still leaning against the doorframe.

'They can call me if they need to. But I want to stay at home with you.'

On the balcony, Haresh tucked the sheet around the mattress and pulled the curtain across. He sat, propping the pillows behind him, and gestured for me to join him. The phone rang, and he groaned, jumping up and rushing to answer it.

Changing into a choli, I pulled on some cotton shalwar and sat on the balcony, popping my Fleetwood Mac tape into my Walkman. Pressing the play button, I slipped on the headphones, listening to *'The Chain.'* In Suhana's room, Haresh had his back to me, and his hand movements were as flamboyant as ever, but more jerky than usual, and I wondered if he was arguing with someone. He shook his hair back and turned to me, frowning. I smiled. He didn't. Shifting my position, I removed one earpiece.

'Mari, come.' Haresh beckoned me. I got up off the mattress and came into the room. He held the receiver out to me. 'Sergeant Mudgalkar.'

'Muddy?' I shook my head, raised my hands, and backed away. 'No.'

With his hand over the mouthpiece, Haresh looked at me. 'You must hear what he has to say. I have taken the time to listen to him, and so should you, darling.'

I took the receiver from Haresh. 'Muddy,' I said.

'Thank you for taking my call, Mari,' he said. The line crackled. 'Are you there?'

'I am. Look, I am genuinely sorry that you got shot, but I don't really...'

'Mari. I believe I have behaved very badly. Haresh Chandekar is a good man, and I was wrong to beat him like that. But I was so jealous. It tore my heart to see you with him, and I went a little crazy.'

'You beat him so badly, Muddy, he couldn't walk for four days. I hate you for that.' Haresh touched my arm, and I looked up at him.

'Even though I saved your life?' Static on the line hissed. 'Can't you forgive me? I thought you liked me, that we were friends.'

'We were friends, and that's what makes it all so much worse.' My voice caught, and I cleared my throat. 'And don't forget that you slapped me too, and you tried to touch me.' Haresh closed his eyes, his lips a thin line. 'And Shanti...how can I call you a friend now that I know what you did, Muddy? Why are you calling?'

'There is something in me that is not good. I know that. I wanted to explain and apologise for everything I have done. I have had some time to think lying here in a hospital bed.' The line crackled. 'I have made sure Shanti is provided for. She will work with Kavita at Sharma's house. And I will change my ways, ask God for forgiveness. Haresh has accepted my apology regarding his sister also. Can't you? Please.'

My initial anger softened, and I thought how hard it must have been for him to make the call, to apologise first to Haresh, and then to me. A wave of nausea flushed over me when I thought of his bullet wound, thinking that it so easily could have been me lying in a hospital. I ran my hand across my face, and sat on the edge of the bed.

'Mari?' Haresh raised his eyebrows. I nodded.

'Is your shoulder recovering, Muddy? Is it painful?'

'It will heal, and of course, I am a hero in town for saving the lovely lady.' I laughed. 'I hope you are happy, Mari. With him. I think he is good for you. My own marriage is next month, and when I have a son and he grows up, I will invite you to the wedding.'

'Really?'

'God promise. I'll ring off now, goodbye. Thank you.'

I put the receiver down and looked at Haresh. 'Bloody hell, I didn't expect that.'

'That was taking some guts. But I accepted his apology in the end because he has admitted his fault. I truly hope he can change, but people rarely do, especially when they are in a position of power.' He stood close, and I breathed in the smell of him. 'Maharani.'

'But Muddy's got away with his involvement in it all, Haresh. He used those girls, passed them to Kiran, who sold them to brothels. Maybe there were more than just Shanti and Suhana.' I gasped. 'Oh God. I think he shot Kiran first.'

'You may be correct. With Kiran dead, there is no way Muddy's involvement could be revealed. And Sharma is powerful, so the whole thing goes away.'

'It's not right,' I said. 'Isn't there something we can do?'

'Corruption is rife in this country. I think we should be focusing on the fact that we have Suhana here. Let Mudgalkar make his peace with himself and his God.'

How could I have been friends with someone like Muddy? God, I'd even contemplated sleeping with him. And in the prison cell, would Muddy have actually raped me if the younger officer hadn't stopped him? Shuddering, I went into the kitchen. After putting some pakoda onto a tray, and pouring two glasses of chai, I followed Haresh onto the balcony, and we sat, the breakfast tray between us.

'I'm sorry I disturbed your sleep again last night, Haresh.' I bit into a potato and onion pakoda, the carraway seeds giving it a hint of aniseed.

'No, no. I'm glad I was there to wake you and to…' he raised his eyebrow, smiling, 'shall we say, comfort you, afterwards. But, tell me, what is this nightmare you have? How did you get that scar?'

'It's a long story.'

'There is always time to listen.'

'Do you remember the first day we met, and I told you my best friend had been killed?' He nodded, his mouth full of pakoda. 'Kate and I taught English in Japan.' I sipped my chai, placing the glass back onto the tray. 'It was really restrictive; we were watched all the time, and they wouldn't let us have our passports back either.'

'That happens also with Indians who go to Dubai or Saudi to work; the passports are returned only at the end of the contract.'

I nodded. 'We didn't really think it was too much of an issue, except that we wanted to leave before our contract ended. Anyway, there was this guy,' I bit my lip, wondering what he'd think. 'and he and I…'

'You were not my first, Mari. Just as I was not yours.' Haresh reached across and touched my face. 'You can tell me.'

Shifting my position, I crossed my legs, adjusting the fabric of my shalwar. I told him the whole story; all the details of how Kate got into trouble with the yakuza, how we were threatened, and how one night she didn't come home. My hand shook as I twisted my hair. Haresh got up and went into the kitchen. Waiting for him to come back, I took deep breaths, trying to steady my heartbeat. Why was it so hard to tell him?

I knocked back the water Haresh gave me. 'I asked for help when she went missing, but…' I pressed the heels of my hands into my eyes. Haresh moved across the mattress, pulled me into his arms.

'Darling.' He stroked my hair, held me while I cried.

I sat straight, wiping my eyes. 'No one believed me, no one would help me. And I hesitated, I didn't know what to do.'

'What could you do?' Haresh sat next to me, his arm around my shoulders.

I shook my head, my face wet. 'When they found her, it was too late. She was dead.'

'It's not your fault. You are right to mourn for your friend, but not to be blaming yourself.'

'I still have regret.'

'*Malaal,* it's the Urdu word for regret, remorse. Malaal is something everyone has, otherwise, you cannot have lived. And something needs to happen for something else to happen. Each one of our stories is written; we all have our own fate.' He leaned across and kissed my lips. 'And that is the nightmare?'

'I was attacked.' Haresh tutted as he traced his fingers along my scar. 'The nightmare is usually about that. But the last few nights Kiran and his gun get mixed up in it. But there's always so much blood.' I stood, taking his hand, and tried to pull him up. 'Come with me. Come to bed.'

'That isn't the answer, Mari.'

There was a knock on the front door. Haresh shook his head, and sighing, went to the front door and opened it.

'Hi, Manu, how are you?' A burst of Hindi preceded the door closing. 'Mari, my phone isn't working again.'

'It worked half an hour ago,' I said.

'I know, it is driving me pagal. Crazy. The office is trying to contact me, so they called Manu.' Haresh stood in the doorway. 'Bloody phone. Get dressed, you can come with me.'

'I'll stay here. I could do with some sleep.' I walked towards him, and kissed him. His mouth was hot on mine, his hands running down my back. I reached down wanting to untie his lungi, but he stepped back, laughing.

'Be two minutes late,' I said.

'You stay and rest. I'll go and come, although it might take some time. A shipment we sent has not arrived, and I need to trace what's happened to it.'

When he'd gone, I bolted the doors closed, and showered. I switched the fan off in the bedroom and straightened the sheets. Taking the breakfast tray back into the kitchen, I washed the glasses and put the pakoda under a mesh basket to keep off any insects.

Transferring the Fleetwood Mac tape from my Walkman into the stereo, I pressed the play button. *'Dreams'* filled the room. I walked out onto the balcony, and moved the curtain back, leaning on the railing. The space below was empty; no children playing cricket or marbles like usual. Where had they all gone? I lay on the mattress and pulled one of the pillows under my head. After everything that had happened, I was in a Bombay chawl, with Haresh Chandekar. I stretched like a cat, memories of his mouth and touch making me smile. And all because of a chance meeting with a girl in a white sari.

Time drifted, and thirst woke me. In the kitchen, I pumped some water from the demijohn, and walked back into the living room with the glass in my hand. Placing it next to the cricket trophies on the cabinet, I pulled out the slim photo album I'd noticed the first time I'd been there. The red vinyl cover was embossed with an edge of gold, worn off in places. I opened the cover and looked at the photos in their poly pockets. Were the young kids Suhana and Haresh? Looking more closely at the faded pictures, I could tell it was them. Haresh looked kind of goofy, uneasy with his own height, perhaps. Suhana looked sweet in her school uniform, the navy-blue shift dress over a white short-sleeved shirt no different from what I'd seen on the schoolgirls in Keshnagar.

Other photos in the album were of a nice-looking couple, which I presumed were their parents. Haresh certainly had his father's height and straight posture. His mother looked kind, with the same expression that he had in his eyes. How sad that he'd lost them at such an early age. It must have been even worse for Suhana, who was only eight at that time. No wonder Haresh and his sister were so close, that he'd wanted to help her when her husband died.

I flicked over the page and gasped. Photos showed a woman in a heavily embroidered red sari, with a gold chain linking her ornate nose ring to her ear and more heavy gold across her forehead. She was sitting next to Haresh. The brocade of his long cream jacket looked rich, and the mandarin collar was partly obscured by the thick garland of roses and jasmine he wore around his neck. His hair was covered by a red turban, the end of which fanned out stiffly on one side. There were several wedding photos like that, with Haresh and his bride in different poses.

What was she like, really? How bad had it been that she'd taken their child and gone back to her parents? I felt sad for him, that she hadn't been able to love him. But mostly because he had so little contact with his daughter.

I flicked through the rest of the photos. They looked to have been taken at Chowpatty or some other sea-front location. The wife, without her fancy wedding get up, didn't look anything special, but she didn't look unpleasant either. Her nose was slightly crooked; perhaps it had been broken at one time. Peering closely, I noticed she had dark circles under her eyes, but apart from that, there was really nothing to remark on.

The last page had one solitary photo of a baby dressed in pink and white. I guessed she was about three months old. With her thick head of hair, the shape of her face, and her large eyes, she could only be Haresh's daughter. My heart fluttered. His child; his Tara. Looking at that photo, I somehow fell in love with Haresh all over again.

Chapter Twenty-Four

London, 2010

THE PHONE RANG, and I grabbed the receiver, almost knocking my coffee all over my office desk. I had a funny feeling something was going to happen. I hadn't expected Sofia to call me at work, it wasn't something either of my sisters did, so when I recognised her voice, I knew it was for a good reason.

'Have you got your test result? Has the IVF worked?' I said.

'We'll find out tomorrow.'

'Then why are you calling? What's happened?' My mouth went slightly dry.

'Nothing,' Sofia said. 'It's about Mum.'

'I'm not having this conversation again, Sof. Please. I'll call you when I get home tonight, okay?' I relaxed, grateful nothing had happened to any member of our small family.

'I just think –'

'Hanging up now.' I put down the receiver.

Shaking my head, I tried to focus on the email I was writing, ready to submit my presentation to another Probus group in the hope they'd fund our new Ethiopian project. My fingers poised above the keyboard, and I lost my concentration for a moment.

My phone rang again, and I hesitated before picking up the receiver. Angie from Oxfam was calling to see if I'd had an update from our local project manager in Senegal. We'd worked in collaboration with Oxfam on various projects over the years, and they handled the press releases.

'Yes, the run-off from the borehole has been a great success. I'll email you the photos Yusuf sent me. The millet is growing well, and the tomatoes.'

'And the maintenance training?' said Angie. 'I really want to include something about that in our next website update.'

'Two successful training programs, and a team of five who cover the whole network of boreholes for that district.' I tapped my pen on the desk. 'Even better, Yusuf's teaching someone basic bookkeeping so that they can collect the water taxes regularly. Then there'll be a fund for spare parts and petrol to actually power the borehole. Win-win. It's gone really well, and we've come in about on target, although Alan probably won't agree.'

'Excellent. Don't mind my ex-husband, you know what he's like. We're having dinner together tonight, actually. Remind him to be on time will you?'

'I will. It's amazing how you two are still friends, really. Quite inspiring.'

'It was for the kids initially, as you know. We're so much better as friends. Funny, isn't it? We actually like each other now we're not married. And I still fancy the pants of him.'

'Too much info, Angie,' I said.

'Alright. Send me what you want me to include in our press release, say, five hundred words? I'll whittle it down. What are you working on next, Mari?'

'It's a campaign for funding school toilets for a village in Ethiopia. Sixty kids are using two squat loos, and of course, there's no running water.' I smiled my thanks at Julie as she placed a steaming cup of coffee and a chocolate muffin on my desk. She'd been to the hairdresser's at lunchtime, and her hair was now pastel pink.

'Launch date?'

'To be confirmed.'

'Lunch? Next week.'

'Definitely.'

'Five hundred words, Mari. By Friday.'

When my phone rang again less than a minute later, I rolled my eyes and picked up the receiver. 'You forgot to say which day for lunch,' I said.

'Sorry?' said a male voice. 'I'm calling from St Brigid's Hospice. It's about your mother.'

For the first time since we'd learned that the latest version of Mum's cancer was terminal, I doubted myself. If she really was in the last stages of her bitter, resentful life, would it be a good thing if I did go and see her? Sipping my half-cold coffee, I made a face. No. She could ask to see me as much as she liked, I wouldn't give her the satisfaction of easing her conscience before she met her God. He may forgive her for being an absolute bitch to me, but I couldn't. I wondered if I'd run out of forgiveness in the same way that doctors run out of compassion. I'd used up a fair share of my forgiveness quota over the years, but never quite achieved it with my mother.

Even Harry managed it, which surprised me after all the terrible things she'd said to him. The names she called him were bad enough, but how he could forgive her for the things she said about me? Family was everything, Harry said, and we were all he had. That pinched my heart. He had more of a relationship with my mother than he did with his own father.

It was almost five o'clock when I arrived. I'd told them I'd be there at five-thirty, but London traffic was never predictable, especially during afternoon rush-hour. The place was easy enough to find; there'd been signage all the way from the M4. Flicking the left indicator, I turned my VW Beetle into the car park and found a space at the far end, near a bank of trees that were already changing colour. Although it was only the end of September, the light had changed, and autumn had well and truly pushed summer out of the way. I sat for a moment, trying to calm my breath, and get myself into the right headspace. Grabbing my bag, I got out of the car.

The modern two-storey building looked welcoming enough, with yellow curtains at each window, and lots of shrubbery around the entrance. It was my imagination, I was sure, but I could feel my mother's disdain, her negativity towards me emanating from the brickwork. Slowly I walked towards the entrance, dread dragging at the heels of my boots, and I stopped halfway across the car park. The sky was grey, and woodsmoke filled the air. Turning, I ran back to my car, fumbling with the zapper to open to door. Inside, I gripped the top of the steering wheel and leaned my forehead on the back of my hands. No. Just no. There was too much hurt, too much resentment over her rejection of me to ever make it right. Jabbing the key into the ignition, I drove towards the exit.

My phone rang, and I braked, pulling into another parking space. It was Sofia.

'Mari. Will and I are on speaker phone, and we have some news.' She sounded breathy, childlike. I knew what she was calling to tell me, but I waited, wanting her to have the pleasure of saying the words.

'Won the lotto?' Tears threatened, and I didn't want her to hear them in my voice, so I forced a laugh.

'We are having a baby.' Will and Sofia spoke together.

'I couldn't wait to tell you, Mari.' Sofia was crying. 'We're so excited. And terrified.'

'That's so wonderful,' I said. 'I'm happy for you, darling. So happy for you both.' I sniffed, blinking the tears back.

'It's early days, but it's looking good. We're going to be parents,' said Will.

'I'm going to have A Bump,' Sofia said.

'So, when's your due date?' I asked

'May twenty-seventh, which is Harry's birthday. And it might be early, or late. And if it's late, it might come on Elena's birthday, June first. Doesn't really matter, as long as it gets past seven months.'

'Sof, whenever they're born, it'll be wonderful.'

'They?'

'Gut feeling, it's twins. You'll have A Twin Bump.'

'Oh, I hope you are right. Look, Stel wants a big celebration lunch at hers this Sunday. You and Harry can make it, right?'

'Definitely. See you there, Mamacita.'

In the rear-view mirror, I looked at the hospice, with its cheery curtains. Heady with the good news, I thought I could handle seeing my mother. I was there, so I might as well see it through. Taking a deep breath, I licked my finger and wiped the teary mascara from under my eyes.

Walking towards the entrance, I pulled my shoulders back and shook out my hair. If I went in with no expectations, I wouldn't be disappointed. If I went in determined not to let her get to me, then I was well prepared, and that was something I needed to be.

Inside the hospice, every step I took felt heavier as I followed the nurse to a room on the second floor. The heat was stifling, and I shrugged off my coat, folded it over my arm.

'Your mother's awake at the moment, so you've timed your visit well,' the nurse said. 'Although she is due some medication in around thirty minutes, so she'll be dozy after that.'

I nodded, forcing a smile to my lips. 'Thanks. I won't be staying that long.'

The nurse opened the door for me, and I stepped inside the room. That frail, scrawny woman laying in the bed wasn't my mother. That wasn't the formidable Anna Garcia Randall who had tormented my whole life. With a deep breath, I stood tall, knowing if pity took over my senses, I'd be lost. The nurse left, closing the door behind her. My mother looked at me, and I saw nothing soft in her eyes, nothing loving or kind, and I wondered why she wanted to see me.

'Marianna,' she said. 'You took your time coming.'

Shaking my head, I could have kicked myself for even being there. '*Hi, Mari. Nice of you to come, Mari,*' I said. 'No? Well, I'm here now. Why did you want to see me?'

'I have things I need to say.' Mum's Spanish accent had never mellowed, despite the fifty years she'd lived away from Madrid. 'Give me that courtesy, please.' She shifted slightly on her pillows, moved her head to look at me. 'Sit, will you.'

A high-backed floral armchair covered with a crocheted blanket had been placed at an angle to the bed. Dropping my coat over the back of it, I moved it further away and perched on the edge. My bag was on my lap, and my fingers gripped it. 'Okay, what do you want to say?'

'You are not my child.'

'Yes, you told me that repeatedly when Elena died. I can't listen to that again.' I stood, ready to leave. 'If you are going to go over the past, and call me evil, cursed, a murderer, and a whore, etc…don't bother. I'd rather you don't say anything at all.'

'Will you listen? I did not give birth to you.' She slapped her veiny hand on the bed, the movement shaking the IV tube and the bag of fluid on the stand. 'That is what I mean to tell you.'

My jaw dropped open. 'What?'

'I am not your mother.' I placed my bag on the chair. 'Did you never wonder why you are all reddish hair, green eyes, and white skin, but your sisters are dark?'

I shook my head. 'Dad was English, I never thought…You're not my mother?' Shock rippled through me, and I rubbed my hand over my mouth. The room was so hot, sweat trickled down my back. 'So, you adopted me?'

'In a way, yes.' She coughed, waved her hand towards the water jug on the cabinet.

'In a way? What does that mean?' Half filling the plastic beaker with water, I held it out to her, but she didn't take it. I placed it on the cabinet.

'I was four months pregnant,' she said. 'We took the ferry to Santander, and drove to Madrid to see your grandparents. But a few weeks later, on the way back, I lost the baby. We stayed in Spain for months after, until I felt ready to return to London.'

'Oh God, that's awful.' I sat in the chair, leaning forwards, my heart softening. 'I'm so sorry. When was this?'

'Listen. I am telling you. Your father confessed to having an affair since before we were married. An Irish girl. He was always like that; he was too charming not to be a womaniser.'

'I think I knew. When I was about ten, I remember you talking to Uncle Saturnino. A woman called Audrey.'

'One of many, Marianna. Can I speak now?' Her eyebrows raised in that annoyed mother kind of way. I nodded. 'This Dublin girl, Jessie, was pregnant and couldn't keep you. She was due a little earlier than I would have been, and after she had you, she didn't register your birth. Nobody in England knew I lost our baby, we'd come back just a few weeks before you were born, and your father told everyone I had a home birth. Then we took you from Jessie, and registered you as our own. Only my family knew the truth.'

'Wait...hang on.' Raising my hands, I took a deep breath. 'So, Dad was my father?'

'Yes. I did not want to raise you as my own, but I loved your father, so I agreed. And then my darling girl, my Elena was born, it was easier to understand that I had no maternal love for you.'

'She was always your favourite, but it was because she was yours and I wasn't?' I wiped my nose on a tissue I found in my bag, and dabbed my eyes. 'That's why you hated me. Why was I never told?'

She shrugged. 'What we did was illegal. Your father wouldn't hear of telling you, didn't want you to think badly of him. You know he adored you. Do you understand now why I could not stand the sight of you? Especially after Elena died.'

'It was an accident, everyone knows that, except you. And thirty years on, you still... shit.' I tilted my head back looking at the ceiling. 'Why are you telling me that you are not my mother now?' *You bitch. You fucking witch. Why now?*

'Because none of it is your fault. It was an accident, yes, an accident. I accepted that years ago, and I wanted to talk to you when you came back from all that travelling in Asia. I was going to tell you that I didn't blame you, and try to be at least friends with you.'

I laughed in disbelief. 'So why didn't you?'

'You know why. Coming back like that. The shame…'

'My God.' My fists uncurled, and I breathed out, wiping my eyes. 'Uncle Saturnino knew, didn't he? That you aren't my mother? That's why he was always there for me.'

'My brother did love you very much. He saw things in you that I couldn't. And when you came back from India… Huh, you are not even his blood and he left you his house for God's sake. And all that money.' She coughed. 'It should have all been Stella's and Sofia's. And then you took them away from me.'

'I didn't,' I sighed. 'I wanted to share Uncle Saturnino's house with them. It was only right they had their share, and they wanted to move in with me. They were eighteen, old enough to decide for themselves. You can't blame me for that. Do they know about Jessie?' Mum shook her head. 'All the years I beat myself up because I had such a strained relationship with you, and you're not even my mother.' I threw my hands up in the air. 'I was content not having anything to do with you, relieved not to have any contact with you. I still don't understand why you are telling me all this now?'

'Because I did forgive you for Elena. But I couldn't forgive myself for hating you. My priest helped me understand, but it was too late.'

'Your priest?' I said. Shame she couldn't work it out for herself.

'I'm also telling you because it's right that you should know everything, in case you want to find your real mother. All I know is she was seventeen and from Dublin.'

My eyes streamed. 'Thank you, I appreciate that. I wish you'd done it sooner though, Mum. We could have avoided all this animosity.' I took a deep breath, and shook my head, moved the chair closer to the bed. I placed my hand gently over hers. 'I tried, Mum. For years, I tried to make the peace, but you always blocked me. You were so vicious, so I stopped trying in the end.'

'I shouldn't have blamed you for your father's...' She closed her eyes, shifted her shoulders. 'But I spent years wishing I did not agree to raising you.'

'That's why it wasn't easy living under your roof. But at least I know why now.'

She sighed. 'You're no picnic either, you know. I'm amazed Harry hasn't moved out. What's he doing with his life anyway? IT they call it, huh. Playing with computers all day, what kind of job is that?'

Leaning back in the chair, I glared at her, letting go of her hand. 'Don't criticise Harry.'

'The way he talks, I don't think he's happy living with you.'

'Don't you dare. You've never accepted him. He was my choice, Mum. Mine. And you treated him like shit for twenty-two years. Harry's kind; that's why he visits you. He comes because I won't, and because he feels sorry for you. And I know damn well he doesn't complain about me.' I twisted my hair, my hand shaking. 'Why do you always have to poison everything?'

'I've said what I wanted to. Now you know. I'm sorry I wasn't a better mother to you. I admit it; I just couldn't like you.' She laughed. 'Marianna, you made me jealous. Your father adored you, and I hated you more for that. He saw his Irish girl in you... and so did I. There are probably more half-brothers and sisters all over the place. Your father –'

'Shut up.' I stood, my chin trembling. 'Don't you dare bad mouth my Dad.' Breathing deeply, I pulled my shoulders back. 'I don't care what his relationship with you was like, he was always a good father to me. Except when you threw me out, but he and I worked that out when I came back from India. Okay, so thank you for raising me as best you could for seventeen years. I'm sorry you hated me.' I walked to the door. 'And I'm glad I know why because it makes me understand that it's actually your problem.'

'Always have to have the last word...' Her words faded as I left the room.

I half-walked, half-ran out of the building, and when I was inside the sanctuary of my car, I finally breathed out. My heart hammered, and with a shaky hand I tried to put the key into the ignition, and failed. Thumping the steering-wheel with both hands, I fought back a scream. I brushed the tears away and sat back in the seat, waiting for my breath to steady.

How could I not have known? Mum was right; I was so very different to my Spanish-looking sisters. Reaching under the passenger seat, my fingers searched for a bottle of water. I took a few swigs, and screwed the cap back on. Calmness took a while to wash over me, and eventually my shoulders dropped. Mum never let Dad forget his affair, and how could she when I was the living reminder of it. The only thing that mattered was that I knew why my mother had struggled with me, and somehow, I didn't blame her. The Irish girl, Jessie, had given me up through circumstance or convenience. Maybe one day she'd come looking for me, but I had no desire to go looking for her.

Chapter Twenty-Five
यात्रा

Bombay, September 1986

THERE HADN'T BEEN any rain for the last few days, so I washed two of my shalwar in a bucket in the bathroom, and hung them to dry on the balcony.

'Let me send them with my things to the *dhobi-wallah*, the washerman,' said Haresh. 'They'll be back in two days. And on the other side of the chawl, the seamstress will iron everything for you.'

'I don't mind.' I stepped into Suhana's room, dodging his embrace and grabbing a few kurtas to wash. 'Anyway, it gives me something to do this afternoon while you're at your office.'

'Ask Suhana to take you for kulfi when she gets back from school.' He grabbed me from behind, nuzzling my neck.

'Ah, kulfi. Oh, yes, I'd love kulfi.' My hands covered his on my waist, and I turned. 'But she likes to rest when she gets back. Like the rest of the chawl. It's the only time it's quiet...every afternoon from about three until five; everyone sleeps.'

'Then go at five, when she wakes.' He smiled.

'Do they have rose and cardamom, like in Kesh–'

'I think not. I know someone close by who has a *mithai* shop, a sweet shop. He is selling all the usual sweets; *gulab jamun, helva, imarti, laddu*. He's from Rajasthan, and sometimes he has *gulkand phirni*. It's made with roses. And cardamom.'

My eyes closed as he kissed me, but I pulled away quickly, rubbing my face where his beard has itched my skin. 'Barber today? It grows so quickly.' I gently pulled at the hair on his face. 'Off you go, I need to finish my washing.'

'How many days left now, Mari?' His eyes were serious. 'When must you leave?'

'Three or four days. That'll give me plenty of time to get to the border. Do you think your train station friend -?'

'I will ask him today. He will know the best way by train. But won't you fly to Nepal?'

'I'm coming back, Haresh. Leaving one or two days earlier won't matter.'

'And then?' He pushed my hair away from my face. 'How long will I be without you?' His mouth on my neck sent shivers through me.

'Maybe a month.' Leaning his forehead against mine, he sighed. 'Haresh, you know the main reason I came to India was to go to McLeod Ganj.'

He nodded, kissed me briefly. 'I know. I will leave now, I don't want to be getting late. I'll arrange everything for you, okay?' Out on the walkway, he winked at me through the kitchen window. 'See you later.'

I waved and went into the bathroom. Crouching by the bucket of sudsy water, I dunked my kurta into it. Swirling it around, I caught the bubbles, pulled the fabric out of the bucket, and pounded it on the bathroom floor. The ezan called from the masjid, and I stopped to listen. The call to prayer didn't make me think specifically of God, but it did make me reflective. All I could think of was one word; happiness. And belief that Haresh and I really could build a life together.

Smiling, I wrung out one kurta and then the other, swilled the floor with the soapy water from the bucket, and refilled it with clean water. After I'd rinsed the clothes, I stood, and the room spun. I leaned one hand against the wall. Shaking my head, I walked towards the balcony, the wet clothes dripping water on the tiled floor.

My hands stopped midway to the washing line, the water snaking down my arms. A cold feeling flowed over me. Kurtas hung on the line, I stepped to the other end of the balcony and dropped onto the mattress. A flash of intuition left me breathless for a moment. As much as I wanted to stay, and as much as Haresh wanted me to, he was wrong; us being together wasn't written. Once I left the chawl, I knew that I wouldn't come back.

'Mari?,' Leyra called from the open front door. Her hair was loose and reached her hips. 'Come downstairs, and drink chai. Don't stay alone here.'

Standing, I wiped my eyes. 'Leyra, I'm fine. Thank you. I need to wash all my clothes.'

'Yaar, bring them.' She slipped off her sandals and walked into the apartment, heading straight for Haresh's bedroom. 'Shall we do them together at the standpipe? Then we'll drink chai. I'll send for pakoda. Or samosa, yes?'

'My clothes are in Suhana's room,' I said coolly. 'I'll get them.'

Leyra took the bag of washing powder, and I followed her downstairs, my arms full of clothing. At the standpipe, two other neighbours joined us. Maybe the ladies had nothing else to do, but I suspected they were curious about me. Hoisting up their saris, they crouched down, sloshing water over one piece of clothing, then another, rubbing them with washing powder, and slapping them against the paving stones.

'We all see the way Haresh looks at you,' Leyra said. 'Nice he is in love with his sister's best friend, nah.' The others smiled.

'Is it?' I said. 'Well, he's so handsome, I expect there are lots of girlfriends in Bombay, probably in Poona too.'

'My husband, Manu, is Bhupinder's cousin, and we heard that Haresh was involved with a woman for a while. Last year.' Leyra dragged her hair back from her face, plaiting it out of the way. 'They were seen everywhere together; Chowpatty, various places. Sometimes he did not come home at night, so he must have been sleeping somewhere with her.'

Ridiculously, jealousy whipped through me, and I had to relax my face and force a smile. 'You all know everything about each other in the chawl?'

'Of course. We're like one big family.' Leyra smiled, gently wringing out my aqua lehenga. 'Sometimes not so happy. But we can't live so close to each other, and not hear what goes on in another apartment.' The way Leyra looked at me made me blush. 'Also, we love to gossip.' The ladies laughed, one of them patting my arm.

Twisting and rinsing, we washed my clothes in less than ten minutes. The shade shifted as the sun moved overhead, and we draped wet kurtas and shalwar over the benches in the courtyard, the colours vibrant in the bright light.

'I'll go and buy us some snacks. What would you like, ladies, sweets or savories?' I said, heading towards the staircase to go and get my purse, and to close the apartment doors.

'Samosa? Is that alright...nice to drink sweet chai with spicy samosa,' said Leyra.

'I know, I love chai and samosa,' I said.

'I'll come with you. Show you a top-class place to buy them.'

Five minutes later, Leyra and I walked along the street outside the chawl, heading towards a row of hole-in-the-wall shops. I bought freshly fried samosas, and some bright orange jalebis. The smell of the spiralled, syrup-covered sweetness made my mouth water.

'Shall we get anything else, Leyra?' I said. 'And while we're here, do you know where I can get some kulfi? I'm craving kulfi.'

'Take that road, and I think the kulfi place is three blocks down. But we'll go home now, Priya Auntie will have the chai ready.' Leyra looked at me sideways. 'You and Haresh, I hope you don't mind me saying...but he has lived here for three years, and I have never seen him so happy.'

'Leyra, he's just happy his sister left her brute of a husband, that's all.' My face flushed, partly at the lie about Suhana, and it was hard not to smile.

'Don't pretend, there's no need. Not even during Ganapati or Diwali festivals is he so happy like now. Diwali is coming at the end of next month. It's the best festival. Will you still be here?'

'I'm leaving soon, hence all the clothes washing, but I could be back for that.' My dream woke, springing to life with hope and possibility, pushing the feeling I'd had on the balcony away. 'Actually, that would be wonderful to experience…especially here…'

'Yes, you should see the chawl during Diwali; lights everywhere, all the balconies, and the walkways, the staircases.' She waved her hand. 'And we usually have music, food, a great celebration in the courtyard. We all make a contribution so that we can all enjoy.'

'Sounds lovely. I'll try and get back here for that.' Smiling, I glanced at her. 'Does everyone know about me and Haresh?'

'No. I was outside one morning, coming back with roti, and you two were on the balcony. The curtain was flapping, and I saw you together. He cuddled you.' She tapped the side of her nose. 'I thought about it, and about how he looks so happy these days, and also that you are alone together after his sister goes to her work. And how the apartment doors are always closed during that time.'

'I'm sorry if you think I don't respect your culture,' I said, shifting the packet of samosa from one hand to the other. 'But –'

Leyra raised her hand. 'If the whole chawl didn't think well of Haresh, it would be different. You would have been cast out for being immoral by now. But nobody knows for sure really. It's all speculation about you and him. The girl, Suhana is living here also, and everyone knows you are her friend. And we all love her. Such a kind, lovely girl. Manu thinks she should divorce, and get married to someone else, but I say, let her have her freedom.'

'I didn't know Hindus could divorce,' I said. My mind was racing and I bit my lip. What was the point in asking? Haresh hadn't said he'd divorce his wife.

'Divorce happens. My sister divorced her husband. He was a bad sort, and so weighing it all up, they divorced. My mother was against it, saying that to end a marriage would affect my sister's karma, but she argued that the children's karma would suffer more seeing their mother beaten and raped by their drunken father.'

'My God, Leyra, that's terrible.'

'She had to live separately from him for more than one year, and even then, it took another three years. So much time with lawyers, and courts.'

'Did the husband not agree to the divorce?' I asked, wondering why Haresh's wife hadn't divorced him.

'He agreed. He wanted to drink, gamble and whore around anyway. But it still took three more years because he wanted joint custody of the children, and my sister would not agree to that.'

Back at the chawl, I sat on the steps of Leyra's apartment, with her and the other ladies, drinking chai and eating the samosas straight from the newspaper. The little ginger and black cat came to me, and I stroked her head, gave her a piece of samosa pastry. She sat and watched me for a while, her almond eyes blinking slowly. I tried not to think too much about Haresh's wife and his little daughter. Perhaps I was wrong to be thinking of coming back to Bombay at all. In reality, there could be no kind of future for us, not when he was legally bound to another woman. It wouldn't matter in England, but I knew I couldn't live with him as his mistress. Would he even want to divorce her? But six months could change everything, and I couldn't imagine not being with him.

The sun moved across the courtyard, and I left the ladies to begin their meal preparation for the husbands and children that would need feeding at lunchtime. In Haresh's apartment, I lay on the balcony, focusing on the thought of Diwali and its celebrations, and drifted into a light sleep.

Shuffling sounds at the front door woke me, and I got up, came inside the apartment. Haresh was in the kitchen, leaning his hands on the counter, his back to me and his shoulders tensed. Glancing at my watch, I saw it was only two o'clock.

'Haresh, you're home early,' I said. 'I'm glad because I want to tell you something.' Haresh turned to me, and his smile was slow, sad even. 'What happened?'

'Nothing, Maharani. Tell me?' I reached up, stroking his newly trimmed beard, and pulling gently at the ends of his hair that still reached the top of his shoulders.

'I drank tea with Leyra, and she was telling me about Diwali. What if I come back earlier from Nepal? I could spend Diwali here, with you.'

Haresh's smile warmed then, and the tension left his shoulders. 'Excellent. I like that idea.' He took a deep breath, and turned to the counter, picked up an envelope. 'Here. Ladies-only compartment to Delhi, and then you'll take another train to Gorakpur. From there it's only three or four hours by bus to the Nepal border.'

'Thank you, but don't look so upset, I'll be back.' I took the tickets out of the envelope. 'I thought I was going to take the bus from Delhi.'

'I don't want you travelling alone on a long-distance bus. So, I booked a ladies-only compartment on both trains. It's safer for you, and I won't worry so much. In Delhi, you can go to the ladies' waiting room at the station. Or find a hotel close by.' Haresh leaned back against the kitchen sink. 'But you need to leave the day after tomorrow. Because you'll lose half a day in Delhi between trains.'

Leyra's face peered around the front door. 'Your clothing is dry,' she said. I smiled and stepped towards her, and she handed me a pile of folded clothes. 'Good thing we washed them, nah? Especially if you are leaving so soon.'

'Thank you so much,' I said, 'but you should've called me; I could've come down and got them.'

'Dhanyavad, Leyra,' Haresh said. 'If you don't mind, I need to rest.' She giggled as he ushered her out of the door and closed it, sliding the bolt home. 'I've left Bhupinder in charge until you go, I told him not even to call me, unless the factory burns down.' I laughed, and he took my hand, leading me towards the bedroom. 'Come, love me a little, before Suhana gets home.'

Once Suhana had gone to work the next morning, I packed my clothes into my holdall, except for my blue and white kurta and the plain blue shalwar that went with them. I'd wear those for the journey the next day.

'If you're only going away for a few weeks, why take it all with you, darling?' Haresh said from the doorway to Suhana's room. 'Leave something here. No need to carry such a heavy bag with you.' His lungi was low on his hips, and my eyes followed the line of hair from his chest to his belly.

'It's not that heavy. I've left some older clothes with Leyra this morning, and she'll give them to someone who needs them. I might leave my lehenga here, and this.' I picked up the sari. 'It's so heavy. Suhana said she'll show me how to wear it this evening when she collects the choli from the seamstress.'

'I can't wait to see you wearing it, Maharani.' He lifted the sari and unfolded the nine meters of fabric. 'Practice wearing it tonight, so that you'll be comfortable for Diwali.'

'And you, what will you wear for Diwali?' I said, taking the sari from him, and refolding it.

'I think I shall surprise you.' Taking me in his arms, he smiled. 'You'll see when you get back.'

Later, Haresh and I walked the few blocks to his Rajasthani friend's mithai shop. The turbaned shopkeeper welcomed us, and we took a seat on the bench outside on the pavement, waiting for the dessert that Haresh had ordered specially for me.

Haresh handed me a terracotta dish, full of a creamy something that was smothered in chopped pistachios. The smell of crushed cardamom seeds sprinkled over the top was enough for me to know I'd like the dessert. I dug my spoon in, pulling up a little dark red gloop from the bottom of the dish.

'Oh, my God,' I said, my mouth half full. Haresh laughed. 'That's rose jam?'

'Rose petals in a sugar syrup, candied, so yes, a kind of jam,' he said. 'And it's a ground rice pudding. I'm so glad you like it.' He spoke to his friend, and they both laughed.

His friend said something at length, arms waving, obviously enjoying whatever he was telling Haresh, who looked at me, and grinned.

'What?' I said, stuffing another spoonful of the rose and rice into my mouth.

'Devindra said that this dessert was a favourite of a beautiful maharani who lived in Jaipur, two hundred years ago.' He took my free hand. 'She married for love, had a strong son, and lived a good, happy life. She brought water to a dry village, people became kinder in her presence, all wrongs were righted when she walked by, and couples fell in love just by being near her.' The expression in his eyes was soft, and my heart didn't need anything else. 'It sounds like you in Shivpur.'

'Ah, but I bet the Maharani's lover wasn't beaten by a jealous suitor. Or –'

'Don't spoil my friend's story, Mari.' Haresh laughed.

'Sorry, my love,' I said. 'I'm going to have to order this every day when I come back from Nepal.' I pointed my spoon at the dessert. 'It's divine.'

'Easily arranged. You called me "*your love*." I'm so happy.' Haresh stood up and swung round, arms outstretched, nearly knocking over at least one passer-by.

'Haresh, don't do your Bollywood dancing now.' I laughed. 'Can we get some of this to take home?' I pointed at the dessert, and he smiled at me. 'For Suhana?'

Carrying the box of gulkand phirni by the string tied around it, Haresh and I walked slowly towards the chawl. We were in no real rush to get back, Suhana was there, and we relished our last moments alone. Of course, there was the night to come, but being out in Bombay as the afternoon heat waned was lovely. The sky rumbled, and I looked up at dark clouds that rolled in from the sea.

'I thought the monsoon was over,' I said.

'It is. Mostly. But it can rain anytime in Bombay, because of the sea. Mari.' Haresh stopped walking, moved me to the side of the street, out of other people's way. 'Yesterday morning…' He shifted from foot to foot, looked everywhere but at me. 'I was going to surprise you when you came back from the north, but I can't wait.'

'What? Why are you acting weird?'

'I told you at Chowpatty that I was making some plans; do you remember?' I nodded. He looked at me, frowning. 'I have learned that we can marry. We have to get a special marriage licence, and it can be only a civil ceremony because you are not Indian or Hindu.' Gasping, I put my hands over my lips. He smiled, his eyes crinkling. 'But we can marry, and then you can apply for permanent residency in India. So, what do you say, shall we have a wedding, you and I?'

My smile faded, reality crashing in. 'Don't we have an enormous obstacle to that?'

'That's just it, Maharani. That's what happened yesterday morning. I called my wife at her parents' home, and I asked her to agree to a divorce.'

'Haresh.' I touched his arm. 'What did she say?' My heart hammered, and my mouth was dry.

'She will think about it, because of Tara. But wife agreed that she and I have no relationship, and divorce might be better for us all.'

'Oh, my God. This is amazing. And Tara? What will happen?' I looked at Haresh, biting my lip. He smiled. 'Maybe you'll be able to see her more if you divorce. The court must give you some rights to see her, as her father.'

'As much as I dislike my wife, I am not wanting to deprive Tara of her mother. Under Indian law, I could demand Tara stay with me, but it's not right for the child. So, my wife and I need to discuss this, with lawyers, of course. I know that with you and Suhana, I can be a good father to Tara. And you can be a second mother to her.'

'I'll be Tara's stepmother.' I smiled. It was easy to imagine Haresh and I walking along Chowpatty with a little girl between us. She'd hold my hand, and Haresh's, leaving a trail of small footprints between our larger ones. I'd teach her English so that when she went to school, she'd have an advantage.

'When I'm free, I want to put sindoor in your hair.'

'Sindoor?'

'Yes, vermillion coloured powder married women are wearing here.' He ran his thumb and forefinger back from my hairline. 'Shall we marry, you and I?'

'Sindoor,' I said, imagining myself as his wife. My head was spinning with possibilities, my heart with hope. 'Does Suhana know? You and she were muttering over dinner last night. I knew you were up to something.' I took a step away from him.

'Please, give me your answer.' He threw his arms out, the box of desserts swaying. 'I am dying here.'

I looked at him, and my heart overflowed. 'My answer is yes, Haresh. Yes, I'll marry you.'

'Really?' He placed the box on the ground, and grabbed my arms, throwing his head back and laughing. 'I want to kiss you, but we are on the street, so I cannot.'

I laughed. 'Me too.'

'You'll marry me. Even if it takes some time?'

'Yes,' I said. Maybe it would be a quicker divorce than Leyra's sister's one had been.

'Suhana said she thought you would wait for me. She loves you; not just because you are her friend, but because you make me happy. And when I gave you the sari, she knew I wanted to marry you.' He picked up the box of desserts, and we walked towards the chawl.

'She told me once that she didn't really like your wife,' I said, 'and that you hadn't married for love.'

Haresh nodded. 'With no parents, I had to marry first so that I could find my sister a good husband. She was so happy last night when I told her I will be divorcing. You know what she said?' He stopped walking, turned to look at me. 'That she has a new life, and that I also a new life, and that you deserve one hundred new lives for the help you have given us. She went prayed to Ganesha to give thanks for all our problems being resolved.'

The drizzle started just as we turned into the waste ground at the front of the chawl. Suhana was on the balcony, and something in her stance made me stop walking. She waved her hands, as if she was shooing us away. Haresh stopped beside me, looking up at her from a distance.

'Why isn't she saying anything?' I said. 'Something's wrong.'

'I don't know, let's go and see.'

'Wait, Haresh…'

Suhana went inside the apartment, and by the time we crossed the waste ground, she met us at the chawl entrance. We stood under the archway, sheltering from the rain. She was tearful, and placed my holdall at my feet.

'Good thing you were almost packed. Everything is inside, your sari, everything. All the train tickets, too. Mari, you must leave.'

Looking from Haresh to me, and back again, I saw the panic in her eyes. Had someone from Keshnagar or Shivpur found her here? Had the chawl neighbours found out about Kiran? But no, it would be Suhana who was leaving if that was the case.

'Tell me?' Haresh's deep voice boomed, and he dropped the box of deserts.

'Your wife, brother,' said Suhana. 'She is here with Tara.'

'Wait here, both of you.' Haresh ran into the chawl. 'I'll go and come.'

'I'll go and find an auto for you,' Suhana said. 'Mari, you need to go. I'm so sorry, my dear friend.'

'I don't understand,' I said. 'Why is she here?'

'She won't divorce him. She came with all her things saying she wants to be a wife to Haresh again.' Suhana blinked and looked at the sky. 'For the child's sake. She says Tara needs her father, and she is so very sorry for staying away. Mari, Tara is adorable. She looks just like my brother.'

I shook my head, disbelief swamping me. 'No. No. We were just talking about getting married, and now I have to leave?'

'Wait here for Haresh, let me find you an auto.' Suhana ran across the waste ground, the rain making her green sari darker.

I waited, but Haresh didn't come down. It took every fibre of my being not to run up to the apartment and tell his wife to fuck off and leave us alone. But there was a child involved; a three-year-old who needed her father. And Haresh, who needed his daughter. Oh God, what was going on up there? Were they arguing? Was she contrite and weeping? Was he telling her to leave, or holding her close?

An auto picked its way past the potholes and the quickly formed puddles. After just five minutes of heavy rain, the streets were awash. Suhana told the driver to wait, and ran back to me still waiting under the archway.

'They're still up there,' I said. 'You're soaked. Go and change. I'll go to a hotel. Tell him…' I ran my fingers over my forehead. What could I say? My mind spun. 'Tell him to meet me on the platform at the station. He knows what time my train leaves tomorrow.'

'Write to me, Mari.' Suhana blinked back tears. 'I'll let you know everything that happens. He'll sort it out, I know he will. He loves you so much. But go now, please –'

'Sister. Please go up.' Haresh came towards me.

I hugged Suhana, and she left Haresh and I standing in the archway.

'She told me. Your wife…' I sniffed.

'I have just seen my daughter. Mari, what a joyful creature she is. You will…one day. But not as soon as we hoped.' Haresh moved my damp hair away from my face, stared into my eyes.

'There is still much that needs to be discussed, but wife has come to live here. And she will not agree to a divorce, because of Tara.'

'But she left you for three years. She didn't think of Tara then, did she? What about all the times you went to Poona to see her?' I ran the back of my hand under my nose, blinked the tears back. 'Did you tell your wife about me? Yesterday, when you spoke to her…did you tell her you love me?'

'I did. Wife said she spoke again with her parents, and that for Tara's sake, they felt divorce wasn't good. And reflecting, they wanted her to come here to me, and give the child a proper upbringing.'

'Meaning with two Indian parents.' I shook my head. 'Does my being non-Indian mean I'm not good enough to help you raise Tara?'

'To them, yes. But not to me.'

'And Suhana? What does *wife*,' I made air quotes, 'think about that now?'

'You are angry, I know. I too.' He raised his hands, dropped them again. 'But what can I do, Mari? She accepts that it is my decision to give my sister a home, she respects that. I think she's saying what I want to hear, but she is looking like she has a lot of remorse.'

'Malaal.'

He smiled sadly. 'Darling, I…' His arms enfolded me, and he held me for a moment. 'I'm sorry. Give me some time.'

'I understand,' I said, moving away from him. 'You can't lose Tara again.'

'No. And her parents divorcing could ruin her chance of a good marriage. I will educate her, find her a good husband, and then…'

'That's fifteen years in the future, Haresh,' I said.

I picked up my holdall and walked towards the auto. The single wiper slapped at the windscreen, the rain heavier than ever, and I was drenched in seconds. Putting my holdall onto the seat, I hesitated, not knowing where to tell the driver to take me.

Haresh ran the few steps to the auto. 'One day, I will send for you. When I am free, I will ask you to come, Maharani. God promise.' He put his fingers to his throat. 'Will you come?'

With the rain pelting down on us, I held his arms and reached up to press my lips to his. Raindrops or tears? Mine or his? I didn't know. We kissed again, knowing these were the last chaste kisses, the last breaths of our love.

'If you send for me, I'll come. God promise,' I said, and touching my throat, climbed into the back of the auto.

The driver turned the auto around, and I looked behind me. Haresh stood in the rain, his hair dripping, his wet clothes stuck to his body, and his wife watched from the balcony.

Three days later, I arrived in Nepal. It wouldn't be a lie to say that I cried all the way there. Kathmandu left me cold, there was nothing that I wanted to see, or wanted to do. My room at the guesthouse in the backpackers' ghetto of Thamel was clean and simple; it was all that I needed to be able to rest.

Desperate for food and water, I went downstairs to get something from the café on the ground floor of the hotel. There wasn't a free table, and a blonde-haired guy caught my eye.

'Hi,' he said. 'Join us if you want.'

Pulling out a chair, I sat with the two guys, and ordered some vegetable *momos,* steamed rice flour dumplings, and a bottle of water. They tried to be chatty, asking where I'd been and where I was going, but I found it hard to hold a conversation.

'I'm just here to get an Indian visa, and then I'm heading to see the Dalai Lama. I…'

'Getting a visa will take more than a week,' said the blonde guy. 'Have you applied yet?'

The room spun, and I thought I was going to vomit. I grabbed the bottle of water, and opened it, sipping it slowly. 'Not yet. Sorry, I'm not feeling great.'

After I'd eaten a few bites of the soft momos, I retreated to my room, drew the dusty curtains, and lay in bed, torturing myself with music. I played and rewound, played and rewound the same song, again and again on my Walkman. '*Songbird*'.

All I could think of was Haresh. I remembered every detail of the month we'd spent together; his deep voice, the things he'd said, the days we'd spent in Dolly Auntie's house. Since the day I'd gone to Bombay to tell him about Suhana, we hadn't been apart for more than a few hours. I lay there, missing his touch, his warmth, his presence. It wasn't heartbreak. It was a grief so profound, it was like my soul had been ripped in half. I turned on my side, the pillow damp beneath my face.

How could this have happened? One minute, I cursed Haresh's wife for coming back, and the next, I praised her selfless bravery for the sake of Tara. It was the same with Haresh; I understood he wanted his daughter in his life, and that he loved me. How conflicted he was, how torn his heart must have been. But it all came down to a choice. And he'd chosen Tara. I had to accept that, hard as it was; she came first, and that was how it should be.

Perhaps the wife would change her mind, and let him have a divorce. I sat up, wiped my face with my hands. I remembered Haresh telling me that they didn't like each other. It could be that after a few days in the chawl, living with Haresh and Suhana, that the wife would realise she was wrong, and that divorce was the best thing for everyone, including Tara. Given some time, things might change. Maybe I could call Haresh from McLeod Ganj, see what was going on. And maybe I'd be at the chawl for Diwali.

Ten days later, I had my new Indian visa and headed to the bus station. The thought of the journey back to Gorakpur didn't enthral me; I'd been so sick on the way up the mountains, and I hoped going down wouldn't be so bad. It was. After a torturous four-hour bus ride, I stopped eating and drinking, in the hope that if there was nothing in my stomach, there'd be nothing to vomit up. The next bus took me from Gorakpur to Lucknow and the next one on to New Delhi. The third day's travel brought more dry retching, but I finally arrived in McLeod Ganj.

The cold wind of the northern autumn had me digging in the bottom of my holdall for my Levi's jacket. Snow capped the mountains in the distance, and brown leaves scuttered down the street. I breathed in the crisp air scented with pine trees, and rubbed my cold hands together, hoping that it was just the early mornings that were so cold. From the bus stop, I walked along the bustling main street, looking for the Tibetan-run guesthouse that was listed in my guidebook. Brass singing bowls and colourful woollen clothing were piled up outside shops, as were cooking pots, plastic bowls and buckets. There were as many burgundy-robed Buddhist monks as there were tourists. Shop signs were in English and Tibetan, and only occasionally Hindi; all three scripts created a feeling of being somewhere that wasn't really India.

The guesthouse owner welcomed me with sweet milky tea, and I drank it in the little reception area, surrounded by coral-coloured pillars, the flowers on their capitals painted yellow and turquoise. The beams across the ceiling were decorated in the same way. My room was at the top of a rickety staircase, and I opened the door. Gasping, I dropped my holdall, and stepped across the room to the window. The mountains were spread out before me, and Dharamshala swathed itself around their base in the valley below. After I vomited once again, I unpacked and went to see the doctor at the local clinic. He sent me to the hospital, half an hour away in Dharamshala, saying he couldn't do the necessary tests. I'd have to tell the hospital about the parasite I'd had in Shivpur, and probably get another course of anti-biotics.

Later that afternoon, I queued behind a group of monks at the phone office on the main street of McLeod Ganj, and placed a call to Haresh. The line didn't connect. I tried again and again, and I jumped when the phone rang at the other end. No one answered, and I placed the receiver back in the cradle, deflated.

For the next week, I wandered the streets around my guesthouse, and through the market area to the phone office. I tried to call Haresh eight or nine times every day, but on the few occasions the line did connect, the call wasn't answered. Between tries, I wiped my eyes, and hung out in Tibetan tea shops or went back to my room, and tried to rest. After the second day, the man in the phone office didn't even ask me to write the number down. It was always the same result; no answer. By the end of the seventh day, I figured if there was ever a time to believe in signs from the universe, it was probably then.

At a travel agency, I booked a flight from Delhi to London for the twentieth of November.

'But I do suggest, Miss,' said the Kashmiri travel agent, 'that you go down to Delhi before then.'

'The weather?' I said.

'It will be very cold here, and maybe, if the snow is heavy, the roads will be blocked. Better you plan to go down at least a week before the flight.'

'Do you know if the Dalai Lama will be at his home before then?'

The travel agent pulled a sheet of paper from a draw. 'No. His Holiness travels so much. He will return in the middle of December.'

I laughed. That'd be right. I'd come all this way in the hope of seeing His Holiness, only for him to be somewhere else.

If I travelled back to Delhi, and used it as a base, I could go to see the Taj Mahal in Agra, and even take the train back to Jaipur. But the thought of travelling anywhere, of unpacking and repacking, of moving around on buses and trains didn't appeal. It would be better to just buy some warmer clothing, and stay in McLeod Ganj for a month, and then do as the travel agent suggested.

'Okay, can I book a bus ticket to Delhi for the week before?'

'Of course. I can arrange that for you, but come back nearer the time.'

Holding the flight ticket in my hand, I looked at the date. I couldn't book an earlier one; the doctor in Dharamshala's hospital had advised me to wait until the end of the first trimester before I flew.

Chapter Twenty-Six

London, 2010

HARRY WOKE ME, shaking me gently from the nightmare. Blinking at him in the soft light from the bedside lamp, I breathed out.

'Sorry, was I shouting again?' I wiped the sweat off my top lip. My heart hammered, and I thought it would burst.

Harry sat on the edge of the bed and held my hand for a while until my breathing calmed. 'At least you didn't try and hit me this time.' His smile was sad. 'Don't you think you should try going back on the meds? They helped before.'

Pushing myself up, I propped the pillow behind me. 'I don't like taking them. They make me feel like someone else.' The irony of my words wasn't lost on me. That was exactly how I'd felt since speaking to the woman who raised me.

'But they stop the nightmares,' Harry said. 'Think of the hours of sleep you've lost over the years.' He smiled. 'Camomile tea?'

Threading my arms through my robe, I got up and patted Harry's shoulder. 'You go back to sleep. I'll go down and make it, and I'll read for a bit until I feel calmer, and sleepy again.'

'Post Traumatic Stress Disorder is serious. Please, call Dr. Shah in the morning and book a session. At least phone him, see what he says.' Harry followed me to the door. 'What do you think has triggered it this time?'

'I don't know. It isn't always obvious.' I threw up my hands. 'It's always just there, ready to bubble over and spill out. I'm used to it, and you know the pattern; it'll settle down.' Denial never helped, and I wasn't obtuse; I knew the onslaught of nightmares was to do with learning that I wasn't who I thought I was. The foundations of my being were shaken by the knowledge my supposed mother had shared.

'Are you sure you're okay?' Harry spoke through a yawn.

'Go back to sleep, Harry. I'll be fine.' I lied.

Downstairs, my hand trembled as I switched on the kettle, I made a cup of camomile tea when what I really wanted was a vat of red wine. I breathed out, my hands on the counter, waiting for the cold feeling in my chest to pass. When I was calmer and more rational, I'd tell Harry that I was the result of my father's affair with a seventeen-year-old Irish girl. But I wasn't ready to tell anyone, not yet.

Two weeks later, Sylvana Randall's funeral was a small affair on a cold, crisp early-October afternoon. The only reason that I cried was because seeing my sisters sobbing and so grief-stricken actually broke my heart. I felt nothing but pity for the woman who raised me, but to everyone at the funeral, I looked like a loving, grieving daughter.

At home, after the wake, Harry took off his black jacket and loosened his tie. It was one of his 'jobs' to light the wood burner, and we needed the warmth; the early evening chill had crept in. He poured us a glass of whisky each, and we sat in the lounge, the wood burner soon giving off a warm glow. Billie jumped onto my lap, purring as she settled her head against my arm.

The doorbell rang, and Harry went to answer it. 'Good, they're here.'

'Noticed you didn't eat,' said Alan, sticking his head around the door. 'Bought us all a Chinese. I'll leave it in the kitchen.'

'I've got champagne,' said Angie. She leaned in to kiss my cheek, a bottle in each hand. 'I know it's not a celebration but…'

'Bubbly is always good, right?' said Jon. 'Although with Issy, it won't last long.'

'Ha ha.' Issy laughed, slapping his arm. She moved a dining chair from the table and sat next to me. 'How are you holding up, Mari?'

'I'm okay. I just feel so sad for my sisters; they've just lost their mother and I never had her in the first place. It reminds me of when Dad died. That's four years ago, but I feel like it was yesterday.'

The champagne cork popped, and Billie flew off my lap. Angie filled the glasses she'd placed on the dining table. 'I know we've talked about it already over the last couple of weeks, but if you want to talk more, we're all here.'

Blinking back tears, I took a slug of the champagne, enjoying the fizz on my tongue. 'Was I right not to tell Sofia and Stella?'

'Definitely,' said Jon. 'Let them remember your dad in the most positive way. You're their sister, whoever your mother was.'

Harry ran his hand through his hair, and it fell back into place. 'What do we call her now? Sylvana? Well, she was so negative about everything.' He stared into his champagne, then glanced at me. 'And nothing that anyone said about you was ever received with any grace or warmth.'

'I never bought it either; the whole thing about it being your fault Elena died,' Alan said. He took a glass of champagne, and sat next to Angie on the sofa. 'Now we know it was just another excuse to focus her anger on you for being someone else's daughter.'

'Yes. It all makes sense now. Easy in hindsight.' I shrugged. 'The thing is, now that I know, I can kind of understand. It must have been awful for her, just having lost a child, then coerced into bringing up the spawn of her husband's affair.'

'Spawn.' Angie laughed. 'It's not your regular step-mother scenario is it?'

'No,' I said. 'You know, I think I'm able to forgive her now. I mean really forgive her for hating me, not just blank it all out.'

'That's progress,' said Harry. 'I know you shouldn't speak ill of the dead, but I didn't like her. I only visited her because I thought I should.' He reached down to stroke Billie. 'She had no filter; the things that would come out of her mouth.' He laughed. 'I used to think there might be some mental illness there.'

'I think she was just a very angry person,' I said. 'And now we know why. If Dad did cheat on her regularly, like she said, she should have left him. But then again, where would she go with four girls? She'd never even had a job.'

'Women of that generation don't leave their husbands though, do they?' said Jon. He placed his glass on the side table, under the lamp.

'And this Irish girl?' said Issy. 'Do you want to start looking for your biological mother?'

'We could all help,' said Alan, heading towards the kitchen. 'Let me put the oven on, or should I just nuke the Chinese?'

'Nuke it,' Jon and Harry said in unison.

'We could look online,' said Harry. 'I know there are agencies too, that can help you track a birth parent. The search engines these days are brilliant. You can find anyone. Actually, speaking of that, I found –'

'All I know is that she was seventeen when she had me, and that she was Jessie from Dublin,' I said. 'But I don't feel the need to look for her. God, is there something wrong with me?'

'It's very personal,' said Angie. 'Don't make any decisions yet.'

'I think if I was fully adopted it might be different. But Dad was my dad.' I shrugged. 'And I've got used to not having a mother for all these years.'

'I think,' said Issy, 'I'd look for her. Don't you want to know where you come from?'

'Your origins are important,' Harry said. 'Especially as you get older.'

'They are,' I said. Gripping my champagne glass, I looked at him, my heart's edges cracking open. Angie and I glanced at each other and she nodded. I took a deep breath, knowing it was the right time. 'Harry, there's something you need to know.'

'It's about India, isn't it?'

'Issy? Did you tell him?' I threw my hands out. In the kitchen, the microwave pinged, and the smell of food drifted through.

'No, he just asked if I knew why you were having trouble sleeping, and…' Issy looked sheepish. 'And you hadn't told us about the conversation with your mum then.'

'Issy just blurted it out,' said Jon, scratching his forehead. 'But only the bit about the wedding invitation.'

'It wasn't malicious, Mari,' said Issy. 'I've kept that secret for so long.' I smiled at her and nodded. 'I didn't think, it just slipped out.'

The microwave pinged for the umpteenth time, and Alan clattered around in the kitchen, swearing and slamming cupboard doors.

'Plates. Plates,' Alan yelled. 'Where are the sodding plates?'

Angie rolled her eyes. 'I'd best give him a hand.' She looked at me, raising her eyebrows. 'Okay?'

I nodded. Harry looked at me, frowning, and I twisted my hair. 'Anyway, the wedding is in less than a month,' I said. 'Alan's given me the time off work, so I'll fly over a week before the three-day ceremony, and I want to stay a bit after.'

Harry nodded. 'I thought you would. I know about the promise.' His gaze was direct, his brown eyes surprisingly warm. My breath stopped short of my lungs, and I bit my lip.

'He's known for years,' said Jon. 'I neither confirmed nor denied any knowledge of it, by the way. Just said he should speak to you.'

'Don't look so shocked,' Harry laughed. 'I overheard you talking to Sofia and Stella about it, more than once.'

Jon stood up, and took Issy's hand, leading her through the dining area to the kitchen. I glanced through the doors to the kitchen, at my four best friends, who were busying themselves with a Chinese takeaway that needed no busying with.

'I'm sorry, Harry.' I said. 'Look, I'm not even sure what that promise means anymore. It was so long ago.'

'Do you still love him? Actually, you don't need to answer that.' He sipped his champagne. 'It's obvious.'

I moved to the sofa to sit beside him. Moving his thick black hair away from his face, I traced my finger along his high-bridged hooked nose. 'I love the memory of what he and I felt for each other back then. And every time I look at you, I fall in love with him again.' Taking both his hands in mine, I smiled. 'Will you come with me to India? Harry Chandekar Randall, it's time you met your father.'

Chapter Twenty-Seven

घर

Mumbai, November 2010

BOMBAY. MUMBAI. I kept having to correct myself, and call the city by her rightful name, but in my heart, she would always be Bombay. The city smelled the same, of ghee and spices and paan and drains. There was more traffic than ever, and the cityscape was dazzling with state-of-the- art skyscrapers.

In my hotel room, I turned away from the window and unwrapped the sea-green silk sari that Haresh had given me. I was glad I'd kept it wrapped in tissue paper and vacuum packed for all those years. It still looked like new. The choli was too tight, and I needed to find a replacement. Glancing at my watch, I repacked the sari and grabbed my bag; Harry would be waiting to have breakfast.

'Morning. I've been awake since about two. Bloody jet lag. I was thinking, I'd like to wear something traditional to the wedding,' said Harry, filling a fork with *masala dosa*, a crispy rice pancake wrapped around spiced potato. 'What do you think?'

I sat opposite him. 'You'll look fabulous in a kurta. We'll need to go a tailor this morning then. It might take a day or so to have it made. You could call Haresh and ask him? He's two inches taller than you, six foot five, so I'm sure he'll recommend somewhere.'

'No. I'll meet him properly at the wedding. What happens after that, I'll just let it happen organically.' I nodded. 'I don't want anything to be forced. When are you planning to meet him?'

'I spoke to him on the phone last night, and we'll meet later today.' I smiled, placing my hand on my heart.

'You look like a fifteen-year-old, Mum, about to go on her first proper date.' He grinned at me, and I tutted. 'You are seriously glowing.'

'I'm trying to stay rational. Twenty-three years is a very long time; a lot can change. Whatever happens, it's now more about you meeting your father more than anything else. Are you nervous?'

'Not really,' Harry said, biting into a piece of the crispy rice flour pancake. 'I feel more excited than anything. I used to crawl under the stairs and look at his photo without you knowing.'

I closed my eyes and breathed out. 'I should have kept it in a frame in the living room. Or given it to you. I'm sorry.'

'Don't be. I always liked the look of him, you know; his eyes were kind and he has such a warm smile.' Harry took a small mouthful of the spiced potato filling. 'I remember you told me when I was about five that you took that photo of him.'

'I did.' I nodded, smiling. 'On the way to find Suhana. At the bus station in Bangalore. Oops, Bengalaru now.'

'As I got older, I recognised the expression in his eyes. The way he looked at the camera, well, at you.' Harry placed his hand over mine on the table, and I blinked back the moisture. 'I could see the love.'

'It was long ago, Harry. He might not feel the same. You are just as soft-hearted as he was.'

'Romantic, Mum, romantic.' He laughed. 'I've been keeping a secret from you for the last few years. I did try to tell you after the wake.'

'What?' I leaned forward, elbows on the table.

'I googled Haresh Chandekar, and found his business website. We've been emailing, but only now and again. Generic stuff, nothing too personal.' I put my hands over my mouth, shook my head. 'I didn't tell you in case it opened up any old wounds.' I looked at him for a minute. 'Oh God, you're angry.'

'No. Not at all. I think it's lovely that you had him to yourself for a while, that you have a bit of a relationship to build on when you actually meet.' I wiped my eyes.

'Stop it, you'll start me off.' Harry blinked, and I was so proud of the man he was.

'Anyway, I'll see Haresh later. And after we finish breakfast, we'll go to a wedding tailor. But let me get some food; I'm so hungry.' I stood, ready to go to the breakfast buffet. I'd seen some paratha I liked the look of, and I needed coffee.

'Are you taking your tablets?' Harry raised his eyebrows. 'Mum?'

'Yes, three times a day. Just to keep to demons away.' I lied. I'd refused the anti-depressants Dr Shah wanted me to take, and we'd compromised on diazepam, although I only took one at night, to help me fall asleep. The packet was in my bag though, in case I really needed them.

While Harry tried on long brocade jackets with mandarin collars, I wondered what Haresh would look like now, aged fifty-two. Would age have greyed his thick black hair? I couldn't imagine that he'd gone bald, but did he still wear it long? Mine was still the same chestnut brown, although it was shorter, falling just beneath my collar bones. Would he have a rounded, pot belly? My waist was thicker than it was twenty-three years ago, my boobs less than perky. Smiling, I chastised myself. I wasn't the girl I'd been, but he was no longer thirty either. I glanced up at Harry, in a pale blue and gold knee-length jacket, and my heart flipped. I knew Haresh's would too when he met his son.

'Madam, this is the nearest colour.' A tailor unwrapped a bolt of sea-green silk, draping it across my sari that I'd placed on the counter. 'It is not exact, but once the sari covers the choli, I think it will do a top-class job.'

I paid the deposit, and with a whole ten hours to kill before we could collect the clothing, Harry decided to go exploring. He hailed an auto and we laughed when the driver spoke to him in Marathi.

My heart swelled as I waved him off, happy that my son was so enthralled with Bombay, with his heritage.

Later that morning, I dressed in new rose pink shalwar, and a pale green and white kurta that I'd just bought in the Anokhi shop a few doors down from the hotel. It reminded me of rose and cardamom kulfi. I draped the pink dupatta across my chest, and over my shoulders. With a deep breath, I picked up my bag and headed towards the lift. My bangles tinkled as I adjusted the dupatta, and I smiled at myself in the mirrored wall of the lift.

Haresh was standing, looking out of the window of the hotel lounge. His hair was shorter, neatly layered into the back of his neck. My hand flew to my mouth, and I stepped towards him. He turned, smiling, his hands flicking outwards.

'Maharani,' he said, his voice richer than I remembered. 'You like it? I decided to be a little nostalgic, and to wear turquoise for you. Like the first time we met, you and I.'

Haresh took my hand. My insides were fluid, my heart mercurial. I looked up at him, noting the silver hair at his temples and deep lines around his eyes.

'I remember,' I said. 'How can I forget; it's still my favourite colour.'

'Shall we sit? I'll order you something.' He led me to a pair of armchairs separated by a low round table.

Haresh was still slim, maybe a little broader in the chest and belly. I looked at him from under my lashes, my heart beating fast. Seated, I placed my bag on the floor by my feet, and he signalled to the waiter.

'What would you like, Mari?' Haresh said. 'I'll take a single malt.' I nodded. 'Two, then,' he said to the waiter.

'You look well, Haresh. Really well,' I said, my eyes moving over his face, drinking in his features.

'And you, how did you not change? You have stayed the same.' He stared at me, ran this hand across his salt and pepper beard. 'This is more difficult than I thought. I have so much to explain to you.'

'No. Nothing needs to be explained.' I smiled at the waiter who placed our drinks on paper coasters on top of the glass table. 'Time makes it easier, and now, Tara is getting married.'

'Yes, and I will finally meet my son. Did he tell you we've had some contact?'

'Yes, and I'm so happy about that. Harry has your character; kind, resolute. I see you in him every day.' My voice wavered, and my chin trembled. 'We talked about him coming to Mumbai about four years ago, just before he went to uni. But then he met a girl and went travelling around Thailand instead. I think he was just a bit nervous then. But he's older now.'

'And this is the right time?' Haresh said. I nodded. He leaned forward, and I couldn't look at him. 'When you left the chawl that day, why didn't you tell me you were having my child? I have never been able to understand.'

'I didn't know; I found out a few weeks later, at the hospital in Dharamshala.' I shook my head, looking up at the ceiling. 'I think I must have conceived the day I told you I'd found Suhana, or in that bloody hotel room in Keshnagar. Anyway, your wife was in Bombay, with Tara. It wouldn't have made a difference. I don't think you would have sent them away to be with me?'

'No.' He breathed out a long breath. 'Regretfully, I couldn't be with you without divorce.'

'I knew that. But when I knew that I was eight weeks pregnant, I wanted you to know, and I called you so many times, but the line would never connect.'

'Bloody phone. Thank you for all the letters and photos you sent via Suhana. It was so good to know about my son's achievements.'

The letters had been penned in my best handwriting, the airmail envelopes' sticky edges licked and pressed down, taking kisses across the oceans. I remembered the bitter-sweet disappointment weeks later when the postman didn't deliver the expected reply. Waiting to hear from him, even via his sister, was romantic and tragic, the stuff of Jane Austen, of TV melodramas set in Victorian times. But that's what it had been like for me. Maybe it'd been like an epic Bollywood movie for him.

'I wanted to share Harry with you, somehow let you be a part of his life, but when he was about twelve, Suhana stopped writing back,' I said.

'Yes, but we thought you stopped writing. It was when we were moving from the chawl to the new house in Bandra, about ten years ago. Wife found all your letters, which wasn't good.' Haresh moved his kurta out of the way, and took his wallet from his trouser pocket. He unfolded a faded photo of me holding a newborn Harry. 'And she also saw this.'

'You carry that with you?' I bit my lip.

'Always, darling, always.' Haresh smiled, tucking the wallet back into his pocket. 'Tara was sixteen then, and the only joy in my life. Wife said she would take Tara away for good if I had any more contact with you. I had to choose between you and my son, who were not in Bombay, and wife and daughter who were. My heart broke every day for you.'

'And Suhana? How is she?' I leaned forwards, picked up my drink.

'She married again. Sadly, too late for her own children, but her step-daughter is eighteen, and her step-son fifteen. You will be meeting them tomorrow. It's a happy story.'

'Yes, she told me she was engaged in one of the last letters I got from her, and that your wife had said all that. I still wrote to her though.'

He frowned. 'No. Suhana told me that she wrote to you from her new address after she married. We devilishly thought you would write to her there, and wife would not know. But you didn't reply.' He placed his hand over mine. 'I was respecting your decision and told her not to send you any more letters. I thought you…hoped that one day, you would arrive in Bombay, and come looking for me again.'

'Haresh…' My eyes were wet, and I ran my fingers under them, trying not to smudge my mascara. 'There's some mistake; I only stopped writing because I didn't get a reply to the last two letters I sent. I thought maybe you'd had another child, or that …' My shoulders shook, and I covered my face. 'I didn't get Suhana's letter.'

'Wife must have intercepted them.' Haresh smoothed the sleeve of his kurta, his face creasing. 'Mari, shall we go to your room. This isn't the place to be talking like this.' He stood and spoke to the waiter. 'Your room number?' I showed the waiter the key fob. 'Send up two more whiskies, please.'

Haresh took the key from my hand and opened the door to my hotel room. He took me in his arms, and I closed my eyes, breathing in the smell of him, of sandalwood. Stroking my hair, he leaned back to look at me, blinking back his tears.

We sat in the armchairs by the window overlooking the city, the small table as huge a barrier as the miles that had been between us for all those years.

'What's Tara's husband like?' I said. 'Did you arrange the marriage?'

'Wife found many boys for Tara, but I would not approve any one.' Flicking his hands out, Haresh laughed. 'I wanted my daughter to have happiness and a full heart. She met Ranjiv last year, at a friend's wedding.' He smiled. 'It is a real love match. You will be surprised; Ranjiv's parents are divorced. It is very common now. If I had known how India would mellow and accept these things…'

'Like two unmarried people in a hotel room together?' We laughed. 'God, what a night that was. Muddy…' I rolled my eyes.

'I was thinking to invite him to the wedding.' Haresh laughed at the face I pulled. 'Joking, Maharani. By the way, being alone in a hotel room is still not allowed, but this is the Taj Hotel, so we won't be disturbed. And I will only be married for two more weeks, Mari. Just two weeks and my divorce will be final. I am a fool; I waited too long.'

'You kept your promise, Haresh. I still can't believe I'm here with you.' I reached across the table, and he took my hand.

Room service delivered our drinks, and Haresh gave the boy some money. 'Don't charge to the room.' Placing the glasses of whisky on the table, along with a small ice bucket, the waiter smiled. I guessed it was a huge tip.

Haresh and I talked for hours; about the past and the future. My stomach rumbled, and he laughed, glancing at his watch.

'I see you are still always being hungry. I'm sorry, I should go, darling. There are wedding preparations I need to see to.'

Nodding, I stood, adjusting my dupatta. 'I need to go and get Harry's wedding outfit. Wait 'til you see him; he's so like you, it's ridiculous.'

Haresh's moved towards me, and his mouth found mine. I clung to him as the years fell away. His kiss ignited a desire that I hadn't felt with anyone else in the last twenty odd years. He pressed himself against me, and I knew it was the same for him.

'Haresh…' I stepped back, still holding his hand.

'This is going to be a busy week, but I'll see you every day.' He looked into my eyes, moved my hair behind my ears. 'It's our time, Mari. You and I.' I nodded and briefly kissed him again. 'We'll talk properly, and make our plans for after the wedding.'

I opened the door for Haresh, but he didn't leave the room, just stood staring into the corridor.

'Harry.' My breath caught, and I reached to touch him. He moved his arm away from me, and I looked from my son to his father and back again. 'Harry…'

Time slowed, and I held my breath. Harry moved towards Haresh, and my heart stopped beating. They shook hands, tentatively smiling at each other. Then my son hugged his father, and my eyes spilled over.

'I feel like I already know you,' said Harry, wiping his nose.

'I hope in reality that I will not disappoint.' Haresh sniffed, and then laughed. 'You are such a fine young man. You did a tremendous job, Mari. Look at my son.' He put his hand on Harry's shoulder. 'Shall we go, Harry, and sit downstairs. We can have chai, and talk a while.' The hopeful look on Haresh's face was childlike.

'I'd like that,' said Harry. 'You okay on your own, Mum?'

I nodded, and my son and his father, the love of my life, walked towards the lift.

Chapter Twenty-Eight

घर

The wedding

SUHANA CAME INTO the room, glowing and beautiful in a gold and apricot sari, and she hugged me for a long time. 'Let me help you dress,' she said. The choli was a perfect fit and the low back fastened with two hooks like a bra. A cord was attached to each shoulder, and she tied them loosely behind me, the tasselled ends bouncing in the small of my back.

I pulled on the long underskirt, and Suhana folded five pleats into one end of the nine meters of aqua silk. Tucking it into the waistband of the underskirt, she adjusted it lower on my hips, and wound the length of fabric around me twice, gathering the heavily embroidered pallu, and draping it over one shoulder.

'I love it. It's more beautiful that the first one Haresh bought me all those years ago.' I smiled, Suhana nodded. 'So many years ago.'

'Like Parvati waited so many years for Shiva. Let me pin the pleats.' Suhana took a large safety pin from her bag. 'It will be easier for you to walk confidently.' Once she pinned the pleats to the underskirt, she attached the pleats of the pallu to the shoulder of my choli with fine pins.

'You can't even see the pins,' I said smiling.

'I have been doing this for a while. Now, sit.' Suhana stood behind me and parted my hair in the centre. Pulling my hair back, she twisted it up, and fixed it in place with two diamante studded combs, attaching a string of jasmine flowers between them. Placing an ornate piece of costume jewellery across my head, she positioned it so that it just covered my hairline.

'Isn't this a bit much? I mean…'

'It's a wedding, not an afternoon tea. Of course, it's not too much. I wore it for my own wedding.' Suhana opened a tiny tin, and took out an aqua and gold bindi, placing it between my brows. 'There. I am so excited about today. Where are your bangles?'

I pointed to the red jewellery box on the bed. 'Haresh sent those over for me this morning. He's been so generous.' Smiling, I put two thick gold bangles on each wrist. Running my thumb over my scar that was white with age now, I breathed out.

'Are you ready?' Suhana looked at me in the mirror. 'You look beautiful.'

'Thank you. I actually feel beautiful.' I stood, and looked down at the aqua silk, at the embroidered edges. 'And so do you, Suhana.'

She grinned. Even with smile lines and creases around her eyes, I could see the girl she'd been, when she'd worn a white sari.

'Come, it's time. We don't want to be getting late.' She ushered me out of the door. 'Harry is waiting with the taxi downstairs. I will see you there.'

Outside, Harry leaned against the yellow and black taxi, the sun catching the gold thread in his cream jacket.

'Wow, look at you!' I said. 'I love you in that.'

'Wow yourself, Mum. Wait 'til Har…Dad sees you.'

Outside the Marriage Registry Office building, a group of men stood wearing red military-style jackets and caps trimmed with gold braid. They raised their instruments and began to play. The drumming started, and the wedding guests clapped and cheered.

Haresh looked like a Moghul prince in his turquoise

embroidered jacket. He smiled, and my heart flipped. Holding on to Harry's arm, I was terrified that somehow the pleats of my sari would come undone, and that I'd trip over the meters of fabric.

'You came, Maharani,' Haresh said, smiling down at me.

'I gave you a God promise, remember?' Looking at him, my heart swelled.

'You look lovely, Mari.' Tara smiled at me, leaning in to kiss my cheek. I squeezed her hand. 'I'm so very happy.'

The Marriage Registry office itself was small, and the wedding guests crowded in. Harry and Tara smiled at each other and stood to one side.

Tara's husband, Ranjiv, shook Harry's hand. 'Good to see you, brother-in-law. How was the trip? Twice in four months; we'll make a Mumbaikar, a local, of you yet.'

They fell into conversation, hushed voices amongst so many others.

'We just need the three witnesses,' shouted the Registrar. 'Everyone else, wait outside.' He flicked his wrist. 'Get out, onto the street; there's no room for you all here.'

Glancing over my shoulder, I laughed as our friends retreated, pulling faces and gesticulating. Haresh put his hand on the small of my back, and stood close. I closed my eyes for a second, hardly believing what was happening.

'I am here. I am the third witness.' Suhana pushed past everyone as they left. She joined Harry and Tara at the side of the room. 'Sorry, to hold you up, sir.'

My heart hammered so hard, I could hear it in my ears. Haresh held my hand as the Marriage Registrar inspected the marriage application. It had taken us ninety days to gather all the necessary paperwork, and have it authorised. Had we missed something? Forgotten something? I breathed out when the Registrar asked the witnesses to sign the papers. With a flourish of a pen, and the thud of an official stamp, it was done.

In the waiting area outside the office, Suhana took the lid off a tiny pot and held it out for Haresh. He dipped the ball of his thumb into the sindoor, and moving my headpiece out of the way, smeared the powder along the first two inches of my parting. .

'I have loved you, Maharani,' my husband said, 'since the first minute I saw you. And I will always love you. God promise.' He kissed my forehead.

'I know,' I said.

'Oh? You know?' He laughed.

'Yes. Because it's the same for me. God promise.'

We followed Suhana, Harry and Tara out of the building. On the street, the band played again; drums, Indian clarinets, and trumpets sounding joyful, if slightly out of tune. Manu and Leyra, Bhupinder and his family, Issy and Jon, Alan and Angie all cheered, throwing rose petals.

'You look amazing, sis,' said Stella, wiping her eyes and hugging me to her. 'Congratulations. I'm so happy for you both.' She waved her mobile phone. 'Sofia and Will and The Twin Bump will love watching this later.'

Haresh put his arm round Harry's shoulders, and they laughed softly. I had no words, just a feeling of completeness, of total happiness.

'Maharani?' Haresh held his hand out for me, and I stepped towards him. 'Come.'

Following the band, we danced down the street, shoulders and arms moving Bollywood style, towards the row of taxis that would take us all to the wedding reception at Haresh's house; my new home.

Acknowledgments

WRITING A BOOK is a solitary thing, but so is dreaming, and both are intensely personal. I wanted Mari's journey to portray my love for India, and my experiences travelling there have inspired the backdrop for this story.

I do have to thank a ticket tout at the train station in Bombay in 1989. His name was Hari, and he wore a turquoise kurta suit. He got me a ticket to Udaipur, and showed me around Bombay for the afternoon. That's where the inspiration ends; there was no romance!

Thanks to my trusted friend and beta-reader, Allie Boller, to Fiona and Chris, and also to Carole Steen of the beautiful Casa Susegad in Goa. Above all, India deserves my thanks for being exhaustingly beautiful, majestic, romantic, frustrating, soul-bearing, and for always calling me back.

Special thanks go to the widows of India, especially those in Vrindavan, without whom there'd have been no inspiration for this story.'

My thanks also to Ken Dawson for bringing my vision to life and creating the beautiful cover for this book, and also for *The Fallen Persimmon*, as well as to Kate Coe at BookPolishers for her skill and patience.

About the Author

GIGI HAS SPENT most of her life living and working in countries all over the world. Her passions are writing and traveling. She loves Asia, and India is a favourite destination. Giving up a career in tourism, Gigi qualified in various holistic therapies and worked in yoga retreats in the Mediterranean for twelve years. Currently, Gigi lives in Wiltshire with Isabella, the cat she rescued from the streets of Fethiye, in southern Turkey.

The third and final part of Mari's story, as yet untitled, will be available at the end of 2023.

Printed in Great Britain
by Amazon